T0289238

Belmour

NORTHWESTERN WORLD CLASSICS

Northwestern World Classics brings readers the world's greatest literature. The series features essential new editions of well-known works, lesser-known books that merit reconsideration, and lost classics of fiction, drama, and poetry. Insightful commentary and compelling new translations help readers discover the joy of outstanding writing from all regions of the world.

Anne Seymour Damer

Belmour

A Modern Edition

Edited and with an introduction
by Jonathan David Gross

Northwestern University Press ✦ *Evanston, Illinois*

Northwestern University Press
www.nupress.northwestern.edu

Copyright © 2011 by Northwestern University Press. Published 2011. All rights reserved.

Printed in the United States of America

10 9 8 7 6 5 4 3 2 1

Library of Congress Cataloging-in-Publication Data

Damer, Anne Seymour, 1748 or 9–1828.
Belmour : a modern edition / Anne Seymour Damer ; edited and with an introduction by Jonathan David Gross.
p. cm. — (Northwestern world classics)
Includes bibliographical references.
ISBN 978-0-8101-2670-1 (pbk. : alk. paper)
I. Gross, Jonathan David, 1962– II. Title. III. Series: Northwestern world classics.
PR4525.D128B4 2011
823.7—dc22

2010038109

∞ The paper used in this publication meets the minimum requirements of the American National Standard for Information Sciences—Permanence of Paper for Printed Library Materials, ANSI Z39.48-1992.

For Piya

CONTENTS

BIOGRAPHICAL NOTE

Anne Seymour Conway was born on November 8, 1749, at Coombe Bank in Kent, and spent her youth at Park Place, Remenham, near Henley-on-Thames.[1] She was the daughter of well-known parents: Henry Seymour Conway served as an army officer and politician, and his wife, Caroline Bruce, née Campbell, Lady Ailesbury, was the daughter of John, fourth Duke of Argyll. Anne retained the aristocratic Whiggish outlook of her parents. Her father's secretary, David Hume, allegedly encouraged her interest in sculpture.[2] When her parents traveled abroad, her guardian was Horace Walpole, who bequeathed his Strawberry Hill home to her as his executor and legatee. On June 14, 1767, Anne married John Damer. After seven years they separated, and he committed suicide on August 15, 1776, leaving her in debt. Damer's career as a sculptress began after this tragic incident, which, as shown in her many letters to friends such as Mary Berry, tinged the rest of her life with melancholy.

Before the death of her husband, Damer commissioned Daniel Gardner to paint her and her friends as the witches from *Macbeth*. He wrote the following poem to accompany the portrait:

> Tales of Old Witches are no longer heard,
> Fictitious legends once receiv'd for truth.
> And wisely here the Artist has transferr'd
> The pow'rs of sorcery from age to youth.
>
> Beware, ye Mortals, who those comforts prize,
> Which flow from peace from liberty, and ease,
> Th' Enchanter's wand, and magick spells despise,
> But shun the witchcraft of such eyes as these.[3]

Of the three women in the painting, Damer is the only one who looks out at the viewer, defiantly.

Anne Damer gave copies to Lady Melbourne and Georgiana, Duchess of Devonshire, as gifts. Each version differed slightly, with details painted into the hem of a garment in the painting, to commemorate the recipient.[4] After her husband's suicide, the group portrait became her farewell gesture to the bon ton, for Damer's father-in-law, the notorious Lord Milton, insisted that she sell her own jewelry to pay the considerable debts her husband had accumulated as a fashionable rake. When her father-in-law also proved unreliable in paying her pension, she lived with her parents for a while and later (in 1778) rented an apartment behind Lady Melbourne's home in Piccadilly, on Sackville Street.[5] Though she seemed anxious to avoid public attention, she attracted onlookers who gawked at this aristocratic woman with a smock and mob cap, working in the damp yards behind her own apartment—a far cry from the fashionable residence she had once kept in London. In the 1770s and for two decades afterward, several caricaturists lampooned her as a lesbian who shunned the company of men, insinuating that she was responsible for her husband's suicide. One particularly cutting sketch of July 1, 1789, shows her gelding the *Apollo Belvedere,* a reference to a statue she intended for the new Drury Lane (c. 1802), which burned to the ground on January 24, 1809.[6] By the 1790s, the playwright Hannah Cowley could depict Anne Damer as a respected artist whose romantic attachment to her own sex symbolized the excesses of the age of sensibility. Despite her jealous detractors, however, Damer was no dabbler. She influenced the perception of Lord Nelson, Charles James Fox, George III, and other figures through her neoclassical busts.

As a sculptress Anne Damer recorded the historical actions of others, but she also became a historical curiosity herself. A pen portrait of Damer appears in Susan Ferrier's *Marriage,* showing her as a cross-dressing woman, complete with riding crop and "worsted stockings and black leather shoes, something resembling buckets."[7] The painter Joseph Farington noted Damer's histrionic farewells to Mary Berry and disagreed with her outspoken opinions on painting.[8] As an actress, she sometimes embarrassed audience members, such as the future Lord Palmerston, who, with the prince regent and the king and queen, attended numerous plays in which she performed at the house of her half sister, the Duchess of Richmond. Nevertheless, the House of Commons ended sessions early so Charles James Fox and William Pitt could attend a production of *The Way to Keep Him* on April 20, 1787, at Richmond House. "So moving were Mrs. Damer and Lord Henry Fitzgerald" in Nathaniel Lee's *Theodosius, or the Force of Love,* that "when the latter fell by his own sword, that Miss Harriet Hobart and Lady Ann Wesley were carried out in a faint,"[9] one audience member observed. Anne Damer helped to design sets, featuring her own sculpture (of Elizabeth Farren, for example) as backdrop; her beautiful costumes received favorable notice in almost every performance.[10] She played Donna Violante in *The Wonder,* by Susan Centlivre; Lady Lovemore in Arthur Murphy's *The Way to Keep Him;* and Lady Freelove in George Colman the Elder's *The Jealous Wife.* She delivered General Burgoyne's epilogue to her father's adaptation of Louis Boissy's *Les Dehors Trompeurs* (*False Appearances*). In Mary Berry's *The Fashionable Friends,* Damer appeared as Selina Vapour, reciting the epilogue written by William Lamb. The play was successful at Strawberry Hill in 1800, but closed shortly after its release in London at Drury Lane, reputedly because of its immorality. Damer's actress friends included Elizabeth Farren and Sarah Siddons, whom she portrayed as the muses Thalia and Melpomene, respectively, in busts exhibited at the Royal Academy in 1789.

Damer traveled to Europe on numerous occasions, keeping a careful record of her observations. She was in northern Germany and the Hague with her parents in 1760–61; in Germany, the Low Countries, and Paris in 1772; and in Paris, the provinces, and Flanders in 1774–75 (when she met Marie Antoinette) and in 1777–78.[11] She visited Rome, Naples, and Florence in 1778–79, 1780–81, and 1785–86, which helped her portray Italian scenes in *Belmour,* especially in the chapters that involve Mrs. Stainville's affair with Lord Raymond. After first meeting Mary and Agnes Berry in 1789, she traveled to Lisbon for her health from November 21, 1790, to March 1791, and seems to have begun *Belmour* in Portugal.[12] Damer visited Sir Horace Mann in Florence and also Sir William Hamilton in Naples, where she met Nelson in 1798. In 1802, Damer traveled to Paris with Mary Berry during the peace of Amiens and met the empress Josephine, Napoleon's mother, and Maria Cosway, who showed her some hidden treasures in the Louvre. She presented Napoleon with a bust of Charles James Fox during the Hundred Days, in 1815.

As an honorary exhibitor at the Royal Academy rather than an official member, Damer contributed thirty-two works from 1784 to 1818, only a fraction of her total output. Walpole encouraged her talent, though his praise led James Dallaway and Alan Cunningham to criticize her work more harshly than they might have.[13] She learned modeling from Giuseppe Ceracchi and marble carving from John Bacon the Elder. William Cumberland Cruikshank taught her anatomy. Among her early works are four wax medallion portraits done in the manner of Isaac Gosset the Elder (1713–99)—of her mother (1777?), her cousin Charlotte Campbell (1777?), Voltaire (1777), and the emperor Augustus (1777). These differ from more fully realized busts, which include Lord Nelson (marble, 1803), Joseph Banks (bronze, 1812–13), and herself (marble, 1786, in the Uffizi Gallery, Florence), as well as a statue she executed of George III (marble, 1790–94).[14] In her lifetime, Alan Cunningham noted inconsistencies in the degree of finish given to her works and concluded that she employed assistants. More recently, critics argue that Damer consciously altered her style from the finished busts of 1784 to the rough and chiseled appearance of Nelson and Banks, which she thought of as closer to the Greek (as opposed to the Roman, mistakenly accepted at that time for Greek). She was not a "dilettante, but . . . an Artist," as she put it in an autobiographical statement, one who traveled often to Italy to study "works of art which are to be found there in order to perfect her knowledge of the true and simple style of the Greeks she has always tried to emulate."[15]

In 1818, Damer moved to York House, Twickenham, where she continued to produce sculpture. She died on May 28, 1828, at her London house, 9 Upper Brook Street, Grosvenor Square, and was buried in the church at Sundridge, Kent, alongside her mother, under a gravestone of her own design. Though her notebooks survived, she ordered all her other private papers, including Horace Walpole's letters to her, destroyed.

Notes

1. I follow the *Oxford Dictionary of National Biography* in listing Anne Seymour Damer's birth date as 1749, though it is sometimes listed as 1748 (see the Noble and Benforado references below). For the most recent information, see Alison Yarrington, "Damer, Anne Seymour (1749–1828)," *Oxford Dictionary of National Biography* (Oxford: Oxford University Press, 2004–9). See also Percy Noble, *Anne Seymour Damer: A Woman of Art and Fashion, 1748–1828* (London: Kegan Paul, Trench, Trübner, 1908), and Susan Benforado, "Anne Seymour Damer (1748–1828). Sculptor" (Ph.D. diss., University of New Mexico, 1986).

2. Alison Yarrington, "The Female Pygmalion: Anne Seymour Damer, Allan Cunningham, and the Writing of a Woman Sculptor's Life," *The Sculpture Journal* 1 (1997): p. 34.

3. George C. Williamson, *Daniel Gardner* (New York: John Lane, 1921), p. 44.

4. Elizabeth Milbanke, *Byron's "Corbeau Blanc": The Life and Letters of Lady Melbourne,* ed. Jonathan David Gross (Houston: Rice University Press, 1997), plate 19.

5. "Albany" in F. H. W. Sheppard, ed., *Survey of London,* vols. 31 and 32, *St. James and Westminster, Part 2* (London: Athlone Press, 1964), plate 115, pp. 367–89. "In February 1785 the Melbournes came to an agreement with their friend, the sculptress, Anne Damer, for her to open a door and window into their garden from the yard of a house in Sackville Street. Mrs. Damer is said to have advised on the finishing of Melbourne House. Lady Birkenhead has written: 'Her knowledge and advice were valued by Lady Melbourne and were of great service to her in the decoration of the house'" (386); see also Mary Berry, *The Berry Papers: Being the Correspondence Hitherto Unpublished of Mary and Agnes Berry, 1763–1852,* ed. Lewis Melville (London: John Lane, 1914), p. 21.

6. Benforado, pp. 192–93.

7. Susan Ferrier, *Marriage: A Novel,* 1818, ed. Herbert Foltinek (London: Oxford University Press, 1997), pp. 42, 48.

8. Joseph Farington, *The Joseph Farington Diary,* ed. Kenneth Garlick, Angus D. Macintyre, and Kathryn Cave, 16 vols. (New Haven: Published for the Paul Mellon Centre for Studies in British Art by Yale University Press, 1978–84), August 19, 1798, 3:1048.

9. Sybil Marion Rosenfeld, *Temples of Thespis: Some Private Theatres and Theatricals in England and Wales, 1700–1820* (London: Society for Theatre Research, 1978), 48.

10. Ibid., 56.

11. Benforado, "Anne Seymour Damer," 44, 271.

12. Anne Seymour Conway Damer, Notebooks, 1791–97. 4 vols., Lewis Walpole Library, New Haven, Conn., 4:71; see also Berry, *The Berry Papers,* p. 27.

13. Yarrington, "The Female Pygmalion," passim.

14. Benforado, p. 15; see also Yarrington, "Damer, Anne Seymour (1749–1828)," *Oxford Dictionary of National Biography* (Oxford: Oxford University Press, 2004–9).

15. Benforado, "Anne Seymour Damer," p. 19.

1749 November 8: Anne Seymour Conway is born.
1767 June 14: Marriage to John Damer.
1776 August 15: Suicide of Anne Damer's husband, John Damer.
1781 Anne Damer travels to Rome; she returns from the Continent on August 31.
1784 Damer participates in the Westminster election of Charles James Fox.
1787 April 20: Damer makes her first of several appearances in amateur theatricals, in *The Way to Keep Him.*
1788 May 23: *False Appearances,* a play translated by Henry Seymour Conway, is produced at the Duke of Richmond's private theater at Goodwood.
1789 April 20: *False Appearances* is produced at Drury Lane.
1790 Damer travels to Lisbon, Portugal, and stays from November 21, 1790, to March 1791; she visits Granada and other cities and returns to London in early May 1791.
1795 July 9: Death of Damer's father.
1797 March 2: Death of Horace Walpole; Damer inherits Strawberry Hill.
1797 April: Mary Berry makes the first reference to Damer's novel, *Belmour,* which she reads in manuscript between April and August.
1798 Damer decides to complete a bust of Nelson in Naples after meeting Nelson, whom Damer calls the greatest historical figure of the age.
1800 Mary Berry's *The Fashionable Friends* is produced at Strawberry Hill.
1801 July: Publication of Anne Damer's *Belmour,* which Damer wrote between 1791 and 1797 during her sojourn in Por-

tugal and Spain. She focused intensely on the novel in August 1797 according to her unpublished notebooks.

1802 Damer and Mary Berry meet the empress Josephine and Napoleon's mother during the peace of Amiens.

1802 Mary Berry's *The Fashionable Friends,* staged at Drury Lane, closes after three nights.

1803 January 17: Death of Damer's mother.

1811 Damer bequeaths Strawberry Hill to Dowager Countess Waldegrave, along with Walpole's prints, books, and furniture included as heirlooms. Damer had lived at this playful monument to Gothic style from 1797 to 1811 and issued tickets to visitors, as Walpole had done during his lifetime.

1815 In April, during the Hundred Days, Damer presents a bust of Charles Fox to Napoleon; she receives gifts from Josephine and a diamond-studded snuffbox from the emperor.

1828 May 28: Death of Anne Damer.

INTRODUCTION

"I am going to pass an hour with Lord Belmour," Mary Berry wrote to Anne Damer. "I dare say we shall both of us think of you."[1] This quotation captures perfectly the autobiographical themes of Damer's only novel, *Belmour*. In this work, she explored romantic passion, the erotic distance between lover and beloved, and the pernicious influence of selfish mentors. Influenced by Ann Radcliffe, Jean-Jacques Rousseau, and, perhaps, Elizabeth Inchbald, Anne Damer began *Belmour* in Portugal. By writing a novel, she could evoke the comforting presence of Mary Berry, confronting her feelings for the young woman in the voice of a male suitor named Belmour. While sometimes read as a window into her private life, however, *Belmour* conceals as much as it reveals.

Twenty years before she published her novel, Anne Damer became the target of personal abuse. Newspaper caricatures blamed her for her separation from her husband, his suicide, and her apparent lack of grief. Hester Thrale linked her to sapphism generally and to the actress Elizabeth Farren in particular,[2] while others fanned the flames. William Combe in *The First of April,* attacked Damer out of pique against the Hertford family, to which Damer was related on her father's side (Hertford was Damer's father's older brother). Jack Cavendish in *A Sapphick Epistle* and observers of her close friendship with the Duchess of Devonshire seemed threatened by and unduly curious about Damer's sexual and financial independence. These rumors circulated from the 1770s until the time she published *Belmour*. Damer countered them through her acting, her sculpture, and, perhaps, her novel, but they never disappeared. Emma Donoghue's *Life Mask* explores Anne Damer's erotic relationship with Elizabeth Farren, while Andrew Elfenbein's *Romantic Genius* explains how rumors about her lesbian identity influenced her artistic career. "As a potential response to rumors of sapphism," Elfenbein notes, "*Belmour* extends the strategy of Damer's sculpture. It denies the marginality that such rumors imposed on her by showing her ability to participate in major literary trends of the day, such as the psychological novel."[3]

Five years after inheriting Strawberry Hill, Damer published *Belmour* along the lines first sketched by Horace Walpole's *The Castle of Otranto,* Clara Reeves's *The Old English Baron,* and Ann Radcliffe's *The Mysteries of Udolpho.* Though set mostly in England, *Belmour* is more cosmopolitan (though no less anti-Catholic) than gothic novels set in Italy. Damer's extensive travels lend authority to the Portuguese and Italian settings of *Belmour,* however much influenced by Radcliffe, who never visited the countries she so beautifully described. Perhaps Damer's work as a neoclassical sculptress (her reading of Epictetus and her assiduous notes taken at numerous museums) led her to look outside of England for literary models. Politically, she was cosmopolitan or Whiggish enough to present Napoleon with a bust of Charles James Fox and to send her bust of Lord Nelson to the king of Tanjore. Most important for *Belmour* was Damer's use of the uncanny and her exploration of the theme of melancholy, which drew on her passionate friendship with Mary Berry first articulated in her Lisbon notebooks. There is no doubt that Damer's life influenced her art. To compartmentalize them is to see how closely they intertwine.

The Work: *Belmour*

Damer's novel appeared in July 1801 and met with a brief but positive notice in the *Monthly Review:* "Considerable talents are here displayed in the support and delineation of characters, accompanied by many just reflections, and a knowledge of the world." Though generally appreciative of *Belmour's* "just reflections," the reviewer questioned the work's morality: "We must except, however, the libertine behaviour of Lord Belmour, in violating the rights of honor and hospitality by his criminal intimacy with Lady Roseberg; a conduct which cannot easily be reconciled with the openness and generosity of his disposition. That man can have little soundness of principle or true benevolence, who is guilty of such a flagrant act of villainy in the house of his unsuspecting friend.—Nor can we commend his virtuous wife, as Emily Courtenay is described to be, her expressions of tenderness towards her former admirer, and still giving him hopes of their future union.—We cannot deem that author's moral sentiments *quite* correct, who holds up such characters as worthy of our perfect approbation and esteem."[4] Despite the reviewer's caveat, Damer had successfully portrayed aristocratic men and women's lives as they were actually lived.

Damer was part of an informal literary circle throughout her life, whether she was performing in amateur theatricals, curating Horace Walpole's library at Strawberry Hill, or adding volumes to her own, reputedly one of the finest in London. She subscribed to *Miscellanies in Prose and Verse* by Catherine Jemmat in 1772, *The History of Miss Meredith* by Eliza Parsons in 1790, and *Contrast* by Regina Maria Roche in 1828. So well known was she as a literary figure that Charlotte Smith mistakenly attributed *Letters of Miss Riversdale* to her. Some even speculate that Damer borrowed Belmour's father's name, Delavere, from Delamere in Smith's *Emmeline,*[5] though it seems more likely that she only advised the author on her style, a task she also performed for her cousin Lady Charlotte Campbell.[6]

Anne Damer read *Delphine* in 1802, one year after *Belmour* appeared. She admired the author's subject, but found Madame de Staël's novel too self-revelatory: "It would be, by no means, I should think, a portrait that one should choose to expose of oneself," she wrote. Damer thought Rousseau, in *Julie, ou la Nouvelle Héloïse,* the better guide: "How differently has Rousseau treated a great passion, and a passion which leaves a ten times deeper impression of its violence on my mind than all the so-often repeated struggles of Leonie and Delphine."[7]

Damer knew the challenge of reining in the "passions," as Staël referred to them in her *Treatise.*[8] What Damer shared with Staël was class solidarity and a thorough knowledge of neoclassicism; they differed in their politics, most specifically in their attitude toward Napoleon, whom Damer admired and Staël, after an initial infatuation, opposed for more than ten years. After 1802, Damer (perhaps following Staël's world-historical example) sought to influence the cultural destiny of France, India, and England as a sculptress more forcefully than she had done before.

In the end, Walpole's influence on *Belmour* was greater than Staël's or Rousseau's. He resembles three characters: Lord Delavere, Dr. Stanmore, and Courtenay. As Delavere, he is a father figure to Emily—prideful, charismatic, but obtuse, insisting that his son marry Lady Clementina Alton (as Walpole mistakenly blessed Anne's marriage to John Damer); as Dr. Stanmore, he encourages Emily's interest in the arts; and as Courtenay, his Gothic Dean Abbey recalls Strawberry Hill. Courtenay resembles the "Horry" of Damer's correspondence, the Walpole of old age whose doddering attachment to Mary Berry proved embarrassing. In her letters to Mary Berry, in fact, Damer called him "the Grim King," underscoring his rather moody and autocratic rule of Strawberry Hill.[9] Anne Damer was "Stick," because of the wooden cane she used after she fell off a scaffold[10] and because she propped up Walpole and his new "wife," Mary Berry.

Anne Damer's notebooks reveal that the inspiration for *Belmour* came, in large measure, from her passion for Mary Berry. Unable to appear together as often as they would like,

Anne Damer and Mary Berry continually imagined meetings and chance encounters.[11] The fantasy of a lesbian life lived to its full sapphic potential haunts the eros-driven adventures of Belmour, whose very name means "beautiful love" in Italian. If she didn't make it up, Damer may have borrowed the name from the widow in Murphy's *The Way to Keep Him* (a part Mrs. Hobart played at the Richmond house theatricals), the libertine Bellmour in William Congreve's *The Old Batchelour,* or the addressee Belmour in Henry Cawthorne's poem "Life Unhappy."[12]

Damer's possible allusion to Congreve's *The Old Batchelour* is particularly intriguing. In this play, Fondlewife is an alderman cuckolded by the handsome Bellmour. Anne Damer might well say with Congreve's character, "Pox choak him, would his Horns were in his throat."[13] As Bellmour cuckolds Fondlewife,[14] so Damer cuckolded Walpole, seducing Mary Berry from under his nose. Other passages from the play also recall Damer's complex relationship with Horace Walpole and Mary Berry. "Why art thee distrustful of the Wife of thy Bosom?" Fondlewife asks Barnaby, who answers, "Because she is young and vigorous, and I am Old and impotent— . . . my inclination was (and is still) greater than my power."[15] These lines add further dramatic irony and may account for Damer's decision to cast herself as a novelistic version of Congreve's libertine Bellmour, seducing young women from the clutches of parasitic old men.

In short, the reader familiar with eighteenth-century poetry and drama cannot help but see Anne Damer as a cross-dressed version of her hero Belmour, a widow who traveled to Lisbon, a person capable of military courage and enterprise. In Damer's novel, Belmour boards a frigate and reveals his personal bravery, just as Damer withstood an attack on her boat crossing the English Channel.[16] As Belmour pursues Emily, so Damer pursued Mary Berry. Emily is artistic, musical, and a sensitive appreciator of picturesque and sublime landscapes in Italy and Portugal. She sketches in Venice, just as Mary Berry (like her sister Agnes) sent landscapes of Pisa back to Horace Walpole expressly for his comment. Damer's love for Berry led her to elide both characters, Belmour and Emily. Mary Berry also addressed Damer in intimate terms, as her other half. "Dear Soul!" Berry wrote, "I am indulging myself in idleness, of body I mean, & not coming to you tonight—This *indulging* myself in *not* coming to you has an odd sound to my ears—but you ought not to be affronted at it when I tell you I am going to pass an hour with Lord Belmour" (April 1797).[17] Deeply immersed in a life with Horace Walpole and Mary Berry, Anne Damer fashioned Belmour from plays and poems by Murphy, Congreve, and Cawthorne, while still expressing her longing for Mary Berry (the Emily of Damer's novel), whom she could not meet in public as often as she would have liked. Perhaps referring to other aspects of this roman à clef, her mother noted the autobiographical sources for the novel, writing a poem in her daughter's voice: "Don't think me a conceited Elf, / I took the Models from myself."[18]

Horace Walpole's letters portray his relationship with Anne Damer in revealing ways. The author of *The Castle of Otranto* and *The Mysterious Mother* cast Henry Seymour Conway's young daughter (for whom Walpole was caring) as a surrogate spouse. "Pray, what have I done?" he wrote to Conway. "Have I come home drunk to my wife within these four first days? Or have I sat up gaming all night and not come home at all to her, after her Lady Mother had been persuaded that I was the soberest young nobleman in England, and had the greatest aversion to play?"[19] In another letter, Walpole also referred to himself as Anne Conway's husband. "She is quite contented with the easy foot we live upon," he wrote. "Separate beds, dining in her dressing room when she is out of humour, . . . who knows but at your return you may find your daughter with qualms and in a sack?"[20] Playful though the letter is, Walpole clearly had a tyrannical side (a darker version of Stanmore, in Damer's novel). He overpraised Damer, inspiring a counterreaction that hurt her career and left her with a dilettante's reputation. "Mrs. Damer has finished a bust of an infant Atys or Paris in marble, that not only surpasses any Grecian flesh, but comes up to the softness and delicacy of Correggio," he wrote to William Hamilton on January 17, 1788. "Yet while her mornings are so Athenian, in the evenings she is a capital actress in comedy; and as I conclude she possesses every talent she pleases I am teasing her to appear in tragedy. She has a pathetic harmony in her voice that Mrs. Siddons wants."[21]

By 1789, the septuagenarian Walpole met the Berry sisters (then in their early twenties). In one of his earliest letters, he signed himself Horace Fondlewives and wrote to them as "Mes très chères Fraises" (April 11, 1789). "As the honeymoon is not over, I hope you will come to me again tomorrow evening," he wrote, signing off as "Your most affectionate and doubly constant husband."[22] Though Walpole only played the part of husband in these passages, he glowered if Damer hinted that she received a letter from the Berrys before him.[23] Walpole piled up wives, neglected them, and apologized for his emotional neediness. In *The Castle of Otranto,* Manfred has two wives, too: he tries to divorce Hippolyta and marry his son's widow, Isabella. There may well have been a bit of Manfred in Walpole after all.

Three months after meeting the Berrys, Anne Damer sailed for Lisbon on November 17, 1790, free for a time from the emotional complications of life at Strawberry Hill, however pleasant in other respects. Traveling in part to restore her delicate health, she was dismayed by the disorder at her residence in Portugal: "You cannot form to yourself an idea of the Portuguese, their indolence or indifference, neither money nor entreaty will bring them. When I came I found two panes of glass broken, and for five days, though the master of the house and my own servants went twenty times a day after the people, I could not have them put in."[24] When she dined at the minister's house, she noted the "fat, vulgar women, and scowling, unknown men. . . . I should like to see something of the Portuguese, which is not very easy for foreigners."[25] Traveling was "really an operation," she noted on December 2, 1790. "There are several only two-wheeled chaises, open before, with leathern curtains that draw; you set out as if on a journey, and go nodding along over the worst pavement possible and up and down very steep hills, on which this town stands, yet these chaises are actually the vehicles best calculated for this tour."[26] She did manage to see an aqueduct, but noted that Portugal's landscape was hardly picturesque. "Here you have a cornfield, an orange garden, a church, and then a house, just as it happens, all jumbled in the same queerest manner that I ever saw. The aqueduct may be called magnificent, but the arches are, I think, too close."[27] Her room, where she ultimately wrote *Belmour,* was "small, white-washed, and a sort of farm-house chimney occupies one-half of it [resembling Emily's small room in *Belmour*]; it is high and built with large, rough stones; there are some shelves, two tables, and many chairs; here I have my books and my writing, and my ideas are not at least outwardly frozen; their substitutes for fires are large cloaks, of the form you see in Florence, which they wear very gracefully, both men and women; they are eternally wrapped up in them, riding, walking, hanging over a balcony when the sun shines, or sitting at home in a state of idleness—a state to which they seem to have a great propensity, by what I hear and by the little I have seen."[28] The cloaks would later find their way into *Belmour,* with the hero sporting a white one in Venice.

In the winter of 1791, Anne Damer visited Lisbon. She noted a "respectable" Gothic church she saw more than once. "One of the most ancient is horrid to look at, almost totally destroyed by the earthquake, little else but the outside walls standing. The Castle, formerly a Moorish Palace, was nearly made a ruin. You see here and there a little bit of a column, etc. stuck in little better than a mud wall, but this her majesty does not think of rebuilding; she has at immense expense built a church called the Convento Nuovo, or the Coracao de Jesu (the heart of Jesus), in the worst taste, adorned by many colossal statues in the Style of Bernini exaggerated."[29] In this church, Damer identified a Raphael which was "miserably painted over, which I gained much credit by finding out, though it is as plain as the nose on one's face."[30] Damer then made a tour of Seville, Granada, Cordoba, Toledo, the Escurial, and Il-de-Fons. At Valladolid, Spain, she visited the cloisters of a monastery of Dominican friars, where she saw Gothic architecture that may well have influenced the portrait of a Portuguese monastery offered in *Belmour.* At Burgos, she visited the cathedral. "Wishing to see it thoroughly, and particularly the Cloister, and not being sure of the same indulgence I met with from my Dominican Friars at Valladolid, I went dressed in Lady Spencer's fashion; this dress, with the large cloak and boots, is what, in point of dressing, the bench of Bishops could not object to."[31] While executing busts of Joseph I, the late king of Portugal, in bronze (the statue was modeled and cast in Lisbon), she continued to gather material for her sculptures and her novel. She traveled to Bayonne and Bordeaux, arriving in Paris on May 3 at the home of her friend Madame Balbi. In Paris, where General Lafayette governed, Damer was visited by the Poissards, a radical element in the French Revolution, and visited the Champs de Mars, then called the Champs de la Fédération. She found this area of Paris spoiled in beauty by the recent political unrest. She attended the Théâtre de Monsieur the following day, went to the Assemblée Nationale, and then drove to see the ruins of the Bastille. Though *Belmour* was most likely composed over a six-year period (1791–97), these travels clearly influenced the setting of the novel. In her room in Portugal, she wrote passionate letters to Mary Berry and recorded Berry's replies. And in Lisbon, her dog Fidele died. So attached had she become to this animal that she requested that she be buried with him at her death, along with her sculpting tools.[32]

Clearly the visit to Portugal was a crucial part of Damer's emotional and artistic development. Free at last from Horace Walpole and his circle, Damer was able to think creatively about the life she had been living at Strawberry Hill. Now, for the first time, Mary Berry came to Anne Damer's consciousness much as Emily Melville comes to Belmour's. Damer addressed Berry as her "soul" and Berry wrote back in the same style. "Tell me all you do & all you see; & above all—all you suffer—such letters are real comforts to me & yesterday I wanted it . . . I long for nothing but to admire this place [Italy] with you, and to see you feel its tranquil beauties as much as I do myself—," a phrase Damer recorded in her notebooks.[33] At the same time, she lived a very public life. Horace Walpole informed the Berrys that she was "received at Elvas with all military honours and a banquet, by order of Mello, formerly Ambassador here (London). It was handsome of him, but must have distressed her, who is void of all ostentation and love of show."[34] Though she attended formal occasions, Damer was very much alone. "From the time I leave Lisbon to the time I reach Madrid, I shall not have a single letter," she wrote.[35] At this time, Damer's sense of personal freedom was very much on her mind. "He may not, as unvalued persons do, carve for himself; Ham," she wrote, quoting *Hamlet*.[36] She puns on the word "carve," reminding herself that even as a sculptress she cannot consort with just anyone, but has public appearances to keep, perhaps because she is the daughter of Henry Seymour Conway and bears letters of introduction from Horace Walpole. The significance of "carve" would not have been lost on Damer, since in this speech Laertes advises Ophelia about how to conduct herself sexually. In a more classical mode, she summoned quotations from Ovid and Terence to teach herself patience, and praised Cicero's letters, while excoriating "Lucan" whom she found "hard and bombastic."[37] "To fortune, strange that thou art never constant, never to be depended upon in thy favors," she noted after reading Terence, a writer she admired more.[38] Her perpetual melancholy led her to quote Shakespeare's *Comedy of Errors:* "He that commends me to my own content / Commends me to the thing I cannot get" (1.2.32).[39] And later, in that same journal, she (or perhaps it was Mary Berry; the attribution is unclear) apologized for appearing happy: "Tell me that you have not been quite alone these two or three evenings—I had a sort of uncomfortable affected chearfullness while with you this morning, which yr low spirits seem'd to make necessary, but which left me, as soon as I left you, & my mind felt a sort of relief in returning uncontrouled to the thoughtfull melancholy which seems too natural to it."[40] Melancholy was clearly a favorite theme in Damer and Berry's correspondence.

By the time Anne Damer published *Belmour,* she had an unsentimental view of life, which was reflected in her fiction. Belmour comes to Emily already jaded. His chief characteristic is melancholy. Having pursued Lady Roseberg unsuccessfully, Belmour feels destined to wander the earth alone. Emily exhibits the same fear in her travels with Mrs. Stainville. Yet Emily's position is even more precarious than Belmour's. For all her beauty, Emily has married a man many years her senior and lived with him, sequestered, for more than a year. Though she declares that she would rather have tended to Dr. Stanmore, and only married Courtenay because Stanmore thought it would protect her financially, Emily hardly behaves in a way that inspires trust, despite Dr. Stanmore's speech at the end of the novel praising her blameless conduct. She encourages

Belmour's advances even while dining with her husband. This comes to a head when Emily encourages Belmour to depart because she fears Courtenay has detected them. Shortly after the lovers separate, Courtenay kisses away the tears Emily sheds for Belmour, and Emily lets him do so, until this hypocrisy becomes too much for her. Courtenay is not innocent of Belmour's attentions, for he comments sarcastically on this topic. Reading the false newspaper report that Belmour has become an ambassador to Russia, Courtenay acknowledges Emily's tact in asking Belmour to leave, painful though this must have been.

For a novel that treats so many melancholy characters, *Belmour* ends happily. Courtenay dies soon enough so Emily can marry Belmour without compromising herself morally. That music and song accompany their reunion—Emily's playing the ancient organ at Dean Abbey that Courtenay's father commissioned—is both predictable and yet disturbing. The very instrument that should bind Emily to her husband's family draws her closer to Belmour.

Damer treats her hero's flirtations with married women as routine. Belmour pursues Lady Roseberg and Emily Courtenay in the presence of their husbands, in both cases becoming the husbands' preferred guest. Lord Roseberg insists that Lady Roseberg invite him to their home. He opens his carriage door to Belmour when he sees him walking along the road. For Belmour's part, "the open, generous candour of his mind, often revolted at the means, which were taken to ensure the continuance of their commerce without suspicion"; though he continues in the relationship with Lady Roseberg, nothing could "reconcile him . . . to the constant scene of deceit and hypocrisy, to which he was hourly witness" (p. 47). Similarly, Courtenay tries to share his German translations with Belmour over breakfast. Though a traditional hero in other respects (he provides for the poor, for example, and unites Wilmot with his lover), Belmour uses Courtenay's own inkwell to write Courtenay's wife a note (a dramatic symbol fraught with Freudian overtones). Courtenay's servant makes the mistake of revealing that Belmour visited Dean Abbey in Courtenay's absence. What might work as farce in a Restoration comedy seems simply sad here, as Courtenay suggests he can trust Belmour because he is a "new friend" (though Courtenay's "sarcastic smile" when he makes this remark [p. 170] indicates that Courtenay knows what is afoot). Despite Courtenay's erratic behavior, Emily knows her own conduct is not beyond reproach: "We must not while we *talk* virtue, *practice* vice," she informs Belmour, before encouraging him to leave (p. 177).

Adding further to the melancholic tone of the novel is the narrator's cynicism. "She had hitherto seen the world in all the gayest colours of spring, and had only read of wintry blasts in the fictitious pages of a novel" (p. 22), the narrator says of the young and vivacious Lady Clementina. Aunt Eliza, Lady Clementina's chaperone, "had the *misfortune,* for a misfortune it too generally is, to become a very considerable heiress" (p. 21). Mrs. Stainville does her best to corrupt the young, even stealing away their admirers (Lord Raymond), while older men make themselves a burden, never more so than when professing the best of intentions. Dr. Stanmore advises Emily in all situations, yet Emily's desire to please him leads her to marry Courtenay. In fact, the misguidance of impressionable youth is one of the narrator's favorite themes. Belmour gives up a parliamentary career supporting the Whigs lest he disobey his father, who needs him to vote with the king to maintain the interests of Belmour Castle; he wished to follow his friend and join the navy but his father "strenuously" opposed this (p. 35); and, most damagingly, Belmour feels incapable of "counteracting his dying father's last request" that he marry Lady Clementina (p. 118). The narrator underscores Lord Delavere's vanity by stressing his relentless pursuit of a marquisate, a "long wished for title" (p. 78); the narrator, who uses the phrase "poor Belmour" on more than one occasion, further tips her hand by reminding the reader that Belmour's father was an only child accustomed to getting his way. Finally, the narrator's descriptions of Emily suggest an older person looking at the young with a mixture of envy and pity. The reader participates in Belmour's burning passion for Emily, since the narrator continually alludes to her physical beauty. Emily reveals her desire for Belmour when she studies his family's portraits at Belmour Castle, hides her catalog of these pictures in a cupboard, and sketches him when he visits the church of the Mendicanti in Venice.

The novel treats homes, abbeys, and castles in some detail, even contrasting them as emblematic of their owners' values. Belmour Castle, located in the west of England, is salubrious, as Dr. Stanmore observes, a "terrestrial paradise!" (p. 183), while Courtenay's ancient Gothic pile, near Cheltenham, is overrun with weeds, with a gate that is rusty and decayed. Belmour's servants greet him and Emily with a rapturous welcome, while Courtenay's are barely present the night he returns with his new bride (even the redoubtable Mrs. Warner cannot manage Courtenay's servants). His indebtedness is a factor in his servants' attitude, for he is a ruined man whose lawyer, Enstine, connives in holding back rent rolls to conceal Courtenay's finances from his prospective wife. Emily only discovers Courtenay's deception when he drops a letter on the floor by accident. She returns the letter to where she found it and never reproaches him with the information she learns. He dies a contented man, informing her that his years with her were the happiest of his life.

The most impressive characters in the novel speak a foreign language (Courtenay and Belmour); the least use their wealth to indulge their laziness (Raymond and Mrs. Stainville). Thus Belmour's knowledge of German, Portuguese, Italian, and classical languages contrasts with the more ambitious and cynical St. Fort, who arranged to have himself named envoy to Munich without bothering to learn German. Where Belmour is as alert to the interior of churches in Venice as Emily is to the inside of Notre Dame, Mrs. Stainville and Lord Raymond overlook the beauty in Naples and other locations completely, absorbed, as they are, in self-centered moods. Belmour and Emily are fit companions for each other: curious, respectful, and scholarly (Belmour was "the allowed best scholar" [p. 38] at Eton and university, while Emily's classical erudition rivals Dr. Stanmore's). Belmour hires a private guide to show him Smyrna, while Mrs. Stainville abandons her intentions to visit sites in Naples and Venice in order to keep Lord Raymond apart from Emily, inventing an excuse of ill health for the purpose ("The sulphureous air of Naples *killed* her; the *oppression* of a *scirocco* was intolerable; and in a *tramontana, with her lungs, how could she breathe?*" [p. 241]). Emily, by contrast, takes no notice of the flirtatious Lord Raymond and cultivates her artistic gifts, particularly her talents for drawing, at the church of the Mendicanti in Venice, and for organ playing, at Dean Abbey. She draws Belmour to her through her beautiful voice, the artistic complement to her physical beauty, which everyone (even the less sensible characters such as Rycot, St. Fort, and others) can appreciate.

As in the novels of Jane Austen, most marriages in Anne Damer's *Belmour* are unhappy. Mr. Rycot curses his wife when he misplaces items in his home and perpetually argues with her. Mrs. Stainville's father uses his daughter's marriage to revenge himself upon his wife: "Nothing, . . . gave him greater satisfaction, than the offer of Mr. Stainville's hand for his daughter; who, being a Roman Catholic, and otherwise, in reality, an unexceptionable match, afforded him an opportunity of plaguing his wife, humbling what he called her absurd bigotry, showing his own superior power, and indulging in what he considered as a proof of his liberal and unprejudiced opinions" (p. 197). Perhaps the most tragic marriage is Emily's parents'; their early death shows the risk faced by young couples without financial support. Dr. Stanmore, an ideal (if asthmatic) physician of the soul, nurtures two generations of impractical Melvilles (Emily's mother as well as Emily herself). Despite his best efforts, however, Emily Melville's future is precarious. Damer's narrator continually offers an implicit critique of a world too vulgar to appreciate Emily's great beauty and gifts.

The only political event mentioned in the novel is the battle of Culloden (p. 126), and the reference to her grandfather's bravery in the battle underscores Emily's noble roots, which make her worthy of the aristocratic Belmour. Emily Dumont (Emily Melville's mother) was originally French, though her family settled in Scotland; she was the daughter of an officer, Dumont, who supported the Stuart cause and tried to place a Catholic Stuart king on the throne of England. Unhappy with his frivolous wife, and of a more studious turn, Dumont took his three-year-old daughter away and died shortly afterward. The mother also died and the child was sent to England to live with Mrs. Dawson, whose large family and husband's ruined fortune led her to give up the child to the wealthy landowner Sir Thomas Melville. The second Lady Melville encourages Thomas to adopt the twelve-year-old Emily (mother of the Emily with whom Belmour falls in love) to tutor her daughter in French but soon grows tired of her and mistreats her. Young Melville falls in love with Emily Dumont and marries her. Disinherited because of this marriage and strapped for money, he subsequently joins the army. Emily and her child are then put in the care of Dr. Stanmore, the surrogate parent: both parents die, the father of a fever, the mother precisely twelve months later of grief. Stanmore takes care of the infant Emily Melville (the heroine of the novel) until she meets Mrs. Stainville at a dance and travels with her throughout Europe. When she returns, Stanmore must travel to Cornwall on business and so Emily, her identity deliberately concealed, stays with Mr. Enstine. She meets Courtenay at a dinner party at Enstine's and marries Courtenay, thinking Belmour has already married his cousin Lady Clementina Alton. Tossed from caretaker to caretaker, from Dr. Stanmore, to Mrs. Stainville, to Mr. Rycot, to Mr. Enstine, Emily finds herself neglected by everyone except Dr. Stanmore, who recognizes her true worth. Emily shows how cultivating the arts and foreign languages can preserve a person's peace of mind. If people let one down, the novel suggests, art never will. And art (music, drawing) can attract like-minded souls in places as far flung as Venice, Bologna, and London.

In addition to exploring the power of art to bring lovers together, *Belmour* includes episodes marked by the uncanny, the return of that which was once familiar but has undergone repression. Terry Castle treats the uncanny in Radcliffe's work in ways that illuminate Damer's *Belmour.* When Belmour visits Emily at Dean Abbey, for example, they go to a music gallery where Emily plays a song that her lover Belmour has previously heard. When Emily visits Belmour Castle, she recognizes Belmour's ancestors as related to the "stranger" she saw in Venice and sketched.[41] When Belmour wanders into Emily's room, he recognizes sketches of scenes he actually visited, indeed sketches of himself. To marry Emily, in other words, is to align himself with a woman who has loved him all along (for the entire length of her sojourn in Italy with Mrs. Stainville, for example). For Emily, Belmour is the "stranger" become familiar, a man who doted over her in secret, exhibiting the kind of sustained attentiveness that augurs for a happy marriage. In what amounts to an extended, two-year courtship in Europe, Emily and Belmour laid the groundwork for their marriage without ever being introduced.

Radcliffe and *Belmour*

Anne Damer drew on Ann Radcliffe's *The Mysteries of Udolpho* and *The Italian* to depict how art draws lovers together in uncanny ways. In both novels, women are mysterious and pursued for that reason. Damer's Emily shares the same name as Radcliffe's heroine. As Emily St. Aubert dreams of Valancourt, so too Emily Melville has thoughts of Belmour. Belmour seems to exist, like Valancourt, in a dream world, in which nothing pleases him so much as hearing Emily sing, watching her sketch, or viewing her portrait (as Emily, in a far more frightening passage in *The Mysteries of Udolpho,* views the veiled portrait). Where Radcliffe explores how her own Emily faces threats of physical violence and intimidation in *The Mysteries of Udolpho,* Damer shows how Mrs. Stainville's careless treatment of the highly sensitive and refined Emily Melville can be no less painful.

There seems to be no extra-literary evidence for Ann Radcliffe's direct influence on Anne Damer's novel. For this reason, perhaps, Andrew Elfenbein concludes that "*Belmour* can be classed with other psychological novels of the 1790s, such as those of Elizabeth Inchbald, which avoid the spectacular incidents of Radcliffe and concentrate instead on tracing characters' interior states."[42] Elfenbein's assessment of Damer's life is one of the most insightful we have, yet it may be possible that Radcliffe's fiction appealed to Damer for other reasons than its "spectacular incidents." *Belmour* includes long descriptions of nature that recall Radcliffe and that create exalted states of feeling that also appealed to John Keats[43] and Percy Shelley.[44] "[St. Aubert, Emily's father] loved the soothing hour," Radcliffe writes, "when the last tints of light die away; when the stars, one by one, tremble through aether, and are reflected on the dark mirror of the waters; that hour, which, of all others, inspires the mind with pensive tenderness and often elevates it & sublime contemplation. When the moon shed her soft rays among the foliage, he still lingered, and his pastoral supper of cream and fruits was often spread beneath it. Then, on the stillness of night, came the song of the nightingale breathing sweetness & awakening melancholy."[45] St. Aubert's worship of nature inevitably leads him to appreciate the nightingale's song and to imitate its sounds. "Sometimes too, he brought music of his own, and awakened every fuzzy echo with the tender accents of his oboe."[46] Emily shares with her lover the passion for music she enjoyed with her father, but like Belmour and Emily, the erotic encounters between hero and heroine are kept at bay by the music that mediates and interprets, one might almost say "refines," the sexual tension between them. Valancourt is brave enough to face down pirates, but sensitive enough to replicate St. Aubert's appreciation of nature. His love of the natural world allows him to resist the dissipations of London. "These scenes, said Valancourt, soften the heart, like the notes of sweet music, and inspire that delicious melancholy which no person, who had felt it once, would resign for the gayest pleasures. They waken our best and purest feelings, disposing us to benevolence, pity, and friendship. Those whom I love—I always seem to love more in such an hour as this."[47] Just as the father St. Aubert shapes a woman, Emily, who can love and be loved by Valancourt, so too does Dr. Stanmore mold Emily into the perfect creature Belmour adores.

Music is closely connected to melancholy moods, and in Radcliffe's fiction directly related to them. In fact, the climax of *The Mysteries of Udolpho* includes a poem, "To Melancholy," that anticipates Keats. In "Ode to Melancholy," Keats instructs his anonymous listener to "glut thy sorrow on a morning rose" (line 15).[48] In this scene, Valancourt, like Belmour, remembers how a musical refrain inspired him to fall in love.

> The sun was now setting on that tract of the Pyrenees, which divides Languedoc from Rousillon, and, placing

herself opposite to a small grated window, which, like the wood-tops beneath, and the waves lower still, gleamed with the red glow of the west, she touched the chords of her lute in solemn symphony, and then accompanied it with her voice, in one of the simple and affecting airs, to which, in happier days, Valancourt had often listened in rapture, and which she now adapted to the following lines:

TO MELANCHOLY

Spirit of love and sorrow—hail!
Thy solemn voice from far I hear,
Mingling with ev'ning's dying gale:
Hail, with this sadly-pleasing tear!
. . . .
O lonely spirit! Let thy song
Lead me through all thy sacred haunt;
The minister's moon-light aisles along,
Where specters raise the midnight chaunt.[49]

In the same way that Valancourt falls for Emily by hearing her play the lute, Belmour hears Emily singing in the church of the Mendicanti in Venice and recollects the Italian air she sings on more than one occasion when they meet again at Dean Abbey. Music becomes a sentimental shorthand that attracts them.

Though this relationship between music and sentimentality appears most often in Radcliffe, one finds it in Rousseau and particularly in the poetry of the time as well. Thomas Warton ("The Pleasures of Melancholy"), Milton's *L'Allegro* and *Il Penseroso,* and many passages by Mark Akenside, James Beattie, and William Collins created an artistic climate that made Damer's *Belmour* possible. "Is there a heart that music cannot melt?" Beattie asks. Radcliffe quotes this epigraph as a chapter heading for *The Romance of the Forest.*[50] For Radcliffe, "Nature's finest instrument" is the "soul," and fancy, as Collins suggests, "points the bleeding Friend."[51] Radcliffe also insists on the relationship between music and morality in the poem she includes in *The Romance of the Forest,* "The Family of La Luc," written by the Yorkshire poet Henry Cawthorne.

> But half mankind, like Handel's fool, destroy,
> Through rage and ignorance, the strain of joy;
> Irregularly wild their passions roll
> Through Nature's finest instrument, the soul:
> While men of sense, with Handel's happier skill,
> Correct the taste and harmonize the will;
> Teach their affections, like his notes, to flow
> Nor rais'd too high, nor ever sunk too low;
> Till ev'ry virtue, measur'd and refin'd,
> As fits the concert of the master mind,
> Melts in its kindred sounds, and pours along
> Th' according music of the moral song.[52]

In the above passage, Clara (the daughter of La Luc whom the heroine Adeline comes across during her wanderings) must learn the regulation of passion from her father, who encourages her to forsake her lute when it interferes with her acts of charity. Before this happens, Clara enjoys the sensuous beauty of music, as Belmour does in both England and Italy.

Sketching also makes its appearance in the novels of Radcliffe, as in this passage from *The Romance of the Forest:*

> When she [Clara] was about sixteen she often selected from her father's library those of the Italian poets most celebrated for picturesque beauty, and would spend the first hours of morning in reading them under the shade of the acacias that bordered the lake. Here too she would often attempt rude sketches of the surrounding scenery and at length by repeated efforts, assisted by some

> instruction from her brother, she succeeded so well as to produce twelve drawings in crayon, which were judged worthy of decorating the parlour of the chateau.[53]

At times the beauties of nature, pictorial art, and music fuse. In *Belmour,* for example, we learn that the hero's mind makes travel particularly pleasant, as it combines the taste for the picturesque, for beautiful art, and for the acquisition of foreign languages. Both Clara, in *The Romance of the Forest,* and Belmour, in Damer's novel, share a love of Italian. "The romantic beauties of Savoy first roused his attention, and, while lost in admiration of the grand features of nature, he for a time forgot his griefs, and fell into a composed and pensive melancholy," Damer writes. "The remains of Grecian and Roman art, so profusedly scattered over Italy, in which the refined taste of Belmour took peculiar delight; music, of which he was passionately fond, and literary science, in which he found constant opportunities to indulge, contributed to soothe and occupy his mind; and his perfect acquaintance with the Italian language gave him every advantage, in the pursuits which he followed" (pp. 59–60).

As in Radcliffe's fiction, Belmour's susceptibility to the beauty of art and music distinguishes him from St. Fort and Lord Raymond, who seem impervious to such charms. Emily Melville's close attention to the interior of Notre Dame, like Belmour's interest in the church of the Mendicanti in Venice, further attract them. It is Belmour's interest in opera, after all, that leads Emily to spot him in Bologna (p. 243). These heightened moments strengthen their relationship, though the hero is equally cautious about meeting Emily too openly, thereby compromising her reputation: "He knew, too, that he was not indifferent to her, but that to preserve that interest so dear to him in her heart, he must, by the sacrifice on earth the most painful to himself, continue to deserve her good opinion, and by a melancholy and probably eternal separation, prevent the possibility of disturbing her peace of mind by his presence" (p. 186). Absenting himself from Emily, by traveling to Smyrna, Turkey, and Greece, is how Belmour proves his love.

Terry Castle provides another explanation for the prolonged absence of heroines in Radcliffe. "Old-fashioned ghosts, it is true, have disappeared from the fictional world," Castle writes,

> but a new kind of apparition takes their place. To be a Radcliffean hero or heroine in one sense means just this: to be "haunted," to find oneself obsessed by the spectral image of those one loves. One sees in the mind's eye those who are absent: one is befriended and consoled by phantoms of the beloved. Radcliffe makes it clear how such phantasmata arise. They are the products of refined sentiment, the characteristic projections of a feeling heart. To be haunted, according to the novel's romantic myth, is to display one's powers of sympathetic imagination; the cruel and the dull have no such hallucinations. Those, who love, by definition, are open to the spirit of the other.[54]

In *The Mysteries of Udolpho,* Emily's father, St. Aubert, does not want to leave his estate because of the continuing "presence" of his dead wife, which has "sanctified every surrounding scene."[55] In a sense, Belmour loves the spirit of Emily, which haunts the gardens, operas, and churches he visits, as much as he loves the woman herself. In the same way that Mrs. Stainville carries the orphan Emily off to Europe, where Belmour accidentally finds her, Emily St. Aubert's aunt carries the orphaned Emily to Toulouse and Emily feels haunted by Valancourt. "A haunted lover can do nothing, it seems, but haunt the haunts of the other," Castle notes. "To love in the novel is to become ghostly oneself."[56]

Writing in the tradition that includes Shakespeare's ghost in *Hamlet* and Tirso de Molina's guest of stone in *El Burlador de Seville,* Horace Walpole had made use of sculptures as weapons and the people they haunt as ghosts in *The Castle of Otranto.* A statue of Alfonso, after all, destroys Manfred's son Conrad. Characters walk out of their portraits, as Alfonso does in *The Castle of Otranto,* and exact revenge upon the unworthy. In *Belmour,* Emily "frames" Belmour through her sketches, just as the paintings of his ancestors she sees at the beginning of the novel allow her to see him anew. To her, Belmour's castle feels both familiar and unfamiliar, home (*heimlich*) and not home (*unheimlich*). The portraits in Dean Abbey, falling out of their worm-eaten frames, recall Courtenay himself, whose neglect of his ancestral home has made of it a hideous ruin.

If the novel is a gothic romance,[57] it earns that title partly because of the eerie feeling that Belmour and Emily have known each other before. Damer achieves this formally, in part, through circular (rather than linear) plotting. Belmour meets Emily as early as the first chapter (p. 13). It is ten chapters later before the reader learns of Emily's history in Italy, Belmour's in Spain and then Italy, and their encounters in Venice and return to England and realizes they've known each other all along ("The narrative would have been better conducted, if the early life of Miss Melville had not been introduced so late, as an episode," the *Monthly Review* complained).[58] In contrast to her cousin Lady Charlotte Campbell's enormously popular novels, such as *Self-Indulgence* (1812), which were stylistically straightforward, Damer plots her novel to heighten the reader's experience of the uncanny.

Though less commercially successful than Charlotte Campbell, Anne Damer participated in the fashionable taste for sensibility, using the word "melancholy" no less than forty-six times. The topic was popular with proto-Romantic poets such as Thomas Gray, who coined the term "white Melancholy" or "leucocholy" in a letter to Richard West (May 27, 1742).[59] "A good, easy sort of state," Gray called it, unlike the state of mind linked in Burton's *The Anatomy of Melancholy* to black bile, one of the four humors. "Following the poets James Thomson, James Beattie, Robert Blair and William Collins, Radcliffe sees melancholy—especially at twilight hours—as healing, restorative and redemptive," Jacqueline Howard notes in her edition of *The Mysteries of Udolpho*.[60] Radcliffe's *The Mysteries of Udolpho* anticipates Damer's treatment of melancholy and beyond it Byron's (an avid reader of James Beattie, whom he invokes in *Childe Harold's Pilgrimage* [1812]).

Freud's "Mourning and Melancholia" (1917) also provides insight into the theme of melancholy Damer develops, although it appeared more than a century later. Freud suggests that mourning is a response to death, but melancholia is an unknown state in which the patient must discover his or her unconscious feelings, sometimes for a mother or father. Mourning is obvious; melancholia mysterious. Psychologically, the melancholic victim might wish for the premature death of a parent (one of many possible scenarios Freud describes), only to feel despair and guilt as a result.

In his essay, Freud describes melancholia as a "profoundly painful dejection, cessation of interest in the outside world, loss of the capacity to love, inhibition of all activity, and a lowering of the self-regarding feelings to a degree that finds utterance in self-reproaches and self-revilings, and culminates in a delusional expectation of punishment."[61] This condition might occur as the result of the death of a loved person, but it might also occur when something has been lost as an object of love, or even when "one cannot see clearly what it is that has been lost."[62] In mourning "it is the world which has become poor and empty; in melancholia it is the ego itself."[63]

In his clinical practice, Freud noted that melancholics often accused themselves of many failings.[64] Freud theorized that "the intense and unreasoning nature of melancholia indicated that what had been lost was not just the external person for whom one mourns but an internalization of the object to which there had been an intense and probably ambivalent unconscious attachment of desire. Such an attachment implies a degree of narcissistic identification. In such cases the loss of the person in the real world then precipitates an internal loss which is experienced as a psychic wound, as a lesion in one's self-esteem."[65]

Lord Delavere's wife is never mentioned in Damer's novel, except to say that she died when Belmour and his sister were young. Her absence might explain the rather dejected outlook of Belmour and Lady Caroline, not to mention Belmour's unconscious anger toward his father. Delavere insists that Belmour marry the insipid but open-hearted Lady Clementina, but Belmour finds himself attracted to the already attached Lady Roseberg. This relationship meets with the father's approval, but Belmour finds his pursuit of Lady Roseberg humiliating, her treatment of him unacceptable. As he chases a married woman, Belmour is enacting the oedipal crisis that led him into the melancholic state described by Freud: he is, once again, the rejected suitor, whose attachment to his mother must find some appropriate replacement. As he wanders the world in a melancholic state, depressed by his father's dying wish that he marry his cousin, he meets the friar in Portugal, Don Juan de Colavrado, whose own act of mourning for the beloved Rosaura expiates whatever sin and guilt attends his mistreatment of her. Though it is not clear that the friar's intense state of melancholy is induced by a lost mother, he nevertheless serves as a double for Belmour; in learning to mourn for a lost love, they become capable of experiencing, through that intense melancholy, a replacement for the primal love object. Belmour meets Don Juan de Colavrado twice: once in Portugal and once in Turkey. In both cases, the result of Belmour's interview with Don Juan is Belmour's decision to return to courting Emily. Don Juan himself draws parallels between their acts of mourning (p. 290).

At least four types of melancholy (natural, affected, religious, and clinical) appear in Damer's novel.[66] Belmour and Emily's natural melancholy (a product of their unhappy experiences in love or their reduced fortune) differs from the melancholy affected by Mrs. Stainville.[67] When Lord Raymond points out "the gloom" of Notre Dame, for example, this leads Mrs. Stainville to "[descant] on one of her most favourite themes, *the charms of melancholy*" (p. 219). In contrast to Mrs. Stainville is the Portuguese friar in his monastery.[68] "If the melancholy of these walls does not disgust you, perhaps you will deign to rest awhile in my cell," he tells Belmour (p. 110), exhibiting a religious version of Belmour's secular withdrawal. Lord Courtenay of Dean Abbey displays a clinical melancholy, bordering on mental illness. He takes long, unaccompanied rides through the forest—anticipating Hindley and Heathcliff in *Wuthering Heights,* incompetent and tyrannical lords of estates that they neglect and mishandle. Courtenay has obtained his wife through the machinations of a lawyer, Enstine. Yet Courtenay's melancholy is genuine and the "dry moroseness in his eye" constitutional (p. 172). When he thanks Emily for the few years of happiness he has enjoyed, the reader is inclined to believe him.

Melancholy was something very personal to Damer. She might never have become a sculptress or a novelist if art did not steady her nerves. As Damer tried to draw close to Berry, the latter withdrew (especially after a public accusation circulated in 1794), meeting Damer only in public and in the presence of others. "Provided I see you again, the languor and melancholy that still oppress my mind make it indifferent almost to me where we meet," Damer wrote. "Of one thing I am convinced, that the first moment my mind will in any degree in reality recover will be when I again see you and press you to my heart."[69] She was willing to play a supportive role for Mary Berry, but felt herself increasingly unnecessary: "Your poor '*Stick*' bids you farewell. It can be a support to nothing, but falls to the ground unless employed in its own service, by you."[70] For her part, Mary Berry regretted the increased dependence on her of a woman (Damer) she had once relied on for advice. "The letters I have had from poor Mrs. Damer but too truly confirm what you tell me of her," Mary Berry wrote. "Her ills of every sort are every day increasing and are alas! absolutely without remedy."[71] Damer, for her part, was unapologetic about her need for human sympathy.

That Anne Damer suffered from extended bouts of melancholy is hardly surprising, but that she wrote a novel involving romance at all seems strange. Her entire life was dedicated to an austere neoclassicism. She "always tried to emulate" the Greeks, she wrote, traveling to Italy "to perfect her knowledge of" their "true and simple style."[72] Yet Damer's cross-dressing shows that this cautious student of John Bacon felt drawn toward more effusive forms of self-expression than her disciplined career as a sculptress allowed.

Anne Damer outlasted her critics. She paid her debts, avoided the dissipation that ruined her husband, and created, because it did not yet exist, a useful place for herself in Regency England as female sculptress and cultural ambassador. Anne Damer moved in aristocratic circles that made her a taste-setter for her generation, influencing such figures as Princess Caroline, Hannah Cowley, and Mary Berry. Her closest friend, Mary Berry, for example, befriended Madame de Staël and set up a literary salon on Curzon Street that attracted Samuel Rogers, Lady Caroline Lamb, Lord Brougham, William Thackeray, and many other literary luminaries.[73] Damer shared John Cam Hobhouse's admiration of Napoleon and knew many of the figures in Byron's extended circle, influencing artistic taste in ways that have not perhaps been fully appreciated.[74]

As she aged, she sympathized with the Romantic, self-expressive heroines she once scorned. "Tho' I am not *Delphine* nor feel myself in any way allied to the race of modern *heroines de roman*," she wrote to Mary Berry on March 8, 1817; "I often find my eyes refuse the task my heart, for relief, would impose on them, in giving you details of what I now feel and what I suffer."[75] *Belmour* might also be read as she suggested *Delphine* should be, as the struggle of "a *Coeur aimant* against the delirium of passion."[76] The first draft of *Belmour* was in her notebooks, after all, which reflect an obsessive mind at war with its own insular and antisocial tendencies. One letter, written toward the end of her life, is typical: "Much it grieves me to think how much I have with my melancholy dashed your comfort," she wrote Mary Berry on March 28, 1803, "for so it is. Not, I know, that you would have had me suppress the feelings from which I suffered, or endeavour to conceal them from you, but writing can never be like speaking, and we have both suffered not only from '*les contretemps*' but from '*les maux de l'absence.*'"[77] In this rich notebook entry, Anne Damer anticipates all the major themes of her novel: melancholy, silent suffering, and the trials of absence, as well as the pain of erotic love. Drawing on the Walpole circle for her depiction of Belmour's life in London and at Dean Abbey, Anne Damer created a novel that celebrates her closest friends. Though she never cast Horace Walpole in marble (a strange omission, even stranger for never having been remarked upon), she did capture his world and her own in *Belmour.* The result is a novel that still holds interest to this day, for its skillful blending of sentimental, romance, and gothic forms.

Notes

1. Anne Seymour Conway Damer, Notebooks, 1791–97. 4 vols., Lewis Walpole Library, New Haven, Conn., 4:71.

2. See Charles Pigott's *The Whig Club; or, A Sketch of the Manners of the Age.* (London, 1794). In June 1790, Hester Piozzi "suspected [Damer] for liking her own Sex in a criminal way" and linked her to Elizabeth Farren. See the "Anne Damer" entry in *Orlando: Women's Writing in the British Isles from the Beginnings to the Present,* ed. Susan Brown, Patricia Clements, and Isobel Grundy (Cambridge: Cambridge University Press Online, 2006; <http://orlando.cambridge.org/> [October 28, 2009]).

3. Emma Donoghue, *Life Mask* (New York: Houghton Mifflin Harcourt, 2004); Andrew Elfenbein, *Romantic Genius: The Prehistory of a Homosexual Role* (New York: Columbia University Press, 1999), p. 108.

4. Anonymous, "Review of Belmour," *Monthly Review,* n.s., 38 (July 1801): p. 314.

5. See the "Anne Damer" entry in *Orlando: Women's Writing in the British Isles from the Beginnings to the Present,* ed. Susan Brown, Patricia Clements, and Isobel Grundy (Cambridge: Cambridge University Press Online, 2006; <http://orlando.cambridge.org/> [October 28, 2009]).

6. Susan Benforado, "Anne Seymour Damer (1748–1828). Sculptor" (Ph.D. diss., University of New Mexico, 1986), p. 222.

7. Mary Berry, *The Berry Papers: Being the Correspondence Hitherto Unpublished of Mary and Agnes Berry, 1763–1852,* ed. Lewis Melville (London: John Lane, 1914), p. 234.

8. Madame de Staël, *A Treatise on the Influence of the Passions upon the Happiness of Individuals and of Nations* (London: Cawthorn, 1798).

9. Berry, *Berry Papers,* p. 141.

10. Ibid., p. 40.

11. See Alison Yarrington, "The Female Pygmalion: Anne Seymour Damer, Allan Cunningham, and the Writing of a Woman Sculptor's Life," *The Sculpture Journal* 1 (1997): 32–44; Damer, Notebooks, 4:passim.

12. Henry Cawthorne, "Life Unhappy, Because We Use It Improperly: A Moral Essay, Spoken at the Tunbridge School Anniversary, 1760," in *The Poems of Hill, Cawthorne, and Hill,* vol. 65 of *The British Poets, Including Translations* (London: C. Whittingham, 1822). The poem begins: "I own it, Belmour! Say whate'er we can, The lot of sorrow seems the lot of man; / Affliction feeds with all her keenest rage / On youth's fair blossoms, and the fruits of age."

13. William Congreve, *The Comedies of William Congreve,* ed. Eric S. Rump (New York: Penguin, 1985), 4:4:12–13.

14. "So am not only forc'd to lie with other Mens Wives for 'em, but must also undertake the harder Task, of obliging their Mistresses—I must take up, or I shall never hold out; Flesh and Blood cannot bear it always" (Ibid., 1:1:142–45).

15. Ibid., 4:1:50–52; 55.

16. Percy Noble, *Anne Seymour Damer: A Woman of Art and Fashion, 1748–1828* (London: Kegan Paul, Trench, Trübner, 1908), p. 73. A privateer captured Damer on her return from Italy in 1778–79. "I am not at all surprised . . . at the intrepidity of Mrs. Damer," Walpole wrote to her mother; "she always was the heroic daughter of a hero" (Walpole, 11:118).

17. Damer, Notebooks, 4:71.

18. "The Author Is Supposed to Speak," a handwritten poem by Lady Ailesbury to her daughter included in the Lewis Walpole Library copy of Anne Seymour Damer, *Belmour,* 3 vols. (London: Joseph Johnson, 1801).

19. Letter to Conway, Tuesday, May 5, 1752; Horace Walpole, *Correspondence,* ed. W. S. Lewis, 37:333 (New Haven: Yale University Press, 1937–83); see also 37:334, 335, 350, 428.

20. Ibid., 37:334.

21. Ibid., 35:437.

22. Ibid., 11:7.

23. Berry, *The Berry Papers,* p. 45.

24. Noble, p. 122.

25. Ibid.

26. Ibid., p. 123.

27. Ibid., p. 124.

28. Ibid., p. 125.

29. Ibid., p. 126.

30. Ibid., p. 127.

31. Ibid., p. 129.

32. There was something Byronic about the burial instructions, the therophilia recalling Byron's monument to his Newfoundland; Damer died in London only four years after he did, to much fanfare, in Greece. Courtenay might also be seen as a figure whose moody and antisocial wanderings on horseback anticipate Byron's "Giaour" and "Marino Faliero." Damer met Byron's friend John Cam Hobhouse several times, and shared his antiquarianism and admiration for Napoleon in

1815. See John Cam Hobhouse, Lord Broughton, *Recollections of a Long Life, with additional extracts from his private diaries, ed. by his daughter Lady Dorchester,* 2 vols. (New York: AMS Press, [1968]), 1:316–17.

33. Damer, Notebooks, 1:1 (January 12, 1791, Lisbon).

34. Noble, p. 129.

35. Ibid., p. 128.

36. Damer, Notebooks, 1:11.

37. Berry, *The Berry Papers,* p. 38.

38. Damer, Notebooks, 1:8.

39. Ibid.

40. Ibid.,1:9.

41. "The drawings in particular attracted his attention: they were views, evidently original, of different parts of Italy, and various buildings, both ancient and modern, of that country, enlivened with figures, and executed in a free and masterly style. Among many of Venice, the church of the Mendicanti was often repeated, and various views given of the inside of the building. On farther examination among the figures on the foreground, one always presented itself so like his own, that he thought—could it have been possible—but it must be fancy—yet it was always represented in the very cloak he wore, on the very bench he sat, where he had often passed whole hours in listening to the divine music repeated from the grated gallery above.—Yet he had sitten for no portrait while at Venice—and again it must be fancy" (this edition of *Belmour,* p. 136).

42. Elfenbein, *Romantic Genius,* p. 108.

43. John Keats, letter to J. H. Reynolds, March 14, 1818, in *Selected Letters of John Keats,* edited by Grant F. Scott (Cambridge: Harvard University Press), p. 102.

44. "Shelleys' Reading List," in *The Journals of Mary Shelley: 1814–1844,* ed. Paula R. Feldman and Diana Scott (Oxford: Oxford University Press, 1987), 2:631–84.

45. Ann Radcliffe, *The Mysteries of Udolpho: A Romance, Interspersed with Some Pieces of Poetry,* ed. Jacqueline Howard (New York: Penguin, 2001), p. 4.

46. Ibid., p. 7.

47. Ibid., p. 46.

48. John Keats, "Ode to Melancholy," in *The Complete Works of John Keats,* ed. Jack Stillinger (Cambridge: Belknap Press of Harvard University, 1978).

49. Radcliffe, *The Mysteries of Udolpho,* p. 665.

50. Ann Radcliffe, *The Romance of the Forest,* ed. with an introduction by Chloe Chard (Oxford: Oxford University Press, 1986), p. 293.

51. "The Thoughts which musing Pity pays,
And fond Remembrance loves to raise,
  Your faithful Hours attend:
Still Fancy to Herself unkind,
Awakes to Grief the soften'd Mind,
  And points the bleeding Friend."

William Collins, "Ode, To a Lady on the Death of Colonel Ross in the action of Fontenoy," in *Odes on Several Descriptive and Allegoric Subjects* (London: A. Millar, 1747), reprinted in *The Poems of Thomas Gray, William Collins, and Oliver Goldsmith,* ed. Roger Lonsdale (Oxford: Longman, 1969).

52. Radcliffe, *The Romance of the Forest,* p. 245.

53. Ibid., p. 249.

54. Terry Castle, *The Female Thermometer: Eighteenth-Century Culture and the Invention of the Uncanny* (New York: Oxford University Press, 1995), p. 123; see also pp. 120–39.

55. Radcliffe, *The Mysteries of Udolpho,* p. 24.

56. Castle, *The Female Thermometer,* p. 124.

57. See Michael Gamer, *Romanticism and the Gothic* (Cambridge: Cambridge University Press, 2000), p. 71, for the difference between "gothic" and "romance": "Gothic, then, does not emerge as a genre separate from romance because it carries with it different gender associations or a different readership; rather, it emerges as a genre separate from romance because reviewers and social critics see its practitioners as committing different and more pernicious transgressions upon the same group of readers."

58. *Monthly Review,* July 1801, article 21.

59. *The Works of Thomas Gray: In Prose and Verse,* 2 vols., ed. Edmund Gosse (New York: Worthington Company, 1890).

60. Radcliffe, *The Mysteries of Udolpho,* p. 651.

61. Sigmund Freud, "Mourning and Melancholia" (1917), in *The Standard Edition of the Complete Psychological Works of Sigmund Freud* [or *S.E.*], ed. and trans. James Strachey et al. 24 vols. (London: Hogarth Press, 1953–74), 14:243–60; p. 244.

62. Ibid., 14:245.

63. Ibid., 14:246.

64. Some of these ideas are explored, in non-Freudian terms, in Thomas Pfau's *Romantic Moods: Paranoia, Trauma, and Melancholy, 1790–1840* (Baltimore: Johns Hopkins University Press, 2005).

65. Robert Clark, "Mourning and Melancholia," *The Literary Encyclopedia,* October 22, 2005, http://www.litencyc.com/php/stopics.php?rec=true&UID=1606 (accessed November 6, 2009).

66. For an excellent discussion of the positive aspects of melancholy, see Eric G. Wilson's *Against Happiness* (New York: Farrar, Straus, & Giroux, 2008).

67. See Diane Hoeveler, *Gothic Feminism: The Professionalization of Gender from Charlotte Smith to the Brontës* (University Park: Pennsylvania State University Press, 1998), which discusses Radcliffe in helpful ways.

68. It is worth noting that Belmour, Stanmore, Courtenay, and Mortimer all retire from the world. In Georgiana, Duchess of Devonshire's *Emma, or the Unfortunate Attachment,* ed. Jonathan David Gross (New York: SUNY Press, 2004), Emma's husband cannot accept her attachment to Augustus Sidney, a man who dies in Russia, and fails to believe second attachments (Emma's attachment to him) possible. He too chooses retirement from Emma until he can accept his place as her second lover.

69. Noble, p. 248.

70. Berry, *The Berry Papers,* p. 255.

71. Ibid., p. 372.

72. Benforado, p. 18.

73. See Berry, *The Berry Papers,* p. 244.

74. Hobhouse, 1:316–17.

75. Berry, *The Berry Papers,* p. 232.

76. Ibid., 234.

77. Ibid., p. 239.

NOTE ON THE TEXT

I have chosen the first 1801 London edition of *Belmour* for the text of this edition. There were four editions of this novel: a first London edition of 1801 by Joseph Johnson, a Dublin edition later that year, a French translation in 1804, and a republication of the London edition in 1827. I consulted the first-edition copy of *Belmour* at the Lewis Walpole Library in Farmington, Connecticut, which is the copy-text for this edition. I have also consulted the copy at the Newberry Library in Chicago.

The first edition of this novel and subsequent editions contain many internal inconsistencies in italics, paragraph breaks, punctuation, quotations marks, and spelling, including spelling of character names. To achieve internal consistency and to make the text more accessible to today's reader, this edition has been edited to normalize usage in some cases. Some changes have been called out in the notes at the back of the book, while others have been made silently. Some unconventional, older, or British forms of punctuation, spelling, and word choice have been retained in order to capture the flavor of the original.

For those interested in variant spellings in the nineteenth-century novel, I have listed the following changes, though many more exist: "doctor Seward" (in the original 1801 edition, see volume 1, page 249) becomes "Dr. Seward"; "Dr. Stanmore" is used here though "Doctor Stanmore" (3:21), "Dr. Stanmore" (3:22) and "doctor Stanmore" (2:27) appear in the 1801 edition. Similarly, "Roman Catholic" is used rather than "Roman catholic" (2:285), "roman catholick" (2:298) and "Roman Catholic" family (3:8). Some honorifics have been altered: "lady Caroline Belmour" (2:263) becomes "Lady Caroline Belmour"; similarly, "lord Raymond" (3:65) becomes

"Lord Raymond"; "Mrs. Rycott" (3:308) becomes "Mrs. Rycot." Other minor alterations include "intreat" (2:250) changed to "entreat"; "imbitter" (2:268) to "embitter"; "anti-room" (3:45) to "anteroom"; "sympathize" (2:295) to "sympathise"; hotels (3:39) to *hôtels;* "Deane Abbey" (1:132) to "Dean Abbey"; "farwel" (2:54) to "farewell"; "any thing" (1:255) to "anything."

Belmour appeared in three volumes and I have retained breaks in volumes since they mark dramatic changes in the narrative. Belmour's father dies at the end of volume 1, and Belmour leaves Emily at Courtney's house at the end of volume 2.

I am pleased to acknowledge Nicole Kirkman, Rebecca Sailor, and Kassia Shaw for providing a digital edition of the novel in 1999. Alex Anderson served as my research assistant in 2008 and made many valuable improvements. Mary Pariscoe assisted with numerous French translations, as did Professor Pascale Anne-Brault of DePaul. My special thanks to Malcolm Kelsall and Jerome McGann for advice about Restoration drama and textual criticism. An anonymous reader for Northwestern University Press suggested the modernized format and also provided a number of helpful comments that improved the final version; Jenny Gavacs assisted, very helpfully, as developmental editor; Alma Reising was a superb copy editor; and Serena Brommel saw the book, masterfully, through all its stages of production at Northwestern.

My special thanks to the University Research Council of DePaul University for financial support. The Lewis Walpole Library provided a month-long fellowship in 2009 that helped me complete this edition. My thanks to the director, Margaret Powell, for making this possible. This book is for Piya, with gratitude for her love and support.

BELMOUR:

A

NOVEL

IN THREE VOLUMES.

LONDON:

PRINTED FOR J. JOHNSON,

IN ST. PAUL'S CHURCH YARD.

1801.

Luke Hanfard, Printer, Lincoln's-Inn Fields.

Overleaf: Anne Damer's *Belmour,* courtesy of the Lewis Walpole Library, Yale University.

✦ Volume I ✦

Chapter 1

IT WAS TOWARDS THE END OF JUNE, when the Earl of Delavere quitted the hot, dusty town, for his castle, in the county of ——, on the western coast of England. The earl, though already in an advanced age, was full of health and activity; and was one of those few fortunate beings, who had been placed precisely in the situation of life, which best suited his taste and capacity, and was best calculated to display the really good qualities of his mind—generosity and benevolence. While his princely fortune served for the gratification of all his wishes, his hand was ever open to assist the indigent; and his pride, which was great, led him still more to the desire of praise for munificence, than to the mere ostentation of riches: but to the nice discrimination of real genius, and unassuming merit, the powers of his mind were by no means equal; he therefore sometimes assisted the less worthy, and afforded his protection to inferiour talents.

Leaning back in his carriage as he drove up a fine double avenue of limes, which led immediately to his magnificent castle, attended by a numerous train of servants, he viewed with a complacent feel of enjoyment the many surrounding beauties of the scene, bestowed by nature, and improved by art, at the seat of his ancestors, together with an unalloyed sense of all the advantages he derived from fortune.

He was accompanied by his only son, Lord Belmour, and his daughter, Lady Caroline Belmour:—turning to the latter, who sat in a pensive reverie by his side, he waved forward his hand to make her remark the increasing growth of the trees, and the fine bright evening sun, that lighted up every object; but finding her inattentive, and that she answered only by a faint smile, after gently pressing her hand, he addressed the remainder of his discourse to Lord Belmour.

They were received at the castle with the accustomed display of grandeur and ceremony. The old porter bowed low at the gate; all the servants "each particular of duty knew," and were exact in the performance of their separate offices. Two fat chaplains attended in the great hall, their faces not a little exhilarated by the earl's being come much earlier than usual, to pass the summer at his castle, and already in imagination devouring the venison and other dainties of his profuse table, which united the plenty of an ancient English baron, to the elegant nicety of the best French cookery.

The earl, after a short compliment to the obsequious chaplains, and a nod of protection, passed on to his study, whither he was followed by his steward, impatient to receive the orders of his lord, and welcome his arrival.

Lady Caroline, although the last day's journey had been but short, feeling herself fatigued, retired immediately to her own apartment. Her fine frame sunk under a pressure of grief and disappointment, and her health was daily impairing. In vain could she seek relief from reflecting on the many advantages she possessed; her high birth, youth, and beauty, with a mind far from uncultivated, as they gave her greater claims to happiness, often made the sad reverse more sensible to her heart.

Her affections had long been deeply engaged, and her too-confiding spirit had left her unprepared against the possibility of indifference or neglect from the man, by whom she had once thought herself tenderly beloved.—It was at Spa that she first saw Derville: he joined to an uncommonly pretty figure the most captivating ease of manners.—Sure of pleasing, by an apparent carelessness he but made his object more certain, and gave a value to the slightest attentions he deigned to pay, although they always tended to some gratification of his own.

The general admiration, which Lady Caroline excited at Spa, first attracted his notice; and as he was then unengaged in any other pursuit, his attentions to her soon became marked, and were received by her in a manner, to which his vanity could not fail of being sensible; for the natural modesty and reserve of her character were little calculated, to impose on one so well versed in the knowledge of the female heart as Derville. He was already known to Lady Newport, a near relation of Lord Delavere's, who had obtained leave of him, to take charge of his daughter for a part of the summer, and carry her with her to Spa.

To Lady Newport, therefore, Derville immediately addressed his attentions, and familiarly claimed an acquaintance, that had, indeed, before been but slight—little more than having seen her at every assembly in town, and having occasionally *honoured* her with a bow, when they met in a doorway.—She on her part was agreeably surprised at having so fashionable a young man in her train, and cared not to what she owed a distinction, that to her appeared so flattering.—Seizing the *ton* of intimacy, with which he addressed her, she presented him to Lady Caroline, with a complacent air of protection, expressive of the *great* acquisition made to their society in a person of Derville's figure, to whom there *could* be no objection. He was from that moment their constant attendant, no party was formed without first consulting him, and Lady Newport soon gave him a general invitation to her house.

She failed not shortly to perceive, what was the real cause of attraction to Derville; but being one of those officious characters, glad to make themselves agreeable at any rate, and sufficiently a woman of the world not to make her intentions too obvious, she without appearance of design encouraged the wishes of Derville, and promoted an intimacy, which she saw grew daily to have more charms for her unsuspicious young friend.—Everything thus conspired, to engage her affections in that dangerous errour, which afterward clouded all the bright prospects of her early life.

The very place, in which she saw Derville, was calculated, to make him appear to peculiar advantage in her eyes. He rode well, danced well, and possessed a thousand personal accomplishments, which could not have been displayed in London; where he found, that to appear an indolent lounging fop, was the easiest road to success. His paternal estate was not very considerable, but what with loading one part of it with mortgages, selling another, and having been fortunate at play, he continued to live in the most fashionable style of expensive dissipation.

Week after week passed on imperceptibly at Spa, and the time settled for their return to England nearly approached. Lady Caroline felt an undisguised melancholy at the thoughts of leaving Derville, tempered however by the idea of his following them to England, which he had declared he should do, whenever they returned thither. His attentions to her had been for some time more marked, and the turn of his discourse often so serious, that she doubted not, but that the inconsiderableness of his fortune, compared to hers, alone prevented his speaking openly to her of marriage; which, far from displeasing her, was, she thought, a mark of the delicacy and truth of his passion; and she was persuaded, that her father would not long refuse his consent, when he found her happiness deeply interested.

Her mother was a considerable heiress, and having died not many years after her marriage with Lord Delavere, almost the whole of her fortune had devolved, according to the marriage settlements, on Lady Caroline, as the only younger child. She felt, therefore, from the generosity of her disposition, much satisfaction in the idea of being perhaps able thus to remove, as she thought, the only objection, that could be made to her marriage with Derville, whose fortune certainly was not so ample, as she might have had a right to expect.

A part of the ensuing winter after her return to England had however already elapsed, without Derville's having come to any direct explanation; when a rich uncle of his, thinking himself near dying, offered to settle his whole estate upon him, provided he would immediately marry. Derville, although he really admired Lady Caroline, and was sensible to her too visible tenderness for him, was by no means disposed to matrimony, and thought with horrour of the immense *trouble* of breaking-off a connection, in which he had been for some time engaged with the wife of his *particular friend,* a woman of a high and violent spirit; to say nothing of a favourite French *figurante,* with whom he actually lived. Yet, as the advantage to himself in the offer of his uncle was so manifest, and as he was at the time somewhat pressed on the score of money, he determined to undertake the management of these separate interests.

Full of this idea, and Lady Darford (for so she was called) being at the time absent from town, he actually made proposals in form to Lady Caroline; taking his chance for what might be the consequence at Lady Darford's return.

The unsuspecting Lady Caroline now thought all her brightest hopes realized, and the high opinion her fond imagination had entertained of Derville's honour confirmed. She knew not the particular circumstances, but merely that Derville was made heir to a great estate, and that he had seized that moment for an explanation her heart had long wished; which left no doubt in her mind of the generous and disinterested motives, that had hitherto prevented him from openly declaring his sentiments.

The earl, her father, although a marriage with Derville did not by any means satisfy his expectations for the establishment of *his* daughter, would not withhold his consent, as she candidly avowed to him the situation of her heart. Lord Delavere however, as he was shortly going for a few months to Ireland, in order to settle some business relative to estates which he had there, begged that all final arrangements respecting the marriage might be deferred till his return.

A short month passed after her father's departure; during which poor Lady Caroline indulged in every flattering hope of future happiness, little foreseeing the storm, that was gathering over her head,—when Lady Darford arrived unexpectedly in town.—Derville had been extremely in love with her, and was still kept in her chains by every effort of the most artful captivation on her side.—She had heard of his intended marriage, but not from himself, and came purposely, full of passion and violence, to reclaim at any rate her captive.—Derville was extremely discomposed at her arrival and it was with the greatest difficulty, that he could at all pacify her, and bring her to consent to a measure, taken merely, as he said, to extricate himself from pecuniary difficulties, and oblige his dying uncle.—But such were the concessions on which she insisted, such her unguarded jealousy of Lady Caroline, whose youth, beauty, and unblemished character, might well excite her fears, that her pretensions soon became too evident to be mistaken.—She followed them everywhere in public, watched every look, and prevented every common attention, that Derville's present engagement with Lady Caroline rendered in a manner unavoidable.

Lady Caroline could not long fail of being sensible of Derville's embarrassment and change of manner. Yet she for some time endeavoured to deceive herself, and was willing to make every allowance for the quickness of her own feelings; till the fresh marks of neglect, with which she found herself daily treated, made it impossible for her any longer to mistake an indifference, which he scarcely attempted to conceal, while he only laughed at her uneasiness as trifling and childish.

A melancholy state of seeming apathy took place in the mind of Lady Caroline, and not a single complaint escaped her lips.—She was now near two and twenty, and knew enough of the world, to be sensible of her own situation; she had too much honest pride, and too much real tenderness, to bear the thoughts of dividing the affections of the man she loved with another; and she plainly saw, that, if she married Derville, she must condescend to become the companion of his mistress, or be wholly deprived of his society.

She determined, however, to wait till her father returned, whose absence had been prolonged from week to week, before she declared her final determination, which indeed the behaviour of Derville more and more confirmed.—He was no longer shackled, or distressed by pecuniary considerations, as his uncle had actually settled his whole estate upon him; and Lady Darford on her part spared no pains, nor hesitated at any sacrifice, that might contribute to render the dawdling attendance on her, to which he had been so long accustomed, and which was so congenial to his disposition, everything he wished. He therefore felt less and less solicitous about his marriage, which he saw would entail on him an endless contest; and he doubted indeed much, whether in any case marriage were, or were not a good thing. He therefore contented himself with honourably declaring, that he was ready to fulfill his engagement with Lady Caroline; and with the most perfect ease and composure trusted the final event to chance.

Lord Delavere at his return would not have much regretted the breaking off of a marriage, which he had never thoroughly liked, had he not been shocked on his arrival at the pale cheek and emaciated form of his daughter; who throwing herself into his arms, with her face bathed in tears, declared in broken and scarcely intelligible accents, that she should henceforward look for no other protector on earth but himself.

Lord Delavere was much affected, for he tenderly loved his daughter; but he knew not how deeply she felt this cruel disappointment;—nor had she any thoroughly sympathetic breast, into which she could pour her affliction. Her brother, a few years older than herself, to whom she was infinitely dear, had been for some time abroad, and the period of his return was uncertain; and indeed much as she required the consolation of his friendship and affection, knowing the extreme quickness of his feelings, she could not but rejoice, that his absence secured her against the possibility of his calling Derville to an account for the failure of her happiness—an idea, that of all others, she most dreaded.

Above a year had passed since this event; during which Derville never took the trouble, to attempt vindicating himself in Lady Caroline's opinion, and was then suddenly married to another woman. Lord Belmour had returned late in the following spring, and the particular circumstances relative to his sister and Derville having been at her earnest request withheld from him, he attributed the melancholy and languor, by which he at times saw her oppressed, in a great measure to the consequences of mere ill-health, an idea she always endeavoured to encourage.

Both Lady Caroline and her brother were glad to leave London, the former to avoid the sight of Derville, which she often found her resolution fail her in accomplishing while inhabiting the same town, and the latter wishing to seek the peaceful and romantic scenes of Belmour Castle; disgusted with the world, from the disappointments his too sensible heart, and too ardent imagination, had met with; although placed by fortune in that envied sphere, in which he was formed to shine a real ornament. It was towards dusk when they arrived—the evening, after an uncommonly hot day, was calm and serene, and the odour and freshness of the numerous *parterres* of flowers, which in the old state of gardening surrounded two *jets d'eau* immediately at the back of the castle, conspired to charm and tranquilize the senses.

Belmour, his mind occupied by many painful reflections, strolled out alone, scarcely knowing which way he went.—He continued for some time walking slowly under a long avenue of trees, that led from the castle, on the side of a part of which, and closely adjoining, was a small strip of garden belonging to the rector of the parish.—Just as he came to this garden, he was roused from the deep reverie, into which he had fallen, by sounds, which, he thought, were not wholly unknown to him, and which seemed the sweetest, that had ever reached his ear.—He heard a soft female voice go through a favourite Italian ballad, with the most touching expression. The well-known words were melancholic, and brought a thousand recollections to his mind; while the plaintive tone, in which they were uttered, appeared to sympathise with his own feelings.—He stopped, and listened with astonishment; at the same time looking through the boughs, which in places were but thinly spread, he discovered a woman sitting, half-reclined, on a bench of turf, with her back towards him.—Just as she ended the air, Belmour's dog, who had followed him, and was hunting among the shrubs near, came running by him barking loudly—she turned her head towards the noise, but appeared not to see Belmour, and getting up walked slowly away.

It was too dark for him to distinguish the person's face; but the tall, slender, and uncommonly elegant form, that he saw moving on before his eyes, filled him with surprise and admiration.—He remained for some time nearly on the same spot, in hopes of catching another glimpse of the figure, but at last concluded that the person he had seen was gone towards the rector's house, and it being then almost dark, he thought it improbable she should return.—He walked on however some way down the avenue, and failed not, after turning again towards the castle, to peep anxiously, though in vain, through the boughs, as he repassed the rector's garden.

When he got near the castle, he could not help smiling at himself, for by that time his imagination had been so deeply at work, and had painted to him in the same being a mind so suitable to the graceful form, which had presented itself to his sight, that a fancied interest had almost taken place in his mind, of which he thought his heart no longer capable.

On his return to the castle, at the bottom of the great staircase he saw one of Lady Caroline's maids, who said, that her lady had had one of her bad fainting fits, and was already gone to rest.—Belmour therefore supped *tête-à-tête* with his father, who was occupied in talking to him on business; this, and a sort of awkwardness, which he felt in beginning the subject, prevented his making any inquiry concerning the person he had seen in the garden, which he had intended doing—but he deferred all inquiry till the next morning, when he proposed to himself to call upon the rector, and concluded he should there receive full information.

The next morning, having risen early, as it was his custom, he had thought the time would never come, when he might with propriety make his visit at the rectory, and was walking to and fro in the great hall, with his watch in his hand, when his father passing that way, and seeing him from the end of the hall, called to him, and, full of a new alteration he was going to make in one of the apartments, taking him by the arm, kept talking to him, and consulting him about what was to be done, for above an hour.

When Belmour at last got to the rector's, a maid opened the door, and said that her master was just gone out.—"When would he return?"—she "could not say,"—and indeed looked so stupid, and so frightened, that Belmour gave up all hopes of gaining any intelligence from her;—and not being in the habit of calling upon the rector, an ignorant, vulgar man, whom he did not see five times in a summer, except on public days at the castle, Belmour could not, without particularity, think of returning to make him a second visit on the same day. Repassing the great hall of the castle, where in summer they often dined, he observed two additional covers, which on inquiry he found to be for Captain Plumewell and Captain Dash, two officers quartered in the adjoining town, who having come to pay a morning visit at the castle, had been invited to dinner by his father.—Belmour felt, that he could willingly have dispensed with any additional company—his sister was low and unwell, and his own mind occupied, not only by many bitter remembrances of events still painful, but by some views for his future establishment in life, which his father had of late pressed with more than usual anxiety, and of which he himself saw the reasonable advantage.

In this disposition of mind he sat down to table, covering as well as he could the thoughtful reverie, into which he was every moment falling, by that politeness and ease of manners, which were peculiar to himself.—In the midst of dinner Belmour was roused from one of these moments of thought by the sharp tone of Captain Dash's voice, who suddenly laying down his knife and fork, and addressing himself to Lord Delavere, said—"Pray, my lord, has your lordship seen the *wonder,* our new beauty?—but I forgot, your lordship has not yet been here a Sunday, and she only appears at church, he! he! he!—the rector locks her up on week days."—Lord Delavere, with a great inclination of his head, replied that he *might* not have seen the beauty in question, if he *had* been longer in the country, unless she had deigned to pay her devotions at his chapel.—"O Lord! beg a thousand pardons, my lord,—I forgot the chapel in the castle—but never was there so handsome a"—"dowdy," interrupted Plumewell, eying with complacency his own trim person.—"Yes, yes," resumed Dash, "*dowdy* as much as you please, but anything more beautiful I never beheld."—Lord Belmour, now all attention, interrupted them in a tone, that, however gentle, commanded a serious answer.—Upon this Dash, impatient to tell the story, silenced his companion, and proceeded to acquaint Lord Belmour with all he knew on the subject, which was, that a beautiful young woman, whose dress was uncommonly plain, had appeared on the Sunday before the last in the rector's pew, where indeed she had been seen before, but not by them, as they had only lately changed their quarters to where they were—that everybody was anxious to know who she was, but that nobody could find out; and that *he himself* had failed in the attempt, and, notwithstanding repeated questions, all he could get out of the rector, whom he said he never suspected before of *standing a siege,* was, that she was with him upon a visit, but as for *who* she was, or *whence* she came, there was no getting a word from him, or *even* from his wife, and still less from the young lady herself, whom he had, he said, accompanied, as it seemed rather against her will, almost half way from the church door to the rector's, till it began to pour with rain, without ever getting beyond a "yes," or a "no,"—that he "thought it d—d odd," but he "believed, upon his honour, that she kept from church the last Sunday *for fear of being admired.*"

"Pray let us endeavour at least to see this *wonder,*" interrupted the earl, smiling.—"Belmour," said he, turning to his son, "I really have some business with the rector, as you know; and it would be but a right thing for us, to invite him and his wife to dinner, for I know not when I can name a time for our public days to begin; and we will not forget, *and their company,* on the card, that we may make sure of the young lady.—These gentlemen, I trust, will do us the honour to meet them."—Plumewell and Dash bowed low—the necessary order was then given for the invitation, and the day named for the following Saturday.

After the company were gone in the evening, Lady Caroline remarked to her brother, as they were sitting together in the garden, how odd the account was, which the officers had given of the young woman, and wondered who it possibly could be.—The rector and his wife, she observed, had neither children nor relations, that she ever had seen with them, and were besides so vulgar themselves, that nothing at all like what had been described could possibly in any way belong to them.

Belmour, on this, recounted to her the *vision* he had seen on the preceding evening—he spoke with so much descriptive warmth and energy, that it extracted a smile from his sister.—"What can you mean?" said he, colouring. "—Ah! my dearest brother," replied she, gently pressing his hand, "beware of romance—remember the views of a father ever most kind to us—his earnest wish to see one of us at least settled," (here a tear started into her eye) "and his project, to which you certainly have *listened* of late, if not *consented*."—"But my dear sister," said he, recovering himself, "what can make you so serious?—can you possibly suppose me so ridiculous?—alas!" added he, mournfully, "the too sensible disappointments of *my* heart tend rather, I fear, to baneful apathy, than to the chance of any new or lively interest."—Here they were interrupted by the voice of Lord Delavere, who called to Lady Caroline, to come in and make his tea, and their conversation was not again renewed that evening.

Chapter 2

IN SPITE OF THE WAY in which Belmour had answered his sister, what she had said did not fail to make an impression on his mind.—The warmth with which he had spoken in describing his adventure, and still more what he had felt, made him appear almost ridiculous in his own eyes.—The two following days, which preceded the Saturday, although he did frequently walk by the rector's garden, and once or twice thought he saw the same figure at a distance through the trees, he made no attempts to see more of her; and when the Saturday came, had by that time half persuaded himself, that he was indifferent whether or not he even saw her at all, *certain* that he *should* see her, he began to believe, that his imagination, assisted by the dusk of the evening, and her unexpected appearance, had deceived him, and that most of the ideal charm would shortly vanish, and some, at best, *ordinary beauty,* present herself to his sight.

A little before the hour of dinner the company were assembled in the drawing-room, when, soon after, the rector and his wife were announced.—All eyes were instantly directed towards the door, when in *rolled* the smug, fat parson, grinning from ear to ear, preceded by his wife, curtseying all round to the very chairs, which she seemed in her confusion to take for lords and ladies—but in vain they expected the young stranger would follow.—The disappointment was general.—Belmour bit his lips, and could scarcely command himself sufficiently, to be commonly civil—all his curiosity, and all his interest in the stranger returned, as the expectation of seeing her vanished.—The earl, making a few steps forward, said—"But we were in hopes you would have brought your company—the young lady, of whom we have heard wonders."—"Much obliged to your lordship," said the parson, "yes, my lord—no, my lord, could not persuade her, my lord—never yet got her to go anywhere but to church, *that,* my lord, you know is quite in *my way.*" This he seemed to think a prodigiously good joke, and laughed at it himself immoderately.—Here the inquiry would for the present have ended, had not Dash, who thought himself now backed by Lord Delavere, skipped up, and with a look that expressed, you *dare* not *now* refuse me, said—"But pray, doctor, who is this stranger?"—"Stranger!" replied he, "almost as much a stranger to *me,* as she can be to *you,* captain, know very little of the young person.—Dr. Stanmore, an old friend of mine, who helped me to this living, by saying a good word to the bishop for me, begged that my wife and I would give her lodging for some time, as his parsonage was painting and repairing, that's all."

At this moment dinner was announced, much too interesting an event to Mr. Rycot, for him any longer to attempt even a second joke, or attend to one word, either Dash or any other person could possibly say to him.—During dinner, though several trials were made, little was got out of the rector or his wife respecting the young stranger, but that her name was Melville. The former was too much occupied by the excellence of the dinner, and the latter wholly taken up by the honour of having been thus invited in private, as she had never dined at the castle before but on public days.—There was, moreover, evidently something like mystery, which the earl was too polite, and indeed too indifferent, to attempt penetrating; and Belmour, from the fear of saying more than he intended, avoided any further inquiry, or even conversation on the subject.—Dash and Plumewell kept up a continual joke about friars, novices, and convents, at which nobody laughed but themselves, and which never advanced them a step further towards the information they wished to obtain.

The dinner over, and the company gone, Belmour took his evening walk as usual, along the avenue, that led by the rector's garden—out of humour with everything, and everybody—all seeming combined in the most teasing manner, to delay the gratification of his curiosity; and still more out of humour with himself for the eagerness of that curiosity, which, although he could not conquer, he was determined not to indulge.—Belmour, though he had never been exercised in the school of *worldly* adversity, yet, as his heart was warm and passionate, his nature confident, open, and generous, a delicacy of sentiment, ill suited to the commerce of a false and selfish world, had early taught him to suffer, and given him a degree of command over himself, which is rarely the portion of the fortunate.—Just as he got back to the door of the castle, he was met by his sister with an open letter in her hand, which announced, as she said, the arrival of Lady Clementina Alton for the next day.—It was then nearly dark, which prevented her in part from seeing the chagrin too visible on Belmour's countenance at this news, but perceiving that he answered coldly, she added, "—My dear brother, you know her coming a little sooner *can* make no difference—and then our aunt comes with her, surely nothing can appear less particular—but, for Heaven's sake! if you *do* dislike it, take no notice to my father.—I have fancied him not quite well of late, and nothing would hurt him so much, as the idea of distressing you on this subject—besides, I am certain, that he knew no more of her coming tomorrow than I did myself, which was not till I opened the letter I have here, which she sent on by *La Croix,* from the inn where she sleeps—'Tis just one of Clementina's freaks!—I suppose she found some ball dull, or the new opera too long!—for she has not the least idea of my father's wishes; if she had, for aught I know, this might be the last place, to which she would direct her flighty steps."

To this Belmour made no answer, but went upstairs to his father, who he fancied looked paler than usual: this, with what his sister had said, was more than sufficient, to make him curb his own sense of vexation at what he had just learned.—He inquired with anxiety of his father, how he found himself, and then talked of Lady Clementina's sudden intended arrival as of a matter of indifference.—Lord Delavere's eyes glistened, and his look tacitly thanked his son for a delicacy of attention, which was not lost upon him.

On the day following, towards the middle of dinner, Lady Clementina's carriage was heard clattering through the courts of the castle.—Lord Delavere made his son a sign, who flew immediately to hand her out—she was accompanied by her aunt Lady Eliza, an unmarried sister of Lord Delavere, who had

had the care of her education, her parents having died young, by which she had the *misfortune,* for a misfortune it too generally is, to become a very considerable heiress.

As she alighted from the carriage, Lord Belmour was struck with her as looking uncommonly handsome, which escaped not her observation, but served to heighten the youthful glow of health, which she possessed in an eminent degree, and added a thousand playful charms to her naturally sweet countenance.—Her fine fair hair was dishevelled, and her whole dress somewhat in disorder, from the hurry of having risen at the *early* hour of ten, to be *certain* of arriving at her uncle's in good time for dinner, as she knew, that he did not like late hours in the country.—As Belmour offered his hand, she seized his arm, and in a familiar way hurried him along, saying—"For Heaven's sake! let us make haste, I am so ashamed of being so late—never mind Aunt Eliza, she will take care of herself—won't you, dear aunt?"

In this manner she entered the dining-room, where she was received by Lord Delavere with open arms, who assured her, that *he* should never complain of the hour, that brought *her* to him.—Seated between the earl and Lady Caroline, she displayed all the gayety of nineteen, that never yet had known sorrow.—She declared herself "*starving,*" devoured whatever was set before her, found everything "charming," everything "delightful."—London, she said, was grown so dull, there was no bearing it with patience, everybody there was stupid—nothing *she* loved so much as the country!—and now she was *determined* to rise every morning at seven, then she should be so well, and *look* so well next winter—and be able to sit up ten times later at all the balls.—What will poor Aunt Eliza do! but she never minds, for she always falls asleep when the first dance after supper begins—never was so good a *chaperon*! They all envy me, for as she never knows what it is o'clock, she never wants to go home.—"Fie, fie! Clementina, how you talk!" cried Lady

Eliza, simpering with delight on her pupil.—It was, indeed, not easy to view her but through the medium of partiality—her faults were those of youth, partaking of the various follies by which it was surrounded, and her native mirth, good nature, and excellent disposition, were yet unsullied by a single self-reproach—she never meant to offend, or knew offence in others but by name—she had hitherto seen the world in all the gayest colours of spring, and had only read of wintry blasts in the fictitious pages of a novel.

Chapter 3

ABOUT A WEEK PASSED without any other occurrence than the arrival of Lord Fenmoss and Mr. Saunter, two fashionable admirers of Lady Clementina, who, finding their time hang heavily on their hands, as the town began to grow empty from the approach of a general election, claimed a slight invitation from the earl, to visit him in the country. One morning, the rest of the company having gone out in various carriages to enjoy a view of the sea, of which the earl was particularly fond, and which was best seen from a distant part of his domain, Belmour alone had remained at home, reading in his room, intending to follow them on horseback. Having finished his book, he went downstairs to replace it in the library. The door happened to be open; he walked thoughtfully on without looking before him, and was half way up the long gallery which contained the books, before he perceived, that there were persons at the other end. Imagining that they were strangers come to see the castle, he was retiring with precipitation, when he saw the rector come towards him, bowing and making a thousand excuses for the "intrusion," which he had "ventured to make, thinking," he said, "that all the family were gone out to take the air, having seen so many of the earl's carriages pass through the village that morning."—At the same time that he saw the rector, Belmour's eye caught a glimpse of the person with him, whom he immediately knew to be the same, whose figure he had indistinctly seen in the garden. Her extreme beauty, and the softness and dignity of her countenance kept him for some time in silent admiration. When he had a little recovered from his surprise, he desired that the rector would present him.—The young stranger had remained on the same spot without advancing; and when Belmour came up to her; he thought he saw a half smile on her lips, which she immediately checked, that seemed at first to indicate some former acquaintance, or recollection—yet he was *very* sure, he never had elsewhere seen her. After the usual compliments of presentation were over, she seemed disposed to take her leave, and was retiring towards the door, when the rector interposed, saying, "Sure, Miss, you will not now run away—my lord can tell you the names of the portraits, about which you were so curious."—Belmour, who on seeing her going, had immediately despaired of finding any possible excuse to retain her, offered himself with eagerness as a conductor, to show her anything she might think worthy of notice in the castle—adding, that "the portraits in question, which she saw over the bookcase, were family portraits merely, and perhaps might be uninteresting to her.—Some of the later heads, indeed," he said, "were by good masters."—"O lord!"—exclaimed the rector, interrupting him, "your lordship's quite mistaken—it was these portraits brought Miss to the castle—thought I never should have got her to come—till last night she by chance lit on the catalogue, explanation, and little history, begun in I don't know what king's reign, and so downwards—your lordship knows—telling the portraits one by one, of all your ancestors.—The book fell off the shelf, as my wife opened the corner cupboard—*whip* Miss here picked it up, and I thought we never should have got her to supper;—though I don't see why she gave herself so much trouble to read, for the moment she saw a name, she knew all about it better than our book could tell her.—This morning she was for coming to the castle, whenever I was *sure* the family were all out."—"Well, sir," interrupted the young stranger, distressed at the volubility of her companion, "do not let us detain his lordship longer than is necessary; since he is so good, I will beg to know a few of the portraits, that are without written names on them, and then we really ought to return home, as it is now late."—Saying this, she kept drawing towards the door, in spite of Lord Belmour's wish to delay her, which, however, he seemed afraid of making too evident. After thus gliding along the gallery, she had come to the head of the great stair-case, which Belmour was offering her his hand to descend, when a confused sound of voices, and rattling of carriages driving up to the door, announced the return of the whole party from the airing.—Lady Clementina was in an instant half way up the stairs, laughing ready to die—when perceiving the stranger handed by Lord Belmour, she stopped for an instant with an expression of the utmost astonishment—then flew up to him, and in a loud whisper exclaimed—"for Heaven's sake! Belmour, who is that beautiful creature? and what are you going to do with her?"—The stranger now appeared a good deal embarrassed, but recovering herself, bowed with much unaffected dignity, and seemed looking for the rector to accompany her home;—but Lady Clementina was downstairs again in an instant, and, hanging on her uncle's arm, insisted on his making the stranger stay to dinner,—"Nay, she had rather have the fat parson too, than let *her* go—Come, dear uncle, and invite them in your *best manner.*"—Lord Delavere was always disposed to do what his dear Clementina wished, and this was, indeed, little more than civility, as the hour of dinner drew near. The rector, thinking his own early dinner long since over no sort of impediment, catched at the proposal with too much eagerness, silencing all attempts the young stranger could make towards excusing herself, on the plea of his wife's expecting them home, to leave her even a possibility of escaping. As Lady Caroline and Lady Clementina were talking to her, Lord Fenmoss rushed by, without taking the least notice of them, upon which Lady Clementina again began laughing. His figure, indeed, was truly ludicrous, as he had half a dozen handkerchiefs tied round his throat, and one of the servant's great coats on.—"Look at him," said Lady Clementina, "he thinks it is all over with him—he is going to take to his bed—was there ever so ridiculous a mortal!—Mr. Saunter," said she, "how could you be so cruel!"—"What could I do!" replied he carelessly, as he was lounging up the stairs—"it was so damn'd hot, I could not hold the reins any longer—they dropped out of my hands, and the curricle tipped over just in a puddle;—not enough, I swear, to wet more than the end of his toe, though he is in such a fright about catching cold—besides, as I told him, he must be used to be up to his knee in water half the year, when he is at his estate in Cumberland.—Faith! I believe it was *that* made him so cursedly angry, for he has done nothing but bounce and fly ever since."—They were interrupted by the arrival of Major Heartley, an old friend of the family, an officer, who after much severe service had retired, with the loss of an arm, upon half pay, with the conscious satisfaction of having *deserved* more of his country, than he ever hoped to receive—and Ensign Melford, a younger brother of a noble family, who had undergone the *immense fatigue* of a campaign abroad, and had returned with all the fashionable disgust for exertions of any sort, and most particularly such as might endanger his own *elegant* person.

In addition to the company above mentioned, Mr. Mortimer arrived, by invitation, to dinner. He was a near neighbour of

Lord Delavere's—had been long a humble admirer of Lady Caroline; but, conscious of the little pretensions *his* rank and fortune could give him to the Earl of Delavere's daughter, he was still proud of the sentiments with which she had inspired him, and voluntarily nourished a hopeless passion in his breast; endeavouring to content himself with seeing, from time to time, the object of his admiration.—He was a man of blameless character, and amiable manners; but his fortune was small, and his health in early youth having been such as to disable him from following the law (the profession for which he was intended) he had retired into the country with an intention of passing the remainder of his life on his own estate, a farm of a few hundreds per annum, and abandoning a world, in which he felt little hopes of success. His passion for Lady Caroline confirmed this resolution; as, without her, he felt all situations must be nearly equal to him, and sought, therefore, only to dispose his mind to the quiet enjoyment of the rational pursuits still within his power.

These gentlemen had scarcely made their bow, when the dinner bell rang; the earliest summons Lady Clementina ever obeyed for beginning her toilette, which often was of more than equal duration with the first course.—That day she declared she would not be a minute; and hurrying away Miss Melville with her, who she said "*must* just come and arrange her hair," away she flew, and did actually return as the company were sitting down to dinner.—Miss Melville, being a stranger, was placed next to Lord Delavere, at the head of the table, and everybody, as if in common accord, left a seat next to Lady Clementina vacant for Lord Belmour, although he usually sat at the bottom of the table.—At first he was not sorry for the change, as it gave him an opportunity of more nearly observing Miss Melville, for whom every instant increased his admiration and interest.—A settled melancholy evidently hung on her fine expressive countenance—her manners were easy and unembarrassed, and though she seemed to cast an observant eye on everything around her, the uncommon profusion of magnificent plate, number of attendants, and general elegance, with which the earl's table was served, appeared as things familiar to her, and to excite in her no degree whatever of surprise.—Lady Clementina exceeded that day even her usual flow of spirits, and her mirth was much increased by several of the persons at table.—Lord Fenmoss, who sat shivering, wrapped up to the chin in a large fur *surtout,* as far as possible from every door or window, inquiring every moment if the physician he had sent for were come, and the *fat parson,* were to her irresistible subjects for laughter. She talked with her innocent freedom continually to Lord Belmour, and leaned familiarly towards him, whispering and endeavouring to make him partake of her jokes.—She had often *wondered,* that Lord Belmour never made love to her—a thing, as she thought, almost of course, from every man of figure and politeness: but she was not in the least offended; she concluded, that one day or other he *would,* but without any further determined idea, or intention of treating him at all differently from the rest of her many admirers.

Belmour, who wanted wholly to occupy himself with observing Miss Melville, was teased and embarrassed by the incessant interruptions of Lady Clementina.—He had caught Miss Melville's eyes, as it seemed to him when she thought herself unobserved, turned towards him with an expression of inquiry;—but it might be fancy.—Towards the end of dinner, a discussion arose between Heartley and young Melford, on the advantages and duties of a military life. The former commonly supported his opinions with more freedom and warmth than he possibly otherwise would have done, from a consciousness of the situation in which he might appear to the ill-judging world, who, from his contracted fortune, and his attachment to Lord Delavere's family, in whose house he in a manner lived, might, without further observation, set him down as a hanger-on, or led-captain, although the real worth and spirit of his character ensured him against the slightest degree of personal offence from anyone.—Melford, after a lively description of the *insufferable ennui,* attending the *fatigues* of service, looked towards Belmour, as if *certain* he should be supported in his argument by *an heir apparent,* who he, of course, conceived *could* think nothing bearable but ease and amusement.—"You should not," said Heartley, "address yourself to Lord Belmour on these subjects.—His lordship has very different ways of thinking, since he voluntarily fought on board one of his majesty's frigates, what I believe *you,* sir, would have thought still harder service than any in which you have been engaged."

Melford stared so long, and with such astonishment, at Lord Belmour, that a general silence ensued; and, he, finding some explanations of Heartley's speech necessary, said carelessly, but with a sigh, that he had taken the opportunity of going out with his friend Captain Harcourt, who commanded a six-and-thirty gun frigate, wishing to see the manoeuvring of a ship of war, having formerly wished to follow the profession himself.—He did not add, that his friend fell bravely fighting, in one of the most brilliant actions of the war, in which he was engaged; and that he, with the courage of a hero, was the first who boarded the enemy's vessel, after the lieutenant had taken the command of the frigate;—and, as a serious look which he assumed after he had finished his short account, at the same time offering to help Melford to some dish placed near him, plainly showed, that he chose to put an end to the conversation, no question was asked on the subject.—But Heartley related to the persons who sat next to him the whole in detail, in a whisper loud enough for Miss Melville, who was listening with particular attention, to hear.—"Don't listen, Miss," said the rector, suddenly turning towards her, "you will be frightened."—Miss Melville's pale cheek was in a moment changed, a deep blush was suffused over her face, and she hastily turned her head the other way, while the rector continued to laugh immoderately at the triumph he thought he had attained in putting her out of countenance.—All this, it may easily be supposed, did not escape Belmour, who lamented inwardly the impossibility he felt of penetrating at all into the sensations excited in Miss Melville's breast, which certainly seemed to be both strong and various during the course of dinner.

Early in the evening, though much pressed to stay, Miss Melville retired, to which the rector consented with a less degree of reluctance, from the extreme impatience he felt, to relate all that he had seen, and all that he had heard, in full liberty.

The moment he entered his own house, he ran up to his wife, rubbing his hands, and chuckling with signs of the greatest exultation.—"I have seen her," said he, "I have seen our new *countess,* yes *countess,* for the earl is to be made a marquis—the Marquis of Belmour, because they have found out it's the oldest title in the family, and Lord Belmour is to take the second title (I know not what) and to be an earl—and they are to be married in the castle—there's for ye!—I got it out of old Worthy, the steward—that is, he did not deny it—and he's as close.—Well, *she is a beauty,* and as gay as a lark, and as frolicksome as a doe.—No wonder my Lord Belmour admires her as he does!—Well, they will be the handsomest, sweetest couple—God bless 'em, say I."—"My dear," interrupted his wife, "I believe the ale has got into your head."—"Ale! where is your foolish head!"—he then, to the best of his recollection, gave her a catalogue of the different wines that were served at table, of the various dishes, and a minute description of the plate, and of every single article of magnificence, with an *attempt* to relate all that was said by every one of the company separately.—The whole with a volubility, that at last put him so completely out of breath, a pause of necessity ensued;—at which interval, Miss Melville took an opportunity to say, that she felt some degree of headache, and should go and take a walk, as the evening was so fine.—"Now, what, the devil! makes her look so *glum*!"—said he, as Miss Melville shut the door—"but some people never *are* pleased—that's sure enough!"—"Nay, my dear," said his wife, "don't say *that,* I am sure Miss always seems pleased and satisfied with everything she has here, though I often think, I don't know why, poor thing! that she has been used to better fare—and as for that, if she does love to sit sometimes in her own room, why, as they say, it's nobody's loss but her own, and better than always being in the way, like some folks!"—"You're a fool, Peggy, so come along," said the parson, twisting his wig straight, which he had more than half rubbed off in the warmth of his narration, and putting on his hat—"come along, I don't care if we *fetch a walk* too, before it's quite dark, for, now I think of it, *my* head feels a little queer, and the fresh air will do me good."—So saying, out he strutted, and soon overtook Miss Melville, who was walking slowly before them.—After their return home, the rector was shortly quieted, by falling fast asleep in his great chair; and Miss Melville sat the rest of the evening at work, little interrupted, as his wife, seeing her more than usually thoughtful and serious, did not obtrude her conversation.

Chapter 4

FROM THE TIME MISS MELVILLE had left the castle, Lady Clementina had talked of nothing but her—her beauty, her manner, and *who* she *could be*—not that it signified, she said, *who* anybody was, when they were so charming.—"Do, cousin," said she to Lady Caroline, the next morning at breakfast, "do let us go and see Miss Melville, it will be but civil, and Aunt Eliza will go with us—she is always *preaching civility* to me."—Lady Caroline, rather gravely, said that she would go with her the next day, but that they *must,* that morning, make a visit another way.

The next morning, Lady Clementina was down at breakfast earlier than usual, protesting that she "*would* go that morning, to see Miss Melville," and collecting all those she could to accompany her on her walk; "for *walk,*" she would, she declared, "it was so near, and so should Lord Fenmoss, in spite of the crick in his neck, and Saunter, in spite of the heat."—Melford was "always ready," he said, "*for expeditions of this sort,*" and Belmour bowed assent—but Lord Delavere, at the same moment coming into the room, told Lady Clementina, that she was welcome to dispose of all the gentlemen that morning except Belmour, who must go with him to meet a person of business, who was then waiting for them at the neighbouring town, at the same time making a sign to Belmour to follow him, as the carriage, he said, was ready.—Belmour, however vexed, had not a word to say, and still less ventured to oppose his father, and object to his proposition, from seeing Lady Caroline's eyes fixed upon him, while the earl was speaking.

The rest of the party, headed by Lady Clementina, proceeded, and were joined by Dash and Plumewell, whom they met in their way.—On their arrival, they completely filled the little parlour of the parsonage. The rector was happily *always* at his ease; but his wife, what with having that day an uncommonly dirty gown on, and a ragged old cap, which she squeezed every moment with both her hands—in vain—she felt it never could set tolerably—and the want of seats for more than half the company, was in a perfect fever.—It seemed to her so *unlucky,* that the honour of such a visit should not have come to her on the day before, or on the day after—any day in the whole year, she thought, would have found her less unprepared.—Miss Melville, who was called downstairs on the arrival of the company, gave her all the assistance in her power. She appeared herself unembarrassed. Her manner, indeed, on all occasions, partook of that ease, which observation, good sense, and a knowledge of the world, alone can give, and which is equally suited to a court and to a cottage.—This manner was, in Miss Melville, accompanied by a native modesty, which gave a gentleness and grace to all her actions.

Lady Caroline made Lord Delavere's excuse for not having been able to pay his respects to her that morning, but said not a word of her brother.—They afterward were led into the rector's garden, where Lady Caroline took notice of the neatness, with which the flowers were tied up, and particularly of an arbour composed merely of willow stakes, but a luxuriant honeysuckle and jessamine were entwined over the little arches with so much taste, and such advantage taken of a fine pyracanthus, which grew near and covered the remains of a bit of ruined wall, that it was impossible to remark it without admiration.—"All *Miss,*" said the rector, "all *Misses* doing.—Faith, she has improved this garden more in six weeks since she has been with us, than our Jemmy, the gardener, in six months—he! he! he!" "—A perfect *Flora,*" said Lord Fenmoss, gliding up to Miss Melville with a familiar and languishing air, who, after this *classic* compliment, of which he felt not a little proud, he thought must, as a person of taste, be flattered by *his* notice.—Lady Eliza could never view the slightest attention paid to any but her dear Clementina, without jealousy, and immediately bustled up to them in order to interrupt further conversation. Lady Eliza had, moreover, a particular predilection for Lord Fenmoss, and would willingly have favoured his addresses to her niece in preference to those of any other—for of all Lady Clementina's admirers *he* was the only one, who ever took the slightest notice of *her,* or ever appeared to perceive that she existed.—*He* would even frequently hand her out of the opera, rather than Lady Clementina; as he knew, that he might keep her snugly standing by a warm stove, till the carriage was actually at the door; while Lady Clementina would unmercifully drag him into the street, among links and footmen, in the open air, in frost and snow, impatient to proceed to some other place of amusement—or *on purpose* to divert herself at his expense, and laugh at him, as his *dread* of catching cold was a standing joke; and, in addition, his finical dress and person never failed, on these occasions, to attract the notice of some honest English by-stander, whose remarks afforded her fresh subject for mirth and diversion.—Then Lady Eliza always inquired *sympathetically* after his health, and recommended *possets, caudles,* and *conserves,* and all the pharmaceutical preparations of a Lady Bountiful, and, above all, *care of himself;* adding, with emphasis, that "*none* of the young men of fashion she saw, were *at all like him.*"—All this not only flattered his vanity, but encouraged his hopes of success with the *rich heiress;* a consideration by no means *indifferent* to his lordship: and he thought it well worth while to submit, to be now and then laughed at, for the chance of a great fortune, and imagined thus cunningly to outwit his antagonists.

After having hurried all over the rector's house and garden, insisting on seeing everything, and so good-humouredly *admiring* everything, that it was impossible to be angry with her, Lady Clementina returned with her followers to the castle, not without having made several attempts to persuade Miss Melville, to accompany her thither, and pass the day—but this she civilly declined.

Lady Caroline, at their return home, found herself so unwell, that, unable to dine below stairs, she immediately retired to her own apartment.—Belmour and his father arrived at the door, just as the rest of the company were sitting down to table, after having waited for a considerable time, every moment in expectation of their arrival, their business having detained them later than they supposed.

The dinner over, Belmour inquired for his sister, whom he found still alone in her room.—He had scarcely had time to express his anxiety about her health, when she interrupted him by asking what could have happened, and why he had an appearance of so much agitation.—"I was not aware of my looks," said he, "nor did I mean, at this time, when I find you so low and so oppressed, to have troubled you with anything merely relative to myself—but lest you should think this something worse than it really is, I will tell you, that my father, during the whole of our long drive, has been pressing me with more than usual earnestness, nay, with eagerness little *short* of violence, on the subject of my marriage, claiming a *promise* which certainly I never made, never could make, never *will* make," said he, rising and walking hastily about the room.—"Why should I voluntarily poison the remainder of a life, which has not hitherto been happy!"—"My dear brother!" said Lady Caroline, with a half-reproving tone.—"No," he replied, "I repeat it, my life has not been happy.—It is not on situation that happiness depends, but on the mind's being adapted to that situation (whatever it may be) in which it is placed.—Mine was not so.—Fortune, it is true, seemed to smile on me—but my heart was often at the moment agitated by anxiety, or torn with grief and disappointment,—deceived, cruelly deceived, in the object of my early affection, I have since wandered vainly about, seeking to curb, nay, extinguish those very feelings and sensations, that I know might have made me blessed.—No, no!"—continued he with much agitation—"if ever I *do* marry, it *shall* at least be a woman of sense, one by whose judgment my own can be both flattered and corrected.—I will not marry a girl, a child—nay, *if* I love her, my own reason must condemn the folly of such a passion.—What have I not already sacrificed to my father!—My disposition led me to the choice of an active life, and from what fatal errours might I not have been saved, had I been allowed a rational and serious occupation!—I wished, earnestly wished, to have followed the profession of the navy—to have accompanied a loved and valued friend in the same pursuit.—He fell!" (here Belmour's eyes were filled with tears) —"In this my father strenuously opposed me."—"I was an only son," he said,—"I knew myself independent.—His commands I might have resisted—his entreaties I could not!—in politics, again with the idea at least of being in some measure serviceable to my country—my youthful ardour would, in a general line of conduct, have prompted me to follow as a leader that one bright genius on whose heart I could repose, should his judgment on any occasion for a moment fail him.—He was in opposition.—Ministry, my father insisted, must always be supported, and he had private obligations, as he said, moreover, that rendered that support, in the present case, indispensable to him;—in short, every view, every prospect he could form, would have been frustrated by my retaining on this subject the privilege to think for myself.—Endless disputes would have arisen, or a coldness have taken place between us, which, from a really kind and affectionate father, my heart never could have supported.—But to become the humble servant of *any*, and *every* minister, and blindly to support his measures, I never could submit—against *that* every honest principle within my breast recoils.—I determined, therefore, wholly to abandon politics.—To this compromise my father, not without some difficulty, consented—but, accustomed to concession on my part, if in this instance he expect obedience, I fairly and openly declare, that he will find himself mistaken.—I know all his prejudices, yet should never, I think, be led to offend him in my choice; but no power on earth shall compel me, to shackle myself for life, without even a possible hope of future comfort or happiness."

Lady Caroline had remained silent—the image of Derville wholly occupied her mind from the moment Belmour uttered the words "deceived by the object of my early affection": it was too forcible an appeal to her own heart!—But by this time, endeavouring to recover herself, she attempted to say something in favour of Lady Clementina; as her father had entreated her to use her influence, to assist in persuading her brother to a marriage he had so much at heart; and in which, indeed, she herself thought she saw many serious advantages.—"Surely," said she, "Clementina is uncommonly handsome, and, setting apart her high birth, her being an heiress, and her near connection with us, always an agreeable circumstance, as it avoids the inconvenience of a thousand new, and, ten to one, troublesome relations, I cannot, when I look round, see any young person to compare to her—she is so amiable! so good-natured! and I am sure, since she has been here, she seems pleased with everything."—"Yes," interrupted Belmour with some vehemence, "pleased with *everything,* and with *everybody.*—You are perfectly in the right, sister, but I must tell you, that, in my opinion, such persons are more to be avoided in a serious connection, even than those who are *pleased with nothing.*—At least, they suit neither my temper nor disposition, except for a common acquaintance, whatever others may think of them.—And this is *really* the strangest fancy in you *all,* to persecute me about a girl, that I am persuaded never to cast away a more serious thought upon me, than on Fenmoss, Saunter, or any other man, that could hand her out of an opera, or would dance a country dance with her!—But I am too warm," said he, "I slurry you now you are ill: forgive me, my dearest sister, forgive me," he repeated, in the most affectionate tone, "let us drop this subject for the present, I will leave you, and come again by and by, if you still remain in your room."—Saying this, he left his sister—went precipitately downstairs, and directly out of the gate, bending his hurried steps towards a wood at some distance from the castle, backed by craggy rocks, which overlooked the sea—a favourite walk of

Belmour's, where he passed many a solitary hour, sometimes fixing his eyes in silent admiration on the vast expanse before him, sometimes lost in endless reverie.—Alone here, and secure from interruption, as the agitation of his mind, from his recent conversation with his sister, began to subside, a thousand recollections crowded on his imagination.—The quiet stillness of the evening, indeed, led insensibly to thought and reflection; no sound reached the ear, but the gentle murmur of the ebbing tide on the sands beneath; the sea was smooth as glass, and the distant little barks scarcely seemed to move on its surface.—The sun, veiled in a light mist, was now already drawing near to the horizon; and the whole surrounding scene was such, as, on a mind like Belmour's, could not fail to make a sensible impression. Yet he felt not half the soothing charm;—no *one* beloved object now filled and occupied his heart.—Young as he was, the airy phantoms of imaginary bliss had long vanished from his sight; and, in their place, appeared to his maturer judgment no flattering hope of more rational enjoyments, such as tempered by reason could satisfy a mind like his, tender, delicate, and susceptible in the extreme, yet confident, open, and generous.—

When Lord Belmour, not then one-and-twenty, returned first from his travels, he came into what is called *the world,* with every possible advantage nature or situation could give.—The grace of his uncommonly fine figure was heightened by all the elegance of dress, and by the most polished manners; and while his native spirit and approved courage made him not less feared than envied by the men, he was courted and idolized by the women.—But to vanity, that could flatter neither his understanding nor his heart, he was little sensible; and although his youth and passions led him for some time to follow, without restraint, the impetuous torrent of dissipation and pleasure, yet, as his mind was naturally both of a serious and thoughtful turn, even in the midst of that perpetual vortex, which is termed *society* in London, he still found moments to indulge his love of reading, and the cultivation of his mind; for Belmour not only left *Eton* and the University the allowed best scholar, but had never discontinued his pursuits in classical learning, and in every other species of elegant literature.—Such moments, indeed, were for some time short and interrupted; but he soon grew disgusted with the insipid bustle of general society; his head, not less than his heart, requiring some more real occupation and interest.—The profligate discourse of his young companions he never could support with patience; and as his known spirit always made him feared, he shortly became a restraint upon them; which circumstance, as he could not fail to perceive it, rendered their company at best but dull and insipid to him.—In this state of mind he first began to distinguish Lady Roseberg, and to seek every opportunity of expressing his respectful admiration of her, for such indeed it was.—He believed her, what she appeared, all that was amiable, all that was virtuous, and approached her with a reverence little short of that due to a divinity;—for though he had followed the allurements of pleasure, his heart was uncorrupted, and he attributed the success, he had hitherto met with among women, to their too great facility, not to indiscriminate vice, and still less to his own merit.

Lady Roseberg was then at the very pinnacle of fashion, admired and respected.—She had been married at sixteen, as it was supposed against her inclination, to Lord Roseberg, who, besides being above sixty, was in his appearance disgusting, and his understanding and manners were by no means calculated to redeem the faults of his person; but he had an immense estate entirely in his own power, no children by a former marriage, and offered *carte blanche* as to settlements.—Miss Rayfield had not sixpence in the world; and the affairs of Sir Samuel Rayfield, her father, were so involved in some East India transactions, not much to his credit, that from him she had nothing to expect; and his only hopes for her future establishment, were to be derived from the bargain made in consideration of her youth and powerful charms.—Lord Roseberg appeared to both the very person on earth best adapted to their purpose.

Miss Rayfield, on her part, had so well profited by the maxims of her father, assisted by certain intuitive principles, inherent in her own breast, that she saw in perspective all the advantages she might derive from such a marriage; and was little less anxious for its accomplishment on the first overtures made by his lordship, than her prudential and calculating father. The marriage was therefore shortly concluded, and, as the whole of the business had passed in the country, where at a race-ball she had been seen, admired, and followed by the enamoured peer, she made her appearance for the first time on the theatre of fashion in London, in the character of *a victim,* cruelly sacrificed to age and ugliness, and was almost as universally pitied, as she was universally admired.

She was received with kindness and attentions even by Lord Roseberg's family, for though they would rather he had not married at all, as they all thought that unavoidable, they were well satisfied that he had not fallen a prey to something much worse, as he was known all his life to have been led by *some* woman—and indeed to be the certain dupe of almost *any* woman, that would take the trouble to impose on him by cajoling and flattery: yet the task was not easy, as the narrowness of his mind rendered him suspicious, and his total dependence on others for amusement and occupation, fretful and discontented.—But once thoroughly lulled into a security, in which he found his own ease, and constant attention to humour his every trifling caprice and fancy, there was little to fear from his penetration.

Lady Roseberg had not naturally a vicious character—she was good-natured and compassionate; and, perhaps, under other circumstances than those in which she was placed, might in some measure have really merited the respect and consideration she for a long time obtained from the world; but an excessive love of pleasure, and a too great facility in its gratification, proved her ruin, and finally overset all the barriers her good sense, prudence, and judgment, had opposed to its violence.—She ceased wholly to respect herself, and shortly after lost the respect she vainly hoped by art and duplicity to extort from others. When Belmour became attached to her, she was in the zenith of her charms; her conduct to her lord had appeared exemplary, and scarcely was the voice of calumny heard louder than a whisper against her. Young men, it is true, were always of her society—but her manner to them was easy and unconstrained, and the first step to admission into her house, was by proper attentions to her husband—and though she followed the full torrent of fashionable amusements, went late to every place, and came late from every place, it was always in company with women of approved character and reputation, near relations of her lord, or such as in themselves, according to the opinion of the world, could but be of advantage to her. In private society, she never was known to show either a shadow of disgust or contempt for her husband.—Some indeed were of opinion, that in her manner to him she carried this forbearance too far the other way, and *must* have reasons for thus affecting, what could not be sincere.—Be this as it may, she had by her prudence gained a degree of consideration, which, united to her youth, beauty, and captivating manner, rendered her the most followed and most admired woman in the bright circle of fashion.

Belmour came a humble suppliant to this shrine of perfection—he had hitherto admired Lady Roseberg only at a distance, but now took an opportunity of being presented to her, as one desirous of being admitted to her society. In consequence he left his name with her husband, with whom, from his naturally agreeable manners, he soon became so great a favourite, that Lord Roseberg was always inviting him to dinner, and soon grew scarcely to be easy, if he passed a day without seeing him. This so well suited Belmour's growing passion for Lady Roseberg, that he willingly submitted to all the *ennui* of his conversation; and, whenever he could flatter himself, that it was not absolutely disagreeable to her, accepted his invitations. For some time she seldom herself invited him, except to her assemblies; and Lord Roseberg at last became peevish at the omission, and asked her, "why she invited a pack of impertinent coxcombs every day, who had neither common sense, nor common civility for *him,* and neglected Lord Belmour, because he was *his friend*?"—She assured him, in the gentlest tone, that she should always invite those, who were most pleasing to *him;*—"You know, my dearest lord, that you choose your own society, and that *my* first study is to make the house agreeable to *you.*"—A look of self-complacency and satisfaction followed from his lordship; he told her, she never looked handsomer, that her head-dress became her, asked her if she had not of late been unlucky at play, put a note of two hundred pounds into her hand, and then limped down to his own apartment, in the most perfect harmony of temper, begging her not to "hurry herself," or come home a moment sooner than she liked on his account.—These, or scenes like these, passed daily, and Lord Roseberg was persuaded, that no man ever was so much master in his own house as himself.

Lady Roseberg, to whom Belmour from the first was by no means indifferent, which indeed had been the cause of her redoubled caution, now saw him oftener at home, and allowed him to be one of her constant attendants in public—but his real and unaffected passion was so evident to others, that it obliged her to greater reserve and appearance of indifference to him, than she showed to most of her followers.—This, poor Belmour construed into disapprobation of his attachment;

and he was frequently tempted, in despair, wholly to relinquish a society, in which he often experienced so much pain and mortification—but as she never lost sight of him, and carefully watched these workings of his heart, a smile, a look were sufficient to recall him ten times more her captive than before.

Still the task on her side was difficult.—He was young, and though his honour, she thought, might be trusted, his conduct might be imprudent.—She knew him to be quick, and believed him jealous—and then his enthusiastic admiration of her *virtues* much *alarmed* her.—What would be the consequence, she reflected, if he ever discovered her *less rigid* principles!—Yet he was not to be given up—*this,* passion had already forbidden in her own breast. Thus the remainder of the winter passed, and her lord had named his day for leaving London, with an intention of passing the early part of the summer at his villa, whither she meant, according to a little plan she had formed, that Belmour should be invited, but *not* by *herself.* Lord Roseberg, she was certain, would insist on Belmour's being of the party.—To him, therefore, she tacitly left the invitation, reserving to herself not to *forbid* his coming, when he should in confidence ask her leave; as, on all occasions of this sort, she well knew, that she might depend upon his delicacy, and that he would rather avoid her sight, than risk offending her; but, as it often happens to those even of the most consummate art, she this time carried her policy a step too far.

Belmour was at her house one evening, only a few days before her intended departure; when Lord Roseberg, who had several times before mentioned the subject to him in general terms, now particularly and directly invited him, and requested him earnestly to accompany them out of town. Lady Roseberg, who was standing close by them at the moment, affected not to hear what her husband had said, but, with an air of carelessness, turned round and walking up to a group of men who were talking together in the middle of the room, began laughing with the greatest appearance of indifference. Belmour, who was quite sure she had from the beginning heard every word Lord Roseberg said, and who was anxiously watching her countenance, in order to discover whether or not he might venture to accept an offer, that gratified his every wish, was so much vexed and disappointed at her manner, which argued, it seemed to him, something even beyond indifference, that after muttering a few indistinct expressions of thanks to Lord Roseberg for his invitation, and casting a look of anger and mortification at her, he suddenly left the room—went home, and ordered horses to be ready for him at a very early hour the next morning, in order to leave town. But whither to go, he scarcely knew—his mind was in a state of restless agitation—he then recollected, that the friend of his earliest youth, and, though a few years older than himself, for some time his school companion, Captain Harcourt, who commanded a six-and-thirty-gun frigate, was just now at Plymouth.—Thither Belmour went, and found relief for his oppressed heart, in the warm and sincere expressions of attachment of the honest tar, who, though he knew not the refinements of modern and sophisticated gallantry, could pity the real sufferings of his friend.

Not long after Belmour's arrival at Plymouth, Captain Harcourt was ordered out on a cruise. Belmour was delighted, on every account, to accompany him. The circumstances followed already mentioned by Heartley—the impression on Belmour's mind was deep and lasting, he had received the last look and dying breath of his friend; who mortally wounded actually fell into his arms.—He was a young man of uncommon expectations; unallied to anything great or powerful.—He had early risen to the rank of captain, and the command of a frigate by his own personal merit and valour.—His character indeed, uniting the most enterprising spirit and undaunted courage to every gentle grace of humanity, did honour *even* to that of a British sailor.

Lady Roseberg, on the morning subsequent to Belmour's leaving her, had with peculiar care attended to every circumstance, that could heighten the elegant negligence of her dress, had *supposed* a bad headache, and ordered only such and such persons to be admitted, among whom Belmour was *not* forgotten. She depended on his coming, and had arranged all she was to say, and all she was to *look*—the whole of which, summed up, was to express, that she *feared,* yet *wished* he should accept of Lord Roseberg's invitation.—No Belmour came—that day and the next passed without her knowing what could have become of him, and her mind already misgave her; when she accidentally heard from Lord Sansterre, whom she met, that as he was returning from the club towards six in the morning, two days before, he had seen Belmour's chaise, with four post horses, galloping out of town;—"What could possess the damn'd fellow?" he asked, "everybody living is in town."—Lady Roseberg with difficulty concealed her emotion.—She was *not mortified,* she too well knew the real cause of Belmour's leaving her, but she was vexed and provoked at herself.—She *ought,* it now seemed to her, to have known Belmour better.—"Yet who could suppose any man, who had ever lived in the world, so absurd?"—What was to be done?—her whole plan had failed—to pass the summer with Lord Roseberg, without one single *interest,* was intolerable even to think of!—She pretended indisposition; retired to her own apartment, where she wrote above a dozen letters to Belmour, all which she one after another threw into the fire; and at last determined to *postpone* this growing and already powerful inclination, and to encounter for the present the unspeakable *ennui* of her husband's constant company, as long as fate should destine her to remain in the country; and rather take her chance of Belmour's returning to her of himself, whenever they should meet, than risk the opinion he might entertain of her, should she, circumstanced as things were, unexpectedly write to him. A resolution once taken, was supported by few better than Lady Roseberg; little alteration therefore was perceivable in her manner, during the few weeks, which they passed at their villa. Yet her mind was by no means equally composed.—The brilliant action, in which Belmour had been engaged, had not failed to fill every newspaper, and for some time to become the general topic of discourse.—She did not require to be *put in mind* of her lover—in fact, she grew every day more anxious and uneasy, and began to fear in earnest she had lost her captive. She was agitated by a thousand various sensations, which, if not new, were at least stronger than any she had hitherto experienced. She looked forward with absolute horrour to an autumn, passed at their chief country seat, surrounded by neighbours and relations, whither Lord Roseberg talked of shortly going; and to the still more painful idea, which now often presented itself, of finding Belmour engaged in some new pursuit, at her return to London.—But it so happened, that Lord Roseberg was suddenly seized with a cramp in his stomach, which excessively alarmed him, and he consulted with Lady Roseberg, whether it would not be more prudent for him at once to remove to town, where he could be certain of every medical assistance at a moment's warning. Lady Roseberg did not fail warmly to second this proposal, and accordingly, in a few days afterward they actually set out for town. As the coach-and-six drove along Piccadilly, almost the first object that presented itself was Belmour, walking slowly along the pavement.—They both saw him at the same instant, and Lord Roseberg, pulling the check-string with vehemence, as soon as he could get the carriage stopped, threw himself half out of the window, extending both his arms, and screaming out in a shrill harsh voice, "Come hither, my dear boy, this moment! we have been lost without you—how could you go fighting there for nothing, when we have so many beggarly younger brothers, that might as well take the chance of being knocked o' the head, as not!—but come along, we have got you again now, and, by G—! we won't let you go a second time."—Saying this, he began making room in the carriage for him, and with a tone of impatience ordered the servant to open the door.—Belmour had advanced bowing, and, as it were purposely, not looking towards Lady Roseberg—when, in speaking to Lord Roseberg, he raised his eyes, and immediately met hers, fixed on him with the softest expression of tenderness and concern.—The dejected appearance of Belmour, the melancholy expression of his countenance, really excited her pity, and she had not time to compose her own looks, or to recover from the surprise of meeting him thus unexpectedly, after an absence that had caused her so much pain.—Nor did she wish it, but now no longer sought to conceal the emotions, which his presence excited.—Belmour for some time remained with his eyes fixed on hers, not hearing a single word that was said to him, and found himself actually seated in the carriage with her, almost without knowing how he had gotten there. Lord Roseberg ordered the carriage to proceed to his own house, and, of course, retained Belmour to dinner, and for the remainder of the day. Poor Belmour drank deeply of that dangerous poison, to which his artless mind exposed him—he for the first time believed himself beloved, not only by the object of his passion, but by the object of his admiration and respect; for he never for an instant had doubted Lady Roseberg's virtues, which, though he might consider them as a bar to his happiness, he still revered.

Day after day now passed with him, in a state of intoxicating joy.—Not a creature at first was in town, and constantly invited as the guest of Lord Roseberg, he passed almost his whole time in the society, for which only he felt the least real interest. An intimacy took place, which rendered him, he thought, supremely blessed: yet from a variety of causes his happiness was by no means without alloy. The open, generous candour of his mind, often revolted at the means, which were taken to ensure the continuance of their commerce without suspicion; though necessary, as Lady Roseberg assured him; and it required all the force of strong passion, the dominion of which he was then under, to reconcile him in any degree to the constant scene of deceit and hypocrisy, to which he was hourly witness. The advantage also taken of the credulity of one, who certainly to him showed every mark of attention and partial kindness, cast a gloom over his thoughtful moments: but there was no alternative; he must submit to what his honest heart could not approve, or for ever lose the object most dear on earth to him. He moreover often looked forward to more lasting ties.—The age and infirmities of Lord Roseberg could not possibly fail to suggest the idea of Lady Roseberg's being one day free to dispose of herself; and his weak and contemptible character, dwindling then into peevish and fretful childishness, the instant he was not indulged in whatever might be the fancy of the moment, made it impossible that she could feel any lasting regret for his loss.

Thus two years passed, during which time every art was displayed on her side, to retain her captive by the only means, on which she could depend to secure his tenderness.—Had she indeed been what she seemed, no *art* was necessary: *his* passion was too sincere not to be constant, while he could think himself not deceived in its object.—This she felt, and felt too her own situation—nay, sometimes even almost wished she had not given Belmour an opinion of herself, which it cost her so much pains to maintain; yet she at other times enjoyed her triumph over his unsuspecting heart, and applauded the subtlety of her own invention, by which she governed the minds either of those who stood in her way, or of those who contributed to her pleasure—but the reign of deceit and falsehood is never lasting.

About this time Belmour, having one day as usual passed the greatest part of the morning at Lady Roseberg's, was standing by the fire, listening to her arrangements for the evening, meaning soon after to take his leave.—When the door suddenly opened, and a man he had never seen hurried into the room without waiting to be announced, ran up to Lady Roseberg, and with an air of the greatest familiarity, taking hold of both her hands, which he kissed one after the other, asked her, if she ever were "so surprised" in her life, as at seeing him. "My last letter did not announce this."—She did indeed seem *surprised,* for she turned as pale as ashes the moment he entered the room.—"I have tired them out, and finished the business," said he, "and am, thank Heaven! returned to the only place on earth, after all, that one *can* live in."—Then only perceiving Belmour for the first time, as it seemed, he eyed him from top to toe, with an inquiring, supercilious glance, not even bowing, and, still holding Lady Roseberg's hands, led her, without the least ceremony, to a window, where a long whisper began between them, during which he sometimes cast his eyes towards Belmour, as if inquiring who he was.—Lady Roseberg had already several times repeated the usual sign for Belmour to retire—he was petrified—at last, however, though unwillingly, he took his leave.—"Who can this be," said he to himself, as he walked slowly from the door, agitated by sensations he could not entirely define.—The person who had thus entered the room was a man rather genteel in his appearance, not young, but tall and well made; his features were marked, and not irregular; but his countenance was sharp and sarcastic.—He was dressed in a foreign surtout, and had the appearance of having lately come from abroad.

Belmour had not gone fifty paces from the door, when he met one of those frequenters of every public place, and of every private society, to which they can obtain admission, who make it their whole and sole business, to dawdle from one place to another, retailers of every tittle tattle lie, and newsmongers ordinary and extraordinary—a Mr. Barnvelt by name, a diligent investigator of all subjects that concerned others, and did *not* concern himself.—"So," said he, familiarly taking Belmour's arm and walking on with him, "St. Fort is come back suddenly, when nobody expected him.—I think I saw him going into Lady Roseberg's not ten minutes ago—but *you* must know, for you are just come from thence, was it not he?"—"Who is St. Fort?" replied Belmour, without answering Barnvelt's question.—"Damn it! *you* must know St. Fort—but no, no, now I think of it, when first you appeared in the world, he was already gone to Munich, having gotten himself appointed envoy, because he had not a sixpence in the world, and was over head and ears in debt.—*Who* he is I cannot easily tell you, I doubt whether he knows that himself, and I am sure *I* do not—but *what* he is I *can* tell you, and that is, one of the damnedest sly sneering rascals that ever existed—Egad! He made himself somehow or other useful to ministry, and was, as I said, appointed envoy to Munich; and now, because it suits him, I suppose, has made them recall him, for no creature expected him back—but you *must* have heard of him at least," continued he, looking Belmour full in the face.—"I never did."—"Humph!"—here the conversation dropped; and Barnvelt, seeing that Belmour was not at all in a communicative mood, pretended that he saw some person on the other side of the street, to whom he must speak, and hurried away.—Belmour was heartily glad to get rid of him; he wished certainly for information concerning the person he had seen; but hated Barnvelt for every single word he had uttered on the subject, which he thought might be all lies, or misrepresentations.—Yet what he had heard added considerably to a thousand teasing uneasy sensations, which tormented him.—He now much quickened his pace, that he might not be stopped a second time by some other impertinent fool, hurried home, went directly up to his own room, and ordered no one to be admitted to him.

Here he paced backward and forward, his mind wholly occupied by confused ideas and painful suspicions, which he dismissed as soon as they were formed—he looked to the hour of going to the opera, where he was to see Lady Roseberg, with an impatience scarcely supportable—yet a dinner in company was to be first endured.—His father (with whom he lived) had particularly desired his attendance that day, and whatever might be the feelings of Belmour, he never, on any occasion, sacrificed to them a single particle of duty or good nature.—At last the hour of the opera came.—When he arrived at the theatre, the first object that presented itself to his sight was Lady Roseberg, quietly and composedly seated in her box.—He looked at her for a few seconds at a distance, before he went to her—she was alone—on his entering the box, she turned round with her back entirely to the stage, and making him a sign to come and sit in a chair close by her, smiled with such perfect ease and unconcern, that Belmour instantly felt ashamed of all he had thought and all he had suffered, and was absolutely in dread of her beginning on the subject of what had passed in the morning, which he had come with such a determination to have explained.—"By the by," said she, "you were in a pretty humour this morning, when you left me—I thought you meant to retain your post on the hearth by force of arms."—Belmour muttered some incoherent sentence, reddening and much embarrassed. "Well, well," added she, "I have no time to scold you now, I have something to say of real consequence to us both, and, God knows! how soon we may be interrupted.—Beware of St. Fort, the person whom you saw this morning."—"Beware!" said Belmour, hastily.—"Do not interrupt me, I know that what you saw must appear strange to you—the whole will be a long story, I know not how it happened, that I never told you all this before, but it is to me a hateful subject—one thing I do *insist* upon, if St. Fort should come into the box, that you will be civil to him—'tis an age ago, when I was first married, and knew nothing almost of the world, that I found St. Fort the established and intimate friend of my lord, who had known and protected him from a boy, as I understood, and he never was out of the house.—At first I really liked him, his talents and knowledge are superiour, and his conversation, *when he chooses it,* infinitely entertaining and instructive."—She paused—Belmour was all attention—"In short, he fell in love with me, or thought he did, which is the same thing—I then could not bear him, *as you may suppose*—on this he grew ill-natured, jealous, and everything that is odious.—Had I at the first mentioned his ingratitude to my lord in attempting to seduce his wife, after all the obligations he owed him, St. Fort would have been forbidden the house, and I should have had no further trouble about him; but he, taking advantage of my good nature, grew quite insolent and overbearing, and under the pretence of *friendship,* and *care for my reputation,* he scarcely would allow me to speak to a creature.—However, as he was *then welcome* to watch me as much as he pleased," (said she with a sigh) "and as I had nothing *then* to conceal—I determined only to continue on my own way, and trust to his being tired first, which so far happened, that, convinced I had no other attachment, he submitted to be on terms of friendship only with me, and grew again tractable and agreeable.—In this state of things he left England, some months before I for the first time saw you.—I dare say that now he does not really care a straw for me, and if you have but common prudence,"—here they were interrupted by the very person of whom they were speaking, and several other men, who at the same time came into the box.—Lady Roseberg immediately introduced Belmour and St. Fort to each other, the latter made excuses to Belmour for not knowing *who* he had the honour to meet in the morning.—Shortly after Belmour, as the box grew full, retired to another part of the house.—The perfect ease with which Lady Roseberg had talked of St. Fort, and the natural manner in which she had accounted for his behaviour, without even attempting *an excuse* for herself, relieved his mind at the moment from the suspicions he had formed; yet he felt uneasy at the thoughts of additional caution, which Lady Roseberg seemed to announce as necessary—already the moments appeared too short to him, in which he was allowed to partake of her society in any degree of liberty, and the idea of such an *observer* as St. Fort was to him intolerable.—All this, however, he kept within his own breast; his first and constant rule was never to distress her, and while she assured him of her tenderness, he was content to bear anything.

Thus a few weeks passed, St. Fort was frequently at Lord Roseberg's, who, however, did not express any very particular regard for him, or taste for his conversation; which showed indeed some genius, and, on many subjects, much information; but he was opinionated, haughty, and obstinate, and, when he was not speaking himself, unless where he wished to please, his look was always sneering and contemptuous. Belmour and he, whenever a discussion arose, whatever the subject, seldom failed to support a different opinion, and often with a considerable degree of warmth.—Belmour always argued from the heart, and St. Fort always from the head. There was nothing, indeed, in St. Fort's manner to Lady Roseberg, that absolutely excited Belmour's jealousy; but he disliked her intimacy with such a character, and though he avoided complaint, he grew thoughtful and melancholy.—A newcomer, too, whom he could not but despise too much ever to think of as a rival, was continually in his way—a Sir Harry Wilburne—one of those fresh-looking half-formed animals, who pass for handsome till they are five-and-twenty, and then become overgrown, fat, unwieldy monsters. This Sir Harry Wilburne had just emerged from his country seat, in the vicinity of a provincial town, where he had shone the brightest star, and left all the misses inconsolable for his loss. On the acquisition of a baronetage, and a very considerable estate, he had come up to London, and, with little introduction, was in an instant generally received into what is called the best company—sought after, and invited to every party.—He was ignorant of the commonest rules of good-breeding, forward and familiar—but he played at all games—cared not what he lost—put down his money to every subscription—made love to every woman—employed the most expensive coach-maker—dressed in the very excess of the fashion, and imitated, as far as his very contemptible genius would allow, the most refined coxcombs and spendthrifts of the day.—Such was Sir Harry Wilburne—yet even Lady Roseberg would allow him to sit by her at public places, whisper in her ear, hang familiarly over her, and often, when poor Belmour stood respectfully waiting to lead her away, he would seize her too willing hand, and brush by with the most provoking ease and self-satisfaction. When at any time Belmour ventured to touch on subjects of this sort, which he never did but in the gentlest terms, rather of entreaty than reproach, he was always told, that she *must* speak to other men, if she spoke to him; that she had rather appear *particular* in public with any man, that was really indifferent to her, than risk the chance of exposing herself to what *he knew* would make her wretched.—The world, she said, was not to be despised; but that was not all, for if ever Lord Roseberg grew for an instant to think he had cause for suspicions, he would immediately forbid Belmour the house.—All this was seasoned with every expression, that the most refined and captivating art could suggest.

It happened one morning, that Belmour had, with more than usual earnestness, pressed Lady Roseberg to meet him at a masquerade, which was given that night at the Pantheon, and was likely to be very numerous.—Lord Roseberg had the gout, and sat at home, which she pleaded as an excuse, saying, that he had "been peevish of late," and complained that she "neglected his society, and could never stay at home unless the room was full of company;"—that she had, therefore, determined to dedicate that evening entirely to sitting with him, and even particularly requested of Belmour *not* to come. To this he reluctantly consented.

At night Belmour, not finding his carriage at the door of the place where he had supped, had walked away, and in passing by one of the shops where there was a display of masquerade dresses, it struck him, that he might as well look in at the Pantheon for an hour.—He entered the shop, and in an instant a variety of dresses were produced.—That of a black-friar struck him as well calculated for disguise, which suited his disposition at the moment, from exposing him less to the plague of impertinent interruptions. He had walked about the rooms for some time, when, sitting down on one of the long sofas placed behind the columns which supported the gallery, he found himself near two persons, who were in very close conversation. The man he thought looked like Sir Harry Wilburne, but the woman (on the side nearest to him) was so completely disguised, that he could not even guess at her, and his curiosity was then very little excited. Shortly afterward he saw St. Fort come, and stand opposite to the two persons who were in conversation.—He could not mistake him, as he was merely in a domino, with no attempt at disguise.—Presently the person whom he took for Wilburne got up, and St. Fort took his place by the lady—he seemed extremely agitated, and spoke with great vehemence.—Belmour then distinctly heard these words, "God d—mn you! if you speak a single word more to that puppy, by God! I will expose you to the whole room—the world shall know, as well as *I* do, *what* you are."—Belmour startled, and concluding St. Fort must be in liquor, was preparing, like a true knight errant, as he ever was in the cause of the oppressed, to defend the lady, though completely, as he believed, unknown to him.—A mask at the moment had so fast hold of him by the sleeve, that for a few seconds he could not disengage himself, and in the interim he saw the lady take St. Fort by the arm and, absolutely clinging to him, lead him away towards another part of the room, whispering in his ear with the greatest expressions of familiarity and earnestness possible.—Belmour was infinitely surprised, that *any* woman should thus submit to such an affront; and, his curiosity being now excited, he followed them.—For some time the crowd, which was immense, prevented him approaching—he at last saw them again seated together, and, as it seemed, their difference settled—then again they got up, and Belmour soon after found himself close to the lady, and pressed on every side by a crowd of masks, he then overheard her say to St. Fort—"let me go home, I entreat you: would to Heaven, I had not come with you! I am frightened to death, and feel that I shall be discovered."—Though she spoke in a feigned voice, somewhat of a well known tone made him shudder.—He listened—again she spoke—the same tone—still it could *not* be—the agony of doubt was too great to bear, and at all hazards he resolved to know the truth.—He followed them closely, just so far off as not, as he imagined, to be observed by them.—They went towards the door—arrived there, a hackney-chair was called, and St. Fort, in an audible voice, directed the chairmen to carry the lady to the Adelphi. On this Belmour for an instant revived—he was however too deeply interested, thus lightly to believe—instantly flipped off his friar's habit and cowl, and followed the chair.—The night was uncommonly dark and foggy—almost breathless he kept up with the chair, directed by the lantern, which one of the chairmen held.—They proceeded—already they had gotten nearly as far as Charing Cross—Belmour was beginning to accuse himself of folly and unjust suspicion—when the chair was set down—what the person within said he heard not, but the chairmen, after several hearty oaths for having been brought so far out of the way, as they said for nothing, took up the chair again, and turning shortly round, hastened along Pall-Mall, and up St. James's Street—Belmour's heart now sunk, and his limbs with difficulty supported him.—Closely however still he followed, till the chair was set down in Park Street, at the door of Lady Roseberg.—He leaned against the rails.—A servant, who had of course stood ready, instantly at their approach opened the door, and, recommending to the chairmen to make no noise again when the chair retired, the door was closed.—Belmour for some time remained motionless, his head resting between his hands, stunned and oppressed with the painful sensations, which crowded on his imagination.

The fog was now dispersed, and day began to appear—the morning was cold, and a drizzling rain fell fast.—Belmour was without his hat, wholly insensible of his situation, or whither he was going.—He walked on for some time with hasty steps, when finding himself suddenly enclosed, and hurried along by an impetuous crowd of people, he was recalled to himself in Oxford road, where the first object that met his eyes was the horrid figure of a criminal going to execution.—"Ah, miserable wretch!" said he to himself, "how wouldst thou wish to change situations with me! yet is that wish almost mutual!—*thy* pains will shortly end!"—He instantly turned from the dreadful spectacle, and getting out of the crowd as fast as he could, made the best of his way home to his father's house, in Grosvenor Square.—His own *valet-de-chambre* was at the door, a Swiss, who had served him for many years with uncommon fidelity and attachment: he was anxiously waiting for his master, and on seeing the disordered state of his appearance, the poor fellow was still more alarmed. "*Oh! mon Dieu! mon cher maître, qu'est-il donc arrivé?—un duel?—Mais non, vous serier plus tranquille—je me rappelle quand.*"—"*Ne parle pas si haut,*" said Belmour, as he lightly stepped upstairs, "*ce n'est rien—va te coucher, Bertram, et laisse moi.*"—But Bertram followed him into his room.—"*Laisse moi,*" he again repeated; and flinging himself as he was, on his bed, he made a sign, that he would be left alone.—In vain did he try to find the repose he so much wanted—a short interrupted sleep for a time, indeed, closed his eyelids; but his imagination, wandering, led him o'er unknown regions and agitated seas, involved in inextricable mazes of endless sufferings.—He awoke unrefreshed, but endeavoured to collect his scattered thoughts—to be at least composed—'twas all he had left to him!—the visions of future happiness were no more.—As he was walking with agitated steps about his room, a note was brought to him from Lady Roseberg, requesting that he come to her.—"Yes I *will* go," said he, " 'tis a last farewell." Then calling in the servant, he sent word, that he should attend her.—It was yet too early—he was impatient for the time—he had no *speech* to frame—no *anger* to conquer—no *resolution* to form—the veil was torn from before his eyes; and the delusion had ceased forever.

Lady Roseberg, notwithstanding his disguise, had recognized him at the masquerade; and at the moment she had spoken to St. Fort with so much earnestness, to beg he would allow her to return home, had perceived Belmour close to her.—Whether or not *he* had heard what she said, she was not certain, or how far she was discovered.—However, taking her part like a true woman of the world, she determined immediately to send for Belmour, make the best she could of what had passed, and trust to his honour for the future.—When Belmour entered the room, the steady and determined look of grief painted on his countenance, his hair disordered, and his fine manly form shaken with agony of mind, struck and affected her more than she expected—she felt a keenness of regret and shame for which she was not prepared. Belmour stood in silence before her—a flood of tears came to her relief, the usual resource!—

she could speak only in broken incoherent sentences.—At last, making an effort, she was attempting to *justify* her conduct, to plead her youth and inexperience, when first she found herself exposed to the dark designing arts of St. Fort, to whom she was *forced* to *allow* she long ago had fallen a prey.—Sir Harry Wilburne, she begged him to believe . . . Here Belmour interrupted her.—"It is immaterial," said he, "further to dwell on painful and degrading subjects—you have deceived me, cruelly deceived me! since others beside myself have been fortunate, or *miserable* enough to please you.—Whether it be St. Fort, or Sir Harry Wilburne, or any others, is to *me* indifferent.—I come to take a last farewell, and to assure you, Lady Roseberg, that with *me,* not only your reputation is safe, but that I would defend you, guard you, even at the hazard of my life."—He paused, unable to proceed—the steps of someone in the anteroom were at this moment heard.—Belmour seized her hand, which he eagerly kissed, and hastily retired, unseen, by the opposite door. He went the next morning to his father, told him that, with his leave, he should immediately go for some months abroad; that he entreated of him not to inquire into the cause of this hasty departure, as he did not feel himself at liberty to speak to him with that openness, that on all occasions he wished.—Lord Delavere was a man of the world; he easily guessed the cause, or near it, of his son's intended departure; and as, in all respects, this happened perfectly to suit his own views and intentions for him, he readily consented.—He was informed by others of Belmour's attachment to Lady Roseberg, and likewise of her character; and though, in a worldly way, he did not at all disapprove of a connection of that sort, which he thought might contribute to form his son, and keep him out of worse company; yet, as she was justly supposed to be extremely seducing, and to possess in no common degree the arts of captivation, he was not at all sorry to find, from whatever reason it might proceed, that Belmour should have broken chains, which began to give him some uneasiness from their duration, and from the fear of such an attachment interfering with the favourite plan of his life, the marriage of his son with Lady Clementina Alton, his beloved niece, who from an infant had been left under his protection, and who in fact he considered as a favourite child. He had placed her, together with his daughter, under the care of his sister, Lady Eliza, when they were children, and had always had the same fatherly attentions for the one, as for the other. Lady Clementina was then extremely young, and Lord Delavere thought, that at Belmour's return she would be more formed, and more likely to please him—he therefore, without any injunctions as to time, allowed Belmour to depart, depending on his own wish for his return. Belmour however a little outstayed his father's expectations, in not coming back to England till nearly two years were elapsed from the time of his departure.

To a mind like Belmour's, a second visit to Italy was likely to be yet more entertaining, than a first had been—to that enchanting country, therefore, he immediately determined to repair, and there to seek, from change of scene, and variety of objects, that tranquility of mind, of which he was unfairly robbed. Stopping at Paris only a sufficient time to procure a passport, he hurried over the uninteresting road, which leads from that capital by Champagne to Lyons. The romantic beauties of Savoy first roused his attention, and, while lost in admiration of the grand features of nature, he for a time forgot his griefs, and fell into a composed and pensive melancholy. The remains of Grecian and Roman art, so profusedly scattered over Italy, in which the refined taste of Belmour took peculiar delight; music, of which he was passionately fond; and literary science, in which he found constant opportunities to indulge, contributed to soothe and occupy his mind; and his perfect acquaintance with the Italian language gave him every advantage, in the pursuits which he followed. Yet still the early lesson of deceit and falsehood, which he had received, weighed heavily on his heart, and he felt the absolute want of that interest in life, which he no longer hoped to find. At his return to England, he found that Lady Roseberg had much lost herself in the opinion of the world; her conduct had been less circumspect, and her manner and appearance, though she preserved her beauty, were considerably changed for the worse.—But as she rested on those steady props to a tottering reputation, an enduring husband and a large fortune, she was still received in most societies, and courted by many individuals, who found their account in the sort of protection it was yet in her power to afford. Belmour was much affected the first time he saw her after his return to England; and on all occasions, where he could do so without the appearance of particularity, sedulously avoided her. He felt this still an effort, and therefore was rejoiced when his father, soon after his arrival in London, signified his intention of going for the summer to Belmour Castle.—Thither he instantly offered to accompany him. This proposition, as it may easily be supposed, was gladly received by the earl, who had previously settled with Lady Eliza, that the moment his niece could be persuaded to leave town, she was to bring her to him.—Thus all his fond expectations seemed to be realizing; for, accustomed only to prosperity, he looked not, where there was a possibility of success, for the failure of a favourite plan; nor did he easily listen to anything like contradiction, or opposition to determinations he had once made. Lord Delavere having been born to an immense estate, and much patronage, all which fell into his hands early in life, by the death of his parents, was taught by those who surrounded him, that he was *always in the right;* this he so firmly believed, that he became the more determined and the more obstinate in the prosecution of all his plans, from a spirit of rectitude;

as those always are led farthest astray, whose errours originate from honest principles.

Chapter 5

WE LEFT BELMOUR in contemplation of the setting sun on a calm sea.—Night was now coming on fast—he had been for a considerable time sitting on a fragment of rock, his eyes fixed on the ocean, but lost in thought, and quite unmindful of approaching darkness, when his dog suddenly called forth his attention by springing up into his arms. The poor little animal, after hunting for some time in the wood close by, had, unheeded by Belmour, creeped gently along, trembling and hanging its tail, till it found itself under the protection of its master; when barking outrageously, and looking towards the wood behind, it obliged Belmour to turn, and among the trees he indistinctly saw the figure of a man, who, as he thought, was endeavouring to hide himself.—Belmour instantly sprang forward, and seized the man by the collar, concluding him to be some poacher, or ill-designing person.—The man, dreadfully alarmed, hollowed loudly, entreating to have his life spared.—"I am a poor man—for God sake! let me go—you can get nothing from me."—"Fool!"—said Belmour, letting go his hold, "dost thou take me for a robber? But what art *thou?*" continued he, "what is thy business here, out of every road or path?"—The man, recovering from his fright, answered rather sulkily, "Why, I'm doing no harm, I lost my way, and I need not be put in fear of my life for that!"—Belmour regretted instantly the alarm he had occasioned the poor man, and in the gentlest tone asked him whence he came, and if he could assist him. "Came," said he, "why I came along with my cattle, left them in yonder field there, for the night, and was going on to doctor, what d'ye call him, at the parsonage."—"Have you business with Mr. Rycot, the rector?"—"And what matters all that, I don't suppose you'll show me the way!"—"Indeed but I will," replied Belmour; "if you will follow me, I will direct you to the parsonage—but it is some way, and you seem very lame—here, friend, lean on my arm, and I will conduct you." "That's main good of you, sir," replied the man, struck with an offer he so little expected. The moon, which had just then risen, allowed him to distinguish the figure of his conductor, which much increased his confidence, and he felt remorse for the surly manner, in which he had at first spoken. Wishing to repair his fault, he of himself continued, "my business is not with the doctor, but I ha' got some letters for the young lady *as* is with him."—"For Miss Melville?" interrupted Belmour hastily.—"From whom?"—"But what right have I," said he to himself, "to pry into the secrets of others?—no matter, no matter," said he, again turning to the man.—The man continued, "Nay, an' please your honour, I don't know *who* it was *as give* me the letters, it was a young gentleman I never *seed* before—at the squire's there, down in Cornwall."—"I often carries letters and parcels for the squire, and for other folks in my way, as I *comes* along with my cattle; there was another gentleman by, too, and they bid me be sure and deliver the letters safe—that's all I knows o' the matter—oh dear! dear! I don't know how I shall get along!—I almost broke my leg against yonder piece of stone there."—After proceeding some little way, the man appeared to be in so much pain, that it seemed impossible to get him on any further, when, finding that they were opposite to a cottage, Belmour proposed to him to remain there for the night, if he could be lodged, and to give him the letters, which he said he could deliver, as in his way home he must pass almost close by the parsonage.—To this proposition the man readily agreed, and a night's lodging was procured. Belmour put a guinea into the man's hand, telling him that he would send the apothecary to him, and then taking the letters in his hand, lightly stepped away.

Belmour, from the moment he had received the packet for Miss Melville, had felt an indefinable sense of pleasure.—He would have done just what he had done for any other person. No scruple therefore occurred to him as to the charge he had undertaken; but as he came to the village, the church-clock struck eleven; this first informed him of the lateness of the hour, which had wholly escaped his notice, and made him hesitate whether or not he should attempt delivering the letters that night, as it was more than probable that the family at the parsonage would be retired to bed.—Still he walked on with quickened steps, and found himself close to the house, before he had made his determination.—Seeing a light in one of the windows, and the casement open, he ventured to knock—no one answered—he gently repeated the stroke—still all was silent, and he was just leaving the door, somewhat unwillingly, with an intention of returning to execute his commission in the morning, when Miss Melville appeared at the open window, and inquired who was there.—She half retired back, on seeing Lord Belmour, with an expression of much surprise; but as he immediately bowed, by which she found that she had been seen, she again advanced, and leaned out of the window. The moon now shone brightly, and its soft rays fell directly on the beautiful face of Miss Melville—her fine flowing hair hung in profusion over her shoulders.—She had on a light sort of wrapping gown, and her airy form seemed to acquire a new grace from the negligence of her attire.—Belmour was lost in admiration—he held the letters in his hand, without speaking for awhile, wholly forgetful of his errand, till recalled from this state of enchantment by the sharp voice of the rector, who had, unperceived, opened a small casement, through which he had thrust his head. Belmour, not without much hesitation and embarrassment, endeavoured to explain the reason of his coming at that hour, and made many excuses for the disturbance he had caused.

The rector, who had been some time in bed, had been fast asleep, and would have remained so in spite of the knocking at his door, had not his wife, with no small difficulty, awakened him, terrified at the noise she so unexpectedly heard. He at last got out of bed, his temper much ruffled at being disturbed, as he thought unnecessarily, from some imaginary fancy of his wife's, convinced no one had knocked at the door; and preparing again to repeat the usual epithets he so liberally on all occasions bestowed on her, of fool and idiot—when on going to the window, by the light of the moon, he perceived Lord Belmour at the door. His sensations became very different, though not less troublesome to himself—his extreme haste to go down and open the door, was counteracted by the unlucky accident of a very *necessary* part of his dress being nowhere at the moment to be found.—In vain did he toss and tumble everything in the room over and over, swear the devil had been there, and abuse his wife;—'twas all in vain—*they* had slipt behind the high-backed arm-chair, that stood by the bedside, and lay completely concealed.—No friendly ray of moonshine then lent its assistance to the discovery.—In this dilemma, with loud vociferation, he entreated of Miss Melville to go to the door, and beg "my lord to sit down in the parlour," till he could wait upon him himself.—She obeyed, and, taking her candle in her hand, descended, and opened the door, but appeared somewhat embarrassed as she spoke, and her embarrassment was not diminished, on perceiving how much Belmour partook of the same sensation.—A situation, so little expected, had thrown him off his guard, and the impression Miss Melville had from the first made on him, heightened at the moment by a thousand circumstances, was too evident in his looks and manner to be mistaken. They proceeded together into the little parlour.—Lord Belmour gave Miss Melville the letters, entreating her to read them. He should, he said, just stay to see the rector, who indeed was calling from above every two or three minutes, to say that he was "*coming*."—She took the letters, looked at the superscription only, saying, she knew "whence they came," and laid them down on the table—a silence followed.—Miss Melville, at last, recovering herself, as well as she could, begged some explanation, relative to the circumstances of Lord Belmour's having been the messenger, who brought the letters. He briefly told her what had happened, and again they were silent.—Belmour could think of little else but the object before him, and his respect prevented his uttering even a word expressive of the admiration, with which he was inspired.—A short time now passed, with only an unmeaning question, or remark, on one side or the other, when Miss Melville was really relieved by the rector's calling out, in a triumphant tone, "*now I am* coming."—"Seek and ye shall find," said he, with emphasis, as he went downstairs, and presently he appeared. The comical smirk of his countenance, his bustle and delight, void of the slightest sense of uneasiness at the ludicrous figure he made, with his clothes half on, and his wig half off, extracted an involuntary smile from them both.—Light he had none, but that of the moon; nor was there indeed ever a single candle burning in the house after ten o'clock, except in Miss Melville's room, and that was a "useless expense," he had often remarked to his wife, with some acrimony, but of which, at this moment, he felt the advantage. After a few moments, Belmour took his leave.—He had not gone many paces from the door, when he saw one of his father's grooms coming towards him; but the moment the man perceived him, he turned short round, and ran back towards the castle.—To this Belmour paid little attention; but a second and a third servant doing exactly the same thing, he wondered what could be the matter. After entering the gates, he perceived the servants were in a sort of a bustle, and when he came into the supper-room, a general look of inquiry prevailed. The supper had been over some time, as half past ten was the regular hour;—the company were, however, most of them still sitting round the table. His father was reading at the other end of the room, and just looking off his book for the time he spoke, asked him dryly, if he had supped where he had been, or chose to have any supper brought.

Belmour now began to tell his story, but perceived such an air of disbelief in every countenance, that he made it very short. Melford, who was walking about the room, came up to him, and with an air of importance said, in a half whisper, "She is a damn'd fine woman, by God!"—"Of whom are you talking, sir?" said Belmour, to him, in the very gravest tone possible.—"Pho! pho!" said Melford, stepping away with an affected air of indifference, but taking care not to address another word to Belmour for the rest of the evening. Heartley, looking down, twirled his knife and fork round on his plate; and Lady Clementina, the most unconcerned of the company, hummed the beginning of half a dozen different opera airs, vowed it was the finest night she ever saw, and that she wished anybody would walk with her.—"I have been taking your part," said she, laughing, "and telling my uncle it was not fair to send after you, as he did, so don't look so glum at me, dear Belmour."—Belmour, teased and provoked at all this, said dryly, that he could "not conceive there should be anything extraordinary in walking out late in such a night," that they knew he frequently ate no supper—"besides,"—"Nay, now, you shall not tell your story over again," said Lady Clementina, holding her hand before his mouth, "for then I *cannot* take your part.—Why should you be ashamed of where you have been? I am sure I only wish *I* had been with you, for"—"Lady Clementina, Lady Clementina," interrupted Lady Eliza, "you *must not* talk so—fie, fie, child, you never consider what you say.—Come, brother, do let us all go to bed, I am sure it is time." Saying this, she got up, candles were brought, and the company retired for the night.

Chapter 6

BELMOUR FELT SERIOUSLY DISTURBED at the manner in which his accidental visit to Miss Melville had been taken. His father, he perceived, thought more of it, than he chose to express, from his wholly avoiding the subject; and the rest of the company, according to their different dispositions, all took it up in a way, that was extremely displeasing to him.—What still more alarmed him, was the growing interest he felt in his own heart, for a person of whom he knew nothing, one too much involved in a cloud of mystery, which, without avowing pretensions neither prudence nor honour could justify, it was extremely difficult to attempt penetrating.—His father's decided objection to any person of inferiour birth, to say nothing of the anxious desire, to which Belmour was no stranger, of his union with Lady Clementina, made him dread the idea of an attachment, which might destroy all the flattering hopes of an indulgent parent, or his own peace of mind forever. He had suffered too much already from passion, not to dread its effects—he wished therefore to curb the sensations of pleasure and admiration, which he had experienced on this occasion, before they gained further power, and determined to avoid any attention towards Miss Melville that might appear particular, and take his chance of future events for their further acquaintance.

Lord Delavere continued his silence, never once touching on the subject of the visit to Belmour; but after that occurrence, appeared more serious and reserved in his manner to him than usual. Belmour, though he had longed to go the next morning to the parsonage, and would, in another case, have thought it but a common attention, in consequence of the sort of disturbance he had occasioned on the preceding night, had had sufficient command over himself not to go, and it was now nearly a fortnight since he had seen Miss Melville, or heard a single word from the rectory, when he happened one evening to go out alone on horseback.—Lady Clementina, as usual, was wanting to make *a party* to go *somewhere,* no matter to her where, and had that evening been able to collect only Heartley and Lady Caroline.—The weather was uncommonly fine, and she declared, that she would take a long walk out of the park, and frighten her uncle, and her aunt Eliza, by coming home late, and "making them think she had *run away.*"—With this determination she set out, accompanied by the persons above-mentioned.—They were scarcely out of the park-gate, when they perceived Miss Melville, taking her evening walk alone. Lady Clementina flew up to her, seized her arm, and protested (in spite of a wink and a grave look from Lady Caroline) that she should not only walk with them wherever they went; "which way that was to be, she had not," she said, "determined; but come back with them, and pass the evening at the castle."—She would take no refusal; and Lady Caroline, seeing that it must be so, out of civility joined her entreaties to her cousin's. Miss Melville, thus taken unawares, and having, in fact, no single excuse to offer, did not long oppose their request. They had continued their walk for nearly a mile, along a narrow by-lane, leading to a small village, when, at a turn, they perceived Belmour at no great distance before them, on horseback; he was alone, unattended even by a groom—his arms were crossed over his breast, and the bridle thrown on the horse's neck; the animal moved slowly on, just putting one foot before the other, with its head carried horizontally before it.—Lady Clementina, looking round to her companions, put her finger to her mouth, in token of silence, and advanced gently till she came, unperceived, almost close to Belmour; then slyly drawing out her handkerchief, she threw it at the horse. The animal thus suddenly struck, made a violent start, then plunged, then reared, and must inevitably have flung any less active, or less expert rider than Belmour.—Lady Caroline screamed, and almost fainted. Lady Clementina put both her hands before her face, and held them close. Miss Melville advanced a few paces, her face paler than ashes; and Heartley stood still, seeing clearly, that no assistance could be afforded.—Belmour first allowed the horse, instigated by fear, to make its various efforts, then checked and brought it back, and gently patting its beautiful shining neck, alighted with the most perfect composure, and smiling at the alarm into which the ladies had been thrown, he thanked them for the concern they expressed, for what he termed his "imaginary danger."—"Well," said Lady Clementina, "since you are safe, and Aunt Eliza is not here to scold me, I don't care, and so come along with us, cousin."—Belmour obeyed, and accompanied them, leading his horse after him. As they passed a few straggling cottages, Lady Clementina saw in the window of a little shop, a ribbon she declared to be "*beautiful.*"—In they went.—*She* had no purse—Belmour immediately produced his, which seemed heavy, and some silver at the same time, which latter more than answered the demand. They came soon after to a small cottage, before the door of which were a few trees, with a rustic bench on one side, and on the other a quantity of fine rose-bushes, growing luxuriantly, half hanging from the cottage-wall, against which they had once been nailed.—The shade and fragrance of the spot tempted them to sit and rest themselves; and it was already growing dark, without their having perceived, that the sun had finished its course. As the conversation had taken a more serious turn than usual, and Miss

Melville had a principal part in it, Belmour was all attention; when in the midst of their discourse, a poor little ragged dirty child, who had for some time, unperceived, stood in the doorway of the cottage, set up a sudden cry, bellowing, "the horse! the horse!" The mother of the child, alarmed, ran in haste from within, to see what was the matter—then, with the bitterest exclamation, repeated, "Oh! dear! dear! the horse! the nasty horse! he has torn, and trampled down all my *bit* of potatoes. Oh Lord! what will Thomas say, when he comes home?—Oh dear! dear!" then, happening to turn, and perceiving the company that were near, the poor woman checked her gushing tears, ready to fall from her full eyes, and supplicating for pardon, hoped she had "said no harm.—I did not see who was here, indeed; indeed, I did not—pray, your honour, excuse me!"—"Good Heavens!" said Belmour, snatching away the horse, and turning it loose, "am *I* the cause of so much pain!"—then catching up the dirty little urchin in his arms, he pressed it closely to his bosom, and followed the woman, who had retired into the house.—He presently returned, still holding the child in his arms, and endeavouring to soothe and comfort it.—The woman again appeared at the door, her eyes streaming with tears, but with tears of a far different expression—surprise and gratitude were too strongly marked on her countenance, to be mistaken.—Belmour, with a look that imposed silence, put the child carefully into her arms—then turning to the company, asked them if they would not "begin their walk homeward, as it was growing late."—They arose from their seats, and Lady Caroline, complaining of fatigue, leaned on Heartley's arm.—Lady Clementina, running up to them, seized his other arm, saying, she "would *help them on,* and now," turning to Miss Melville, "I leave *you* Belmour, and his horse, all to yourself, to make the most you can of."—Belmour, having consigned his horse, which Heartley had already caught, to the care of the woman of the cottage, till he should send his groom for it, said, that *the horse* at least should not be troublesome, and that he should be happy in offering his services to conduct Miss Melville.—As she took his arm, she felt him tremble.—The road was in many places rough, and the evening so far advanced, that they could scarcely discern their way—often did Belmour, as he thought, merely to save her from the danger of falling, press her arm closer to his beating heart, but with an expression so authorised by respect, that it could not offend.—They followed their companions, who walked slowly, on account of Lady Caroline, scarcely speaking during the whole of the way.—Their thoughts were too much occupied by the singularity of finding themselves in a situation they a few hours before had so little expected, either to admit of indifferent subjects, or of indulging in more interesting conversation.

When they arrived at the castle, contrary to Lady Clementina's expectation, she found her aunt, Lady Eliza, perfectly at ease on her account, from knowing her with Lady Caroline and Heartley, on whose conduct and protection she could depend; and from being herself deeply engaged at the moment in a pool at commerce, some of the neighbours having come on a visit to the castle, and remained there for the evening, which, with the addition of Saunter, and her dear Lord Fenmoss, had enabled her, much to her satisfaction, to make up a party. Determined one way or another to torment her aunt, Lady Clementina insisted on *buying in,* to win the pool from her, as she said, because she saw, she thought herself "*sure.*"—"Belmour," said she, leaning back, and holding out her hand, "give me your purse again, for you know I have none of my own."—Belmour immediately put his hand into his pocket, then recollecting himself, said, he had not his purse.—"Well!" said Lady Clementina, "was there ever anything like that? Why you took out your purse at the shop, as we went along.—Can you say you have *no purse* now?—I believe you think I mean to embezzle your money!—Come, come, give me your purse, you shabby creature."—"I have none," said Belmour, "but I will fetch you immediately what gold you want."—"No, no," replied she, "I can get money enough from my uncle, or from Aunt Eliza here, though *she* won't much like to give me hers—but, mercy on me! I begin to guess—no, you could not give your purse to that fright of a woman, at the cottage!—I never saw such a poor starved-looking creature, nor such a dirty ugly child."—Belmour coloured, and the laugh became almost general against him.—Lady Clementina, with her usual flow of spirits, and some humour, began an account of their *adventures* that evening—but his eyes, at the moment, met Miss Melville's, and how was he not repaid!—The look of sympathy, and somewhat more than approbation, which she seemed not even to wish to disguise, touched him to the very soul.—Lady Clementina continued her narration—*he* heard her not. The pool at commerce was shortly finished, and Lady Eliza victorious, which put her into such good humour, that, although at the risk of the supper, which was announced as ready to come, being cold, she did not oppose Lady Clementina, who, taking Miss Melville by the arm, and leading her towards the piano-forte, declared that she *must* hear her sing, for she knew "she could." Miss Melville, with that composure and simplicity of manner, which heightens the grace of every action, said that she should obey instantly, not to give her the trouble of repeating her orders.—A music book was placed before her, with the favourite Italian airs of the preceding season. Several of these she went over, accompanying herself with uncommon spirit and expression.—Her voice was touching and harmonious—all were lavish of their praises, Belmour excepted—*his* admiration was *felt,* not uttered. She then, on being desired to continue, sang several plaintive airs in the Venetian dialect.—Belmour begged of her to sing one of those airs, he was, he said, "*sure*" she knew; a faint blush o'erspread her cheek as she began, "*Perche amor mio ben nascondi,*" the very air, Belmour, unseen, had first heard her sing in the garden.—The blush, however faint, and a somewhat of increased tenderness in the tone of her voice, did not escape him—to what could he attribute this? to the recollection of some absent and interesting object?—How painfully did Belmour already feel this conclusion!—Still too, as in the garden, Miss Melville's voice seemed to convey to his ear sounds not wholly new to him; yet this, he thought, *must* be fancy. Supper, a second time announced, interrupted the music, and Lord Delavere, who had involuntarily, with the rest of the company, been delighted, offered his hand to Miss Melville, and led her into the supper-room. During supper, the conversation turned on various literary subjects, on all of which Miss Melville seemed perfectly well informed, and spoke with taste, precision, and judgment, whenever her opinion was called for. Italy was then mentioned, in praise of which she dwelt, it seemed, with peculiar interest. "Lord!" exclaimed Lady Clementina, "have you really been in Italy? How I envy you—well, I should like to see the pope—and what amazing good fun it must be to walk about all night in the open air, without having Aunt Eliza thinking it necessary to come and smother one up with a nasty fur-cloak—don't you hate fur-cloaks, Miss Melville?—but were you long in Italy?—*that* I am not sure I *should* like." "I was abroad nearly two years, madam." "Two years," repeated Belmour, half aloud, and half to himself. "When, may I ask, did you return?"—Someone, at the moment, speaking to Miss Melville, prevented her hearing, or at least answering his question, and, as it grew late, she soon afterward begged leave to retire.—A carriage was called for, but, as she expressed her wish rather to walk, the company, Lord Delavere and Lady Caroline excepted, all insisted on seeing her home. The night, indeed, was so warm, that even Lady Eliza could not fear catching cold. Lady Clementina was no sooner out of the first gate, but she proposed a circuitous walk to the parsonage, saying, it was "much too fine to go home to bed."—Belmour, who was walking by Miss Melville, seconded this motion, and it was past twelve o'clock, before they got to the parsonage.

The rector was pacing backward and forward before his door, with his wig in one hand, and a handkerchief in the other, with which he kept wiping his head; and the heat from which he suffered seemed to be considerably increased by his impatience for the return of Miss Melville, that he might, as he called it, "*shut up shop;*" an *elegant* metaphor, which he was accustomed to use on many occasions. The moment he saw Miss Melville, he tossed on his wig, and, waddling on forward some way to meet her, cried, "so Miss, you are come at last!—I suppose you think folks ha' got nothing better to do, than to wait for you, he! he! he!—however, I knew where you were, so there's no harm done."—He then made a thousand bows and *curvettes* to the company in general, and to Lord Belmour in particular, hoping his lordship was well, and begging pardon for what he had said. Then, with a loud laugh, he added, nodding and winking, "but you know, young women must be looked after, and Miss is under my care."—Miss Melville, colouring, entreated not to detain the company, but, shortening the usual compliments as much as possible, thanked them for the honour they had done her.—They retired to the castle, to luxury and magnificence;—she to her humble dwelling—yet, if "sweet be the slumbers of the virtuous mind," to such she had a right.

Chapter 7

THE NEXT MORNING, Lord Delavere, at breakfast, announced his intention of going immediately to town, as by letters which he had just received, he had learnt, that his patent for the marquisate he had been long soliciting was made out, that it would appear in the gazette that very week, and that he had now only to kiss hands.

He told Belmour, that he should keep him but a very few days, but must take him with him; "though," added he, "*you* must not kiss hands, for I am in doubt between two titles of almost equal antiquity in our family, and cannot yet decide which to choose for you.—I shall the less be disposed to stay in town," continued he, still addressing himself particularly to Belmour, "as our men of business are arrived here this morning, with all the papers relative to settling our exchange of lands with your pretty cousin here, and they will not like waiting long—however, wait they must, for a few days, till we return."

Belmour was by no means pleased with this sudden departure; however, as he began now to indulge in the idea of knowing more of Miss Melville, the opportunities of which, from the probability of her visits at the castle being repeated, he trusted, would in future be frequent, he felt less pain in acquiescing in his father's proposition; to which, indeed, he had no reasonable objection to oppose. He had moreover of late observed Melford's attentions to Lady Clementina appear to take a more serious turn, and she seemed at least to *listen* to him.—This helped to encourage a thousand vague ideas, which he ventured not to search his own heart sufficiently to define.

An early dinner was ordered, after which they set out—the carriage driving through the village had not failed to attract the attention of the inhabitants, and the rector was one of the first, who sallied forth from his door to see them pass.—In vain did he repeatedly try to stop some one of the servants, in order to inquire the cause of this unexpected departure.—They flew after the chaise, in which for celerity the earl now traveled, driving all before them, and shortly disappeared in clouds of dust.—The rector still was not disposed to give up his inquiry—on he walked towards the castle, from the outermost gate of which, as he approached, he saw the two lawyers issuing.—They were in quest of some person, to show them the way to the inn, where they expected to find their baggage, which they had ordered to come down by stage.—Rycot was in quest of intelligence from the castle, they soon met, and preliminaries were instantly settled. The rector was to show them to the inn, and then give them a bottle of his best ale at the parsonage.—He had not gone ten paces in company with them, when a *luminous ray* shot across his imagination—"it must be so—it *is* so," said he, muttering to himself, and eyeing his companions from top to toe. "I think, gentlemen," said he, pulling up his breeches, "I guess *your* business,"—"*Our business,* sir, will soon be settled, I fancy." "Huzza!" cried Rycot, attempting a jump, and actually clearing the ground with his feet, "huzza!—well God bless them, say!—soon be settled?—aye, I'll warrant ye!—all agreed, no falling out there!—And when, tell me the day—I'll see why, if we be not all ready." "*The day,*" replied one of the lawyers, with an expression of much surprise at the vehemence of the rector, "*the day,* sir, we cannot exactly tell, but the writings will be drawn up within a fortnight; and as the parties seem perfectly agreed, there will only be to—" "Say no more, say no more," interrupted the parson, in a perfect ecstasy.—"Come along, and you shall drink their healths in a bottle of such ale as, I must needs say, who should not say it, you never tasted in your lives."—The rest of his discourse, which was chiefly in broken sentences, was wholly unintelligible to the lawyers, and they both, by significant looks to each other, expressed that they thought him a little crazy.

From the inn, they all proceeded to the parsonage, where they found Mrs. Rycot and Miss Melville in the little parlour.—The former was still sipping her tea, and the latter sitting by her at work. The rector having ushered in his company, with as much form as his joy would permit, bustled up to his wife, and, in a half whisper, said, "mind you're civil now to these gentlemen. I shan't say any more—all's settled—d'ye hear that, *old girl,* all's settled—but *mum*—mind what I say to you, that's all—*to be* in a fortnight.—Why thou look'st as stupid, woman!—I say they are to be married in a fortnight—don't understand *that*?"—At this instant the bells accidentally began ringing—"never mind, gentlemen; sad crazy old affairs, I know—one of them quite cracked—but never mind, I say, all shall be in order—set your hearts at ease."—The lawyers looked at each other with astonishment.—"*Lard,* my dear," cried Mrs. Rycot, at the moment catching hold of Miss Melville's hand, "you look very pale, what's the matter? sure you an't well?"—"Some folks never are," muttered the parson, "when other folks are pleased." "Come along with me into the air," continued Mrs. Rycot—"there lean on my arm, my dear, mercy on me! why how you change colour!"—Miss Melville got up with some difficulty, and left the room with her conductress, owning that she felt herself unwell, and begging leave to retire to her own room. "Here then," said the rector, calling after her, "take this letter, Miss, I have had it in my pocket for you all day, and forgot to give it you.—I don't know who it comes from—there, take it with you—my *sarvice,* and good night, since you're not for coming back to us."

"A very beautiful young lady that," said the younger of the lawyers, as the door shut.—"Pray, doctor, who is she?"—"*That,*" replied he, rather testily, "I have been often asked, but never yet could tell; when I *can,* I will—but come, let's drink and drive care away."—"We will pledge you in one glass," said they, "but must be gone immediately.—We have much to do, were up early. This morning, and must be up earlier tomorrow, as we mean to make a visit from miles off, at a gentleman's, where we have business, and then meet my lord at his return, and have besides many things to settle together tonight, which *good company,* sir, would interrupt—and so, you will excuse us." Rycot, though rather disappointed at their leaving him so soon, had nothing to oppose to their determination, and felt so well satisfied with his day, that he the more easily consented to their going. Having seen them to the door, he returned to his little parlour, where, after finishing his bottle of ale by himself, he as usual fell fast asleep in his arm-chair.

Chapter 8

BELMOUR, FROM THE MOMENT he left the castle, had felt his spirits sink, and as he proceeded on his journey, became more and more thoughtful and melancholy. His hopes of improving his acquaintance with Miss Melville seemed to fade—and, if he did, to what must that not lead?—He no longer deceived himself, as to the sentiments with which she had inspired him, but dreaded the consequences of finding his heart further engaged, before he could know even to whom.—Much less if there could ever be a chance of anything but misery for him, in such an attachment.—Yet voluntarily to give up seeing her, was an effort he felt not disposed to make.

Everything appeared tiresome and uninteresting to him in town, and after a very few days, as the business on which they came appeared settled, and that his father was in possession of his long wished for title, finding that he proposed making a visit of some days more near town, Belmour determined to return without him. The marquis did not *object,* but showed some signs of surprise at his son's proposition, and fixed his eyes at the moment on him, in a manner that brought the blood into Belmour's face.—Nothing however further was said, and the next morning, Belmour, with an agitated feeling of impatience, threw himself into the chaise, that was to convey him back to the castle. On the morning of the third day after his departure, he arrived there.—Caution had by this time given way to the soothing idea of again seeing the object of his admiration.—As he alighted, his sister and Lady Clementina flew to meet him.—He thanked them for their eagerness—inquired after their health with more than usual warmth, and asked every question but the only one he was really anxious to have answered. Lady Clementina, however, so far shortly relieved him; for, turning to Lady Caroline, she said, "My dear, don't you think we might send for Miss Melville, to come to us this evening? We have not heard of her these two days, and, poor thing! she looked wretchedly the night she was here, though she would not allow she was ill, and sang more like an angel than ever."—To this proposition Lady Caroline assented, and Belmour took courage to say, that he would be their ambassador, and carry their message to Miss Melville.

The moment dinner was over, Belmour, with a beating heart, flew to the parsonage—he found the rector walking to and fro before his door, who immediately came up to him, bowing with even more than his usual obsequiousness.—"Humbly thank your lordship for this honour—just come, I find—left my lord marquis well, I hope—but pray, my lord, walk in—or would your lordship please to rest yourself first on this bench?"—Extending one hand forward as he held his hat in the other—"I am always happy to wait on you, sir," Belmour politely replied, "but my visit this time was intended for Miss Melville—to whom I bring a message from Lady Clementina and my sister—may I be allowed to see her?"—"Miss Melville!—O dear! my lord, Miss Emily went this morning—bird flown, my lord," said the rector, smiling with complacency at his own *lively* mode of expression.—"Went this morning!" repeated Belmour, endeavouring to conceal the painful surprise he felt.—"When does she return?" "O! my lord, Miss Emily does *not* return.—I received a letter from Dr. Stanmore, the day after lordship and my lord marquis went, to thank me, as he was pleased to say, for my care of Miss Emily, and telling me, that she was to leave us immediately—thought, indeed, we should have kept her here all summer, which to be sure would not have been *quite* so convenient, as they say, but glad to do anything for Dr. Stanmore, my best friend.—Worthy man, my lord—got me recommended to the bishop for this living—glad, indeed, as I was saying, my lord, to do anything for him, and I know he loves Miss Emily as much as if she were his own child—nay, some think she is so, not that I believe it—though we all are young at one time or other, he! he! he!"

Belmour gravely resumed, with an affected air of indifference—"Miss Melville is, I conclude, returned to Dr. Stanmore's."—"No, my lord, no, Miss said she was going for the present to a relation's in town—*whom* she did *not* say—some folks, you know, never like talking of themselves, and *I* never like asking questions others don't choose to answer.—So I took a place for Miss Emily in the stage, at her desire, and off she went.—My wife there was whimpering and crying to part with her—but she's a fool!—beg your lordship's pardon." Seeing that Belmour continued to listen, the rector, highly flattered by being encouraged to continue his conversation, wished inwardly that he had known more on the subject than he did; for this, owing to various circumstances, was in reality very little: but what he did *not know,* he endeavoured to supply the place of by surmises and *innuendoes;* so that after a rhapsody of nearly a quarter of an hour, poor Belmour was left more in the dark than before, as to any essential part of Miss Melville's history.—It was evident to him, that some mystery hung over her birth and education, which Dr. Stanmore had not thought fit to explain to the rector.—Having no hope therefore then of further intelligence, and wishing to free himself from so unpleasant a companion, Belmour took his leave.—He had gone but a few paces, when the rector, with his short arm thrust to the bottom of his coat-pocket, skipped after him, saying that he had forgotten a note, which Miss Melville had left for Lady Caroline, and desired might be delivered.—"With your lordship's leave I will take it up to the castle?"—"By all means, sir," Belmour replied, for guessing it to be merely a formal compliment at parting, he felt little curiosity as to its contents, and was not sorry, that *another* should first carry the news of Miss Melville's departure to the castle.—He was sensible, that the chagrin he felt would be but too visible on his countenance, were he to expose himself to more penetrating eyes than the rector's, before he had had time to compose the agitation of his mind. He flew to his usual refuge, when his mind was affected, a solitary walk, and directed his steps to the terrace already mentioned, overlooking the sea.—The evening was cloudy, cold, and blustering, and his favourite scene overcast—a few distant sails only appeared in the horizon.—He went on hastily to the further extent of the cliff, which there surmounts the coast; and then returning, slackened his pace as he came within sight of the castle.

Belmour was naturally romantic (a disposition frequently inherent in noble minds), of quick perception, and lively feelings.—The circumstances, therefore, which had attended his short acquaintance with Miss Melville, and the mysterious cloud, which enveloped her history, added not a little to the interest she inspired.—Yet this half-formed passion, though it much agitated his heart, left him not without the use of his reason.

Even the clue was now lost, by which he might have traced her steps—and, were it not, on what pretence could he follow her?

The teasing combination of untoward circumstances in which he felt himself involved, and the degree of uncertainty, which, in spite of reason and propriety, he experienced, how to act on an occasion, which something whispered to his mind *might* decide the future of his life, embarrassed and confused him.

By this time he drew near the castle, doubtful still whether he should enter; but on seeing his sister at the window of her own apartment, it occurred to him at the moment, that possibly the note left by Miss Melville, which Lady Caroline must have long received, might afford some light respecting her sudden departure; and judging his sister to be alone, he went directly to her room.

Lady Caroline came forward to him, holding the note in her hand, with an expression of more *surprise* than *regret* on her face.—"Was there ever anything so strange!" she exclaimed, "as this sudden flight (I know you have seen the rector).—Well, these mysterious doings do not look well for our *beautiful friend*!—which I am sorry for," she added, rather as if she *could* have said, I am *glad*.

"Your remark, sister, is not very charitable," replied he, dryly—"but pray give me the note." "Not a single word or hint did she give of her intention, though, by the rector's account, she *must* have known of her going, when she was last with us"—continued Lady Caroline, endeavouring to make good her story.

Belmour was attentively reading over the note, which contained nothing but an acknowledgment of the civilities received, expressed in the most polite terms.—She then ended, by wishing that it might at some future time be allowed her farther to excuse the, perhaps, seeming inattention of not having waited on them to take leave in person, and to explain the causes, which had prevented her.

"Well," said Lady Caroline, "and is not *this* strange, brother? I must think," continued she, "as Mr. Cranford said, who was here this evening to make a visit, just as the rector came, and who particularly knows the Melville family, that she must have taken that as a name merely to conceal her own, or be at best some natural daughter; for Cranford protests, that he never heard such a person ever mentioned among them." "Sir Charles Melville," he said, "always resided at his estate in the north, and has only one sister.—They are immensely rich; and *you* will allow, brother, that it is not probable, were she indeed of that family, that they should wholly neglect *such a relation,* were there not some cause, that cannot well be to her honour."

"This is a subject," returned Belmour, "my dear sister, on which we are not likely to agree, therefore at present we will say no more upon it.—I know what has given an asperity to your expressions, not natural to you—but all this is quite unnecessary; you may, believe me, be *candid* without fear, I am no knight-errant"—saying which, he left the room.

It was now the usual time for assembling in the evening at the castle, and candles were already lighted.—Belmour, wishing on this occasion to avoid any appearance expressive of the sensations of his heart, went directly into the music-room, where the company often passed the evening.—There he found Lady Clementina dragging her aunt Eliza about the room, in continued fits of laughter, and protesting she should dance an *allemande* with her, which a servant of Belmour's, who touched the welch harp admirably, was, in obedience to her commands, then playing.

The moment she saw Belmour, whom she thought *rather* a better subject for her purpose, she flew up to him, and seizing his arm, told him he must take her Aunt Eliza's place.

Belmour made no resistance, he danced inimitably, and on *no occasion* thought it a mark of *good breeding,* to refuse when he was called upon.

On Lady Caroline's coming in, who vainly pleaded fatigue, and Heartley, who arrived at the same time, as vainly the rheumatism, the *allemande* was converted into a Scotch reel, and from one dance into another, in the wildest flow of spirits, did

Lady Clementina continue till supper-time.—She had been *quite melancholy* at hearing Miss Melville was gone—but ten minutes after almost forgot Miss Melville had ever been there.—At supper, however, she resumed the subject, ending by saying, she was certain, that Miss Melville would turn out to be some princess in disguise, or some fairy sprite, for she surely seemed no common being.

Chapter 9

TWO DAYS AFTERWARD, and before he was expected, the marquis returned.—He no sooner saw Belmour, than he told him, that he was sorry to send him away, but that his presence was absolutely necessary for a day or two in town, on particular business, and to sign some deeds of consequence. "It's your own fault though," he said, "for you would have avoided this journey, had you only stayed quietly with me, and not have been in such a prodigious haste to return hither."

Belmour had wished, he scarcely knew, or would not allow to himself, why, for any excuse, that might serve to carry him to town; for his going at that moment, he was aware, must be thought particular, without an assigned cause.—When his father therefore made his speech to him, he could scarcely conceal the relief it brought to his mind.

Imagination soon suggested the possibility of again seeing Miss Melville, should chance favour him, and from that moment his whole thoughts were occupied on various plans to enable him to discover where she had taken up her abode in town. Belmour was to set out, by his father's desire, in two days' time; he again tried the rector for intelligence—but in vain.

The stage coachman (whom he saw under the pretext of having some books, of which he was particularly careful, conveyed from town) was next tried; and, with the assistance of Bertram (pretending it was at his sister's request) he actually did, in part, succeed in his inquiries. On his road to town, he found, that Miss Melville had stopped a day at Exeter, it seemed, by the innkeeper's account, from having been unwell.

On his arrival in town, having previously informed himself where the Exeter stage put up, and feeling pretty sure of not being known, he without delay went himself to the inn. The people there could give no account of any such person as he described having been seen, but the innkeeper, at the last recollecting himself, said, "our Jack" (meaning the stage coachman) "may perhaps know, and he's in town today—only just stepped out a bit."

The man soon after returned, but so drunk, that it was impossible to get a word out of him, and the stagecoach was to set out that very night. Belmour, vexed, unable to turn his thoughts to anything, and believing his father's business might very well be delayed for a day, would not even go home, lest he should be stopped and prevented from prosecuting his present intentions, but walked about the streets in the neighbourhood of the *Swan with Two Necks,* anxiously waiting for the time, when he thought the coachman likely to be in a state to answer his questions.

On returning to the inn, he found the man stretched on the bench where he had left him.—On their rousing him, rubbing his eyes, he asked with an oath, why he was to be disturbed before his time.—"G—d damn ye, why ye know, I never have but to shake myself, take a *snack,* and away!"

But on Belmour's addressing him, whose figure always commanded involuntary respect, he begged "his honour's pardon," and seemed anxious to give him every information in his power.

The man was naturally intelligent, and, on Belmour's description, seemed perfectly to recollect the person in question—he told him, "the lady *as* he talked of had stopped at Staines—though," said he, "she was *quite* genteel, and paid the same as *though* she had come to London."

Belmour's prudence almost wholly now forsook him, to find that he was again disappointed.—That but the day before he had passed through the very place, where he might have received intelligence, nay, where possibly Miss Melville might actually be!—This was too much, and he determined, at all events, to return to Staines, trusting to the best excuse he might be able to make for his appearance, should he be fortunate enough to see Miss Melville.—He however first sent to his father's agent, with whom he appointed a meeting, and for that purpose delayed setting out till sometime in the day following, hoping thus to finish his father's business in town; but the agent talked of some days more, at least, before the papers could be ready for signing. Waiting for this, Belmour considered as impossible to his impatience; leaving word, therefore, that he should be in town again in a day or two, he set out on horseback, accompanied only by Bertram, for Staines.

On his arrival, he found no difficulty in procuring what information the landlord could give him, who was loquacious and communicative.

It appeared, that Miss Melville (for by description and coincident circumstances it could be no other) had been met, on her arrival at the inn, by a young man, and that a chaise had been ordered for them to go away together almost immediately; but that she had found herself so ill, as to be unable to prosecute her journey, and that, having inquired for a private lodging near, she had gone thither, and *he* believed the lady and gentleman were there still, "and *like* to remain."

Belmour's colour went and came during this account—when the landlord ended, he desired to be conducted to the house, where the lady was—" 'Tis just out of the town, my lord," said he, "I'll show your lordship the way."

Belmour, though struck with the idea of all the innkeeper might surmise, and ashamed of his own folly, was unable to resist the impulse of his heart.—He walked on with hurried steps, till they came within sight of a sort of cottage, surrounded by a small garden, enclosed with a low paling—"That's the house," said the man, pointing towards it, "and there's the lady *a walking*."

Belmour made him a sign, that he need follow him no further, and walked up towards a small gate opening into the garden.—It was indeed Miss Melville: she was leaning on the arm of the young man who was with her.—On Belmour's appearing (and he was certain she had recognized him) she turned away, and, walking slowly, went directly into the house—the door was shut.

The young man having seen her into the house, walked up to Belmour with some quickness, just as he laid his hand on the latch of the garden-gate, with a design to enter.

"Do you want anything here, sir?" said he, speaking rather in a foreign accent. "I wish, sir, to say a few words to that lady," replied Belmour, somewhat surprised at the manner in which he had been addressed, "and shall beg leave to wait on her now, or at her own time."

"*That lady*, sir, is ill, and cannot see anybody." "Sir," resumed Belmour, eyeing him from head to foot, "I shall however take the liberty of sending her a note, and of asking at least this favour from herself." "If you please, sir, but she will not see anybody."

The person who spoke seemed to be between twenty and thirty, his face was hard and much pitted with the smallpox, but his figure was manly and fine—he had a black stock round his neck, and a short hanger by his side—his appearance was somewhat that of a seafaring person.

Belmour seeing him so little disposed to enter into conversation, and fearing to create any suspicion, that might injure Miss Melville, if he then further intruded, took his leave.—The young man only just touched his hat as they parted, and standing at the gate till Belmour was out of sight, seemed desirous to make sure of his not returning.

Belmour, beyond measure chagrined, went back to his inn.—A thousand painful ideas assailed his mind.—It seemed evident that Miss Melville avoided him; yet he wished for further certainty, though to what purpose he dared not ask himself.—Note after note was written and torn; at last one, that, as he thought, could not give offence, was finished, which he was just folding up, deliberating whether he should send it that night, or wait till the next morning, when the sudden clattering of a chaise was heard in the court, and presently a voice not unknown to him repeated, "Lord Belmour! Lord Belmour! you say is here! O! show me in to him."—The door instantly flew open, and scarcely leaving Belmour time to huddle the note into his pocket, St. Fort appeared, a being of all others he would least have wished to have seen at that moment.—He knew him to be penetrating, curious, and malicious; while he asked Belmour carelessly how he "came to be *settled* there!" inquiry lurked in his eye.—Belmour, reddening, answered, that he had expected to meet a person there on business, whom, not finding, he meant the next day to return to town. "Well," said St. Fort, "I am lucky, for I felt d—mn'd tired and little disposed to go on tonight, yet the thoughts of a *solo* in a dirty inn staggered me, and *now* (bowing) if I am not troublesome to your lordship, I shall certainly not think my evening *dull.*"—There was no possible excuse to be made; poor Belmour was therefore forced to submit to hear histories of persons he did not know, and scandal he did not believe, told, it was true, with much dry humour by St. Fort; but so little adapted to the state of Belmour's mind was this sort of conversation, that he could no way keep up his attention to one half of what he said.

St. Fort announced his intention of setting out the next morning on his road to Weymouth, at eight o'clock; this suited Belmour, as nine, he thought (being prevented that evening) would be a proper time to send his note to Miss Melville.

At about eight o'clock the next morning, Belmour heard a chaise drive out of the inn-yard: he doubted not but that it was St. Fort's, and rising immediately, he dressed, and came down-stairs, with the note in his hand.—Calling to a waiter, he had begun explaining whither the note was to be carried, when St. Fort appeared.—Belmour started; the waiter, half frightened at the instantaneous change in Belmour's countenance, stammered.—"The *lady*, and please your lordship, I believe it is she your lordship means, that lodged just out of town, had a *chay* from our house this morning at eight o'clock, and I believe she's gone, my lord, but *master* knows better."—St. Fort, who clearly had heard all that was said, brushed by, with a half-checked sneer on his face, and going directly into the room where they had passed the evening together, the door of which stood open, walked up to the window, and leaning out, began humming an air with affected unconcern.

Belmour, whom no man dared to question, when he decidedly forbad it by his looks, followed St. Fort into the room, and ordered breakfast.—St. Fort, rubbing his eyes as he sat down, said he had overslept himself—the breakfast was tacit on both sides, and shortly afterward St. Fort actually did set out. He was no sooner gone, than Belmour, giving way to the impulse of passion, determined to follow Miss Melville, and try to satisfy his curiosity at least, as to her present destination, which he fancied might afford lights to assist him in his future conduct towards her. He inquired which road the chaise had taken, then mounting his horse, and at the stage following, easily procured the same intelligence; but when he came to the second stage, on the Hertfordshire road, he was told that a chaise, to whom belonging they knew not, had come up to the door of the inn, and that the gentleman and lady he inquired for were "gone off together."—What road did they take? "*That,* your honour," said a waiter, pointing to a sort of by-lane, turning out of the great road, "I *see'd* them go up yonder hill."

Belmour, shaking the reins on his horse's neck, set off in a swift gallop.—He continued for some miles, plainly tracing the recent track of wheels, when suddenly the lane ended, along which he had gone, and opened into a wide sandy common, cut by fifty different roads.—He was forced to stop—no possibility seemed now to remain of discovering which way the carriage had gone, one only miserable cottage appeared in sight, at which he could inquire. Thither he went, but could learn nothing—a poor old wretch, in tattered garments, was spinning at the door, so deaf, that he could with difficulty make her hear, and by no means comprehend what he said—she seemed hardly to know what *a chaise* meant, but always answered—"Nay, farmer Blade's cart han't gone by today."

Belmour, though himself in despair, forgot not to assist the wretched, but dropped a guinea into the hand of the old woman, as he turned away his horse from her door, and was followed by her benedictions, till the sound of her feeble voice was lost in the wind.

After vainly riding round and round the common, in hopes of catching again the lost track of the wheels, Belmour was at last forced to seek the lane by which he came.

Thus foiled every way in his search, he felt a degree of anger against the cause of so much, hitherto, fruitless inquietude.—He was evidently, he thought, avoided by Miss Melville, why he knew not; and arguing from the sensations of the moment, it seemed, to him ridiculous not to give up all further inquiries after her, and not to endeavour at least to obliterate the impression, which, unauthorised by hope or reason, she had made on his heart.

In this state of mind, harassed and fatigued, Belmour was met on his return to Staines by Bertram.—"*Mauvaises nouvelles milor,*" said he, taking hold of the bridle with a trembling hand, as Belmour alighted from his horse.—"Good Heavens!" said Belmour, "my sister is ill."—"Non *milor,* non—not Lady Caroline—my lord marquis—he is very ill indeed."—"Who brought the news? where is the servant?" said Belmour in an agony.—"Thomas, the groom, he brought the news, my lord, but he's gone on to town for milord's physician.—I *see* him luckily as he was changing his horse—for he thought your lordship was in town—but he could not stop, as he *says* it was Lady Caroline's order to lose no time, but bring the physician—and indeed they think *he come* too late, for the doctors from ——, who are with him, think he cannot live many hours."—"Order instantly a chaise," said Belmour, in a fiercely articulate voice.—"A chaise, and four of the best horses they can give—you, Bertram, I shall take in the chaise with me, be quick."—Bertram flew, and having ordered the chaise, while it was preparing, silently put something to eat before his master, who, he judged, as was the fact, had touched nothing since breakfast.—He dared not speak, but as he put down what he had brought on the table, the poor fellow cast a suppliant look towards Belmour, so expressive of his solicitous care for him, that it brought the tears, ready before to start, into his eyes.—"I thank thee, Bertram," said he, "I will try to eat," and waving his hand to be left, he sat down to the table.

The chaise was soon at the door, and from that moment, Belmour stopped only to change horses, till he came to Belmour Castle.

When he alighted, he saw a general gloom spread over every face—he asked not a single question, but hurried to his father's apartment.—At the door of the bedchamber he was stopped by his sister, who, coming to meet him, held up her hand in sign of silence—she gently shut the door,—"My father is just dropped asleep, make no noise."—"Oh God!" exclaimed Belmour, throwing himself on her neck—"I shall then again see my father!"—"Yes, my dearest brother—but I fear there is little hope," Lady Caroline mournfully resumed.—She then told him, that their father had been seized by a sudden and violent attack, the symptoms of which, although not clearly understood by the physicians who had hitherto seen him, were by them pronounced to be very dangerous; that, however, he did not now appear to suffer much; and that it was their opinion, that he might live for some time. The marquis's own physician, who shortly afterward arrived from London, and who, at Belmour's particular request, remained to attend him, confirmed this opinion. Every resource of medical art was in vain exercised with consummate skill, for the possible chance of his recovery—six weeks had now passed since the first seizure, during which Belmour had anxiously remained in the exercise of the most tender and unremitting attentions to his father, when meeting the physicians in the morning just after their first visit that day, he was told by them, that the marquis appeared so much refreshed by the more than usual repose he had gotten the preceding night, and so much himself, that, should he have a second night as favourable, they should not be without hope of a final recovery.—Belmour, revived by this encouraging speech, went immediately into his father's room, and sitting down by his bedside, with a glow of satisfaction on his countenance, to which it had now long been a stranger.—"I rejoice," said he, "to hear so good an account of you."—"The physicians flatter you," returned the marquis, with difficulty raising his heavy eyelids, and looking towards his son—"I say *flatter* you—few fathers in this age, I fear."—Belmour's face was in an instant covered with tears.—"My child," continued he, stretching out his arms—then holding his son for a long time closely pressed to his bosom—"be assured, that your affection—the recollection of your constant tenderness, and unremitted duty towards me, now softens all I suffer, and makes even these moments more than tolerable—but I affect you too much," said he, seeing Belmour choked with tears, and unable to utter a word—"compose yourself, my son, I have lived happily—die happily, and trust in the mercy of that Divine Power, that doubtless watches over us—what moral can say more?—Something yet I would request," he continued, "but I fear to distress you"—his voice almost failed him.—"You know my earnest wish—Clementina, the child of my adoption—but no more—I wish your happiness; only, my son, be not too hasty in your choice—*this* I do entreat, and it may be a weakness, but a long line of honoured ancestors, whose pedigree remains hitherto unsullied, I would wish not to think, even in that particular, could ever be disgraced by you—but I am fatigued—go, my son," said he, leaning back on the pillows which supported him, and stretching forward his hand, which Belmour affectionately kissed—"go, my son, farewell."—Again waving his hand, his eyelids closed as Belmour left the room—he scarcely spoke again after this last farewell of stupor, in the course of the following night, to appearance without point or effort, expired.

The marquis was sincerely regretted, not only by his children, but by all his domestics and dependants, to whom he was kind and generous. His pride, though excessive, being always accompanied by benevolent attentions and politeness of those, who were subordinate to him in rank, rather served to increase respect and deference, than to give offence.

Belmour was much affected at the death of his father, and his last words made a serious impression on his mind—he wished even, could it be consistent with his own future happiness, fully to comply with his dying request.

Lady Clementina had remained at Belmour Castle, unmindful of all her youthful vanities, in constant and affectionate attendance on her uncle and Lady Caroline, whose health visibly declined: her eyes were sometimes filled with tears at their sufferings, and sometimes she relieved their drooping spirits by her natural and unaffected flow of mirth and gayety.—Treated with the affectionate familiarity of friendship by this lovely and amiable girl, Belmour, at times, almost thought he loved her, and the image of Miss Melville, for the moment, faded on his imagination; but before these impressions were ever sufficiently strengthened, to allow him to take a decided resolution, some sudden and childish sally of Lady Clementina's, or some mark of thoughtless indifference for him, at once destroyed them, and made him doubly sensible how much his heart required sympathy, both of character and feelings, to render a serious engagement in any degree conducive to his happiness.—Then again that image, ever most dear to him, returned with renewed power, although he feared to yield to what he rationally considered might be only the effect of delusive passion.—Thus passed about a fortnight after the death of his father, when the state of Lady Caroline's health grew so considerably worse, that immediate change of climate was recommended by the physicians as the only chance of saving her from a decline. Belmour, alarmed for his sister, instantly determined to accompany her to Lisbon, and from that moment, was wholly occupied with preparations to make the journey as easy and tolerable as possible to her, who, naturally of a gentle, timid nature, was now, from illness and depression of spirits, wholly incapable herself of making the least exertion. In little more than a month from the time of their father's death, they set out on their road to Falmouth, taking leave of Lady Clementina, who had remained at Belmour Castle, and would not quit them till their departure, but gave them the last farewell with streaming eyes, and saw them actually drive from the door, before Lady Eliza could persuade her, though sometimes scolding, and sometimes soothing; she had repeatedly remonstrated against crying, which she said was at once the worst thing possible for the health, and the most unbecoming to the complexion, and, raising her voice, "Lady Clementina, my dear," said she, sobbing herself, "if you cry so, you will not be able to show your face at Weymouth" (whither they were going for the latter season), "and I hear that all the world is to be there."

Thus the cousins parted, and, taking opposite roads, bade adieu to Belmour Castle.

✦ Volume II ✦

Chapter 10

LADY CAROLINE BORE THE JOURNEY but ill, and on their arrival at Falmouth complained of extreme fatigue and depression of spirits. Belmour, having placed her in the quietest apartment he could find at the inn, as it was then towards the close of the evening, walked out in order to make inquiries concerning the packets, and to arrange everything so as to render the voyage as little subject to inconvenience as possible for his sister, who, with difficulty, restrained even her fears on the occasion.

He learned that two packets were ready to sail immediately, and that they only waited for the wind, at that time unfavourable; that the cabins of one were already taken by different passengers; but that the other vessel was unoccupied, and wholly at his disposal. Belmour, having made his arrangements, was returning back to his sister, when, at a little distance, he thought he saw a figure, that was not unknown to him; but it being now dusk, he did not immediately recognize the face: presently afterward, drawing nearer, and the person pulling off his hat to him, he discovered it to be Derville. Not having the least expectation of meeting him at Falmouth, Belmour was a good deal surprised, and by no means agreeably. He had never been much acquainted with Derville, but thought him a coxcomb, and disliked him; and, though the circumstances relative to his former engagement to his sister had always been carefully kept from him, still he knew enough to make him more than suspect, that she had suffered much from her attachment for him. The cold manner, in which Belmour returned his salute, by no means escaped Derville, but he affected not to perceive it; and, as it happened to suit him, put on in return an air of easy familiarity: he had then been detained for above a week at Falmouth, where he had not yet met with a single acquaintance, or anything that *he* called *human,* and was by that time a good deal tired of himself, and still more so of his wife; he was therefore glad to have his *ennui* relieved in any degree, he cared not by whom. After informing himself of the cause of Belmour's appearance at Falmouth, where he so little expected "the good fortune of meeting him!" he, in return, told Belmour, that Mrs. Derville had been for some time unwell; and that Dr. Patchum had recommended Lisbon as affording the most likely chance for her recovery: but he did *not* tell him, that the cause of this ready acquiescence on his part to a plan so little calculated, as he thought, for his own amusement, was owing to the circumstance of a rich relation of his wife's, from whom, in her right, he expected a considerable accession of fortune, and who, it was believed, was not likely to live long, having earnestly requested to see them. This relation, who had honourably acquired a considerable property by trade, and had resided for many years at Lisbon, having no nearer descendant than Mrs. Derville, it was naturally supposed, from this sort of summons, meant to make her his heiress; and to objects of interest Derville was by no means indifferent, however often he might appear unmindful of the future, when occupied in the pursuit of present gratifications.

Belmour, after taking leave of Derville, who lodged at the separate inn, deliberated with himself on his way home to his sister, whether or not he should mention having met with him: he feared the least agitation of mind in her present weak state, both of health and spirits, and, as Derville and his wife were not to sail in the same packet, he thought she might as well remain ignorant of a circumstance, which, he doubted not, would distress her, till she arrived at Lisbon. But, on his return, the first question Lady Caroline asked, was whom he had seen? On this Belmour thought it would seem affectation, not to mention Derville, and, in the end, distress her more. She made no remark in answer, and the room being nearly dark, imagined she had escaped any observation from her brother. The next morning the wind being still contrary, Lady Caroline said she required a little air, and proposed walking with her brother. As they came near the sea, and were continuing their walk along the harbour, Derville appeared just returning from the vessel, in which he was to embark, where he had been to view the accommodations. He instantly came up to Lady Caroline with an air of interest and seeming pleasure at thus unexpectedly meeting her, familiarly offering his arm for her to lean on, which she readily accepted; "two arms," said he, "are better than one." Belmour, on whose arm she was at the moment leaning, frowned, but she was too much hurried and occupied at the moment to remark it. Derville and his wife, by Lady Caroline's invitation, passed the evening with her, and Belmour was forced, however reluctantly, to partake of this society.

Three days passed nearly in the same manner; when at length the wind proving fair, the two parties embarked in their separate vessels.

Belmour, as the ship quitted the harbour, cast a melancholy look towards the shore. He had for some time been standing on the deck, his arms folded across his breast, lost in vague reverie; at that instant the painful recollection of having quitted Miss Melville, probably forever, rushed on his imagination: he fixed his eyes, with a sentiment of tender melancholy, on the parting coast, till it was lost to his view. Night soon afterward came on, with a high and tempestuous, though not contrary wind, and a rough sea; the same weather continued till the fourth day, when the wind lowered, and the sea became gradually calm and smooth: and on the seventh day from their sailing, the two packets entered the harbour of Lisbon. The extreme beauty of the scene charmed and delighted the elegant taste of Belmour:—Lady Caroline, wholly occupied by the renewal of sentiments fatal to her repose, which the unexpected meeting at Falmouth had occasioned, from the moment of their arrival, thought only of the means of seeing Derville—she considered herself as dying—pride and resentment vanished from her gentle bosom; she dignified the sensations of her heart with the name of friendship, and willingly suffered herself to be deluded by this specious errour.—Circumstances, indeed, favoured the delusion. Derville himself, accustomed to please, careless by nature, and by habit unused to occupation, would, out of mere idleness, dawdle after any pursuit, which, even without occupying his senses, would employ his time; he therefore, on this occasion, where his vanity too found so much gratification, was forward in every expression of interest, and in those attentions, which so naturally captivate the unwary mind of innocence and truth.

Mrs. Derville was a *fine lady,* without one grain of heart to *molest* her, but no fool; she was convinced, early after their marriage, that she was not to pretend to any place in her husband's heart or affections, and being moreover perfectly easy on the subject, sought only to make an indifferent and fretful temper, the seeds of which she plainly perceived in his disposition, subservient to her own views and pleasures. The first object of her care was, therefore, always to accommodate herself to any society he might prefer, in order that she might, unmolested, choose her own: at Lisbon, of course, seeing which way the bent of his inclination lay, she made it her business, by every little art and attention in her power, to engage Lady Caroline in an intimacy with her; in which she easily succeeded; they shortly became inseparable, with the addition of a Mrs. Marsden to their society, a widow who had long resided at Lisbon. She was one of those *good sort* of women who never speak or think ill of others, but shut their eyes to vice or folly, wherever it appears, that they may not have the trouble of attempting to correct or avoid it. She wanted neither common sense nor common information; was blessed with good health and good spirits, which none of the nicer feelings of a more delicate mind ever disturbed; and thus, always cheerful, always obliging, and always willing to be pleased, she was eagerly sought after as an agreeable companion by those, into whose society she accidentally fell.

The mornings were passed by Lady Caroline with these companions, accompanied constantly by Derville, and sometimes by other gentlemen, who occasionally joined their party, in drives and rambles, or sometimes excursions by water on the enchanting bay, to visit the surrounding coast, and view the city from the different points on the opposite hills, from which its beauty and magnificence appear most striking; and, in the evenings, the same company generally assembled at Lady Caroline's, whose health obliged her to confine herself to the house after sunset.

Mrs. Derville, who was what is called a pretty woman, and had great pretensions to please, had at first cast an eye towards Belmour: this she thought would have been a perfectly *good arrangement,* but his pre-occupied looks, distant civility, and decided melancholy, soon convinced her, that to make anything of him, would take her much more time, than she had any probable chance of passing at Lisbon; and a genteel handsome young *fidalgo,* who, under the pretence of teaching her Portuguese, was become her constant attendant, and was received familiarly into her house, appeared much better suited to her purpose.

Belmour, to whom the whole of this society was insupportable, was grieved and mortified to see his sister thus forgetful of herself, as it appeared to him; yet unable farther to remonstrate with her, since the gentle and affectionate hints he had given her, had been received by no means in a way to encourage any farther attempts on the subject; and her health but too visibly declining, made it impossible for him to risk anything, that could even in the slightest degree distress or agitate her mind. He passed as little of his time as he could with them, except when he thought himself of use to his sister. He even made a journey into Spain, in the course of nearly six months, which had now passed since his leaving England; besides frequent excursions to Cintra, where he had hired a small house, in one of the most beautiful situations of that romantic and singular place. There he passed whole days alone, sometimes rambling among the mountains, the craggy sides of which are partly covered with luxuriant evergreens, partly with majestic cork-trees, and varied in their fantastic forms—sometimes he would sit for hours pensively viewing the infinite beauty of the ocean in all its varied tints—then swiftly mount with agility to the very summit of the highest of the mountains, where still are to be seen the picturesque ruins of a Moorish castle, the last refuge whence the gallant people were driven by victorious Spain. "Alas!" would he exclaim, "why is chivalry no more—why are the genuine sentiments of the heart no longer ennobled by the imagination!—Have we gained by the change? by circumscribing them within the narrow limits of cold calculation?"

One day after a solitary ramble of this sort, Belmour was returning to his cottage, when casting his eye accidentally along a sort of winding valley enclosed by mountains; the belfry of a church appeared, which till then had escaped his notice; though he thought, that not a building, scarcely a single spot of that romantic place was unknown to him. Thither he directed his steps—a green path, hedged closely on each side with lauristinus, myrtle, and orange-trees, led to a small church, placed on an eminence, to which he ascended by several flights of steps. On entering the door he judged it to belong to some convent of Capuchins, from the simplicity of its appearance, as the severity of their order admits of no gilding, no metal, no ornaments; and the plain ungaudy altar, with its row of wooden candlesticks, was here adorned only by a picture of Velasquez, which might indeed well have engaged the attention of a stranger; but at that moment the sensations of Belmour's mind were still more excited by the peculiar manner, in which the church was ornamented and enlivened by flowers.—Some *padre* fond of gardening, it appeared, had placed earthen pots with plants growing luxuriantly in them, not only in all the windows, but upon a sort of ledge, that went round the inside of the church. The colour of the earthen pots assimilated perfectly with the brown sobriety of the place, while the vivid and tender green of the plants they contained, many of which flaunted down the walls, seemed to prove the impossibility of rivalling the gay decorations of nature, and conveyed to the mind more agreeable, more graceful ideas of ornament, than could have been done by all the stucco, marble, or gilding in the world.

Belmour stood for some time reclined against one of the piers of clustered columns, which supported the arched roof of the building—all was silent, and he thought himself alone; when turning his eyes towards the farther end of the church, he perceived a figure kneeling on the pavement—it was a friar—his body was bent forward, and his arms closely embraced a low monumental urn, on which his head rested.—Belmour felt a secret awe at the appearance before him, mingled with surprise, and, scarcely venturing to breathe, remained riveted to the spot where he stood.

Shortly afterward the friar rose; he stood for some time before the urn, then, taking up a small basket in his hand, which was by him on the pavement, he walked slowly on towards the door, by which Belmour had entered. Before he had turned his head, Belmour had retired so as to conceal himself behind the pier, but at the same time to have a distinct view of him as he passed. It was a face of dignity and beauty; his figure was tall, and appeared graceful as he walked slowly by, his arms folded across his breast; he seemed to be about fifty, his countenance was composed, and bore rather the marks of habitual melancholy than recent grief. Belmour followed him, still unseen, to the door of the church; then, having seen him turn towards the gate of the monastery, he returned back into the church, and flew with impatient curiosity to the monument, which the friar had just quitted.—It was recently strewed with fresh flowers—the urn was of fine gray marble, its form simple and elegant; no other inscription than these few words on the urn, "*Rosaurae Sacer,*" then followed "*posuit,*" and only some initials. Belmour, as he contemplated the monument, felt a tear steal down his cheek.—"Death here," said he to himself, "has surely been accompanied by some unusually aggravating circumstance;"—at the moment a distant sound of voices chanting a requiem, struck his ear, and he soon perceived the monks advancing two by two from behind the altar to their places in the choir.—He returned to his cottage, his mind deeply impressed with the scene, to which he had just been witness: he regretted being obliged to return the next day to Lisbon, and longed to inquire further after the friar and the monument, which inspired him with so much interest: but he had promised his sister, to see her again on that day, and indeed having of late thought her more unwell and more depressed than usual, his own anxiety made him desirous of returning to her.

When he got to Lisbon, he found that several mails long due were arrived by the packet.—In them were some letters from his principal steward, who, by chance an honest man, earnestly requested his presence for the settlement of various concerns relative to his estates, which his short residence in England after his father's death had hitherto prevented; and, among other articles of private and public intelligence, his sister informed him, that she had received letters from Lady Clementina, announcing her intended marriage shortly to take place with young Melford.—Lady Caroline as she spoke looked at her brother with a kind of half reproach on her countenance, which plainly said, "You might have prevented this:"—but Belmour heeded her not—he felt a relief from the circumstance, which by no means sympathised with his sister's ideas—the conversation on that subject soon ended between them, and Lady Caroline then, with some hesitations, said, "But my dear brother, I am sure you ought to go to England; you left everything unsettled, and by what Barnard tells me—" "My dearest sister," interrupted Belmour, with the most affectionate expression of kindness, "I shall not leave you: my going to England is, believe me, immaterial; a mere matter of form, and six months or a year will make no difference; whatever good Barnard, our steward, may say, I beg you would not ever mention it again."

"But, my dear brother," said Lady Caroline colouring, "I have a little plan that—" at the instant in burst Mrs. Marsden—"Well, my dear, have you told Lord Belmour our scheme? he must approve, I am sure—nothing so good as change of air—and then, you know, he may do just what he likes; we can take care of you; and we will not delay setting out, lest the weather should grow too hot, which I am sure it is not now, for nothing ever was so delightful—then we will all set out together, travel through Spain, sail from the most convenient port to Italy, see Rome, and pass the winter at Naples; and as you are to be under my particular care," continued Mrs. Marsden, taking Lady Caroline's hand, "should Mr. and Mrs. Derville travel too fast for you, you know I am always to be commanded by you, and at your devotion—never was so good a plan! I have always died to see Italy—and to travel in such society!—nothing ever was so delightful!"

Belmour was all astonishment—he had not imagined, that his sister was in a state to venture undertaking a journey even of fifty miles; but all he found had actually been arranged during his short absence at Cintra. Yet, although the plan perfectly suited his own convenience and disposition of mind at the moment, he felt inexpressibly chagrined and vexed at the part he saw his imprudent and unwary sister was acting—but how effectually to remonstrate he knew not. Lady Caroline was of an age, to judge and to decide for herself; and moreover, though one of the gentlest of beings, she was not on all subjects easy of control. All that Belmour could do, and on what he absolutely insisted was, that he should settle everything for her as to the arrangement of her journey, which he did in a manner that made her wholly independent of the Dervilles. Mrs. Marsden was to accompany her, and a physician, whom Belmour had brought with him from England to attend her; a sensible and intelligent man, who had travelled over most parts of Europe, and was thoroughly acquainted both with Spain and Italy. Thus with the addition of couriers, proper servants, and her own separate carriages, nothing could oblige Lady Caroline to depart in the slightest degree from what best suited her own convenience on the road; and Belmour, making the extreme delicacy of her health a pretext, earnestly entreated of her to travel separately with Mrs. Marsden and her own suite, and meet her other friends only at the different towns, where they might stop for some days. This was in part promised; for ashamed of the weakness of her own conduct, and awed by the well-known rectitude of her brother's mind, Lady Caroline avoided as much as possible all discussions on the subject.

The real origin of this whole plan was Derville's growing tired of Lisbon. Mrs. Derville's relation had finally settled everything on her and her husband, and being likely to linger, perhaps for a considerable time, Derville, who had never seen Italy, thought it a good opportunity to make the tour of that country; particularly as his extravagance had made his living in England just then not so agreeable to him, as he expected to find it, when in possession of the future increase of property, to which he now looked with certainty.

In a little more than a fortnight everything was in readiness for the journey.

Belmour was much affected at parting with his sister, who, when she received his last embrace, was drowned in tears; and at the moment wished she never had consented, thus voluntarily to quit such a protector: but the die was cast.

Belmour had accompanied his sister across the harbour to Adeya-Galega: when he returned, the evening was calm and serene, the sun-beams still played on the surface of the water, and no sound met his ear but that of the oars, as the boat glided gently along—the quiet stillness, that reigned, well suited the melancholy train of meditation, into which he had fallen—he had determined before he returned to England again to visit Cintra; and the idea of the friar contributed not a little to confirm this resolution—his fine dignified figure often presented itself to his imagination, and the deep melancholy of his countenance, together with the singularity of the attendant circumstances, excited an interest in his breast, beyond that which mere curiosity could inspire.

Having nothing that detained him at Lisbon, Belmour went the very next day to Cintra, and that evening walked to the church, where he had seen the friar.—He appeared not—another of the brothers was saying mass at one of the altars: and after having walked round the church, and again read the inscription on the urn, Belmour retired. The next day, however, he was more fortunate; on his way to the church he saw the friar just coming out of the door; quickening his pace he soon came up to him, as he was turning to go towards the monastery. After accosting him with a "*Salve Domine,*" he walked on by his side, and presently asked him in Portuguese (in which language he had during his stay in Portugal made no small proficiency) if, without being troublesome, he might accompany him on his walk, at least to the gate of his monastery. The friar raised his eyes, which were fixed pensively on the ground as he walked along, and turning them towards Belmour with a placid look of inquiry, as if somewhat surprised at the proposal, bowed assent, and they walked on together.

A short silence ensued—the friar then, with that ease which rarely belongs to any but persons of the world, asked Belmour a few questions concerning his coming to Portugal, seeing, as he said, that he was a stranger: but it seemed more from civility, and not wholly to avoid entering into conversation with him, than from curiosity; by the time, however, that they had reached the gate of the monastery, the tone of Belmour's voice, the unaffected mildness of his manner, and the melancholy of his countenance, had so far created an interest in the breast of the friar, that he wished at least for a less abrupt parting—he turned—hesitated—and after heaving a deep sigh, gently smiling, said, "If the melancholy of these walls does not disgust you, perhaps you will deign to rest awhile in my cell; a few dried fruits and a bit of bread are indeed all I have to offer, but you will favour me by the acceptance: and," added he, "if you be curious in objects of antiquity, this building may deserve your attention. The monastery you now see," continued he, pointing to its mouldering walls half covered with ivy, "is but a poor remnant of former magnificence, and must, by the ruins still to be seen, have been at an earlier period of time very considerable; it is said too that the original monastery, dedicated to the order of St. Benedict, was built on the site of an ancient pagan temple, which I am led to believe from several broken columns, and fragments of sculpture, not Gothic, which I have here and there traced not far from the place, half sunk in the ground and covered with plants.—But the sun is already high—you will be cooler within;" saying this he led Belmour into a beautiful cloister of the purest Gothic architecture, which surrounded an open court, planted with orange and citron trees; in the middle was a fountain of limpid water, with everywhere a profusion of the finest flowers.

"These beautiful flowers," said Belmour, "I believe, father, you make your particular care, for even with the luxuriant growth of this climate, I have yet seen none so fine." "*My* care!" said the friar, fixing his eyes on Belmour with a look of questioning penetration—"never, my son, surely till now have I seen you, nor can you know aught of me."—"Pardon me," resumed Belmour, instantly aware of having said more than he intended, "you have indeed never seen *me* till now, but"—here they were interrupted by some of the friars coming by; on which the friar bowing, made a sign to Belmour to follow him. They passed on through a small door into a long dark passage, on one side of which were the cells of the friars, each separate, their size not ten feet square, a bench on which a mat was stretched (their only bed), a table, and a lamp, and crucifix, were all the furniture they contained: in that which they entered indeed, there was the addition of a shelf, which contained some books; "and is this damp cell your habitation?" said Belmour, with an expression of compassion.—"Our order is severe," replied the friar, "but of that I complain not."

They were no sooner seated, but the friar, who had been struck with Belmour's exclamation on seeing the flowers, seemed desirous to know whether it were accidental, and without further meaning, or whether by any chance he really knew more concerning him.

Belmour ingenuously related to him all that had passed; begging his forgiveness for what, he said, he feared must seem unwarrantable curiosity; "but," said he, "the interest excited in my breast by the scene, to which I was accidentally a witness, believe me, father, deserves a better name."

"Strange," said the friar after a few minutes' pause, "that a silence nearly of thirty years should be thus broken! that to you, an utter stranger, I should relate what I have never once been tempted to utter, since these walls first became my sad refuge—but no matter," said he, laying his hand on Belmour's, which he gently pressed—"something of sympathy—something, my son, there is between us, which it would be even painful to me to resist, and my story may be remembered by you as a warning against that fatal errour, worldly and inconsiderate pride."

"My name," continued he, "is immaterial, suffice it to you to know, that it is among the first in Spain. After the death of my beloved mother, whom fate cruelly snatched from me; my father, incited by the jealous and turbulent spirit of a second wife, with whom he was passionately in love, shortly after their marriage withdrew all his former fondness from me; and, as it was given out, for the advantage of my education; but, in fact, wishing to remove me from his presence, sent me, accompanied by a governor, to Lisbon; where at that time some of our family had retired, being under a temporary banishment from our court. There, among various other acquaintance, I made that of a worthy merchant, whose house was ever open to me, who treated me with parental kindness; I, in return—" here his breast heaved, and his countenance was disordered; recovering himself, he continued, "I, in return, planted a dagger in his bosom. He had one only daughter, beautiful as an angel, fresh as the new-blown rose—she was thoughtless, gay, and happy—the love she inspired me with, she participated with all the innocence of pure affection; and, judging *my* passion by her own, she never doubted, but that we were to be united by sacred and indissoluble bands.—Educated in innocence, and ignorant of the prejudices of a bad world, she never dreamed of doubts or obstacles to our future union. I was, she saw, approved of by her father; and to him she had ever looked, not only as to the most kind and virtuous of men, but as to the most honoured. With difficulty could I restrain her, by a thousand falsehoods and artful subterfuges, from openly avowing the innocent sentiments of her heart: I, on the contrary, was born in a corrupt court, and early initiated in vice. My young companions were men of profligate manners, who laughed at all morality, and, too fatally for me, succeeded in stifling those seeds of virtue, implanted in my breast by the divine hand of our Maker, and so difficult wholly to eradicate. I had, as I said, succeeded in persuading her, that for reasons, which I should afterward explain, our mutual sentiments must, for the present, remain secret; though what were really my views I had never dared to ask myself; when I unexpectedly received letters from my father, by which I learned, that a marriage was on treaty for me with a lady nearly allied to the blood royal, famous for her beauty and accomplishments; and, though indifferent to his son, my father was, through pride and vanity, anxious for the honour of his house, and the manifold advantages he foresaw might accrue to it from this connection: he therefore desired my immediate presence at Madrid. Stunned as I was at this most unforeseen event; and in despair at leaving my Rosaura, I dared not venture to withstand my father's positive command. Taking therefore a hasty leave of all I loved, under the pretext of sudden business, (for I told her not the true cause of my departure) I left Lisbon, uncertain of my own future determinations—but to be brief—on my arrival at Madrid, assailed on every side by objects too powerful for my pride and vanity to withstand, I, for a while, forgot all that I had left behind me. Rosaura, after writing less frequently, had for some time omitted to write at all; this I interpreted into indifference; yet the latent flame, which still remained in my bosom, roused by her supposed neglect, recalled her dear image with double force to my imagination: when a sudden change of ministry taking place at the court of Madrid, my marriage, which had never been finally settled, was abruptly broken off. I felt a sincere joy, which I scarcely could conceal from my father when he announced the news to me; and, having obtained his permission, flew back with rapture and impatience to Lisbon. I hurried to the house of my old friend, determined to throw myself at his feet, confess my former errours, and formally, at all hazards, ask his lovely daughter in marriage—too late, alas!—I found, to my surprise, the house shut up, and was told, that he had left Lisbon some time since, in grief on his daughter's retiring, no one knew why, suddenly to a convent, with a determination to take the veil, in spite of all his entreaties to the contrary. During this affecting relation, I endeavoured to restrain my emotions: Rosaura could not yet, I knew, have taken the last vows, and still I hoped. I waited not for the delay of sending a messenger, but immediately set out myself in search of her: in my way to the convent (distant but a little from this monastery) as I passed the church, a melancholy bell was tolling; I continued but for a few paces, when a sudden and involuntary impulse made me return, and enter the church—need I proceed?—my life! my joy! my everything! was then a clay-cold corpse!—I was her murderer!—a sudden and sullen grief took possession of my soul—without a tear I then saw buried those dear remains, over which my eyes have since shed torrents—but that time is passed—I am composed," said he, holding his hand awhile closely pressed over his forehead—"you will guess at the rest—the world was lost to me; and having obtained leave of the superiour to raise the small cenotaph you saw (as I pretended to the memory of a beloved sister) in this mansion I took refuge—would it could have been from myself!—but the divine will be done," said he, devoutly raising his eyes to Heaven. "That I was the murderer of my Rosaura," continued he, "I can have no doubt. It happened some time after I had professed, that I was called to confess one of the nuns of the neighbouring convent, to which Rosaura had retired, who, after enlarging on many trifling errours, which her timid imagination estimated as sins, told me, that it weighed heavily on her mind, that a letter, given to her in secret by a dying saint (so she termed my Rosaura) had never been delivered to the person, to whom it was addressed, through fear, she said, of the superiour. She knew me not, for here to all I am unknown; and when I sent my renunciation to my father of all my paternal rights, in favour of my half brother, which he not unwillingly received, only reserving to myself a donation to this monastery, I kept the place of my retirement concealed from him, nor do I believe he has since ever wished to discover it.—Stifling my extreme emotion, I took charge of the letter—to me, I need not say, that it was addressed—what were my feelings, when, on reading the gentle dictates of my lofty Rosaura, I was told, without reproach, that my inconstancy had hastened her fate! She forgave, and blessed me!—oh! torture of the mind—recollection which ages cannot obliterate!—for," added he, "the ever-blooming image of my Rosaura fades not before me—still is that image present to my fancy.—Had she lived, time might have effaced, in part, those outward charms, at least, which captivate the senses; but my regret is equalled only by my penitence: silence and solitude have, however, composed my distracted mind. The cultivation of flowers, once the innocent delight of Rosaura, forms my recreation—ought I to complain?—oh! no, I praise a merciful God, for having allowed me time for penance; and hope, finally, to rest in peace. All of my sad story, I think, my son, is sufficiently explained.—Forgive me if I have dwelt too long on past remembrances—farewell, for I hear the bell, which summons us to prayers—I must attend—let me again see you before you leave this country, before we part, I fear, forever!" Saying these words he hurried out of the cell, and hastening with Belmour to the outward gate, bade him adieu.

Belmour walked pensively from the monastery, his mind entirely occupied by what he had heard; he was touched beyond measure at the story of the friar, and the sufferings of a passionate lover were rendered but the more affecting, by the composed dignity with which they were related.

Nothing now detained Belmour in Portugal, but the expectation of letters from his sister; as he wished to know, before he left Lisbon, how she had supported the first part of her journey. Soon afterward he heard of her having reached Madrid, where the whole party proposed passing some weeks. Lady Caroline wrote in spirits, although the account from the physician was less favourable than her own: on Belmour's part, however, nothing further could be done; he therefore secured a passage in the packet which was next to sail for England. He did not fail, as it will easily be supposed, to visit the friar before his departure, in whom he found a mind uncommonly well-informed, and less warped, even with respect to the opinions and customs of the world, than could have been supposed after so long a seclusion from society.

Belmour, when he took his leave, inquired by what means they might keep up some sort of correspondence.

"I cannot," said Belmour, "flatter myself with ever being of use to you; yet the idea of not being wholly ignorant of your future welfare would make this parting less painful." The friar, shaking his head with the most touching expression of settled melancholy on his countenance, replied,—"I will not deceive you—you will hear no more of me—to silence and oblivion my life has now long been devoted; nor, I confess it, would I venture to engage my sad heart in any new interest on earth.—No!—buried in the tomb of my Rosaura are all my hopes, thoughts, and wishes; and when I strew her monument with flowers, the solemn purpose must be still performed by an undivided mind:—forgive me," said he, "and know my son, that 'tis not in these deep solitudes, as in the vortex of the world, where, excited by passion ever changing its objects, hopes, fears, and interests rapidly succeed each other in the breast, and often, like the waves of the ocean passing over the sandy beach, leave no lasting impression behind.—All here is serious: strong feelings govern and occupy the mind, or apathy prevails.—Still I would be remembered by you—" (an involuntary tear here started in his eye) "you will not be forgotten in my orisons—farewell!" said he mournfully, as he folded Belmour in his arms—"farewell, and take my blessing." He stood at the gate of the monastery, where they had parted, following Belmour with his eyes, and often, as he saw him look back, waving his hand, till intercepted by the trees; as Belmour entered the path which led from the church, he lost sight of him forever.

Chapter 11

A FEW DAYS AFTER BELMOUR had taken leave of the friar, he quitted Lisbon, and embarked for England. Twelve days' sail, in the most prosperous weather, brought him to Falmouth.

He felt not that joy, which should have accompanied him, on his return to his native land, where every advantage fortune could bestow was showered upon his head. When he reached Belmour Castle, however, the seat of his ancestors, he experienced a sensation of unspeakable pleasure at the natural expressions of satisfaction and joy, which his presence occasioned among all those, by whom he was surrounded;—he felt they were sincere—felt that he deserved them.—His pride was of that genuine, noble nature, which secures respect from man to man, in whatever situation or rank of life he may be placed; added to this, his benevolence and generosity, with the polished gentleness of his manners, had ever made him adored by his father's tenants, domestics, and by all the surrounding inhabitants of the country, and his return was looked to, as the promise of every good: but when he turned his thoughts inwardly to his own susceptible heart, he there felt only a melancholy blank—felt himself alone in the world.

"Is this happiness?" cried he,—"alas! alas! to others, indeed, I may, in some measure, be the means of dispensing it—but to myself!—" Occupied with these reflections he had been for some time walking to and fro in the gallery of the castle, when, throwing himself on a sofa, his eyes met a portrait of his sister.—It was herself as once he remembered her, smiling in all the bloom of health.—"Poor sister!" exclaimed he, "how art thou changed! now perhaps no more! and what real interest remains to me on earth?" His eyes continued fixed on the portrait, till they were dimmed by tears.—"But," continued he, as he passed his handkerchief across his eyes, "why should I not endeavour at least to seek relief from the activity of my own mind, and, if possible, avert this baneful apathy, an evil hardly less pernicious than ungovernable passion?"

The advice which the friar had given him, and earnestly and solemnly repeated, against worldly pride and prejudice, had made a deep impression on his mind.

"Vain world," cried he, "what indeed art thou and all thy charms, when compared with the only earthly happiness worth seeking—the union of two hearts mutually blessing each other?—I have too long delayed this search, too long trifled with feelings I can never obliterate."

To all ideas of happiness, the image of Miss Melville had, since first Belmour saw her, been constantly united in his imagination, and no obstacle now seemed to oppose his researches after her; as the marriage of Lady Clementina had relieved him from the painful dilemma, either of counteracting his dying father's last request, or uniting himself to a woman, for whom, with all her charms, he felt only indifference. Full of the determination of satisfying his mind as to Miss Melville, Belmour gave notice, that he should shortly set out for London; where, indeed, it might naturally be supposed, after so long an absence, and the circumstances under which he left England, that he had business.

Determined as he was in his intentions, the means of discovering Miss Melville's retreat were not easy: he turned a thousand projects in his head, which were dismissed almost as soon as formed.—From the rector nothing was to be learned; he, Belmour found, had not heard from Dr. Stanmore (the only source of intelligence) since Miss Melville's departure; and Belmour was moreover cautious in his inquiries of him, as fools are ever curious, and he wished to avoid the suspicion of any particular interest on the subject.

Belmour, though anxious to get to town, on his arrival there found himself no nearer any intelligence on the subject of Miss Melville than before. Dr. Stanmore he considered as his last resource; for having no acquaintance with him, inquiries, the result of which were uncertain, might, he feared, appear impertinent: on this measure, however, he had in a manner determined; and some unavoidable law business, relating to the settlement of his father's affairs, now alone detained him in town. His mind was in a state to make the society of indifferent persons rather a pain than an amusement; he therefore rejoiced at finding scarcely any of his acquaintance in town, knowing that the consequence of meeting them must unavoidably be numberless invitations, which he felt in no way disposed to accept. In this disposition of mind, he had one evening strolled out early after a solitary dinner, not knowing in the least whither he was going, merely to dissipate for awhile the melancholy of his reflections; when happening to pass the theatre in the Haymarket, the first night of a new play, he found himself suddenly involved in the crowd, and forced near one of the doors. Naturally fond of theatrical entertainments, it immediately occurred to him, that he could not at that moment do better than, without resistance, follow the stream. The door of the theatre, by which Belmour had entered, led to the pit; he there found all the seats occupied, and therefore stood for some time surrounded by others in the same situation, who could not find better places, attentively occupied by the performance. The first act over, on turning his head he perceived close by his side the very person, whom he had seen in the garden with Miss Melville, when he went from the inn at Staines with an intention of visiting her. The person happening to turn his head at the same moment, his eyes met Belmour's; he bowed slightly, and then immediately looked another way. Belmour, after taking a few minutes to recover from the surprise of this unexpected meeting, with his usual politeness of manner, begged leave to ask him after Miss Melville's health, and where she was. The man, with a look of some astonishment, and a half sneer, replied, "*Miss Melville,* sir, is, I believe, at her house in Portland Place." There was something so rude and forbidding in the looks and manner of the person who spoke, that Belmour did not feel tempted to renew any further conversation with him—and, indeed, all he wished to know seemed to be comprised in the few words he had already heard—he could now no longer fix his attention to the performance, and as it also occurred to him, that he might be seen by some of his acquaintance, which he wished to avoid, he quitted the theatre.

The joy and relief which Belmour felt from this unexpected information, mixed at the same time with a thousand doubts and fears, wholly occupied his mind. When he left the theatre, he was irresistibly led to Portland Place.—It was not, he thought, a proper hour to make a visit, but he wished to assure himself, that in reality Miss Melville had a house there; that there was no mistake. As he walked along the broad pavement, meaning to make his inquiries, a bright enamelled plate on the door of one of the most considerable houses, with *Miss Melville* in large letters on it, struck his eye.—He stopped; at the moment a carriage drove up to the door, which was, on knocking, instantly opened by a porter, dressed in a handsome livery, and several other servants appeared in waiting.—This is indeed a change in circumstances! said Belmour to himself: some event, he doubted not, had placed her in a situation better suited to her merit, than that in which he had seen her.—He now felt dissatisfied with himself, for thus having delayed to express the sentiments of his heart, till they no longer might carry with them that undeniable certainty of disinterested attachment, which could not have been mistaken, had he addressed her in the humble station, in which he first saw her placed. He however flattered himself, that, in time, the circumstances, which had occasioned his silence, might be explained; and, occupied with these ideas, he passed the night in forming a thousand plans, which the following day might authorise, or forever destroy.

The next morning, at the earliest hour at which he thought a visit admissible, with a note ready prepared in his hand, to ask admission for some other time, in case she should not be at home, Belmour, with a beating heart, stepped into his carriage, and ordered the coachman to drive to Miss Melville's in Portland Place.—On his arrival at the door, there was a demur, as it seemed, whether or not he was to be admitted: but his card having been carried in, the doors were instantly opened, and he was conducted upstairs, and through a large apartment. As he entered the last room, the groom of the chambers, who had ushered him in, bowed respectfully, and said that Miss Melville would wait on his lordship immediately. Nearly a quarter of an hour, however, passed, before anyone appeared, during which time Belmour had leisure to observe the furniture, which was new and very expensive; at last two folding-doors flew open at the further end of the room, and a lady tripped lightly on towards him, whom he had never before seen. She was plain, and her countenance unpleasant, but dressed in the utmost excess of the fashion.—"I beg ten thousand pardons, my lord," said she, shrugging up her shoulders, "for making your lordship wait, but I was under the hands of that *goth,* la Minaudière, who would not let me stir till he had finished my hair, and who regularly comes at the most inconvenient hour possible—but I entreat of your lordship to be seated.—I am sure, my lord, I am much flattered by this honour. Shamly, I conclude, who promised to *scrape-up* all the dancing men he could for my ball, has been obliging enough to mention my name to your lordship.—I ought, I am sure," continued she, simpering, "to apologize for having troubled your lordship to come upstairs, but I could not refuse myself the pleasure of thanking you in person for the honour of your visit."—Here the lady, as it seemed, having come to the end of her speech, stopped as if expecting an answer. Belmour, with difficulty recovering from his painful surprise, after some hesitation, begged pardon, saying, "that there was some strange mistake—that he had been told, that this was the house of Miss Melville, whom he had formerly the honour of seeing, and to whom he had meant to pay his respects."—"Might I be informed," continued he, colouring, "if Miss Emily Melville live here, or where she is now to be found?"—Here the countenance of the lady present underwent a very considerable change—the corners of her mouth were instantly drawn down, and her eyebrows elevated—then, tossing her head over her left shoulder, with a sneer of the utmost contempt, she replied,—"This, my lord, is *my* house, I know of no other *Miss Melville:* there was, indeed, a person, who claimed some relationship with our family, with whom certainly, I think, *your lordship* never could have had any acquaintance—a strange incoherent story," continued she, softening her looks again as she turned towards Belmour, "of which *I* never could comprehend a word—but she is married now, and not likely to give us any more trouble."

Belmour, during this speech, had remained silent—the pang he felt on the close of it is not by any words to be expressed—he instantly got up, and muttering excuses for the trouble he had given, took his leave.

"You will not forget *the fiveteenth,* my lord; though I owe this honour, it seems, to a mistake, I shall send my card," screamed a shrill voice after him, as he went downstairs.

Poor Belmour had not felt disposed to ask another question of the lady he had seen; her words, and the tone in which she had spoken, were too expressive of spite and prejudice, to give him the smallest encouragement.

One part of her intelligence was too probable, he thought, to doubt. Yet what might not be doubted from the mouth of one, who spoke with such perfect ignorance of Emily!

Dr. Stanmore seemed now, indeed, his last resource; and, unable longer to support so painful an uncertainty, Belmour ordered his chaise to be ready within two hours—slept that night at ——, and setting out early again the next morning, arrived in the evening at an inn, within half a mile of the village where Dr. Stanmore resided.—There Belmour left his carriage and servants, and having inquired the way, walked on alone to the parsonage.

On his approach, he was struck with the uncommon appearance of neatness and cultivation, which everywhere prevailed—numbers of small white cottages were here and there scattered about: each with its little garden, which he observed, as he passed, to be not only stocked with vegetables, but adorned with flowers, and their walls covered with jessamine and myrtle, of which the vicinity to the sea admitted. At a little distance beyond the parsonage appeared the church-steeple, and the village, prettily backed by a wood, which rose gradually on the side of a hill, broken and rocky towards the top, and terminating on the opposite side in a sharp cliff, which overhung the sea. As Belmour crossed the small garden of the parsonage, which led to a low porch, the entry of the house, he saw a person, whom he immediately guessed to be Dr. Stanmore, rise from the porch where he was sitting with a book in his hand, and advance to receive him.

Belmour was struck with the dignity of his appearance.—He was tall, and rather corpulent; a quantity of fine white hair covered his head: and his countenance was expressive both of sweetness and penetration. As he drew near, the natural surprise on the intrusion of an utter stranger seemed tempered by politeness and good breeding. Belmour bowed and hesitated—he felt the awkwardness of his situation; which Dr. Stanmore, however, seemed willing to relieve by a cordial invitation to enter, as he called it, his humble habitation.

They stopped, as it were by mutual accord, in the porch, where, after they were seated, a short silence ensued. Dr. Stanmore waited for an explanation of the visit he received, and Belmour knew not how to begin—his real feelings upon this occasion were not easy to be reduced to the tone of *conversation*. At last, however, after mentioning his name, at which Dr. Stanmore gave a slight start, and making the proper apologies for his intrusion, Belmour proceeded to explain the motive of his visit; "wishing," as he said, "to inquire after a lady, whom he had had the honour of seeing at Belmour Castle some time past, and of whom he had accidentally received an incoherent account from a person of the same name."—"I am not surprised," said Dr. Stanmore, after a faint smile of contempt, "at any account given to your lordship by the person, to whom you addressed yourself for information, which could be no other than Miss Eliza Melville, on whom the family estate, a large property, devolved on the death of her father. Emily Melville, the child of my adoption, is the daughter of his elder brother, who died young; and she, from motives quite unnecessary to explain, has been ever unfortunately considered in an insidious light by those of her family, who were not bound to protect her.—But no matter, her undeserved sufferings, are, I trust, at an end. Mr. Courtenay, to whom she is now married, sensible of her merit, will, doubtless, reward her virtues: and if my most earnest prayers can aught avail," said he, raising his eyes to Heaven, with an awful expression of the most fervent devotion, "my child will be happy!"

Belmour's colour here totally forsook him—a deadly paleness overspread his face—he rose, sat down, and rose again, in visible agitation. There was something in Dr. Stanmore's manner, which, however tempered by politeness of expression, and mildness of manner, seemed to oppose further inquiries: and Belmour, who feared, lest his anxious desire to know more of Emily's history should be the very means of precluding him from further information, knew not how to continue the subject—a short silence ensued.—Dr. Stanmore then rose, and inviting Belmour to take some refreshment, opened the door which led into the house—Belmour remained seated. "I had hoped," said he—"and still, if it were not too great a liberty, should request"—his voice faltered—"might I," continued he, in some degree recovering, "be allowed to ask a few particulars concerning the family of Miss Melville, of which I have hitherto obtained only so erroneous and imperfect an account?" Dr. Stanmore had looked at him with compassion while he spoke; he then, after a few moments, as it seemed of doubtful consideration, advanced towards him; and taking his hand, which he pressed between both his own, insensible himself of what he did. "I know not," said he, "the precise motive which excites your present interest in Emily, though I by no means affect total ignorance on the subject: and it was not, I confess, my intention at first, to have entered further into the particulars of her life;"—he paused—"Yet," continued he, leading Belmour into the house, who had risen on his coming up to him, "if you will deign to be my guest for tonight; and indeed even now it would be late, were you to return to the inn; I will endeavour to satisfy the desire you seem to express, of information concerning her."—Poor Belmour's countenance, still more strongly than his words, expressed his gratitude for a favour he had so little expected, from the manner in which his inquiries had at first been received by Dr. Stanmore.

They passed through a small neat parlour, into a library, filled with well-arranged books, and commodiously furnished, but with uncommon plainness and simplicity. After they were seated, Dr. Stanmore continued—"Having told you the conclusion of Emily's history, I shall now begin with some circumstances, which preceded her birth; and endeavour," said he, with a sigh, "not to make my story too long—it is but a melancholy tale!

"Emily Dumont, her mother, was of a family originally French, but long ago settled in Scotland; and the daughter of an officer, who, thinking the cause a just one, had assisted in the attempts to re-establish the house of Stuart on the throne of England. He with difficulty escaped, after the battle of Culloden, where he had distinguished himself by an unavailing bravery, and fled to France, where he subsisted on the remains of a very slender fortune, which his friends found means, from time to time, to transmit to him. His residence was chiefly at Bourdeaux, where some years after his flight, he fell in love with, and married, the daughter of a considerable merchant in that town, (but who afterward went broke) and he was otherwise not very fortunate in his choice. His wife, although uncommonly handsome, and by no means wanting in natural powers of mind, from an early love of admiration and pleasure, and from that general want of principle, too common to many of her nation, could not long contribute to the happiness, or even constitute the real comfort of a man, whose character differed so wholly from her own.—Dumont, for that was his name, was of a retired and studious turn, simple in his manners, gentle and unsuspecting: but once roused by offence, determined in his purposes. He for some time witnessed, in silence, a conduct he much disapproved; but when, after repeated and gentle remonstrances, he found his efforts to reclaim his wife unavailing, and that the levity of her manners daily increased, instead of diminishing, he avoided her society, and retired to a small villa he had near the town, carrying with him his only daughter, then about three years old, his favourite child.

"Dumont continued to reside at this villa for some time, when finding his health rapidly declining, and foreseeing the probable event, he dreaded for his daughter both the education and example she must unavoidably receive from her mother, were she left to her care, and listened to the proposal of a distant relation of his in England, who offered to take charge of the child.—Thus was the little Emily consigned to the care of strangers, and sent, as it were, an orphan into the world, which indeed she shortly afterward actually became, by the death of both her parents.

"Mrs. Dawson, the person with whom Emily Dumont resided, having, from the death of her father, received no remittances from France for her support, or any assistance from her other relations, who after a time ceased even to notice applications on the subject; and having herself a large family, and a ruined fortune, had formed an intention of retiring with her husband into Wales.—From which circumstances she began to consider Emily as a charge, which added much to their embarrassment: yet how to dispose of her they knew not; when chance threw an opportunity in their way, which appeared calculated to relieve them from their difficulties, and afford to Emily, in some degree at least, that support, of which she was so nearly destitute.

"In the neighbourhood of the place where Mrs. Dawson resided, was the seat of Sir Thomas Melville (a name, doubtless, not unknown to you;) a man of immense property—he had been twice married, and had then a son living by his first wife, also a son and a daughter by his second wife, the Lady Melville then living. Sir Thomas was a man of weak capacity, sickly and infirm, and wholly governed by his wife; who, to give you her character in few words, answered exactly the description of a *stepmother,* in the worst sense of the epithet.—Her chief object, in which she fatally succeeded! was to detach Sir Thomas from his eldest son, a youth of superiour talents and the greatest expectation."—Here Dr. Stanmore paused, as it seemed, to recover from a visible emotion.—"Well did I know his worth!" continued he, "for when yet a child, he was placed under my care by his mother, the former Lady Melville, and again sent to me here, after his leaving school, to prepare him for the university.—In fact, no opportunity was lost by his mother-in-law, of removing him from home, as she dreaded his growing virtues, his spirited and amiable disposition, and the power he might, in spite of all her influence, one day obtain by the natural affection of a father, thus defeating her deep-laid schemes for the aggrandizement of her own children.

"Emily Dumont was now about twelve years old; when it happened, that Lady Melville, who passed almost the whole of the year in the country, forced, in that particular, to give way to the humour of Sir Thomas, being anxious to complete in all respects, according to *her* ideas, the education of her daughter, was in search of some young girl, who might serve her as companion, and with whom at the same time she might converse in French. Emily, who had by no means forgotten the language she had learned from her cradle, appeared in all respects exactly what was required; and Mrs. Dawson being known to several of the families in the neighbourhood, who visited Lady Melville, easily obtained an introduction and recommendation to her, in favour of Emily, who in consequence was shortly afterward taken into her house, with a promise that she should thenceforward never want protection. With these general terms, Mrs. Dawson found it convenient to satisfy her conscience, and set out for Wales, persuaded that she had fully done her duty towards her charge, and placed her beyond the probability of future want or distress.

"Emily was at first delighted with her new situation. Amiable and engaging, she was encouraged and caressed by all: Lady Melville *protected* her; and Miss Melville, pleased with the novelty of such a companion, existing, as she supposed, only for her service and amusement, would scarcely suffer her to be for a moment out of her sight. But it was not long before the pride and ill-temper of Lady Melville, and the caprice of her daughter, made poor Emily sensible of her subservient situation.—The natural gentleness of her disposition, however, and the thoughtlessness of youth, supported her, and made her more grateful for its advantages, than affected by what she might occasionally have to suffer—and her quickness of apprehension, and aptness to improve every talent she possessed, rendering her useful to her patroness, she was not without her share of favour and moments of approbation.—For above five years she continued with Lady Melville upon this footing; when, she knew not why, she saw her favour daily decrease with Lady Melville.—She was unaware of the envy and jealousy her growing charms excited in the breast of the mother, from the praises lavished on her wherever she appeared; while Miss Melville, in spite of her utmost efforts to attract and captivate, when Emily was present, often remained almost unnoticed. Miss Melville, too, adopting her mother's ideas, and growing tired of a companion, whose superiour merit, and propriety of manners, prevented her from treating her as ill as she was inclined, from natural insolence, and mortified pride, affected only indifference and contempt.

"Poor Emily mourned in silence.—She had not, on earth, a friend to whom she could complain, or a hope of assistance, should she be forced to quit Lady Melville's house.

"The family was just returned from a short excursion to town; during which, Emily had been treated with more than usual severity; when young Melville, whom his mother-in-law could not prevent from passing some little time at his father's, previous to his going abroad, arrived at Melville Hall. He was then just twenty, his person uncommonly fine, of a noble, spirited disposition, and his only fault (that my partial eyes at least could discover) was a too great warmth of temper.—But how would not that fault have been softened by reason, had fate but granted time for its maturity!—Yet, though every way formed to gratify both the heart and pride of a parent, Melville was, as usual, received by his father with coldness and indifference: at which, though unaccustomed to his tenderness, he felt particularly mortified, as he now came to take leave of him, and his absence from England, he understood, was intended to be of some years.

"On his arrival at Melville Hall, having inquired if there were any company in the house, and having been answered by the servant to whom he had addressed himself, that there was none, only the family; when they were assembled in the drawing-room before dinner, I have often heard him declare, that no surprise ever equalled what he felt, on the entrance of Emily. He had scarcely seen her since she was a child; as his visits, which had been very rare, to his father were chiefly made in town, whither she had not then accompanied Lady Melville; and her figure was so much altered and improved, that he at first did not guess who she was—nothing could surpass her beauty, or the natural grace and elegance of her manner.—" "But your lordship," said Dr. Stanmore, "has seen her daughter, who is indeed the image of her unfortunate mother."—Belmour coloured, but was silent.—Dr. Stanmore continued: "Young Melville, hurt at his father's cold reception, and his mind assailed by many painful ideas, was preparing to pass most unpleasantly the time previous to his departure, when, as you will already have guessed, the sudden and unexpected appearance of an object, formed every way to charm and captivate, with the addition of that sympathy, natural to persons placed under similar unpleasant circumstances, failed not shortly to excite an interest in his breast, which terminated in love. Emily, unaccustomed from her early infancy to the soothing care and tenderness of a parent; alone, and a stranger, as it were, in a bad world; born with a heart alive to every soft feeling of virtuous affection; knew not how to oppose the sentiments excited in her breast by the attentions, interest, and tenderness of Melville; who, though young, evidently possessed a decided steadiness of character, which inspired confidence and security. In him she saw a friend and protector.

"To his family, her ties of obligation were small; she was treated with insolence and contempt, for the mere casual superiourity of fortune, and, indeed, owed them little more than her subsistence, in return for the employment of her time, and her utmost endeavours to please, exerted in their service. She could in fact, therefore, feel little scruple in listening to the dictates of Melville's avowed and sincere passion—circumstances too materially contributed to excuse both her and Melville.

"Lady Melville, his mother-in-law, on his first attentions to Emily, had redoubled her watchful observation on his every look, and the harshness of her dry and sarcastic manner towards him; but shortly afterward, a change in her whole behaviour took place, for which he was at a loss to account. She gradually became soft in her manner, and almost caressing both to him and Emily, artfully throwing out her praise, separately, of each to the other, so as to persuade them of the interest she affected to take in their welfare: added to which, while carefully avoiding the appearance of premeditation or design, she gave them every possible opportunity of being together. Unexperienced as they were, it was impossible they should escape the snare.—Melville, encouraged by the kindness and altered manner of his mother-in-law, ventured to hint to her his passion, and begged her interest and good offices with his father.—She affected surprise: but told him, she thought Sir Thomas *might* be brought to consent to their union, as fortune *ought* not to be an object with him, and that Emily certainly could to no family be a disgrace. Sir Thomas was at the time, in addition to his usual indifferent health, suffering from the gout, which rendered him so fretful and uneasy, that, except Lady Melville, whom he scarcely allowed to be out of his room, few dared venture to approach him.—However, the time of young Melville's intended departure drawing near, he determined, supported as he thought himself by Lady Melville's powerful interest, to take courage, and speak to his father on the subject nearest his heart; meaning to declare himself ready to submit to any delay, or any terms whatever, that his father should think proper to impose, if, finally, he might hope, with his consent, to be united to Emily.—Trembling, he entered the apartment of his father.—He was received by him with the most forbidding looks, and scarcely allowed time to explain himself, before he was loaded with every term of reproach, for attempting to disgrace, as he called it, his family, and think of marrying a French beggar, who had subsisted, he said, only on his bounty: but of *her* he should *take care.*—Lady Melville, at the instant, entered the room, on whose countenance a malicious smile was so evident, that Melville's eyes were in an instant opened; he saw himself betrayed, and without uttering another word, left the room. The next day Emily, with five guineas in her pocket, was actually ordered to leave the house; an order with which she immediately complied, retiring to a neighbouring farm-house. Thither she was followed by Melville, who, in addition to his passion, felt the dictates of honour instantly determine him never to abandon one, of whose forlorn situation he thought himself the sole cause.—They immediately set out for Scotland, where they were married. On his return, Melville found all intercession with his father vain—his estates were wholly in his own power: and he not only withdrew his son's allowance, but at the same time declared him disinherited. The army was his only resource, in which, by the assistance of his friends, he obtained a commission; but having at present neither house nor retreat, he claimed from my early friendship, and assured attachment, a protection for his wife; and in terms at once the most manly and affecting, deplored the cruelty of his situation, which allowed him not for the moment to ensure her even from positive want and necessity.—Could I refuse! I had ever considered Melville more as a son than a pupil: and his errours, bearing the character of imprudence, not of vice, could but excite my pity.—Shortly after their marriage, Melville came to me with his wife, who, beautiful as an angel, was also the image of purity and innocence.—Six months were passed by them under my roof in quiet and content—their last farewell, alas! to happiness on earth.

"Melville's regiment was then ordered to the West Indies; fain would Mrs. Melville have accompanied him thither, but the objections to this measure were too strong.—He had only his pay to subsist on, and the idea of exposing her, then too in a state of pregnancy, to the many dangers and difficulties he might have to encounter, was intolerable to him. It was settled, therefore, that till his return, which it was supposed would be within a twelvemonth, Mrs. Melville was to remain with me.—Thus they parted; and, though with the most affecting expression of regret, still, on his side, with the youthful hope of future happiness; but on hers with a despondency she vainly endeavoured to conceal.—A deep melancholy took possession of her, softened, indeed, by the natural sweetness of her disposition: but almost her first smile was on her infant, born a few months subsequent to her husband's departure, and whom, after her mother, I named Emily.

"Two years had passed in vain expectation, without any determined time having been fixed for Melville's return, when his letters announced, that within a few days he was to set sail for England.—He requested of his wife to meet him on his landing: saying, that he should be his own messenger, and directing her to accept of an invitation she would receive from a friend of his, who had a house on the coast near Falmouth.—Thither she repaired, and day after day from the Strand, where she took her constant station, did she watch the coming of the vessel, which was to bring her only joy.—At last the vessel was descried; it was known to be the expected packet.—With beating heart and eyes, strained towards the yet distant sail, did she wait in its approach.—The sea was calm and serene—nearer and nearer it approached—at last she saw a boat put off, which rowed directly towards the spot where she was.—A sudden dimness overspread her sight: she with difficulty supported herself, leaning with one hand on a piece of broken rock, while with the other she grasped the hand of her child, whom she had led to meet its father's first embrace.—Again her eyes opened, as the boat drew near—better for her, they had been closed forever!—The first object, that struck her returning sight, was Melville's servant, a lad who had followed, and shown particular attachment to him, in deep mourning. I have little more to add," said Dr. Stanmore, observing Belmour much affected—"the servant brought the fatal news of Melville's death, who had been attacked by a sudden and violent fever, just as he was about to embark; he, however, had strength to write a short letter, in which he entreated his dear Emily, to live for the sake of their child.—He also sent her his portrait, saying, that thus only could he fulfill his promise of returning to her—and closed his letter with a sad farewell. The particulars I mention, I learned from the friends she was with—to me she returned in a state of stupor: from which, however, she at last succeeded in rousing herself, and endeavoured to fulfill the dying wishes of her husband, and live to cherish and support her child.—But the blow was too severe—her fragile form sunk under its weight. On the very day twelvemonth, on which she had met the fatal news of her husband's death, she expired in my arms—leaving her dear infant to my care. I have fulfilled the sacred charge, and watched over it, I may say, with parental interest and affection: and well have I been repaid! for a mind more enlightened, or a heart more open to every noble, every tender feeling, never was more conspicuous than in my Emily—and, perhaps, never were such force and energy of mind united in the same character with such softness and affection."—Here Dr. Stanmore leaned back in his chair, to appearance much fatigued with having spoken so long.—Belmour entreated of him not to continue.—"Notwithstanding the pleasure I have in hearing you," said he, "I must beg of you now to rest—another time, perhaps."—Dr. Stanmore thanked him.—"I am, it is true, fatigued," said he, "nor can I ever recall these melancholy scenes to my mind, without renewed suffering.—As you are kind enough to be my guest for tonight, we will for the present dismiss the subject, and tomorrow I shall have more strength, and finish, which is not much, what remains for me to say."

The rest of the day passed in conversation between them on various topics, on all of which Dr. Stanmore talked not only with intelligence, as a man of sense and erudition, but as a man conversant with the world. He informed Belmour, that early in life he had travelled with a young nobleman, who afterward died abroad, not only over France and Italy, but into Greece.

"I had in my youth," said he, "a rambling spirit, and, I must confess, a strong predilection for the army; and submitted, with reluctance, to the judgment of my father, who earnestly pressed my going into the church, where he had hopes of procuring me considerable preferment; and much," continued he, with a smile, "was he distressed for me on the failure of those hopes.—But where may we not find content!—certain it is, that I would not now exchange this simple dwelling, and moderate situation, where the power of doing good to others has not been denied me, for palaces and riches."—At night they separated, having risen mutually in each other's opinion as they conversed. Belmour, however, said little—too deeply affected with what he had learnt from Dr. Stanmore; of himself he could not speak, nor of the only object, which had now so long occupied his mind.

He was conducted by Dr. Stanmore to a neat apartment above-stairs, the whole furniture of which was white, and the wainscot also white, adorned with drawings, in neat but simple frames.—Belmour was no sooner alone, than, on casting his eyes round the room, he was convinced that he was actually in the very apartment formerly occupied by Miss Melville.—The sudden sensation, the long train of ideas, which this circumstance excited in his mind, are not to be described—every part of the room was carefully examined by him, stepping lightly on the floor, lest his footsteps should be heard in the small and thin-built house. The drawings in particular attracted his attention: they were views, evidently original, of different parts of Italy, and various buildings, both ancient and modern, of that country, enlivened with figures, and executed in a free and masterly style. Among many of Venice, the church of the Mendicanti was often repeated, and various views given of the inside of the building. On farther examination among the figures on the foreground, one always presented itself so like his own, that he thought—could it have been possible—but it must be fancy—yet it was always represented in the very cloak he wore, on the very bench he sat, where he had often passed whole hours in listening to the divine music repeated from the grated gallery above.—Yet he had sitten for no portrait while at Venice—and again it must be fancy. To get rid, however, of an idea, which puzzled and occupied his mind, he in vain endeavoured to rest—his eyelids were no sooner closed, than all he had heard from Dr. Stanmore pressing, as it seemed, more strongly on his imagination, precluded all hope of sleep.

Belmour rose early the next morning, impatient again to see Dr. Stanmore, and planning within himself the many questions he meant to ask him relative to Miss Melville, and her present situation; but concluding that he would not yet be up, he determined to wait his hour of breakfast in the garden.—The sun was newly risen, the air soft and serene, and the fragrance of the flowers, with which the little garden was plentifully stocked, delightful. In the arrangement of the whole place, he remarked an elegance and propriety of taste, which left him no doubt, by whom it had been planned. Thus surrounded, as he was, by objects which brought the image of Emily so forcibly to his mind, his admiration of her seemed every instant to increase with his anguish for her loss.

"To me," said he, mournfully, "to me, she is lost forever!—yet I must see her again—I must assure her of my respect, my admiration, since I dare not, alas! of my regret."—Occupied with these ideas, he advanced with a quickened step towards the house, hoping now to find Dr. Stanmore below stairs. At the door he was met by the maid, who, dropping an awkward curtsey, said—"that her master begged his honour's pardon, but that he was too unwell to come down stairs, and hoped he would excuse him—and breakfast is ready, your honour, in the little parlour," said she, leading the way. Belmour followed, with a feeling of disappointment, which he knew scarcely how in any degree to conquer.—He had hoped to learn many particulars relative to Emily's history, and to have had many circumstances explained, which had so much excited his curiosity; he wished, likewise, to have farther improved his acquaintance with Dr. Stanmore, whose sentiments and conversation inspired him with peculiar interest, together with a respect and reverence, to which his situation, and the simple dignity of his figure and manner, necessarily contributed.—"Am I then," said he to himself, "destined to burst in ignorance! and is there, indeed, some spell formed eternally to counteract and oppose my wishes, on the only subject which really interests my heart!"—He had learned from Dr. Stanmore, in the course of their conversation, that the seat of Mr. Courtenay was in Gloucestershire; and recollecting, from the name of the place, that it was remarkable for an old ruin, which many persons travelled purposely to see, he determined to take advantage of this circumstance, and, under pretence of the accidental curiosity, which might be supposed to have brought him there, ask permission to see Emily; which, he thought, without any appearance of particularity, he was authorised to do, from their former acquaintance at Belmour Castle.—What were his designs, or what his expectations from this visit, perhaps he hardly dared to ask himself—for the moment it promised him a sort of indulgence, or at least relief, and his mind was not at present in a state to look farther. Thus determined, as he was preparing to leave Dr. Stanmore's, having previously endeavoured to express his obligation to him for his reception, in a letter which he desired might be delivered to him after his departure, just as he passed the door of the little parlour, he met Dr. Stanmore, coming slowly towards him.—"I cannot," said Dr. Stanmore, speaking with much difficulty, "suffer you to go without one farewell from me, nor without expressing my sincere wish, that we may, at some future period, improve our acquaintance—forgive," continued he, taking both Belmour's hands, which he pressed—"forgive the liberty I take, but something tells me, although till now we have never met, that we were not destined to be always strangers to each other."—Belmour expressed his obligation with so much warmth and affectionate gratitude, that it brought a smile on Dr. Stanmore's countenance; which smile plainly said, "thou hast a tender heart!"—"Much it grieves me," continued he, "to be thus seized at this moment, when I almost flattered myself you would somewhat have prolonged your stay; but, though by no means at present dangerous, as I am told, these attacks of a sort of asthma, to which I have many years been subject, completely disable me, when they come, for several days, and render me nearly incapable even of speaking."—Saying this, he advanced into the room, towards an arm-chair, supported by Belmour, who, as soon as he saw him quietly seated, fearing that his staying longer might be troublesome, with sincere regret took leave of his host.

Chapter 12

BELMOUR, DURING HIS WALK to the place where he had left his carriage the day before, arranged his plan, in consequence of what he had learned from Dr. Stanmore, and found that he could not, without difficulty, arrive at the Post Town, distant however only a few miles from the seat of Mr. Courtenay, till the next evening.—Having accordingly, on the following night but one, slept at ——, he proceeded on the subsequent morning to Dean Abbey.—Passing, as he went, through a park of considerable extent, though too much occupied by his own thoughts to be very observant of the surrounding objects, he was struck with an air of neglect which reigned throughout. It was with difficulty, and not till the postillions had repeatedly hallooed, that admittance had been gained at the first gate, which was opened only by a common labourer: when, after having traversed the park, he arrived at a large iron gate, which led into an open court before the house, he waited above a quarter of an hour before the key was brought; and then, from the immense weight of the iron gate, and rust of the hinges, it seemed for some time doubtful, whether or not it could be opened at all. The house, evidently part of an ancient abbey, had an air of picturesque grandeur, but a great part of the building was an absolute ruin, the walls of which were, in many parts, covered with ivy of immense growth.—"Is this the ruin which is shown to strangers?" said Belmour to the servant, whom he followed into the court.—"No, my lord," replied the man, who had glanced his eye over the coronet, which was on Belmour's carriage.—"No, my lord, the ruins as *some comes* to see, is about a mile off, up yonder in the park" (pointing to a steep rising ground).—"I thought as how your lordship asked for my master."—"Is Mr. Courtenay at home?" said Belmour. "No, my lord, master is gone out since morning."—"Is Mrs. Courtenay at home?" continued Belmour, coughing, in order to disguise the agitation of his voice.—"I ain't sure, my lord; but if your lordship will walk there a little, upon *that there* terrace, I will go and inquire."

Belmour passed on through a small door in the wall, which on that side of the house crossed a broad high terrace, from which there was a distant view of the country. The ground falling abruptly in that part, and the soil being rocky, formed a sort of natural rampart, which continued for some way along the house. As he walked along this terrace, waiting for the return of the servant, he accidentally cast his eyes up to an open window above, where, leaning on her arm, in a pensive posture, he saw Emily.—It could be no other—nor did it require the quick sensation of a lover to recognize her figure.—Belmour remained for some time in the place where he stood, earnestly looking towards her—during which, she once turned, as it seemed, on some person's entering the room where she was, but again resumed her former attitude, and appeared lost in thought: the servant whom he had sent up with his name, then coming towards him, Belmour advanced to meet him.—"Please ye, my lord," said the man, "my mistress is not at home."—"Not at home!" muttered Belmour to himself, with a look of disappointment; then, after musing for a few seconds.—"Might I, sir, beg to have pen and ink brought me?"—"O yes, my lord, I'll fetch your lordship pen and ink, and some paper in a moment: please ye, my lord, to walk into the great hall, and your lordship may look at the paintings there the while, they are reckoned very curious."—Belmour having thanked the servant, followed him into the hall.—The *paintings* which the servant talked of were shields and armorial bearings, with banners, and a quantity of old armor, which were all suspended under the high arches of a fine ancient Gothic roof, beautifully worked; the whole of the panels below had evidently also been highly carved and ornamented, but were defaced and fallen to decay.—Belmour cast an inattentive eye over these objects as he walked about the hall, when suddenly his notice was attracted by the conversation of two servants, who entered the hall at the opposite end.—One had a chaise-seat thrown over his shoulder, and the other, coming up to him, cried,—"Why, John, where are you carrying *that there chay-seat*?"—"The *chay-seat*? why to be mended: don't ye see here, it wants a lock, and the side's cracked; our old Allen will have enough to do to get it ready by Tuesday, when mistress goes to Cheltenham."—"To Cheltenham! What is mistress going there?"—"Yes, the doctor ordered her: you know she *have* been but poorly ever since she came here.—God bless her! say I, she's a sweet lady."—By this time they had passed Belmour some way, who had remained listening with the utmost attention to their conversation; but before they got to the door, he distinguished little more, except a doubt whether Mrs. Barbara liked going or not, and, that Mrs. Barbara was "a pretty girl, but *d—d proud*."

Shortly afterward the servant, whom he had commissioned, brought him pen and ink, and, bowing, asked if "his lordship would walk into the parlour, where there was a table?"—"I thank you much," returned Belmour, putting some money into his hand, "and am sorry for all the trouble I have given you, but I find it unnecessary to write from hence.—You will, if you please, present my respects to your lady, and say, that I regretted not having the honour of seeing her": saying this, he hurried out towards his chaise, into which he threw himself.

Chapter 13

IT HAD INSTANTLY OCCURRED to Belmour, as the reader may, perhaps, guess, on the conversation which he overheard between the servants, that by going himself to Cheltenham, to which place he was nearly in the direct road, he would have an opportunity of seeing Emily without any appearance of particularity, and in a manner far beyond any expectations he could have formed for himself.—When he arrived at the inn where he had left his baggage, and where Bertram, his *valet-de-chambre,* had remained, he found him pacing about the court in expectation of his return.—On seeing the carriage drive up, he flew to open the door for his lord—"*Milor n' aura pas dine?*"—Belmour, smiling, said, "*n'est pas tard, Bertram mais ordonne moi à diner, et dis que je compte passer la nuit ici.*"

This was beyond Bertram's expectations—he had often remarked to himself, that, in travelling, his master, nine times out of ten, would pass by a good inn, and go on to a worse, as it appeared to him without the least consideration upon this *weighty* subject.—Now the kitchen, rooms, and beds of the present inn, all which he had had time fully to examine during his master's absence, conducted in form by an obliging and officious host, having appeared to him *superexcellent;* when the hostess, after he came downstairs, presenting him at the same time with a glass of wine, held forward between the middle-finger and thumb of a very white hand, hoped that his lordship, the marquis, would not think of going further that night, as the roads were bad, and the stages long: and, indeed the quality that came to visit the ruins of Dean Abbey seldom passed her house, without stopping a night at least.—Bertram shrugged up his shoulders:—"I like your *ouse,* madam," said he, "and would stay *for week vit* pleasure; but I cannot answer for *mi lord; e* come *e* go *ver* he please—but I follow *im* to dee end of *dee verld, par Dieu*!"

Belmour had determined to remain for that night at ——, merely as a place where he could pass some hours alone, and was in no haste to arrive at Cheltenham, as it was then only Saturday, and, by the account of the servants, Emily would not leave Dean Abbey before Tuesday.—The moment he had dined he strolled out, and, taking a distant walk over the country, returned not till long after it was dark; on these occasions Bertram was always sure to be met by him, hovering round the door, with evident marks of anxiety and uneasiness on his countenance, which he often, through fear of offending his master, endeavoured to conceal by a thousand ludicrous attempts at expressions of ease and unconcern;—all this was at times troublesome to Belmour, and excited his impatience; yet, as honest expressions of unalloyed zeal and affectionate attachment, his heart was not insensible to them.

On the following day, Belmour left the inn at ——, and towards evening arrived at Cheltenham, where he soon settled himself in a small house, taking his chance for being near where Emily might lodge.—Established at Cheltenham, in expectation of Emily's arrival, thought on thought crowded on his imagination:—to what real advantage this farther renewal of sentiments, which had already given him so much pain, could tend, he did not venture to inquire of himself.

Chapter 14

BELMOUR, THE NEXT MORNING, walked to the well. It had not occurred to him, that he was likely to meet any of his particular acquaintance at Cheltenham; and so indifferent was it to him, one expected, *whom* he met, that he had not thought of making any inquiry on the subject—he was therefore surprised, though not disagreeably, at seeing, among a number of unknown figures, his cousin, Lady Clementina. She was walking slowly up to the well, leaning on Melford's arm: but the moment she saw Belmour, she flew towards him, dragging Melford after her—"My dear cousin!" cried she, "who could have expected to have found *you* here!—But I am quite rejoiced to see you again; and, for Heaven's sake, tell me something of Caroline, how she does, and where she is; for I never can understand from her letters what in the world she is about.—I depended on her returning to England with you; what could be the reason she went, the lord knows where, by herself, when she said her health was better?"—All these questions Belmour answered in the best manner he could, and it was easy to satisfy Lady Clementina; she knew not suspicion; she was herself all truth and frankness, and believed others to be the same: and when, by chance, she took "*an aversion,*" as she called it, to anyone, she always herself *wondered why.*—"Amiable being!" (thought Belmour to himself, as he looked at her with the kindest expression of affection)—"how happened it that *thy* charms, however powerful, could never reach my heart?"—"I really am quite glad to see you again, Belmour," resumed she; "and I think we shall agree much better together than we used to do, for you have no notion how grave and sober I am grown; quite a pattern," said she, laughing.—"Here have we been living for these three weeks quite alone; for I only just come to the well in the morning, and then see no more of these good people" (making a face) "for the rest of the day: and yet I never have wanted company.—When I am tired in the evening, I make Melford read to me sometimes, though to be sure he don't much like it."—Melford gaped, and made a slight effort to release his arm, of which she had hold; but she, without taking the least notice of this, only held it the tighter.—"Well," continued she, "but you dine with us today; for, though we like to be alone, we shall like *your* company still better; and I have got a monstrous comfortable little habitation out of the street."—Melford cordially joined in this invitation, that is, as far as a *very fine* gentleman *can* be *cordial;* for his time, of course, hung heavily on his hands, and he was glad to have the addition of a person with whom *one could live* to his society.

From that moment Belmour was the constant guest and companion of the Melfords, his own solitary walks excepted, which he never omitted; and, from being in the habit of rising early, he had always leisure time to himself. Tuesday, Wednesday, and Thursday passed, without Emily's appearing.—Belmour grew almost in despair.—"What is the matter with you, my dear cousin?" Lady Clementina had a thousand times repeated.—At last, on the Friday morning, as Belmour walked out of his own house, which happened to be in the same row with Lady Clementina's, at the very next door he saw a woman uncommonly busy washing and dusting, and cleaning everything about the house.—"You seem very busy, good woman," said Belmour; "do you expect company?"—"Yes, your honour, we *expects* Madame Courtenay here tomorrow; and I'm sure I don't know how in the world I shall get the house ready; for these Jew-people that were here are so nasty, there's no getting things clean after them: *howesever,* if our Martha comes to help, we shall do pretty well."—Saying this, she twirled her mop almost in Belmour's face; and clattering up to the passage of the house, with a high pair of pattens on her feet, in an instant disappeared.—Away went Belmour, and *that* day Lady Clementina had no occasion to ask him, "What was the matter with him:"—for to a thoughtful, and sometimes almost absent expression, when not exceeding certain bounds, she was with him so well accustomed, that she took it as a thing of course.—On the day following, just as they had done dinner, a post-chaise passed the window of the room where they were sitting, and stopped at two doors off, which was the very house where Belmour had seen the woman cleaning everything on the preceding day.—Lady Clementina saw the post-chaise, heard it stop, and, bouncing up, flew to the window.—"There is an arrival!" said she, "for this house was empty yesterday.—I must see who it is.—Men have no curiosity; there you sit like two stocks!"—By this time her face was close to the window: then, throwing the casement open, she exclaimed—"Well! mercy on me!—I protest it is!—Yes, it is!—I am not mistaken, it *is* Miss Melville!—Mrs. I don't know what, for she is married now; but I will go to her this moment, and do you follow me at least."—Saying this, she darted out of the door, and was in the other house just as Emily, with a look of some fatigue, was seated in a little parlour near the door.

Belmour soon followed; and Melford, after some arrangement of his cravat, and a complacent look of examination, cast over his own person, carelessly joined them.—When Belmour appeared at the door, where he stopped, bowing respectfully, Emily rose and came forward, desiring he would not remain thus at the door, with a look of much sweetness, though not wholly free from embarrassment. "You see I have told you truly," said Lady Clementina, "here we are, met together once more, was there ever anything so odd! and I am *sure so lucky*!"—She then went on with a string of questions, the sum total of the answers to which was, that Emily had been for some time unwell, and that Cheltenham had been strongly recommended to her by her physician—that she had taken that opportunity of coming, as Mr. Courtenay, who did not in general like leaving home, was under the necessity of passing a fortnight or three weeks in town, on some particular business.—"You do indeed look pale," said Lady Clementina, "but we will take such care of you here, you will soon be well.—Come, I must insist on your passing this very evening with us; our house is literally within two doors of you, it cannot fatigue you to walk thither."—Emily endeavoured at first to excuse herself for that evening, but Lady Clementina would not be refused—"Come, come," said she, "we will split the difference: we will go and take a walk, or a drive in the sociable, and call for you at our return."—Emily bowed assent.

The evening was passed at Lady Clementina's, with the addition of no other visitor than a Mr. Reeves, a *hanger-on* and flatterer of Melford, but of the inoffensive sort, whose only object was a good dinner, and a recommendation to the same in *any* other house. Belmour had no sooner seen Emily, than he experienced a species of relief from the unsettled state of mind, into which he had so long been thrown, which seemed to him like happiness; and the prospect of now forming a part of her society was still a blessing so much beyond his past expectation, that for the moment he almost forgot the indissoluble tie, which, by uniting her to another, had in reality separated him from her forever.

As Emily had expressed much surprise on first seeing him, and said that she thought him still abroad; Belmour found, that she had not been informed of his coming to Dean Abbey: and it immediately struck him, as he was anxious to avoid any appearance of particularity, that it would be better not to mention his visit to that place, although he did not attempt making a secret of having seen Dr. Stanmore; as from himself, indeed, he concluded she would have been informed of that, in the course of their correspondence.—It was, indeed, true, that Emily knew not of his having been at Dean Abbey; she had been unwell the day he came there, and was sitting at the window as before mentioned, when the servant entered the room; and, guessing that he came to announce a visit, having heard a carriage drive up to the door, she, without asking who it was, said that she was not at home—and afterward, wholly indifferent as she supposed the subject, had not thought of inquiring who had been there.

Chapter 15

NEARLY THREE WEEKS had elapsed in that state of quiet society, which is seldom found, but when persons of congenial, or at least *accordant* dispositions and tastes, meet in some place distant from the scenes of their different cares and anxieties.—Lady Clementina, really occupied by her passion for her husband, seemed to forget her former vanities and love of general admiration, and her naturally good and amiable qualities shone forth in all their true lustre; and Melford, though his character was weak and unsteady, was still sufficiently captivated, to be flattered by the attentions of such a woman, and with the addition now made to his society, was tolerably well secured from *ennui,* the inherent evil of the idle and trifling; and what with his curricle, in which Lady Clementina was daily paraded about with him, his sociable, of which the rest of the society partook, his saddle-horses, and an excellent table, he contrived to get tolerably through the day.

Belmour sought every opportunity of improving the advantage fortune had thrown in his way, and wished, at least, to feel an attachment, which he could not conquer, justified by reason.

Emily rose daily in his opinion—the superiour strength and energy of her character appeared so blended with affection, and every gentle feeling of the mind, that while it commanded his respect, it increased his admiration.—The sympathy, too, of taste, which existed between them, led insensibly to that confidence and intimate communication of ideas, which are at once the charm and the support of intelligent minds.—Yet on the subject nearest his heart Belmour never ventured to breathe the slightest hint, nor was his curiosity concerning the particulars of Emily's history in any degree satisfied.—Her disposition was evidently open; yet, if he attempted to touch on the occurrences of her past life, as far as they were known to him, and particularly when they happened to be alone, a sudden expression of melancholy overspread her fine animated countenance, and a something like reserve took place in her manner, which precluded further inquiries.

Of Dr. Stanmore, indeed, she often spoke, and always with the tenderness and affection of a child for a beloved parent—dwelling with delight on the recital of his virtues, and on all the obligations, she said, she owed him, for the quiet enjoyment of a happy infancy, and for the improvement of such powers as her mind had under his tuition acquired.

It was now the middle of July, and the weather uncommonly fine.—Emily frequently strolled out, carrying with her implements for drawing, and amused herself with sketching the many picturesque and rural spots in the immediate neighbourhood of Cheltenham.—Belmour had, one day, accidentally met her, and as she appeared not displeased at his approach, he ventured again the next morning to join her, finding her occupied in the same manner, and, from that time, they habitually met, nearly at the same hour Emily seated herself on the trunk of a tree, and Belmour on the ground by her side.—He was one day seated in this manner, occupied in cutting the pencils ready for her use, when the conversation was naturally led to her talent for drawing.—"I saw several drawings of yours," said Belmour, "when I was at Dr. Stanmore's, which, I am sure, prove your perfect knowledge of perspective."—His eyes were fixed on the pencil he was cutting, as he spoke, and his voice trembled—he was conscious, that he meant something more, than his words seemed to imply.—Emily continued silent—when, on lifting up his eyes, they met hers turned towards him, with a look of so much softness, tenderness, and pity, that he was for a moment lost in the unexpected feeling of delight he experienced.—Emily then, as it were, suddenly recollecting herself, turned again to her drawing, and, not without some confusion, began talking of the view she was taking, and of the difficulty of representing all its beauty.—At that moment, Lady Clementina came running up to them with a note in her hand.—"Lord!" said she, "I have been hunting for you in every room of your lodging—did ever anybody go out so early, but my *quiz* of a cousin there!—now don't look so grave, dear Belmour, for you know, that if you are a *quiz,* you are the handsomest *quiz* in the world, and when that is the case, nobody need mind what they are—but here I have an invitation from Seeres, the nabob, and one for you, and all the company I please to invite—he gives a ball at Presbury tomorrow se'n-night, and there is to be a temporary ball-room erected, and all the stage-coaches are coming down filled with cooks and confectioners, and the Lord knows what!—and *Monsieur Paris* is to preside and order everything, and we are to have bowers and *bosquets,* and fountains and *jets d'eau* all made of paper and tin: in short, the ball is to be delightful, and all the neighbourhood are to come for fifty miles round.—Young Seeres is now in my room, come in grand form to invite me, and make excuses for his father, who, *out of respect,* as he said, did not venture himself to do so sooner.—Reeves, who came with him, kept telling me all this before him, in his droll way, and making such faces behind his back, that I thought I should have quite misbehaved, for I was ready to die with laughing at Seeres's awkward bows, and his foolish fat face.—But I must run back, for Melford, who is just come down to breakfast, won't thank me for leaving him alone with such company—I shall say, that I have found you, and that you will come, Belmour, of course, as I may ask all the men I please; but you had better now come home with me, and give your own answer."—"I fear," replied Emily, "that this day se'n-night I shall not be here, for I expect Mr. Courtenay in a day or two now, and I think he will be impatient to return to Dean Abbey."—"Not here! but indeed you will be here for as long as I stay, and so you may make up your mind to that, and Mr. Courtenay too, if he comes—come, come along, and don't talk such nonsense!—not go to the ball! that would be a good joke indeed, to go away just before the day!" Belmour cast a look of dejection towards Emily, which she appeared not to observe, but taking Lady Clementina's arm, which she offered, walked on with her, seemingly attending to all she was saying, and all she was planning, in consequence of this intended *fête;* which was to be given with all the lavish expense of Eastern magnificence, in honour of the marriage of the nabob's daughter with a newly created Irish peer.

A gloom overspread Belmour's countenance all that day—the idea of parting could not indeed be new to him, but he had thought the period more distant—and though the morning following that day, Emily, after the arrival of the post, announced to Lady Clementina before him, that she found Mr. Courtenay would be detained by his business in town longer than he had expected, and that she consequently should attend her to the ball; he could not recover that feeling of enjoyment, which, however temporary, had soothed his mind, and enabled him to appear with that degree of animation and gayety, which was natural to him, and which formed one of the great charms of his character.—He now grew anxious in the extreme, to discover, before they parted, whether or not he were wholly indifferent to Emily; and with the doubt returned to him all the melancholy, which so long had preyed on his soul.—Could he but again behold that look of tenderness, which so enchanted him!—could he but think he was even pitied by Emily; all, it seemed to him, would become supportable!—But the fear of offending, of losing the degree of intimacy and friendship, which he then enjoyed, rendered him cautious to avoid every expression of his sentiments, that might betray the secret of his heart.

Chapter 16

THE DAYS, WHICH PRECEDED THE BALL, were passed without any new occurrence, in the same easy and familiar society.—On the eve, as they were at supper, Lady Clementina declared, that she should take charge of Emily's dress—"I have," said she, "sent for two dresses from town: they are of the same make, only of different *colours,* and one I destine for you, my dear," turning to Emily, who smiled with a look of surprise—"yes, for you," she repeated, "I shall be affronted, indeed, if you won't wear it; and you know, Mrs. Barbara, your maid, can make any little alteration required: and I myself shall take charge of arranging your head.—Melford's *valet-de-chambre* is the best *coiffeur* I ever saw, and always arranges my hair on grand occasions: he shall exert all his skill for us both—but was there ever such fine hair as you have! my dear Emily," said she, taking out the comb which supported her *chignon.*—"I must see the length of it;—mercy on me!" getting up, and standing as far off as she could, extending her arm from her, "was there ever such a length, and so immensely thick!—But you do bundle it up so without the least care or attention!—Well, no matter! tomorrow I will have my own way in everything. Lord! I forgot I must dance with that odious Seeres—he was told, I suppose, to request the *honour* of *my hand* by his *papa.*—I don't care, you, Emily, must dance with Belmour; for Melford, I know, hates dancing; and you know there is no change of partners here, which is lucky, as *Miss Nabob,* and lord—I don't know what his name is, must dance together—but I assure you, my cousin, should he not have forgotten, is the best dancer by far I ever saw.—Nay, don't make a face, Belmour, for you know you are."—"I was very fond of dancing," said Belmour, "and by no means wish to deny it, and," continued he, turning his eyes towards Emily, by whom he was sitting, "on this occasion, I shall think I am so still."

Lady Clementina shortly afterward declared, that they must all go to bed, that by a good night's rest, they might be able to sit up all the night following.—Belmour, as it was his custom, offered Emily his arm, in order to attend her home.—When they got out of the door, the moon shone so brightly, spreading its soft rays over all the surrounding objects, and the stillness and uncommon warmth of the night was so inviting, that Belmour ventured to propose their walking first across the meadow, which leads to the well.—Emily consented—they continued to walk for some paces in silence, when Belmour, almost imperceptibly pressing her arm, which was within his, said—"May I hope that you will allow me to be your partner tomorrow?"—"Why should you doubt it," said she, gently smiling, and turning her eye towards him.—"Because," resumed he with some emotion, "I doubt all I most wish."—"Does *Lord Belmour* say that!" quickly resumed Emily.—"Who then can boast of happiness!"—"Does happiness depend merely on situation?" mournfully replied Belmour.—"It does not," said Emily, "but such advantages, as *you* possess, to a well-constituted mind are never subjects of indifference, but ought to be considered as real blessings."—Belmour sighed—"And does Mrs. Courtenay think *me* happy?" continued he.—"I sincerely wish you to be so," said she, with much warmth and eagerness.—"I thank you," said he, pressing her hand, which he continued to hold till she gently withdrew it.—They were now again at the door of her house.—"The night is charming," said Belmour, still hoping to prolong their walk.—"It is, indeed, but it is late," said Emily, "good night, and till tomorrow, farewell."—"Good night then," repeated Belmour, bowing respectfully, after he had conducted her to the door.—"O! could such moments of delight be continued to me!" said he to himself—"but they are passed, never to return! yet still will they be dear to my latest recollection!"—He again walked across the meadow—again returned to the house—all was silent—the moon now sunk apace, and a light, which then appeared at the window of his own house, and Bertram, whom he saw stretching his head out of it, as it seemed in expectation of him, reminded him, that it was time to retire.

Chapter 17

THE DAY FOLLOWING WAS, on Lady Clementina's part, wholly occupied by preparations for the ball, in which she also engaged Emily so much, that Belmour had less opportunity of seeing her than usual; but when in the evening they met in the parlour at Lady Clementina's, dressed and ready to set out, Belmour, accustomed as he was to Emily's beauty, whose native charms required indeed no ornament, was beyond measure struck with her appearance, and gazed at her for some time, with so much surprise and delight, that he was recalled, by a rising blush on her cheek, to the recollection, that he must not longer indulge in his admiration.—He immediately turned to Lady Clementina, who stood ready to receive his share of praise.—"Never did I see anything so beautiful and so brilliant as your dresses."—"Have I not done wonders?" said Lady Clementina; "and look here at her head," turning Emily round, "I thought I never should have made her consent, to wear this diamond *bandeau* of mine, which so prettily unites these feathers; is it not charming? We are both, as you see, dressed exactly alike."—"Charming! indeed," repeated Belmour—and nothing certainly could exceed the elegance of their appearance.

Belmour too, who was so much more dressed than usual, had heightened the accustomed grace of his fine figure—in short, when the group arrived in the ball-room, which Melford by no means disgraced, being what is called an uncommonly pretty man, all eyes were fixed on them; but after the dancing began, Emily and Belmour alone seemed to attract the attention of the company; they both danced inimitably, and the admiration they excited, was buzzed about in a manner, which they could not fail to hear.—Belmour was in a state of enchantment, which nearly made him forget all prudence—thus to hear his name joined to that of Emily, with such expressions of applause and admiration, overpowered his sense with ecstasy and delight.

The room grew extremely crowded, and he had ceased to attend to distinguish the by-standers; when, just as he got to the bottom of a dance, he was surprised, and by no means agreeably, at seeing St. Fort among the lookers on, and Barnvelt by his side.

St. Fort waited till Belmour came pretty close to him, and then advancing a step, with something like a sneer on his countenance, said—"This I did *not* expect! how long have you been returned to England?"—Belmour answered him so coldly, that

Emily was struck with his manner, and, laughing, said in a whisper, "Pray, tell me who that is? some person, I am sure, that you dislike."—Belmour smiled; "You are not wrong," said he, naming St. Fort.—St. Fort was then no more thought of by them, till, seated at supper, they saw him placed precisely opposite to them at a narrow table.

His eyes, during the supper, were fixed on Emily, with a freedom of admiration, that bordered upon impertinence; then on Belmour, first with a look of inquiry, and then of certainty. All this escaped not Emily's quickness, but evidently distressed her; the degree of gayety and ease, which the amusements of the evening, admirably conducted, had naturally inspired, suddenly vanished, and gave place in her manner to a degree of reserve, which damped poor Belmour's temporary bliss. He plainly saw whence it arose, and dreaded the effect, which ideas, perhaps newly excited in her mind, might have on her conduct towards him, and the probability of this circumstance, however trifling in itself, putting an end to the unexpected moments of happiness he had enjoyed. He felt too a degree of anger and vexation against St. Fort, which he could scarcely command; yet the more endeavoured to restrain, from conviction, that nothing would so much gratify his malignant spirit, as having an opportunity slyly of indulging that spite towards him, which he dared not openly avow.

The supper over, Lady Clementina rose in a flow of spirits, and insisted on the promise she had obtained from Emily of dancing the *menuet de la cour* with Belmour. "I will dance a simple minuet with him first," said she, "for I never could learn it, and then you shall dance with him, I am determined; so make no objections."—There was no possibility of refusing; but though the excess of merited applause, which they received from every by-stander, might well gratify their vanity, they neither of them could recover that feeling of gayety, which they had enjoyed the former part of the evening.

After going over all the walks, which were lighted up in the prettiest manner, and omitting no part of the entertainment, Lady Clementina at length proposed to return home. The morning had already dawned before they entered the carriage, and the rays of the sun shortly afterward spread a sufficient degree of light, for Belmour clearly to distinguish the beautiful, though pale cheek of Emily; her look was thoughtful, and almost dejected, and her fine eyes were less frequently turned towards him, than he was accustomed to see them. When they stopped at her door, Belmour trembled as he alighted to hand her out of the carriage, and scarcely ventured to press her hand, as he took leave of her.—"I have been fast asleep," cried Lady Clementina, rubbing her eyes, "and so I believe you have all been, for I have never once heard the sound of your voice the whole way.—You will come to dinner tomorrow, as usual; and you, cousin, I don't *ask.*"

Chapter 18

THE LATENESS OF THE ENTERTAINMENT of the preceding night left Belmour little hope of meeting Emily in the morning; he, however, rose, and walked at the accustomed time to a romantic little valley, a favourite scene of Emily's, where, seated at the foot of a tree, he had first seen her drawing.—"Scenes of the happiest moments I have passed," exclaimed he, casting his eyes around, and sighing bitterly; "still, still with pleasure I behold you, though my foreboding mind whispers to me, that the charm which bound me to you is lost perhaps forever!"—For a considerable time he stood with his arms folded across his breast, and lost in thought—then suddenly recollecting himself, "Yet," said he, "she is not gone from me, I shall again behold her—but will her eyes be turned to me as usual, with the gentle expression, at least, of friendship?—for thus I have seen them!"—Again he sighed—he was vexed and angry with himself—he felt conscious, that his prudence had in some measure forsaken him the preceding evening, to which a thousand circumstances had unavoidably contributed.—How could he explain?—how could he attempt at an excuse, when he dared not avow the cause of his errour?—The feeling of suspense which he now suffered was intolerable; and after walking about for some time, he was going towards home, with an intention, as he passed, of inquiring at Emily's door whether she were up—when, just as he turned, he perceived St. Fort at a distance, as it seemed, coming towards him.—"Curse on thee!" said he to himself, "that thus, like an evil genius, crossest me wherever I go!"—He knew that if he did not instantly avoid St. Fort, he would tack himself to him, and follow him wherever he went. Pretending, therefore, not to see him, he turned quickly into another path, and by crossing two or three different meadows, easily escaped. It was not doubtful, but that St. Fort would call on Lady Clementina, and that she would invite him to her house, as he was a man of the world, and known to everybody. Belmour therefore in idea already saw him established in their society, and dreaded him as a malicious spy over every look, every word he might utter. After rambling about for some hours, Belmour called at Lady Clementina's door, and at Emily's, but was told by the servants, that they were still in their rooms; he therefore gave up the hope of seeing Emily that morning, and expected the hour of dinner, when he depended on meeting her at Lady Clementina's with anxious impatience.

When Belmour, at the accustomed hour, arrived at his cousin's, she ran forward, the moment he entered the room, with evident marks of disappointment on her countenance.—

"Would you believe it, Belmour," said she, "Emily," (for so she familiarly called Mrs. Courtenay) "has sent me an excuse, and will not dine here today?—Mr. Courtenay," she says, "is just arrived; and though I wrote her word, that I begged she would bring him, she will not come, but entreats of me to *excuse* her.—Indeed but I do *not* excuse her!—and I think it quite disagreeable of her.—I am sure, if I be not to see her as usual, because Mr. Courtenay is come, I shall wish him hanged! What sort of man is he? does anybody here know him?"—At the instant dinner was announced, St. Fort and Barnvelt, whom Belmour at first had not perceived, came forward, and with two other men followed into the eating-room.

Poor Belmour felt a degree of vexation and disappointment, which is not easily to be expressed, and which the presence of St. Fort redoubled, as he saw the necessity of appearing unconcerned.—They were scarcely seated, when St. Fort leaning backwards in his chair, and negligently resting his hand on the table, said, turning to Melford, whom he sat by—"Pray, how came this beautiful creature to marry that damned fellow, Courtenay?" Melford was preparing to answer with a look that plainly said, I neither know nor care; when Barnvelt, interrupting him, asked St. Fort whether it were the same Courtenay they were at school with?—"I conclude so," replied he.—"Why surely then," said Barnvelt, "he is a very gentleman-like man, and I remember was reckoned an excellent scholar, and uncommonly clever when he was a boy.—I have since seen him accidentally, but not indeed now for some years, nor did I know what was become of him: but I believe, St. Fort," continued he, laughing, "that you remember the old story of the mutton pie, when you peached out of spite to a poor boy, who had, innocently you know, gotten you a whipping, and Courtenay took his part, and set all the boys against you, and it passed by a regular vote, that you should be sent to Coventry."—"Poh! poh!" said St. Fort, colouring, "I know a great deal of Courtenay, and lived a great deal with him, when he first came to London, and a fine life he then led!—he *was* completely ruined—what he *is*, I know not, for I have never seen or heard of him since I first went abroad, which is now many years—but he has all the pride commonly attached to the collateral branch of a great family; the supercilious insolence of a freethinker, which I know he is; and an infernal temper, from which, however, he suffers more himself than he makes others suffer; as no one ever knew better how to conceal their faults than he does, which he has certainly both sufficient sense and command over himself to do completely, whenever he chooses it, or thinks it worthwhile for any gratification of his own."—Having finished this speech, St. Fort took a pinch of snuff with much composure, and began his dinner.—Poor Emily! said Belmour to himself, is she then united to such a being?—Yet an involuntary feeling of something like relief stole on his imagination, on the reflection that Mr. Courtenay was not *too charming*. The dinner over, Barnvelt proposed a walk, which, as the rest of the gentlemen agreed to, Belmour, who, in expiation of his imprudence of the night before, was now become all caution, did not refuse.—Lady Clementina declared, that *she* should go to Mrs. Courtenay, and either walk or sit with her, as *she* chose. "And I think you are all very shabby," said she, "for not coming with me, at least to her door, and offering to do the same."—Saying this, she flew downstairs—Belmour followed her, presenting his arm, and accompanied her to the door of Mrs. Courtenay's lodging, then bowing gravely, he left her.—"What is the matter with you, the Lord knows!" said she, as he walked away, "but I can't stay to inquire, and so farewell till by and by, when I hope I shall find you in better humour."

Belmour felt his spirits so much oppressed, that he sought not to see Emily.—"All is now over," said he to himself, "and I remain the melancholy insulated being Fate seems to have destined me to be—a few short days will rob me even of the sight of all my soul holds dear on earth!" With these melancholy ideas, Belmour had retired to his own lodging in the evening.—On the following day, however, having received a message from Lady Clementina, he obeyed her summons to dinner.—When he arrived, he found the company just sitting down to table, which consisted of the persons named on the preceding day, with the addition of Emily, and a man he had never before seen, and whom, of course, he knew could be no other than Mr. Courtenay. His figure was genteel, his face plain, his eyes sharp and penetrating, but a sort of scowl, which hung over his brow, made his countenance less agreeable, than it would naturally have been.—The place by Emily, which Belmour was accustomed to occupy, was still vacant.—Belmour hesitated, when a look from Emily instantly decided him, and he seated himself by her side.—Yet was he not flattered, for the look, though with an expression of much gentleness, merely said, "And why not sit by me today, as usual?"

The company, some from one cause, and some from another, had remained uncommonly silent till towards the end of dinner, when a dispute on German writers arose between St. Fort (who premised that he was no German scholar, and knew little more of the language, than to ask for what he wanted at an inn, or scold the postillions on the road) and Mr. Courtenay, who till that instant had not uttered a word.—The former inveighed against the grossness of the pictures, and exaggeration of sentiment, which the theatrical pieces, in particular, he said, presented to the view.—"But they represent Nature," said Courtenay, with some warmth; and then, smiling ironically, "Nature," said he, "indeed may be too gross; and as for passion, with which they certainly are replete, that must appear bombastic to most men of the world."—Belmour, who had hitherto been silently listening to their conversation, addressing himself to St. Fort, said, "Surely, St. Fort, we may *admire*, but we should be cautious in *condemning* from translations.—

Passion is, indeed, of all languages, and may therefore be easily translated; but how difficult fairly to render the delicacies of idiom, which alone can express delicacy of feeling!"—"Your lordship, I fancy, understands German?" said Mr. Courtenay, bowing.—"I have studied it a good deal," replied Belmour, "and am, I confess, a great admirer of the force and energy of the language, to say nothing of the merit of writers, which even, when viewed through the medium of indifferent translations, still retain sufficient force to be read with interest, and even admiration, in spite of all their real, or supposed faults." St. Fort, who with a look that expressed you are two to one against me, and perfectly welcome so to be, taking out his snuff-box, turned to the other end of the table, and began talking about the opera for the ensuing season. Mr. Courtenay continued for some time in conversation with Belmour, on the merit of the German writers, with evident pleasure at finding himself so well understood. Dinner was no sooner over, than coming up to Emily, he said, "I must beg of you to present me to Lord Belmour, though I fear I shall profit little by his acquaintance, as we are going hence so soon, unless you, Emily, can prevail upon his lordship, to honour us with a visit at Dean Abbey.—It is a strange romantic old place," continued he, addressing his discourse to Belmour, "which in that style has its beauties, but it would require the riches of a nabob, to do all that is wanted there."—"Those are the first of beauties any place *can* have in my opinion," said Belmour, "and I shall hope to express my admiration of Dean Abbey, long before the nabob's *improvements* take place."—At this moment, Lady Clementina called to Emily, whom she followed into the drawing-room. From that time, Belmour and Mr. Courtenay were much together for the few remaining days they passed at Cheltenham, and it was agreed between them, that Belmour should come to Dean Abbey on his return from Wales, whither, in reality, he had accidentally said he was going, on being asked one day, somewhat suddenly by St. Fort, what brought him to Cheltenham, and whither he was going afterward.—Belmour had no opportunity of inquiring particularly of Emily, whether his visit to Dean Abbey would be agreeable to her; and the offer made him by Mr. Courtenay he felt an indulgence, that he could not resist; it secured to him, he thought, the liberty from time to time of seeing Emily, a blessing of which he had lately wholly despaired.—As a *friend,* said he to himself, I may one day hope to interest her, and every sentiment, that can offend, shall be carefully secreted within the last recesses of my burning heart.

The society at Cheltenham separated with real regret on the part of Lady Clementina and Emily, the former declaring, that, if Mr. Courtenay were so *stupid,* as not to come to town in the winter, she should come and *torment* him at Dean Abbey.—St. Fort made several vain attempts, to renew his former intimacy with Mr. Courtenay, who openly treated him with the greatest coldness; and Barnvelt, in his usual way on such occasions, tried to attach himself to *all,* or any of the party; which in the present instance, unfortunately for him, so wholly failed of success, that he could not even get a companion to bear half the expense of his hackney-chaise to town.

Chapter 19

THE SOLITUDE OF BELMOUR'S TOUR in Wales, the romantic scenes which had been presented to his view in that country, were by no means calculated to lessen the force of the impressions, with which he left Cheltenham.—He arrived at Dean Abbey in less than a month from the time when he parted with Mr. and Mrs. Courtenay, and alighted with a beating heart at the gate, by which he had before entered, but which was now, as well as the house door, thrown immediately open for him. Mr. Courtenay he found in the hall, who came forward to meet him.—"This is kind indeed," said he, and after shaking hands he led him upstairs.—"Emily," he continued, "is expecting you, I am sure, as by your letter we counted upon your arrival before dinner, for the roads at this time of the year are excellent."

Belmour was happy, that he had little more to do, than to bow, in answer to this and many other civilities expressed in the most cordial and polite terms by Mr. Courtenay, as they ascended an immense old stair-case, traversed a long gallery, and several other rooms, till at last they came to that, in which they found Emily.—She advanced towards them with a look so expressive of the pleasure she had in again seeing Belmour, that he could not doubt, but that his coming was at least not considered by her as an offence.—Yet that look was so placid, so indicative, as he thought, of a mind composed and serene, that it inspired him with a degree of shame for the perturbation of his own, which added to the embarrassment he already felt.

"I know not how I have ventured to invite you," said Mr. Courtenay, "to this strange uncomfortable place, where we live almost like hermits—for neighbours we see none, and so small a part of this old mansion has yet been furnished since I came to my estate, that I have very few rooms to accommodate visitors; and I will confess," continued he, advancing his chin, and drawing down the corners of his mouth, "that I do not feel impatient to have better, at least *more* apartments to dispose of.—I *have* lived in the world, and know what *the world* is."—At this moment dinner was announced, which put an end to Mr. Courtenay's discourse.

During dinner, as Belmour anxiously watched every look of Emily's, he plainly perceived those traces of melancholy on her countenance, which had struck him from the first of their acquaintance, much increased.—"Strange!" said he to himself—"I know not how to wish her happy with another, yet cannot bear to think she suffers!"

The rest of the day passed in conversation, in walking, and in examining the building, which had been immense and now, the greatest part being in ruins, presented on the outside the most beautiful and picturesque object imaginable, to the eye of taste.—Such was Belmour's, and his unfeigned admiration and praise seemed to please Mr. Courtenay, who was evidently vain of its antiquity.—"Emily," said he, "finds many subjects here to exercise her pencil, which the trim walls of a modern building would not afford.—She shall by and by show you some of her drawings."—"I know," said Belmour, looking at her with some earnestness, "that Mrs. Courtenay succeeds not less in her drawings of buildings, than in landscapes."—Emily coloured, and without looking at him, shortly afterward changed the discourse.—She had not forgotten what had passed at Cheltenham, where Belmour had hinted at the same subject,—"You must now come to my garden," said she, leading them towards the very terrace from which Belmour had seen her at the window—"where we shall find a seat, for I am really fatigued, and the evening is so warm and so delightful, that I think it will be pleasanter there than in the house."—"You always think it *pleasanter* there, than anywhere else," said Mr. Courtenay, smiling; "and I must confess, that you have made the most of all the old rose-bushes and honeysuckles, which they say were planted by my great grandmother. She lived, I believe, to near a hundred, and for the last fifty years of her life never once stirred from this place. Her whole and sole amusement and occupation were planting flowers on the sides of that terrace, to which, latterly, she used regularly every day, whatever the weather, to be carried, when from extreme old age she could no longer walk. And there," continued he, holding out his arm and pointing as they advanced on the terrace, "is her arbour, as it is called, though, I believe, like the good ship *Argo,* it retains the honour of its name, long since the existence of any remains of its component parts."—They were by this time come to a bench, near which were quantities of honeysuckles of immense growth, twining over a broken piece of old wall, which joined the house.—Here they seated themselves, and the calm stillness and warmth of the evening, increasing the odour of the flowers, rendered the situation more than usually agreeable; from that side of the building only, indeed, was there any sort of prospect, and this prospect was chiefly over the tops of trees (the terrace being raised above them), and thus extended to the view of a distant country; for, notwithstanding its picturesque beauties, nothing could be more gloomy than the situation of the Abbey, which stood detached from any town or village, in the middle of a large park, ill kept, and for the most part overgrown with thorn trees and furze. A long dark avenue of sycamores led to the principal gate, and, except that part of the house immediately above the terrace, the whole building was surrounded by lofty trees irregularly placed, the branches of which in some places hung over the roof. The inside of the house entirely corresponded with the outside; and of the habitable apartments those, that were furnished, contained the remnants of ancient magnificence—tattered arras, high-backed ebony chairs, heavy, carved, and almost immovable tables, covered with faded Persian carpets.—Family portraits were everywhere to be seen; some really curious, others destined to cover the white-washed walls of the long passages, which communicated from one apartment to another, many of them half dropping out of their worm-eaten frames.

Belmour had for some time remained silently seated by Emily, who herself appeared absorbed in thought, when Mr. Courtenay observed, that the dew was falling fast, and that it was almost dark; "And we will sit, my dear Emily," said he, "if you please, in your room; for Lord Belmour is, I find, as fond of music as I am; and I should much wish him to hear the organ, which you have had placed there. It is one," continued he, turning to Belmour, "which my father had made by that famous maker—I forget his name—but it is on the instrument.—My father was a great musician—but indeed he scarcely ever lived here, and it has, for ages past, been little used till now." He then led towards the house—they followed.—After traversing the great gallery, they found at the end of it a door, opening into the room of which Mr. Courtenay had spoken, and which Belmour had scarcely entered, before from its position he guessed it to be the same, at the window of which he had seen Emily.—"This room, I see, looks to the terrace," said Belmour, putting his head out of the window. "It does," replied Emily, with a look rather of surprise at his eager manner in making, what appeared in itself a remark of so much indifference.

Shortly afterward, at their desire, she sat down to the organ.—The instrument was admirable; capable, notwithstanding its force and fullness, of being reduced by certain stops to the softness necessary to accompany her divine voice. Belmour sat enraptured, with his eyes fixed on her in silent admiration, at times wholly unmindful of the presence of Mr. Courtenay.

In the course of the evening he ventured, not without a heavy sigh, to ask for some of the airs, which he had heard her sing at Belmour Castle. She immediately began, and sang over most of them, without having recourse to her music book: but seemed purposely to avoid looking towards Belmour.

Mr. Courtenay, who had then walked into the gallery, returning into the room, requested her to repeat the song she had just finished as he entered.—This she did, singing with the most peculiar softness and expression—her eyes too then involuntarily, as it seemed, met Belmour's with a tender expression of melancholy, which penetrated him to the heart.

The evening over, when Belmour retired to his apartment, all that he had seen that day, with the addition of a thousand painful reflections, crowded on his imagination.—He sat lost in thought—his arm resting on a table, and his hand closely pressed before his eyes—then, withdrawing his hand, he cast them round the room—it was large, and rendered so dark by its furniture, that the two candles, placed in the massy silver candlesticks, which stood on the ebony table on which he leant, scarcely extended their light beyond the space immediately surrounding them. Belmour, taking up one of the candles, walked slowly round the room. At one end was a bed of dark green velvet, with a broad gold fringe, which was in absolute tatters—the tester nearly reached the ceiling, and the head was ornamented with the family arms, embroidered in gold, silver, and coloured silks, but so tarnished and faded, that little but the design was to be distinguished. The hangings, which were in the old style some way from the wall, were of tapestry, but fallen into decay. The chairs, glass frames, and other furniture, &c. were of ebony, and the floor from age, being of oak, nearly the same hue. This room, indeed which was plainly the state-room, perfectly accorded with the remainder of the apartments. "Good Heaven!" exclaimed Belmour, throwing himself on a chair, "and is Emily destined to pass her days in this gloomy mansion?—Oh fate! have I deserved this?—duty,—affection for a father, have undone me!—but Courtenay is perhaps beloved—if so, 'tis well—may she be happy!—I will not repine.—Yet, why does fortune mock me, by showering down so many vain gifts on my head, while she thus robs me of the only blessing, which, in my estimation, could have given them value?—Emily! Emily! didst thou but know how thou art beloved!"—Thus did Belmour continue for a considerable time in an agony of grief and passion, and the morning began to dawn, before he had thought of taking any rest. The daylight, which appeared through the many openings and crevices of the shutters, reminded him at last of the hour: he then threw himself on his bed, where, exhausted by fatigue, his eyelids were closed by an interrupted sleep.

Chapter 20

BELMOUR AWOKE MUCH LATER than his accustomed time. Bertram was already in his room, but judging, from his master's looks, that he was not disposed to speak, he prepared what was necessary in silence, not without much curiosity to discover what had disturbed, as it appeared something had, his master's rest, and why he had not undressed on the preceding night. Belmour, when he entered the drawing-room, found Emily already seated at the breakfast table. Mr. Courtenay, getting up, said, "I have for some time been expecting you, knowing your lordship to be an early riser; but I fear you have not slept well, our bedchambers are but uncomfortable." "I have slept perfectly well," replied Belmour, seating himself at the breakfast table. "I had gotten some of my German translations ready," continued Mr. Courtenay, "and, I confess, had a plan of showing them to you before breakfast for your criticism, as Emily, though as good a classic scholar as Dr. Stanmore himself, in this cannot assist me; and I meant for that purpose to way-lay you, as you came out of your room; but we shall, I trust, have time sufficient. You will not, I hope, think of leaving us soon? I have indeed ventured on this supposition, and asked Barnvelt to meet you here; he is a very old acquaintance of mine, a good-natured fellow as ever lived, and I understand a particular friend of your lordship's." "Not particularly so," replied Belmour. "Humph? I thought he was," said Mr. Courtenay. "But

I certainly do not require any society at Dean Abbey," continued Belmour, "but that I have already had the honour of being admitted to: and while I am allowed to enjoy *that* society, I shall think myself sufficiently fortunate." Emily, while they were speaking, examined Belmour's wan, dejected countenance, with a look of interest, but joined not in the conversation.

Breakfast over, Belmour, who was examining the pictures, had walked into the gallery. Mr. Courtenay, as he left the room, following him with his eyes, said, "I really pity that young man—with every advantage nature or fortune can give, it is hard to suffer, as I plainly see he does, from an unhappy passion."

Emily changed colour—Mr. Courtenay, still looking towards the door, continued, "Barnvelt told me the whole story.—I wonder, when the lady had been detected, and after so long a time, that he has not conquered his passion—but there is, after all, no accounting for these things.—I am not apt, as I believe you know, to take fancies to people, but anyone so well informed, with evidently such superiour talents, and so unassuming as Lord Belmour, I think I never saw and indeed new friends," continued he with a sarcastic smile, "are often better than old ones, because we trust them less, and therefore we are less likely to be deceived." This soliloquy was interrupted by Belmour's returning to the room. Mr. Courtenay then proposed riding, to which Emily and Belmour assented, and Mr. Courtenay went out of the room, saying he would order the horses.

They remained for some time silent—Emily could not immediately recover from the agitation of mind occasioned by what Mr. Courtenay had just said.—That he should be so much deceived, far from giving her any satisfaction, seemed to awaken self-reproach in her breast; a sensation to which she was wholly unused.

She looked towards Belmour, who seemed as if expecting that she should speak to him, then towards the window, near which she was sitting, and then, to Belmour's infinite disappointment, got up, saying, that she should go and tie up some roses, which she saw had fallen from the wall. After a deep sigh, Belmour followed in silence. He was now accustomed to find a temporary relief even from the violence of his passion in the charm of Emily's conversation, which he at that moment felt particularly to require. Such, indeed, was her superiour sense and reaction, tempered by mildness and sensibility, that Belmour sometimes, while he listened with rapture to her conversation, thought that he could be content only to continue thus her friend. Vain imagination, which the subsequent moment destroyed!

Belmour, after assisting in tying up the roses, ventured to ask Emily, as she still neither spoke, nor looked towards him, whether anything had disturbed her.—"Nothing worth mentioning," said she.—"Nothing, I assure you.—I shall be better after my ride.—I fancy the horses are by this time nearly ready;" saying which, she walked again towards the house; and, as she evidently avoided his inquiries, Belmour dared not further insist. The day passed much as the preceding one had done, ending, as it was Emily's custom, with her favourite terrace, where she constantly walked, or sat on the different benches, till it was time to retire for the evening to the house.

Nearly a fortnight passed without any particular incident, except the arrival of Barnvelt, and, as it seemed by no means to the satisfaction of Mr. Courtenay, of St. Fort; who, Barnvelt wrote word, was his companion on a tour he was making, and he *concluded* he might bring him. After reading the letter from Barnvelt, announcing their coming, Mr. Courtenay threw it on the table towards Emily, with an expression of ill-humour and violence, which made her start—"There," he said, "as usual! *one* can never allow *one* fool or knave to come within one's doors, but he is followed by half a dozen more! But, by *God*! I shall soon again adhere to my own system!"

It was the first time since Belmour's acquaintance with him, that Mr. Courtenay had been betrayed into any similar impetuosity, although Belmour often thought, that St. Fort was not wholly mistaken in the character he had drawn of him. That he was uncommonly sensible, it was impossible not to perceive; but although his manner, when he chose it, was even captivating, there still lurked a dry moroseness in his eye, which seemed plainly to indicate, what he *might* be, if offended.

To Emily he always spoke with kindness, respect, and attention, and evidently showed for her the greatest admiration.—After reading the letter, Emily said, "It is but for a few days." "True, it is but for a few days," continued he, recollecting himself, and apparently ashamed of the warmth, into which he had been led—he then endeavoured to laugh off what he had said, as a mere joke; which Emily, though by far too clear-sighted to be deceived, from prudence affected to believe. Belmour was, in his heart, as much provoked at this intrusion of St. Fort's, as Mr. Courtenay—he dreaded both his penetration and his malice, and once thought actually of leaving Dean Abbey before he came; but not having sufficient resolution, he persuaded himself that Mr. Courtenay would think it uncivil.

It was now some days since the arrival of Barnvelt and St. Fort, during which time the latter had, without the least success, exhausted the secret and dangerous poison of his sly and artful flattery, in the hope of ingratiating himself with Emily; whose powerful charms failed not to affect his senses, though none could reach his cold unfeeling heart; when, breakfast being just over, a servant happened to bring Mr. Courtenay a letter from some one of the neighbours, which required immediate answer. Mr. Courtenay got up, and after searching about with some impatience, exclaimed—"Where is the inkstand, which I have often so positively ordered should be left here? if one do not use a thing of this sort every day oneself, it is sure to be taken away."—"I did not take it, your honour," said the servant, looking frightened; "I will ask Thomas."—Thomas, at the moment came into the room.—"His honour wants the silver inkstand."—"The silver inkstand? why 'tis here to be sure!" muttered he to his companions, then to himself—"but it is *not* here,"—then lifting up his hand with an air of triumph, "but I *know where* it is—sure enough it is behind the window shutter in the great hall, and has been ever since I carried it down to my lord there—the day *as* his lordship came here, before my mistress went to Cheltenham—I will see in a moment, and fetch it up."—"Thou art distracted," said Mr. Courtenay to the man as he went out.—"What can the fellow mean?" continued he, looking full at Emily.—"I really cannot guess," said she, with a look of the utmost astonishment.—"I always understood, that you had never seen this place, till I had the honour of showing it to you?" said Mr. Courtenay, turning to Belmour—Belmour, colouring violently, said, "I never did—that is, I only called in my way to Cheltenham, to pay my respects to Mrs. Courtenay, when I had not the good fortune to find her at home—and I remember taking the liberty to ask for a pen and ink, to write my name; which is, I suppose, what the servant means."

Mr. Courtenay did not appear perfectly satisfied with this explanation, but made no remark. The servant returned with the inkstand, and setting it down directly before his master, looked at Belmour; "Your lordship remembers, I am *sartain,* that your lordship said you wanted to write a letter; and then when I brought the pen and ink into the great hall, where your lordship was walking about: your lordship said *as how* it was no matter, and that you would not write—" "Enough," said Mr. Courtenay, peevishly, "leave the inkstand, and get about your business."—St. Fort, without turning his head, cast a significant glance towards Barnvelt, who had fixed his eyes on the table before which he was sitting, and did not choose to raise them—a general silence ensued, and, when Mr. Courtenay had finished his note, the company dispersed. As they were all going different ways, Emily came up to Belmour, and in a tone of half-reproach asked him what could be the reason, that he had never mentioned to her his having been at Dean Abbey.—"Alas!" said he, "what has long been *the reason* of anything I have done, but the fear of displeasing *you*? (of deceit you cannot suspect me) and now," continued he, "that poor hope deserts me! you are, I see, offended."—"Indeed, I am not *offended*," resumed she, "but I must speak seriously to you, you have made it necessary—it is not now a time—you are expected—I shall join you all by the time the horses are ready," continued she, turning to go towards her own apartment.—Belmour, who had changed colour several times during this short conversation, unable to reply, offered not to detain her. "I know my fate," said he to himself, "and my own imprudence has undone me." Belmour however determined, if possible, not to encourage the impertinent surmises of St. Fort, which had by no means escaped his observation; and for this purpose, by a thousand vain attempts at ease and unconcern, endeavoured to conceal the real anguish of his mind. The day following was appointed for the departure of Barnvelt and St. Fort, which accordingly took place.

Belmour had talked of the same period for his departure, but still lingered on, unable to resolve on leaving Emily, although everything tended to convince him of the necessity of that resolution. Mr. Courtenay had, of late, but slightly opposed his going, and had treated him with a coldness and reserve of manner which, however tempered by perfect politeness, was the very reverse of that cordial expression of sentiment, which he had experienced from him on their first acquaintance.

Emily he could not consult—he felt it every day more impossible for him, to attempt speaking to her in the calm language of friendship.—Ill, indeed, was the habit of seeing Emily, in which Belmour had of late indulged, calculated to reduce a passion, which, in its infancy, had resisted both time and absence, to the sober dictates of reason and prudence.— The peculiar elegance of her figure charmed in every action; whether she rode, or danced, or walked, the unaffected grace of her beautiful and airy form could but increase that admiration, with which he had been inspired from the first moment he saw her; while the superiour charms of her conversation, enlivened by a brilliant imagination, and accompanied by an unassuming modesty and simplicity of manner, secured the affections of a heart like Belmour's, capable of the purest and most delicate passion.—This passion he now no longer wished to conquer, but rather considered the melancholy void, which he must then feel in his breast, as a misfortune—for too deep and too serious was the nature of his attachment, to admit either of change or substitute.

Chapter 21

TWO DAYS HAD NOW PASSED, since Barnvelt and St. Fort had been gone, still Belmour remained, and could not determine on going—Mr. Courtenay began, he thought, to appear less reserved to him, than he had done of late; and he flattered himself, at some moments, with the hope of fixing a period for his return.—At others, all hope faded before his imagination—"Never," he repeated to himself, "shall I see her more—we now part forever."—Impressed with this idea, he had not sought any opportunity of particular conversation with Emily, feeling convinced from what she had said to him on the day which preceded St. Fort's departure, and from other expressions which, at different times, he had collected from her, that she meant to speak to him on the subject of his leaving Dean Abbey.

Occupied with these painful reflections, Mr. Courtenay having taken his leave after breakfast, saying, that he had a visit to make a few miles off: Belmour had, for some time, been walking to and fro on the terrace already mentioned, which, at the further end, terminated in what was called the labyrinth walks, formed of thick yew hedges, with here and there recesses, in which there were benches. Belmour, almost unknowing which way he went, had strolled beyond the terrace into these walks; when suddenly, on turning his head, he perceived Emily pensively seated on one of the benches.—His first impulse, thinking himself unobserved, was to retire; when finding that he was seen by her, he advanced.—"Were you avoiding me?" said she, "but I really must speak to you."—Here she paused, making him a sign to sit down by her—Belmour obeyed in silence, and with his eyes fixed on the ground—then, after gently raising them, and turning towards Emily, he started—"You are not well," said he, "what, for Heaven's sake, is the matter!"—"I am not *well,* indeed," she replied;—"*can* I be so?—Belmour," continued she in a solemn tone—" 'tis in vain we attempt longer to deceive ourselves—we *must* part."—It was the first time she had used this familiar appellation; and to be thus addressed by Emily, for an instant charmed, as it were, his every sense—he then turned pale—"Let us," said she, endeavouring to force a smile, "let us hope one day again to meet, and not by an ill-timed delay prevent the possibility of ——" "No, no," said Belmour, "we meet no more!—I see my fate, and submit!"—he then covered his eyes with his hand, and was going—"Stay, I conjure you!" said Emily, taking hold of his arm, "you do not, I am sure, wish to make me more wretched—let me at least suffer for one I can approve, and restrain for my sake this violence of passion, which would disgrace the feelings of the heart." The suppliant expression of her countenance as she spoke was so touching, that Belmour, falling at her feet, begged her forgiveness, and in a tone of resignation said, "I *will* obey thee—whither shall I go?"—"*That* I cannot direct," said she, bursting into tears, " 'tis enough, that I have bid you leave me—I do not wish to deceive you," said she, recovering herself, and making him a sign to rise and again sit by her,—"the attempt indeed would be vain! or affect an indifference for you, which my heart cannot feel—but—*hear me,*" continued she, seeing that he was going to interrupt her—"how much more does not this avowal increase the necessity of our parting! we must not, while we *talk* virtue, *practice* vice—no, my friend," said she, gently pressing his hand, "you would not have Emily thus degraded; thanks to that benevolent power, who has hitherto protected, guarded, and supported me, I have never known guilt, and now its weight would be intolerable to me—save me, therefore, and by your ready acquiescence, spare me, the necessity of still more painful exertion. You know, too, Mr. Courtenay—his opinion of me, and his confidence—can I hazard losing this, and becoming a prey to suspicion and mistrust!—I will say more—I mistake, or of late he has not been wholly free from suspicion, though not a hint has yet passed his lips on the subject. He is, I know, conscious of the quickness and violence of his temper, and at constant war with himself, to curb its baneful effects—but I hear someone coming—think of the immediate means of separation—remember I *depend* on you." "This is not," said Belmour, starting with agony, "a last farewell!"—"It is not," Emily hastily replied, "tomorrow order your chaise; I will then for a moment see you first—" "You promise;"—"I *promise.*"—By this time the footsteps drew near—Belmour rose, and with precipitation turned down a close walk, which secreted him from the view of the person he heard coming: but walking with hurried steps, unmindful of which way he went, he was suddenly met by Mr. Courtenay, who stared at him in a way plainly to indicate his surprise at the disordered looks of poor Belmour. Mr. Courtenay, however, after considering him for a few seconds, passed on, saying, coldly, that it was a fine day.

The footsteps which had been heard were those of a servant; who, having delivered his message to Emily, had retired; and she, when Mr. Courtenay came up to her, (thinking herself alone) was sitting with her handkerchief closely pressed to her eyes. "You seem unwell," said he, with an inward and agitated voice.—Emily started—"I did not see you," said she, somewhat in confusion. "I *believe* it," replied he, dryly, and with a half-sneer on his countenance, "but I deferred my intended visit, on finding since, by a letter which I received, that I am to expect a person here on particular business, either today or tomorrow."—Then, as it seemed recollecting himself, he inquired about her health with an expression of interest—"was it the headache?"—She said it was, and that she had been, in addition, oppressed by a dreadful lowness the whole day. Mr. Courtenay then drew nearer to her, offering her his arm as she rose from her seat, which she accepted; and finding him almost imperceptibly press hers to his side, as they walked on together, her tears flowed fast, dropping on her hand, he raised it to his mouth, affectionately kissing them away: this was too much, and Emily hurrying on towards the house by a walk, which led immediately to one of the doors; she entreated of her husband to allow her to go to her room, saying, that being alone would best recover her—that she shortly should be better.

Belmour, who determined in everything to obey Emily, and to avoid, to the utmost of his power, all chance of wounding her future peace of mind by any imprudence, that might escape him from the pain he felt at this cruel parting, behaved throughout the day, while in the presence of Mr. Courtenay, with apparent unconcern, and asked his commands for London, whither, he said, he was going, with composure. The paleness of his cheek, and dejection of his eyes, might indeed plainly have shown, that some hidden uneasiness preyed on his mind, even to one of less penetration than Mr. Courtenay;

but he either did not, or affected not to observe anything particular in Belmour's looks, or manner; keeping however only to the strict rules of good breeding in his *regrets* at his going, and *hopes* that he would return.

Belmour's conduct on this trying occasion was not lost on Emily. "I thank you," said she, at a moment when she was not overheard by Mr. Courtenay; "*this is* kind indeed; and be assured, that *such* marks of real attachment will ever be remembered by me with the most grateful satisfaction." Belmour answered only by a sigh. The remainder of the day passed nearly in the usual manner, except that the evening's music (Emily's singing, accompanied by the organ) was somewhat prolonged by Belmour's having several times entreated to have some of the airs repeated, finishing by that he had first heard her sing, when unseen himself, at Belmour Castle; this was almost too much for poor Emily, who, however, with the most pathetic expression, got through it, and supper having been for some time announced, the evening closed.

On the morning following, Belmour's chaise was ordered to be ready immediately after breakfast, and he thought only of the last farewell he was shortly to take of Emily. Breakfast over, and nothing apparently preventing Belmour's going, Emily grew thoughtful, revolving in her mind how she should accomplish her promise, when she was relieved from her embarrassment, by a servant whispering to Mr. Courtenay, that a person was come from town, who wished to speak to him immediately. "Show him into my room," said Mr. Courtenay, with a look of some agitation. Belmour immediately, on a hint which Emily gave him, held out his hand to Mr. Courtenay, saying, he begged not to detain him, that his chaise must be ready, and that, with a thousand thanks for all his kindness, he took his leave. Mr. Courtenay, after a moment's hesitation, shook hands with him, then left the room, saying, that he still hoped to return before he went, and again wish him a good journey, but that he must instantly speak to the person who was in his room, as he knew that he was pressed for time.

Emily immediately rose from the table, before which she was sitting—"I have, you see, performed my promise," said she, casting a look of pity on Belmour; "and now let our farewell be brief,"—her voice faltered—"Again I thank you," continued she, holding out her trembling hand to him, "for this touching mark of your affection, I now have a least *one* heartfelt consolation in the remembrance of our faultless character."—Belmour gently pressed her hand to his clay-cold lips, but spoke not.—"Farewell," she mournfully repeated, as he stood motionless before her—"farewell,"—then waving her hand, she left the room.

Belmour for a time remained fixed to the same spot where he had stood—then fearing Mr. Courtenay might return, and sensible that he ought by all means avoid being seen by him in the state of agony and disorder, in which he felt himself, left the room, hurried downstairs, and after casting a last melancholy look towards the Abbey, threw himself into his chaise, which stood waiting at the gate, and stopped not till he came to London.

Chapter 22

ARRIVED IN TOWN, as he alighted at his door, Belmour was by chance met by Dr. Seward, who, begging pardon for his intrusion, followed him into his house.—"You must excuse me, my dear lord," said he, "but I cannot resist this opportunity of just inquiring after you, it is such an age since I have seen you, and," taking his hand, "you will, I am sure, forgive me."—Belmour, as he looked at him, felt his eyes filled with tears, the first he had shed since he left Emily.—Dr. Seward had been the favourite and confidential physician of his father, was the person sent for from London to attend him during his last illness, and had again returned to Belmour Castle just before his death, since which period, Belmour and he now met for the first time.—"You are kind," said Belmour, returning his salute to him, "I am very well, I thank you." "I fear otherwise," replied Dr. Seward, looking steadfastly at him, and still holding his hand.—"Come, come, my dearest lord, you shall not thus escape from an old friend, but sit down, I entreat it of you, in this parlour."—Belmour allowed himself to be led into the parlour, where he was scarcely seated, but he fell back senseless in his chair.—Dr. Seward calling for the immediate assistance of his servants, saw him carried to his bed.—Here he remained in an almost hopeless state for nearly three weeks, a raging fever, accompanied by delirium, having manifested itself immediately after he was put to bed, and but too well justified the physician's apprehensions.—Dr. Seward giving up almost all other attendance, scarcely quitted Belmour's room, or even his bedside, during this long period of imminent danger, for such it was; judging it absolutely necessary, that every turn of the disorder should be watched with the most minute exactness and feeling, and that if others surpassed him in skill, none could rival him in his sincere and anxious wishes for the welfare of his patient, so that he took the whole responsibility on himself.

On the first return of reason and recollection, Belmour expressed much uneasiness at what he might in his delirium have uttered.—He feared, for the sake of Emily, lest the secret of his heart should have been revealed!—"Rest secure, my dear lord," said Dr. Seward, immediately comprehending his meaning, "I have myself constantly attended you, and you have not, on my honour, uttered a single expression, that even an indifferent person might not have heard.—You frequently, it is true, in your delirium, called on some beloved object, whom you even at times thought present, but named her not." "I thank you," said Belmour, raising his languid eyes towards his friend, "this was indeed kind, and since *you* have watched me, I care not what I may have said."—The doctor then fearing greater exertion might, in his weak state, fatigue him, forbade any further conversation.

The next morning, perceiving him considerably refreshed by the rest, which, during the foregoing night, he had been able to take, the doctor ventured to give him several letters, which had been brought at different times for him during his illness.—On receiving the letters, he eagerly seized on one of them, which with uplifted eyes he pressed to his lips.—"This is indeed a balm!" said he—he then made a sign to the doctor, that he wished to be alone, who immediately retired.—Belmour was no sooner alone, than with trembling hands he opened the letter, which it will be easily guessed was from Emily.—It had been written and sent to his house a few days after his leaving Dean Abbey.—The words of Emily were kind, tender, and impressive.—She entreated of him to take care of himself—to remember her as *she deserved*—but at the same time exhorted him, not to attempt writing to her, or seeing her, as he valued her future quiet and peace of mind.—This, she said, was the last time he was to expect to hear from her.—"An *indifferent* letter I would not," added she, "receive from *Belmour,* and a clandestine correspondence, such as ours must become, *never* can be carried on with innocence."—She then, after some details relative to Belmour and herself, ended by saying, "if we cannot be happy, let us, my friend, *deserve* to be so, and trust to that Divine Power, who, never wholly abandoning innocence and virtue, will restore peace to our bosoms."

Belmour, with a look of resignation, after repeatedly kissing the letter, put it into his bosom.—"I could," said he, sighing, "have wished once to have thanked my Emily for this unexpected favour; but she will have it otherwise, and the future care of my life shall be, since I cannot contribute to her happiness, at least not to disturb that peace of mind, which she so justly values."

Chapter 23

BELMOUR'S RECOVERY WAS SLOW; an extreme languor succeeded the violence of his disorder, which still did not leave the physician without serious apprehensions for him, though not such as threatened immediate danger to his life.—On Dr. Seward's proposing to him, to remove to the country for change of air, Belmour communicated to his friendly physician his intention of going abroad, the moment his strength would allow him to undertake a journey.—This the doctor highly approved, saying, that a few months of the approaching winter spent in a better climate, would be of infinite service to his health; "and then," continued he, "in the spring you may visit your own beautiful castle, for I know not a more salubrious air, and as to the place it has ever appeared to me a perfect terrestrial paradise!—How my good old lord used to enjoy it!—Well, he surely deserved blessings by his own enjoyment of them, and by his desire to dispense them to all around him. I have heard him called proud—and *proud* he was; but his pride led him always to support, with real honour, the high station in which he was placed, and to treat all those subordinate to him with benevolence.—Had all our noblemen *such pride,* the world would go better than it does with us!—But as I was saying, my lord, the winter months abroad, and the spring and summer at Belmour Castle—and I will answer for your health—but you must not travel alone."

Belmour shook his head.—"Indeed, but I must travel alone," said he, "I am unfit for society, and shall be long so." Seeing that the doctor was going to argue the point with him, he stopped him, saying, "let us not, my good friend, dispute on that subject.—I thank you for your kind intentions, but I am determined, and for reasons I wish not to explain, I must also entreat your secrecy.—Owing to your attentive care, having judged it necessary, I have seen no creature, nor, I believe, has my illness been much known of, or even my being in town. I mean to take advantage of this circumstance, and set out quietly the very first moment I am able.—The procuring letters of credit from my banker, and some other necessary preparations, I shall entrust to your friendly care."

Dr. Seward was a man of sense and penetration; from the determined manner, therefore, in which Belmour had spoken, and other circumstances which he had observed, during the course of his attendance on him, he judged it by no means advisable, to attempt any further opposition to his intentions.—Change of climate he had himself intended to propose, and as to the mode, although he had regretted Belmour's expressions on the subject, as he thought they proceeded from some temporary impulse, he paid less attention to them, and considered only what to him appeared most necessary for the immediate benefit of his health.

Belmour, aware of his situation, no longer attempted to combat feelings he could no longer wish to conquer, but endeavoured only to exert the powers of his mind, to oppose the more baneful effects of despondency.—He felt an indifference, and even disgust for everything, that had not an immediate reference to the object of his passion; and considered total change of scene, and variety of objects, as the only means, by which he might, in time, at least, hope to acquire that composure of mind, which belongs even to the unhappy, when not labouring under the pressure of self-reproach.—"The hope of being of use to my country has hitherto, from circumstances, been denied me," said he to himself, "nor could I now attend to politics, were I united with the characters I most admire!—Belmour Castle, the delight of my early youth, is become insupportable to me!—too strongly is my mind now impressed with the idea of all it might have been to me!—What then remains? or whither shall I go?—Oh! Harcourt!" he mournfully exclaimed, "my much valued friend, hadst thou been spared to me, I might now have flown for refuge from myself to thy protecting bosom, and followed in the path of glory, where thy bravery would have led, or fallen honourably by thy side."

From Lady Caroline, Belmour seldom heard; her letters, when she wrote, were short, and described her as much engaged and pleased in the society of a large party of English, which had met at Rome.—To this sort of society, Belmour found himself so perfectly unequal, that he gave up all thoughts for the present of joining his sister.—Of her health she herself always gave a better account, than was entirely confirmed by her physician, who, though he allowed all immediate danger to have been removed by change of climate, still considered her as in a very precarious state.

Belmour, who tenderly loved his sister, shed many tears over the letter, which he wrote to her on the eve of his departure; in which he told her, that, for reasons which hereafter, when they should, as he hoped, one day meet, he would entrust to her, he was now bidding farewell to England; and that it was his intention to travel into Greece, a part of the world he had always much wished to visit.

And now having settled with Dr. Seward about the very few correspondents, whose letters he would have sent after him to such places as he should name, and other business of the same sort, two months after his leaving Dean Abbey, Belmour, accompanied only by his servant Bertram, on whose fidelity he could rely, set out with an intention of immediately crossing France to Marseilles, and thence continuing his journey in whatever way opportunity or inclination might suggest. The better to avoid all chance of society being forced upon him, he determined to conceal his name, and to take one less subject to remark—in short, to forget if possible himself, and remember only the dear object of his passion.

It was not now with him as when he had quitted England after his father's death, his mind occupied by that recent and melancholy event, and by the illness of his sister, who, in her then helpless state, from him, as her sole protector, seemed to claim every care, thought, and attention.—The uncertainty too and doubt, under which he had remained with respect to Emily, made it then seem to him folly and inexcusable weakness, not to endeavour to combat the passion, which her appearance had excited in his breast during their short acquaintance at Belmour Castle.

Subsequent events had now afforded him more than sufficient reason, to justify the sentiments, with which she had from the first inspired him; and admiration of her character was superadded to that respect, esteem, and confidence, which can alone render attachment permanent.—He knew, too, that he was not indifferent to her, but that to preserve that interest so dear to him in her heart, he must, by the sacrifice on earth the most painful to himself, continue to deserve her good opinion, and by a melancholy and probably eternal separation, prevent the possibility of disturbing her peace of mind by his presence.—Many circumstances of her history to the period of her marriage he had heard at different times from herself, in the course of that intimacy, in which they had now for some time lived together, first at Cheltenham, and then at Dean Abbey.—Her blameless life, indeed, left her little difficulty in its recital; for the early habits of virtue and reason, instilled into a mind by nature prone to every good, saved her from those errours, into which youth and inexperience are too often led by passion, by thoughtlessness, or by dissipation, and which fatally tend to embitter their future days.—Emily's education had begun, it may be said, almost with her birth, and in the school of adversity; for when, after the death of her unfortunate parents, she remained under the care and protection of Dr. Stanmore, the playful hours of infancy were scarcely over, before she became of necessity acquainted with the cruelty of her own situation; a situation, which it required that strength of character, with which she was endowed by nature, aided by the sound precepts of philosophy, set before her by her kind monitor, to support with composure and resignation.

By birth entitled to affluence, and all the enjoyment fortune can bestow, she found herself an outcast from her family, owing even her subsistence to the benevolence of one in no way related to her.—Dr. Stanmore's affection and tenderness, indeed, supplied, as far as it was possible, the want of parents: yet still, as her heart expanded, Emily could not but feel the privation of those natural ties, which endear life to us—and often did she envy the helpless infant of the poor beggar at her door, when she saw its little arms encircling the neck of its mother, and pressed tenderly to her bosom.—The melancholy fate too of her parents rendered them doubly interesting to her—she wished she had but even seen her father; and the recollection, however faint, of her mother, so early torn from her, was treasured up in her bosom with inexpressible tenderness.—These genuine feelings of the heart were never discouraged by Dr. Stanmore, whose eyes often filled with tears at the mention of her parents, and often would he look with rapture on Emily, when he saw her most affected by sensations so congenial with his own.—Well-calculated, too, were the constant habits of charity and benevolence, in the exercise of which she was admitted to assist him, and the gratitude of his parishioners, expressed in terms little short of adoration, to excite and encourage every genial affection in her heart—and the hours dedicated to instruction and science, under the tuition of such a preceptor, were soon sought after and attended to by Emily, with as much eagerness as the gayest scenes of amusement and dissipation could have been. Yet Dr. Stanmore, whose sound judgment and sober sense guarded him against the enchantments of enthusiasm, into which the warmth of his heart, and energy of his taste and genius, might naturally have betrayed him, failed not to set before the eyes of his beloved pupil, the duties, the occupations, and the rational enjoyments of common life; endeavouring to make her sensible on what these enjoyments really depended, and to divert prejudice and passion of their borrowed and dangerous ornaments.—The growing beauties of her form, the natural elegance of her manners, together with her superiour understanding, seemed well to entitle her to the hope of contracting some marriage, that might place her in that rank of life, to which by birth she had a right—yet this was an uncertainty; and the total want of fortune, the cruel neglect, and, indeed, treachery of her nearest relations, increased the chances against her.—Dr. Stanmore, therefore, made it the great object of his education, to render her mind equal to any situation, in which she might be placed, and to establish, upon an immutable basis, those principles of action, that love of truth, and confidence in Heaven, which place their possessor in some degree beyond the reach of fortune.

The vicinity of the village where he lived afforded little society but the occasional visits of a few country squires, their wives, and daughters; and the neighbouring town, being neither gay nor opulent, boasted only of an annual ball and a monthly card assembly during the winter season, which were however occasionally attended by some considerable families in the neighbourhood.

To one of these balls, Emily, at Dr. Stanmore's desire, who was ever anxious to promote her amusement, had gone, under the protection of a Mrs. Morton, a respectable lady of the neighbourhood, and an old acquaintance of Dr. Stanmore's, who had solicited to accompany her thither.—Emily was then seventeen; and though she had only had a few occasional lessons of dancing, she had so well profited by the instructions of her master, an itinerant Scotchman, so perfect was her ear, and so graceful her every motion, that as her light steps moved, it seemed in air, the admiration she excited was general; a murmur of applause ran through the room as she went down the dance, and from the spectators on each side, frequent and more audible expressions of surprise and approbation could not fail to be distinguished by her. The dance ended, she perceived a lady, whom she had before observed sitting negligently in a half-reclined posture, listening, as it seemed, with no great attention, to the discourse of two or three men, rise and come up to Mrs. Morton, who instantly advanced to meet her.—Emily, who was going to her chaperon, stopped not to interrupt them, and the more particularly as she saw by their looks, that their conversation was about herself.—"Come along, my dear," said Mrs. Morton, making Emily a sign to advance, "Mrs. Stainville desires me to introduce you to her, an office I certainly shall perform with peculiar pleasure," continued she, simpering with an air of satisfaction at the idea of the essential service she was rendering her young *protegée*.—Emily blushed, she felt a degree of timidity, which she had not before experienced.—The extreme elegance of Mrs. Stainville's dress and appearance, so superiour to anything she had yet seen, inspired her not only with admiration, but with a species of awe; she wished to please, but felt an awkwardness, which she feared must wholly defeat her purpose. Mrs. Stainville by her manner, perfectly that of a well-bred woman of the world, soon relieved Emily from her embarrassment.—She inquired, with an expression of interest, after Dr. Stanmore; he had, she said, once done her the honour to be her guest—but it was long ago—she feared he had forgotten her.—They were here interrupted by several gentlemen, who, coming up to Mrs. Stainville, said that a cotillion was to be formed, that there were two ladies ready, and two others only wanting.—Mrs. Stainville, with a negligent air of half refusal, said, that she had given up dancing, but that if Miss Melville would be one, she could not refuse.—Emily blushed, and felt mortified at being obliged to confess her inability, never having even seen *cotillons* danced.—"I don't quite believe you," said Mrs. Stainville, "but if you do not choose dancing, I shall also refuse, and we will go into the tea-room together."—"That must not be," said a young officer, advancing and seizing Mrs. Stainville's hand, who *suffered* herself to be led away, " 'tis enough that we are deprived of *that lady,*" casting an affected glance at Emily, "*you,* madam, shall not escape us."—A fourth lady shortly having joined them, the *cotillon* was begun.—Mrs. Stainville, little more than *walked* the dance over, but with a graceful air of ease, which left the by-standers in little doubt of her talents for dancing, were they exerted.—She then, coming up to Emily, complained of *extreme fatigue,* and entreated of her, to come and sit with her on a bench, where she might lean.—Mrs. Stainville's conversation was lively, intelligent, and agreeable, and her manner even fascinating, when she wished to please, which being now the case, Emily was enchanted with her.—Mrs. Stainville too, in addition to these advantages of manner, was not wanting in understanding; and having acquired a considerable degree of superficial knowledge on many subjects, and learned the precise and proper terms of praise, disapprobation, doubt, and enthusiastic admiration, not only on works of art and literary productions, but even on philosophic disquisitions, she knew so well how to introduce her remarks, and keep back her ignorance, when it existed, that she seldom failed to give those, with whom she conversed, a high opinion of her character and abilities.—It was not therefore to be wondered at, if Emily, unknowing of the world, was pleased and flattered by the marked attention, which she showed her, particularly as Mrs. Morton seemed highly to encourage this new acquaintance.—Supper being announced, Mrs. Stainville begged to be allowed being of Mrs. Morton's party, on which many mutual compliments having passed between them, they proceeded together into the supper-room, followed by a train of men, who bustled about Mrs. Stainville's chair, and seemed to vie with each other in offers of service.

The supper over, minuets were proposed.—Here again, poor Emily experienced a second mortification—she had never been taught a minuet!—"Impossible!" cried Mrs. Stainville, then turning to the next person near her, "was there ever a figure so formed for a minuet!" said she, throwing her head back, and shrugging up her shoulders.—"O! Miss has time before her enough to learn!" said a fat fresh-looking man, with a droll sly countenance, who stood near.—This remark did not seem to be particularly relished by Mrs. Stainville, although so encouraging to her new friend.—She was herself, not without considerable solicitation, prevailed on to dance a minuet, which she did with ease and elegance, but declared, when she had finished, that *positively* that was the last time she ever would *expose* herself before so many people.—Country dances then again began, and Emily, pleased with the distinction shown her, danced with additional spirit.—Mrs. Stainville, when she saw Emily about to retire from the ball, and return home with Mrs. Morton, got up in haste from her seat, and coming up to them, renewed the many obliging things she had said to Emily, adding, that, "as she had her permission," she should no longer than the day following, delay waiting upon her at the parsonage.—Emily was no sooner seated in the carriage with Mrs. Morton, whose house was about half a mile on the other side of the parsonage, and who was to convey her home, than she inquired of her, who Mrs. Stainville was.—"I never saw anything so agreeable," said Emily, "as she appears to be; are you, madam, much acquainted with her?"—"O yes," replied Mrs. Morton, with a consequential toss of the head.—"I used frequently to go to their house, when her husband was alive.—Mr. Stainville often invited *poor* Mr. Morton and me.—Mr. Stainville kept an excellent table—nobody better served—and Mrs. Stainville is indeed a most elegant woman—where she now lives in this county, is only a small farm left to her by her late husband—but she has a very considerable jointure—the family-seat, where she resided with her husband, is a matter of ten miles off, and they lived there winter and summer for many years, and commonly had a house full of company.—They did not visit much about themselves, but our house, when *poor* Mr. Morton was living, was not a mile from them—the park reached quite to our garden, and I have often seen her out of my window, strolling about with a book in her hand—she is vastly fond of reading, and all those sort of things.—Mr. Stainville though, I should tell you, was a Roman Catholic, but it was in the marriage articles, that she was never to be disturbed in her religion, and so she is a Protestant.—Lord! I saw her when first she was married, and a sweet beautiful creature indeed she *was*—nay she *is* still a very fine woman, though, to be sure, not quite so young."—"Her appearance and manner are uncommonly pleasing," said Emily, "and to *me* she does not look above thirty?"—"O! more than that—more than that!" said Mrs. Morton, with a significant nod, "but no matter—what signifies anybody's age, as I always say, why how one looks is everything—*poor dear* Mr. Morton used always to be talking of *age*—and I remember one day we were standing together, looking out of my window, when Mrs. Stainville happened to walk by in the park, leaning on the arm of a relation of Mr. Stainville's, *a nabby,* I think, they called him, and my husband flew quite into a *puff*—to see a woman (said he) that pretends to sense, dawdling about with a boy young enough to be her son! 'Lord, my dear! where's the harm,' said I, 'why, people are not the more wicked for being young, surely!'—'You're all alike,' said he, swearing a great oath! for, to be sure, my poor dear husband was a little apt to be choleric! Well! Heaven rest his soul! I am sure, I regret him day and night.—I shall never see his like, after all!—Well, but my dear," continued she, after passing her handkerchief, which she took out of her pocket for the purpose, across her eyes.—"I am sure, that Dr. Stanmore will be quite pleased, that I have *brought* you acquainted with Mrs. Stainville, for, as I was saying, she is a most charming woman, and nobody more respected.—For the latter years of his life, Mr. Stainville lived more alone, as his health declined, and had no company, but a relation or so, staying with him—but Mrs. Stainville never left him!"

After a few more anecdotes in the same style from Mrs. Morton, and remarks *equally judicious,* the ladies found themselves at the door of the parsonage, where, after many expressions of thanks from Emily to her companion for any trouble she might have given, they parted.

Emily found Dr. Stanmore quietly sitting over a Greek tragedy in his little library: he had, as it was his custom on such occasions, which indeed were very far from frequent, sitten up till she returned.—"Are you not gone to bed, yet?" said Emily, running up to him, and embracing him.—"No, my child," replied he, "not till I have seen you safely returned—but come," continued he, smiling, "sit down by me, and tell me all you have done, and all you have seen, for you look pleased."—Emily then told her little history with youthful warmth, dwelling with peculiar eagerness on her account of her new acquaintance.—"I am glad thou hast been amused," said Dr. Stanmore, "young people should be so; and, indeed, could I procure thee more amusements than thou hast, I would most willingly do it—for it is an invariable maxim with me, that to give what is called *the world* its just value, we should at some time of our life have known it; we are then less likely to sigh after its imaginary charms, or to consider its follies in too strong and too melancholy a light.—Mrs. Stainville I have heard always highly spoken of as a very superiour woman, and, indeed, remember (as she mentioned to you) to have seen her at her husband's, but it is long ago—to your acquaintance with such a woman as I imagine Mrs. Stainville to be, should she indeed wish to improve it, I can see no objection."—Emily's countenance expressed the delight this account gave her.—"Heaven bless thee!" said Dr. Stanmore, with the kindest expression of tenderness—"I love to see thee look gay—thou art often too much otherwise—but it is late; good night, my child, and all good angels guard thee!"

Chapter 24

MRS. STAINVILLE'S PROMISED VISIT at the parsonage was, as it may be supposed, impatiently expected by Emily.—She rose even earlier than usual that day, decorated the flower-pots, which she constantly placed in profusion over every part of the house, with peculiar attention; her own dress, too, was more carefully attended to than usual, although, in this respect, little trouble was either necessary or possible; for the simple style of dress, which, as becoming her situation, she had adopted, while it spared both time and expense, seemed but to heighten the native beauty and dignity of her figure.—At eleven, Emily was prepared to receive her visitor, but twelve, one, and even two o'clock, their usual hour of dinner at the parsonage, came, but no Mrs. Stainville.—This, as it seemed to Emily, accorded so ill with the flattering expression of impatience to see her again, in which Mrs. Stainville had been lavish, that she thought there must have been some mistake, and that some other day was intended for her visit.—"Fine ladies," said Dr. Stanmore, smiling, "of which order I take Mrs. Stainville to be, never know hours—she will come by and by, I make no doubt.—In the meantime, we might as well have our dinner brought."—The maid at the instant was actually, unbidden, bringing in the dinner, it being so much past the usual hour, when a carriage was heard driving up to the house; on which, setting down the dish she had in her hand on a table in the passage, she flew to open the door—Emily was there almost as soon—Mrs. Stainville, immediately perceiving her own blunder, put up both her hands to her face.—"I am ashamed of myself," said she, "I know not how I could come so late—I waited for the carriage—I am always early—but I must insist on your going to dinner, and not minding me;—nay, if you would allow me to sit down with you, I can't say how hungry I am—this is the only hour at which one ever *ought* to dine."—Dr. Stanmore saying, "*she* certainly must command," led her into their parlour to a plain neat dinner.—From his table profusion and luxury were indeed equally banished; but every real comfort was to be found at it, which moderation could desire.

Notwithstanding her *hunger,* Mrs. Stainville ate little—but she knew precisely the excuse, that was to be made for her want of appetite—threw all on the delicacy of her health—longed to eat more—then the comfort of the rooms—the freshness of the air! sweetness of the flowers!—everything was *enchanting*!—in short, she was determined to be pleased, and *to please;* which latter determination no one knew better how to support, when she chose it, and *while* she chose it, than herself.—Formed for the world, Mrs. Stainville was all that *the world* required a woman should be, to excite both admiration and interest.—Her understanding was of sufficient depth for *the world*—her sentiments and feelings, such as might sympathise with those of others, without making too strong, or too lasting an impression on her own mind, ever materially to affect her happiness—her figure was tall, graceful, and well proportioned, and the natural expression of her countenance soft and pleasing, with somewhat of a languid cast; which, in order to render still more interesting, she sometimes, it must be confessed, heightened to a degree bordering on affectation. Her education had been rather strict than moral, as her father, a professed freethinker, preached the doctrine of plenary indulgence for all transgressions, while attention to appearances was properly maintained, and no established form violated; which last he considered as merely intended to keep fools in awe, and allow wiser people to profit by.

Her mother, on the contrary, *meant* to be a warm advocate for real virtue, and true religion: but as she always made her *own* virtue, and her *own* religion, the standard and prototype, from which no possible deviation was to be admitted, and had herself a very limited understanding, it happened, unfortunately, that in all arguments, disquisitions, and disputes on these subjects with her husband, which were extremely frequent, she was constantly defeated.—He considered her, indeed, much as a wig-maker does his block, a something on which he might display to advantage the proofs of his talents; and on all occasions, when he wished to shine, and set forth his favourite tenets, he would purposely excite the poor good soul to begin the unequal combat, in which she was certain to be foiled, and generally left the room in a flood of tears, while he, with a cold sarcastic laugh, strutted about triumphant.—Mrs. Stainville was their only child, and the darling of her father, who spared neither trouble nor expense in her education; his particular care and pride being to render her just what *he thought* a woman should be, the very reverse of her mother, whom he had married in early youth, at a moment of passion, and despised ever after as a fool.—Nothing, therefore, ever gave him greater satisfaction, than the offer of Mr. Stainville's hand for his daughter; who, being a Roman Catholic, and otherwise, in reality, an unexceptionable match, afforded him an opportunity of plaguing his wife, humbling what he called her absurd bigotry, showing his own superiour power, and indulging in what he considered as a proof of his liberal and unprejudiced opinions.—Mrs. Stainville had profited, as may be supposed, by the education she had received, and through life conveniently suited the doctrines of her father (to whom she had always looked up with a species of veneration) to her own taste and purposes.

The dinner being over at Dr. Stanmore's, Mrs. Stainville expressed much impatience to see the garden; it looked, she said, "so charming, the shrubs flourished with such peculiar luxuriance!"—"To the vicinity of the sea," said Dr. Stanmore, "and Emily's care, its chief merits are owing—your walk will not fatigue you."—Saying this, they all then proceeded into the little garden, where, throwing herself negligently on a bench overshadowed by the thick branches of a lime, then in full blossom, Mrs. Stainville, having requested of Emily and Dr. Stanmore to sit by her, descanted, with no small degree of eloquence, on the charms of quiet and retirement.—She then suddenly recollected, that she had appointed a friend of hers to call upon her that morning, "and it is now above an hour past the time," said she, taking out her watch, "there is no help for these things—she will wait, and I must, with your permission," turning to Emily, "settle some time for my seeing you again."—Emily looked towards Dr. Stanmore, whose countenance expressed only signs of approbation.—Various plans were then alternately started and rejected by Mrs. Stainville; at last it was agreed, that she should come in her carriage the second day following, and take Emily home with her, to pass the day.—Thus began an intimacy, which, in its consequences, materially influenced the future tenour of Emily's life.

Volume III

Chapter 25

MRS. STAINVILLE FAILED NOT in her appointment;—with Emily she appeared every moment more and more charmed. As they alighted from the carriage at Mrs. Stainville's door, she stopped—"Will eight o'clock be too late?" said she, taking Emily's hand, "or may I venture to keep you here till that time? The evening will then be cool, and our drive back pleasanter—but you know not," continued she, "what a dull day you are going to pass. I am almost frightened at my own confidence, for proposing such a party to you. I see no company; and except Mrs. Barford, whom, I conclude, you know, there is not a chance of our seeing a creature—she too was doubtful about coming."

Emily, with the sweetest expression of truth and natural politeness, assured her, that she required no other company, but thought herself too happy in being thus honoured by her. Mrs. Stainville then led her into the house—"Such a place!" said she; "an absolute nutshell!—but it is clean, and I think you will find this little room cool, and tolerably comfortable."

The room, indeed, was small, but furnished with a sort of negligent elegance—sofas, chairs, and tables, plain, it is true, but admirably executed—several shelves for books, on which were placed classic authors in various languages—Voltaire, and above all, Rousseau, was conspicuous—one of the tables, in particular, was covered with maps, drawings, prints, books, letters, and letter-cases, innumerable—in one corner of the room stood a piano-forte, and in another a harp. Emily had not been long in the room, before the harp attracted her notice—it was an instrument of which she had often heard, but never had seen. "O! I am a wretched performer," said Mrs.

Stainville, "and the harp is quite out of tune, half the strings wanting. Do you play on the harp, Miss Melville?" Emily replied in the negative. "On the piano-forte, then? for I am sure you are a musician." Emily modestly answered, that she was extremely fond of music, and had received some instruction from an organist, who inhabited the neighbouring town. Mrs. Stainville immediately insisted on her sitting down to the piano-forte; was enchanted with her playing, and with the melody of her voice.—"Half a dozen lessons from *Spinetti,*" she exclaimed, "would make you perfect! The simplicity of style, in which you sing too, *I* delight in! It is just as English should be sung; but how you would sing Italian!"—

In this manner, what with music, conversation on various subjects, walking, viewing the arrangements of the house, &c. eight o'clock came to their mutual surprise, although their *tête-à-tête* had been uninterrupted either by Mrs. Barford, or any other company; and after a pleasant drive to the parsonage (Mrs. Stainville having insisted on conducting Emily home in person) they parted much charmed with each other.

Mrs. Stainville was not many days without renewing her visits at the parsonage, which shortly became more and more frequent. She was delighted with Emily, and that something, which she thought *romantic,* in thus unexpectedly meeting with a creature so superiour, lodged hitherto in obscurity, added much to the interest, with which she was inspired for her. Dr. Stanmore's conversation, too, was so uncommonly lively; so instructive without pedantry; so improving without harshness; and he contrived to introduce into his discourse, with unaffected gentleness, such encouraging views, such consoling sentiments of the purest religion and morality, that his hearers left him always better pleased with themselves, for having been pleased with him. A love of virtue stole imperceptibly upon them, as vice shrunk abashed from his presence.

Mrs. Stainville had naturally taste sufficient to be sensible, in a great degree, of the charms of such a society, and as nothing then happened to occupy her too versatile mind, or call her off to the pursuit of less rational enjoyments, she made it her sole object to please her new acquaintance, and to convey to their minds a favourable idea of herself.

Mrs. Stainville, as it was before remarked, although she had no depth of knowledge whatever, was by no means ignorant on literary subjects. She had heard them continually agitated while living with her father, before her marriage, and afterward with her husband, who was uncommonly well-informed, and who took a pride in *his* wife's appearing to advantage in the society he had chosen for himself, which consisted chiefly of a few men of learning and information, who thought it worth their while, in consideration of his hospitable house, and excellent table, to give him a portion of their time, and to conform to many rules and formalities peculiar to his mode of living.

Mr. Stainville was of an ancient Roman Catholic family, proud of his descent, and jealous of the diminution of consequence, which he knew he must undergo by living in the world, while his religion was a bar to every avenue of power or aggrandizement, to which his very considerable fortune would otherwise have allowed him to aspire.

He resided habitually at his family-seat, making, however, occasional visits to the Continent, where he had relations settled, some in France, and some in Italy. This he considered as diversifying his otherwise too monotonous life; but the difference was, in reality, less sensible than might have been supposed, as the same formal style and apparatus followed him, wherever he went; and so far from amusing himself with the diversity of manners of other nations, he suffered no individual to keep company with him, but such as would conform exactly to his own. Mrs. Stainville had accompanied her husband on several of these journeys, which he had continued to make for some years after their marriage, but had by no means participated in his undeviating partiality to his own habits. At Paris she acquired that well-bred ease of manner peculiar to French women, and their elegance of dress was adopted, and afterward constantly adhered to by her. In Italy everything rendered her an enthusiast. Sculpture, painting, music, the enchanting climate, the diversified scenes which nature presented to the view, from the grandeur of the Alps and Apennines, to the quiet and luxuriant plains of Lombardy—for all by turns she was passionate, and had always returned to England with regret; a regret for which, however, she, in some degree, comforted herself, by *sentimentally* exhaling in the silent groves of Harberry, sometimes alone, and at other times more to her satisfaction, when chance threw some *sympathetic soul* in her way. But she always knew precisely how far these flights of fancy might be indulged, without offending the opinions of the world, or giving even the slightest degree of umbrage to her husband, whose vanity, indeed, rendered him little subject to suspicion.

On the death of Mr. Stainville she determined on the most rigorous observance of every form established on those occasions. She was left by him with discretionary power of inhabiting any one of his houses, of which he had several, the family mansion not excepted; and a jointure of three thousand a year, beside a small estate wholly at her own disposal. Thither she immediately retired, formally relinquishing to the next heir all further rights and pretensions to the other houses. This place had long been called *her farm,* and had, with Mr. Stainville's concurrence and approbation, been ornamented and embellished with much taste. At this farm, and in almost total solitude, Mrs. Stainville had passed above eighteen months, when her acquaintance with Emily first commenced. The period of remaining there was, in her own mind, fixed to two years, at the expiration of which time she had determined again to go abroad: but as she thought it by no means necessary to entrust the world (notwithstanding her respect for it) exactly with all her thoughts and intentions; and as she conceived the appearance of retirement and solitude, situated as she was, to be particularly *interesting;* she forbore speaking of future plans, and talked of herself rather as having given up the world, and wishing to dedicate the remainder of her days to *sentimental retirement.* To the ball, where she had first seen Emily, she had been *forced,* most *unwillingly,* but *never* knew how to resist the solicitations of her friends, and hated not *always* to give way in trifles, which others were sometimes kind enough to think of consequence, where *she* was concerned. But never, she would say, was her complaisance so repaid to her as on the present occasion, since it had afforded her an opportunity of making *such* an acquaintance as Emily.

Mrs. Stainville had, when she chose it, not only the power of accommodating herself to the dispositions of those, whom she wished to please, but of almost becoming, for the time, everything they most approved; and Dr. Stanmore's maturer judgment was scarcely less biased in her favour, as their intimacy increased, than Emily's youth and inexperience. Scarcely a day passed now but Mrs. Stainville came to the parsonage, where she frequently remained, ordering her carriage to fetch her again at night. She read, conversed, and walked with them, and partook of all their little amusements. Sometimes, in return, she would ask of Dr. Stanmore leave to carry Emily home with her. When at the parsonage, she often accompanied Emily on her visits to the neighbouring cottagers, listened to their tale of gratitude for the blessing they enjoyed in their pastor, and was lavish in her charitable donations, on the slightest appearance of distress among them.

She inquired, with interest, of Dr. Stanmore, into the particulars of Emily's real situation, and shed unfeigned tears at his affecting recital of the melancholy history of her parents, and the unprotected state, in which she had been left by her numerous relations. Having thus, by degrees, paved the way, Mrs. Stainville ventured to hint to Dr. Stanmore an idea, which had early, on her acquaintance with Emily, offered itself to her imagination; this was no other, than to obtain leave of him, to allow her to take Emily abroad with her. Her health, she said, obliged *her* to pass the next winter out of England, and seek a milder climate. Dr. Stanmore paused.—"Nay," continued Mrs. Stainville, "I will *engage* on your summons, should I even wish to stay longer than a year myself, to bring back Emily to you. You will not refuse? It will be so delightful to me. May be of some advantage to her. I have not, however, even mentioned my plan to Emily, nor shall I, if I cannot obtain your consent, be assured."—"You are all kindness and attention," said Dr. Stanmore, gently pressing her hand—"forgive a moment's hesitation," continued he, with a sigh—"but be assured of one thing, that I shall make no *terms* with one to whom I trust my Emily; nor would wish, by any means, to confine you as to time. I am indeed aware of the many advantages Emily would have in your society, and of the delight she would experience in the course of such a journey; nor shall I ever oppose what I think conducive to her welfare or happiness. Previously, however, to a final determination, I shall think it a duty, to inform some few of her relations of this intended step. It is more than probable, that my letters, like the many I have already written to them, will remain unanswered, in which case I shall not long withhold my consent to your flattering request, but take upon myself the authority, as Heaven knows I feel the tenderness, of a father." As he uttered these last words, his voice trembled, and his eyes involuntarily filling with tears, he gently waved his hand and left the room.

Chapter 26

AS DR. STANMORE HAD PROPHESIED, the letters which he wrote to Sir Thomas Melville, and some other of Emily's relations, remained unanswered. Sir Thomas, indeed, under the *laudable* pretence of his health then being in too weak a state, to venture the possibility of any sudden shock, or the least pressure of business, was never suffered to open a letter; and Lady Melville, (then living) to whom all letters whatever, addressed to her husband, were carried, took care, on this occasion, that *he* should not even know of the application. Such pains, indeed, had she taken, to spread the belief among Sir Thomas's relations of his son's never having been married to Emily's mother, whom she pretended had been discovered to be the daughter of a low adventurer, and herself a worthless abandoned creature, that this infamous story was generally received by them; and having once gained ground, no one of them had taken the trouble to inquire further into it. Dr. Stanmore's character, it should have seemed, would have been a sufficient evidence, to contradict these falsehoods; but he was at a distance, little known to them, and believed to have been himself imposed on by the art of Emily's mother, or to have conceived a mere doating fondness for the child; and their indifference, indeed, on the subject, made them blindly follow the idea first taken up by the head of their family, whom many of them, for obvious reasons, feared to disoblige.

The delight which Emily experienced, on the first intimation of a plan so calculated to gratify her every wish, and on a prospect of entertainment so wholly beyond her utmost expectations, may be partly imagined. But in addition to the lively curiosity, and eager search after novelty, common to youth, Emily possessed a thinking mind, and already a considerable share of information; this intended journey, therefore, conveyed to her imagination not only the idea of agreeable variety and change of scene, but of peculiar satisfaction, in having it in her power to compare the present state of the countries into which she was going, with all she had read of them, and collected from Dr. Stanmore's discourse and observation. Emily had, indeed, a quickness of perception, and a facility of comprehension, which made her immediately seize the essential points on any subject submitted to her understanding; and to these mental perfections she added an accurate and retentive memory, which had been confirmed by habit, and improved by rational exertion, under the tuition of Dr. Stanmore. His favourite occupation had ever been the instruction of his child, and his endeavours exerted to supply, as far as it was possible, the absence of every other master. He would often repeat to himself, "It is only by instilling into her mind sound principles of religion, virtue, and philosophy, that I can hope to render it equal to meet the rough blasts and buffets of a bad world—for, alas! how uncertain her future lot! how invariably has fate hitherto frowned upon her!"

When Dr. Stanmore could no longer expect an answer to his letters from Emily's family, he gave his full and entire consent to the plan proposed by Mrs. Stainville; and from that moment the intended journey became the chief subject of conversation among them.

Mrs. Stainville, whose visits at the parsonage had been for some time still more frequent, employed most of the evenings in reading, particularly French, in which she excelled; and theatrical subjects were chosen by her to improve, or rather perfect, Emily's pronunciation, who was already far advanced in the knowledge of that language, having, when a child, been sent by Dr. Stanmore's care to a day-school, set up in the neighbouring town by excellent French teachers. An uncommonly good ear, joined to the facility natural to children in acquiring a language, had shortly enabled her to speak with fluency, and the more elaborate part was afterward followed up by Dr. Stanmore, an accurate and profound grammarian, whose knowledge and researches had been by no means confined to the ancient languages.

Thus several weeks passed to their mutual satisfaction; but as the time of her departure drew near, Emily felt her heart sink at the idea of leaving her old friend, and only real protector. She had at first considered the bright side alone of the pleasing prospect, so unexpectedly opened to her view; and as in making the little preparations for her journey, or in the different conversations on the subject, Dr. Stanmore had never touched, with the slightest expression of regret, on his own loss, but, on the contrary, encouraged every idea that could tend to heighten the gratification she might hope from the intended plan, the painful image of absence from what is most dear to us, then new to her mind, had but faintly presented itself.

She now fancied Dr. Stanmore looked unwell, that his spirits were not so good, as he seemed to wish they should appear. In short, a thousand fears seized on her gentle affectionate heart, and she almost wished he had never consented to her going.

On the eve of her departure, her spirits almost wholly failed her, and it required all the well-judged exertions of Dr. Stanmore's kind intelligence, to support them. As she looked at him, the traces of sickness and age seemed to her never before to have been so evident. "Oh! were I to think this a last parting," said she to herself, "the world could not now tear me from him! kindest, best of mortals!" And on the morning following, when Mrs. Stainville's well-dressed courier was heard, galloping up to the door, loudly cracking his whip, to announce the approach of his lady, Emily sunk almost lifeless on Dr. Stanmore's bosom; then raising her head, and drawing herself a little back, she fixed her eyes on him with the most affecting expression of anxiety. "Fear not, my child," said he, reading her thoughts, "I *will* live to see thee again." The carriage was by this time at the door, and Dr. Stanmore, fearful of increasing her uneasiness by betraying all the pain he felt himself at this separation, led Emily gently forward, and after holding her some time pressed to his bosom, unable to speak, put her into the carriage. Mrs. Stainville, seeing how much she was affected, attempted not foolishly to *console* her, but taking her hand, which she kindly pressed, begged of her not to restrain herself. After a time, Emily turning to Mrs. Stainville said, "I beg pardon, madam, I am wretched company!"—"I judge not thus," replied she, "such marks of sensibility can but endear you to *me:* but, I insist on it, all constraint must be banished between us. When your spirits are somewhat recovered, we will then talk, or not, as we may be disposed: at present, I shall take my book." Saying this, she drew a small volume of Rousseau from among a number of other books, with which the pockets of the carriage were filled, and leaning backward, appeared wholly occupied with what she was reading, leaving Emily to pursue her own train of thoughts in liberty.

The separate meditations were, however, after no very long time, interrupted by a violent scream from Mademoiselle Jaqueline (Mrs. Stainville's new French *femme-de-chambre*)—"What is the matter," said Mrs. Stainville, starting.—"*Ah! mon Dieu! nous allons perir,*" exclaimed Mademoiselle Jaqueline. Emily, perceiving no danger near, was all astonishment.—"What is the matter," repeated Mrs. Stainville, in rather a more authoritative tone than before. No explanation still from Mademoiselle Jaqueline, who then sat squeezed up in the corner of the carriage, with one hand before her eyes, and the other extended towards the coach window. It was at last discovered, to the no small amusement of Mrs. Stainville and Emily, that Mademoiselle Jaqueline's terrour had proceeded from the carriage, then descending a hill, on which there was a slight declivity, having gone a little on one side.—"Upon my word, Mademoiselle Jaqueline," said Mrs. Stainville, "these freaks of yours must not return, or our journey will be strangely disturbed."—"*Comment!*" replied Mademoiselle Jaqueline, "*Madame n'a pas peur en voiture!*"—"Not I," said Mrs. Stainville.—"*Mon Dieu!*" continued Mademoiselle Jaqueline, "*Madame la marquise, que je viens de quitter, crioit toujours encore plus fort que moi, toutes les fois que la voiture panchoit seulement de côté. J'y suis si habituée que.*"—"*Il faut vous deshabituer, Jaqueline,*" said Mrs. Stainville, with as much gravity as she could command, "*ou vous courez risque de crier toute seule, avec nous.*—For you, my dear Miss Melville," continued she, turning to Emily, "are, if I mistake not, as little subject to fears of this sort as myself."—"Indeed," replied she, "I am not subject to *fear* of any sort; but in that *I* have little merit!"—A resigned, but dignified expression of melancholy, overspread by her countenance, as she uttered these last words, which escaped not Mrs. Stainville; but willing to draw her off to more cheerful ideas, she took no further notice of what she had said, than by a kind look of sympathy, and then began talking on other subjects. Emily by degrees entered into conversation—she was void of affectation, and always *willing* to be pleased. The variety of objects, as they travelled on, served considerably to dissipate the gloom which hung over Emily's mind, for to her all was new; yet never for an instant did her attention remit to her absent friend; her first care, on her arrival at every destined post-town, was to inquire for letters, and to dispatch hers to Dr. Stanmore; to whom, according to agreement, she sent a faithful and detailed journal of all that befell her, of all she saw, all she felt, and of the various sources of amusement or interest, that occurred during the course of her absence.

They stopped merely a few days in London, which were passed chiefly at the *hôtel* where they lodged, as Mrs. Stainville wished to avoid the trouble of unnecessary visits, being impatient to arrive at Paris. There she proposed, with much idea of satisfaction to herself, passing at least six weeks; and it being then only the very beginning of September, she considered this arrangement as no way interfering with her plan of spending the winter at Naples.

The voyage and journey were performed without accident; and Emily had the comfort, a very few days after her arrival at Paris, of receiving a very kind and consoling letter from Dr. Stanmore, written with the warmth and interest of true friendship. He entered into details of all she was to see, and pointed out to her the different objects of curiosity, most worthy of observation, that she was likely to meet with; exhorting her at the same time to profit of the advantage fortune had thrown in her way, by thus offering the means, not only of improving her taste, and enlarging her ideas, but adding to a well-informed mind that knowledge of the world and human nature, which travelling, and the habit of conversing with persons of different nations and variety of character, alone can give. He then added, after the most affectionate expressions of anxiety for her safety and welfare—"against what is called the *allurements* of the world I need not guard my Emily—too well, my child, I know thee!—but against thy own too tender, susceptible heart!—remember well my lessons!—and now *wrong* me not, by feeling a regret too keen at this absence, on my account:—for how much have *I* not to thank Heaven, while I enjoy the thoughts of thy gratification and pleasure, and the future hope of thy return!"

Chapter 27

MRS. STAINVILLE, HAVING ALREADY PASSED many months at different times at Paris, when abroad with her husband, who had some near relations established there—persons of the first rank and distinction, had only on her arrival to renew her visits to them, and was immediately received into several of those select and intimate societies, which form the charm of a Parisian life, and to which it is by no means easy for foreigners to obtain admittance. Private boxes at all the theatres were instantly at her command for every night in the week, and pressed on her acceptance by her different friends.

The ladies were all *enchantées* to see her again, and hoped she meant to *passer au moins l'hiver* with them. In short, Mrs. Stainville was caressed, flattered, *embrassée,* and *recherchée,* by all the Parisian ladies of her acquaintance, and the men were universally polite and obsequious to her.—"*Mais qui est cette jeune personne?—une parente apparemment?—elle est charmante!—mais charmante! belle comme un Ange!*"—were the exclamations generally uttered, and loudly repeated on perceiving Emily, who always modestly stood apart, while the first effusions of mutual joy took place on the appearance of every former acquaintance of Mrs. Stainville's.

Emily was, indeed, *charmante,* and her extraordinary beauty excited additional admiration, from the novelty of her appearance among a people *then* accustomed to a stated form and precision of dress, from which little deviation was in general admitted. The perfect symmetry and natural grace of Emily's form were heightened by the simplicity of her attire, and her fine hair unconfined and hanging loosely in natural ringlets, partly over her forehead, partly tied upon the back of her head, or flowing over her shoulders (a mode she had adopted originally merely for convenience, and which, except on particular occasions where form was required, Mrs. Stainville insisted on her continuing) gave her, as they said, "*l'air d'une belle statue;*" and as such, even the most insensible gazed at her with surprise. She was followed by admiring crowds in the public walks, and wherever she appeared, and generally went by the appellation of "*la belle Anglaise.*"

Emily was sought after by all Mrs. Stainville's most particular acquaintance. Parties were made purposely to show her to others. In short, nothing was so much talked of as *la belle Anglaise;* and her appearance had made more *sensation* than that of any other stranger, in that generally frequented metropolis, where something is always the wonder of one day, and forgotten the next.

Mrs. Stainville was flattered by the attentions shown to her young friend and *protegée,* and felt a complacent satisfaction at what she considered as a proof of her own judgment and penetration, setting apart the interest, which, according to her character, she then really felt for Emily herself. Sometimes, indeed, her satisfaction on this subject was not *quite* so complete, when, as it now and then happened, in their walks on the *boulevards,* or in the gardens about Paris, she heard muttered among the many, who actually followed them, purposely to gaze at Emily, after the usual compliment—"*ce sont des étrangères: apparement que c'est sa fille!*" (pointing towards Mrs. Stainville)—but Mrs. Stainville was easily put into good humour again, by the constant repetition she failed not to hear in all *good company,* of—"*Mais je vous trouve rajeunie et embellie, jamais je ne vous ai vu si bien!*"—to which, being the remark of persons who *must* be the better judges, she gave full credit.

In this manner, lodged with Mrs. Stainville in one of the best *hôtels,* engaged in a round of elegant amusements, managed without fatigue or hurry, which at Paris even in the gayest circles it was possible to avoid, did Emily pass her time; yet, though every way pleased with the scene before her, she remained unintoxicated by its charms, considering and enjoying it only as a gay vision, the performance of which could not long exist to her.

Emily had now passed above a month at Paris, without having been otherwise distinguished by the men, than by expressions of general admiration. Among those, indeed, whom they saw most frequently, everyone had *chacun sa chacune,* although this *appropriation,* from the perfect decorum of manners always observed between the parties, was rarely perceivable to those unaccustomed to Parisian manners. It was, moreover, decided, that Emily was not "*coquette;*" and whether or not she were "*sensible,*" as an unmarried woman, no Frenchman *de bonne compagnie* would attempt to discover—*honour* forbad that.

It therefore commonly happened, that the attention of the men, in the societies they frequented, were more habitually directed to Mrs. Stainville (still really handsome) than to Emily. There were indeed, as usual, many English at Paris, but none that were particularly known to Mrs. Stainville; who, as she said, "not going abroad to hunt after her own countrymen, however *charming* they might be at home," gave a general order to the porter, on her arrival at Paris, to admit only French visitors.

When one evening at the *Marquise de Bellevue's,* where she was to sup, as Mrs. Stainville was in the midst of a conversation with the Marquise, on the subject of a new metaphysical publication, she heard her suddenly exclaim—"*Ah! vous voilà donc de retour.*"—And, on turning her eyes towards the door, where the *Marquise's* were directed, she saw a tall genteel-looking young man, whose figure was wholly unknown to her, advancing into the room. The Marquise got up, and went forward to him, extending both her hands, which he separately and respectfully kissed, bowing gracefully several times to her, and then round to the rest of the company.—"*Mais vous êtes bien aimable de revenir,*" said she, "*nous ne vous attendions pas de si tôt—convenez en, vous vous êtes ennuyé à Vienne?*"—Then turning to Mrs. Stainville—"*vous connaissez surement le petit Raymond, vôtre compatriote.*" Mrs. Stainville replied in the negative—"*il faut donc que je vous le présente—c'est le meilleur enfant du monde!—venez, Milor, que je vous présente.*"—The proper bows, and proper compliments for the occasion, were then immediately made on each side.

Lord Raymond had a gentle, and rather melancholy cast of countenance, which instantly interested Mrs. Stainville in his favour. She invited him to make her party at cards, and talked much to him during supper, where he was placed next to her; but, though he was perfectly polite, and listened with complaisance to all she said, he spoke little himself, and his chief attention seemed directed to Emily, who sat opposite to them—his admiration was evident, and, though his looks were soft and respectful, his eyes were often so intently fixed on Emily, that she could not meet them without a blush; this occasioned her seldom to look that way, and gave him a still better opportunity of examining charms, which to him appeared beyond any he had yet seen.

Supper was no sooner over, than Lord Raymond drew towards Emily, and stood near her for some time, occasionally conversing with indifferent persons, withheld by a certain awe, with which the unaffected modesty of her manner inspired him, from addressing her directly; at last, however, seeing her seated, he ventured to place himself in an empty chair, which stood by her side.

The *Marquise de Bellevue,* whom all this had not escaped, came across the room to Mrs. Stainville, who was at play, and, leaning over her shoulder, in a half whisper, communicated to her her remarks—"*le voilà amoureux de vôtre belle Demoiselle,*" said she, "*mais savez vous que ce seroit le plus joli parti du monde pour elle—il faut que nous arrangions cela ensemble—il est riche, et n'a personne à consulter que lui même!*"—Mrs. Stainville looked round and smiled; she had no determined project of captivation for herself in the present case, and felt rather pleased at the idea of such a conquest for her friend—"*Mais vous y allez bienvite, ma chère amie,*" said she, laughing.—The Marquise heard her not; she had flown to receive some late comer, whom she discovered at the moment in the anteroom, and thought no more that evening, either about Emily, or her *aimable* Lord Raymond, whose unexpected return had so delighted her.

Chapter 28

THE NEXT MORNING Lord Raymond failed not to present himself at Mrs. Stainville's door; and, as she on her side had not failed to take off the before-mentioned general *interdiction,* by specifying to the porter an exception in his favour, he was admitted.

Lord Raymond had not been long in the room, when Mrs. Stainville's servant coming up to her, asked if her carriage were still to wait; on this he instantly got up to take his leave—"I beg you would not think of going," said Mrs. Stainville, "we are in no sort of hurry, and, indeed, I expect the *Abbé de Bellevue,* who promised to escort us this morning. Perhaps, my lord, should you have nothing better to do, you would not dislike to be of our party, as the day is fine?"—Lord Raymond bowed assent—"At least," continued she, "to the *Tuilleries,* where we mean to walk—after that I am going to show my young friend here *Notre-Dame,* which, as your lordship must have seen twenty times, I will excuse you."—He never had seen Notre-Dame, and begged to be allowed to accompany them there also. At this instant the *Abbé de Bellevue* flew into the room, passing with precipitation the servant who was announcing him—"*Mille et mille pardons, Madame, je suis honteux!—je le vois, je me suis fait attendre!*"—"Not at all," she replied; "you have done me a favour, for, had you come sooner, and been more exact to your appointment, I should have been deprived of the honour of seeing my Lord Raymond."—"*Ah, Milor!*" exclaimed the *Abbé,* on perceiving Lord Raymond, "*charmé de vous revoir!—rien de si triste, que Vienne, à ce que l'on dit—la société du monde la plus choisie, à la vérité—mais d'une tristesse! d'une monotonie!—c'est vôtre païs, par example, qui est beau!—je regrette encore le temps, que j'y ai passé!—j'étois bien jeune alors!*"—"I have been little in London," said Lord Raymond, carelessly, "our country-seats, are, I think, pleasant."—"*Rien de si charmant!*" said the *Abbé,* pulling up his collar, as he looked full at himself in a large glass placed over the chimney—"*rien de si charmant!*" still looking at himself.—"But, *l'Abbé,*" continued Lord Raymond, half smiling—"have not our English country-seats some of the faults of which you accuse Vienna?"—"*On trouve moyen d'y remédier,*" said the *Abbé,* turning his head round, and casting a soft, significant glance at Mrs. Stainville, who coloured, and, as it seemed, wishing to put an end to this conversation, got up instantly, saying that it was late, and that they ought to set out. Lord Raymond, who was standing by Mrs. Stainville, offered her his arm, and the *Abbé* skipped up to Emily for the same purpose with a forward familiar air, undaunted by the extreme gravity of her looks at the moment; and as he put her into the carriage, squeezed her hand with so little reserve, that she withdrew it with a marked look of disapprobation. Emily continued silent and thoughtful for some time.—What passed just before they had left the *hôtel* had not escaped her quickness. She wondered how Mrs. Stainville could suffer, nay, as she often did, *encourage* such a coxcomb as the *Abbé*—for it was by no means the first time she had been struck with the freedom of his manner, and the familiar ease with which he often treated her friend. During their walk in the Tuilleries, Emily, when she spoke, wishing to avoid the impertinence of the *Abbé,* addressed herself chiefly to Lord Raymond, which the *Abbé* perceiving, and never interpreting anything to his own disadvantage, concluded was owing to its being "*une affaire arrangée*" between them.

When they arrived at the church of *Notre-Dame,* Emily was struck with the grandeur of that venerable pile, and anxious to examine the objects of curiosity, which it contained; but on this subject she procured little assistance from her companions. Lord Raymond seemed surprised, that she took the trouble even of looking at any of the objects separately—"There is nothing the least worth seeing here, I believe," said he: "the dark gloom of the church, indeed, is fine."—This Mrs. Stainville took up, and began descanting on one of her most favourite themes, *the charms of melancholy.* Lord Raymond listened to her with attention, agreeing in all she said—and the *Abbé* being engaged in conversation with a person, who had accidentally entered the church at the same time with themselves, Emily had full liberty quietly to observe every thing there worthy of remark.

On their return home, when they were alone in the carriage, Emily, who still bore in mind the *Abbé's* looks to Mrs. Stainville, took an opportunity, after complaining of his impertinence to herself, of expressing in general terms her dislike to the freedom of his manner.—"You are a child, my dear," said Mrs. Stainville, gently tapping her on the cheek; "the *Abbé* meant nothing earthly by what you call *impertinence*—and as to his manner, he is spoiled—that's all—His aunt, the *Marquise de Bellevue,* perfectly idolizes him—'tis enough to turn any head; besides, he is universally admired, and has an uncommonly pretty figure. I formerly saw him in England," continued she, after a *hem* or two—"he came to our house in the country, invited by Mr. Stainville.—I wonder I never happened to tell you." At this moment the carriage stopped at the door of the *hôtel*—Mrs. Stainville darted instantly out, and running upstairs, called to Emily, saying, there was but just time for them to dress, as the lady she expected, who was to carry them out to dinner, she knew was very exact.

Emily retired to her own room, but not immediately to dress: *her* dress, indeed, required little time, and she felt not at that moment disposed to any unnecessary preparations of the kind. The occurrences of the day had left a sort of unpleasant impression on her mind, which rendered her careless of indifferent objects; yet, on consideration, as she was naturally most unsuspicious, she attributed this rather to her own want of knowledge of the world, than to any other cause.

The evening was passed at the *Marquise de Bellevue's,* with whom Mrs. Stainville was become almost inseparable. *She* was her oracle, and nothing was done without consulting her—*her* opinion, which was always decided, whatever the subject, was received as a law, not only, indeed, by Mrs. Stainville, but by the whole of her society, to which an obsequious deference to whatever *she* uttered was the most unerring passport. The *Marquise de Bellevue's* society was at once one of the most brilliant, as well as one of the most numerous in Paris.—She was herself a *bel esprit*—corresponded with Voltaire—yet admitted of the *magique* of Rousseau's eloquence—and (professing herself on all subjects free from prejudice) she admired Hume, who, she said, was "*le philosophe des ames integres*"—a sentence nobody ever understood, but that everybody admired. The Marquise was *d'aillieurs,* a woman of the first rank, possessed a large income, and occupied one of the finest and most elegant *hôtels* in Paris. Her manner perfectly corresponded with the brilliancy of her situation. She was, in short, a complete *Frenchwoman,* and had regularly passed through that discipline, and taken those *degrees,* long established, and strictly adhered to in French society by all persons of distinction. She had quitted her nursery and her *bonne* for a convent, where she received her education—was married at fourteen to a man she never before had seen—passed the first two years after her marriage under the immediate care and inspection of her *belle-mère,* and having then *duly* produced a first-born son and heir, was launched out into the world to use her own discretion. The *happy pair,* then, after living for nearly twenty years together upon the best footing, *à la française,* seldom meeting in their own house, except by chance on the great stair-case, when they always *kindly* inquired after each other's health, and passed on to their separate engagements, found out that, in spite of the liberty mutually allowed, they should live still more agreeably apart; and *Madame, en conséquence,* by agreement remained in possession of the *grand hôtel,* where she saw her own society, while *Monsieur* retired to the *petit hôtel,* with a favourite *figurante,* where he lived in that expensive style of luxury and *recherche* known only at Paris.

When Mrs. Stainville and Emily entered the room, the first object that presented itself to their view was the *Abbé,* seated, with an air of triumph, by a young lady, who, having just glanced at them as they entered, and risen with an affected air of *nonchalance* from her chair, into which she almost instantly dropped again without saluting them, continued listening to him.—"*Vous êtes étonnée, n'est-ce pas, mon coeur, de voir Madame de Vermont ici?*" said the *Marquise* in a whisper, as she came up to Mrs. Stainville, but loud enough for Emily to hear—"*mais c'est mon neveu qui l'a voulû,*" continued she, shrugging up her shoulders, "*Il me gouverne, comme vous savez!*"—A closer whisper then followed, the last words of which only reached her ear (an exclamation from the *Marquise*)—"*Oh! elle est coquette comme on ne l'est pas!*"—Mrs. Stainville seemed to receive what was said to her with indifference, and shortly afterward sat down to cards. Emily, after remaining for a little time by her, looked for a place in another part of the room, where there were persons not at play.

Lord Raymond soon afterward entered the apartment. His eyes instantly sought Emily, but he went not up to her, although there was an empty chair by her, but stood carelessly leaning with his back against the side of the room, sometimes *answering,* rather than talking, when anyone happened to address him. Towards the end of the evening *Madame de Vermont,* who had without interruption been playing off all the *graces* of affectation, started up, saying, she was "*perdue*"—the hour of supper at the "*Duchesse de Malbranche's,*" she said, "was come, and she should be too late, *ce que la Duchesse ne pardonne jamais—mais je suis d'une étourderie!*"—The *Abbé,* with a tender glance, signifying *must I lose you,* seized her hand, and screaming out as they swiftly passed the anteroom, "*les gens de Madame de Vermont!*" led her to her carriage.

Lord Raymond, who at last had taken his resolution, was just advancing towards Emily, by whom had still remained the empty chair, when the *Abbé,* quicker than lightning, flew back after having put *Madame de Vermont* into her carriage, and without looking to the right or to the left, darted into the chair which had for the whole evening remained unoccupied—"*à la fin!*" said he, adding in a lower tone some *fade compliment.* Lord Raymond bit his lips in anger, and retired again to his post, all which Emily had not indeed observed; but soon tired of the unmeaning *jargon* of the *Abbé,* she rose, and at the same moment supper was announced. Lord Raymond then advanced, and offering his hand, begged leave to sit by her at supper.—"Are you much acquainted with the *Abbé de Bellevue*?" said Lord Raymond, after they were seated—"I see him often," replied Emily, "but *acquainted* with him I think I never could be."—"I ought not," continued Lord Raymond, his countenance brightening, "for an instant to have supposed it possible! Yet I see him so sought after, and so admired by persons, whom I should so little suspect *such* a being could please, that I am sometimes tempted to doubt my own senses, and believe *white teeth and cherry cheeks irresistible.*"—"You forget," said Emily, smiling, "one half of his *merits,* a more than common share of forwardness and self-sufficiency." Their conversation was at that moment interrupted by the *Marquise,* who called across the table to Lord Raymond to inform her—"*Si on nourissoit les vaches en Angleterre comme en France?*"—Lord Raymond having satisfied her question, continued wholly occupied in conversing with Emily during supper. Her evident contempt of the *Abbé* (whose *white teeth* and *cherry cheeks* had sometimes stood in his way) flattered his vanity, and gave him a higher opinion of her taste. She had at first sight inspired him with admiration; but he now felt a desire to please, and unaccustomed to withstand any impulse of his mind, he sought not to conceal the impression Emily had made on him.

Lord Raymond, from the natural bent of his character, was easily captivated, but difficult to fix. He had been from his cradle nourished in the lap of adulation, reared and cherished by a fond doating mother, who, from the hour of his birth, saw but *him* in the universe.—She had been many years married to her lord, and all hopes of an heir seemed a blessing, that was to be denied them: hence, therefore, having on earth no other cause of complaint, arose all their lamentations—"For whom shall I plant or build! For whom improve my estate!—My interest in the country!—All will perish with me when I die!"—would the earl often exclaim with bitterness. His next heir was a distant relation, of whom he knew little, and for whom he cared less, and his *title,* (*the earldom*) fatal thought! was lost with him. The countess too, in her way, was little less solicitous upon the subject. Should anything happen to her lord, where was her consequence!—Could *she* retire to a melancholy jointure-house, accustomed as she had ever been to the world, to bustle, and to the most brilliant situation!—From Tunbridge to Spa; from Spa to Pyrmont; from Pyrmont to the sea, all was repeatedly tried—in vain—when, shame on foreign assistance! it happened at last, just after the bustle of a contested election, in which the earl had come off victorious, that, in addition to his triumph, a pregnancy was announced to him by his countess, which crowned all his wishes; and in due time a son was born, to the ringing of bells, roasting of oxen, blazing of bonfires, and general rejoicings of his numerous household and tenantry. Expressions of joy and congratulations were, indeed, received from the whole county, where the earl's popularity was much increased by his having, on the late election, triumphed over an upstart ministerial candidate.

The boy was at first but weak and puny; however, the constant exclamations from all who saw it, of "*Lord! what a fine child!—how large and strong for his age!*" comforted in a great degree its doating parents, and more than half persuaded them, that he was indeed of Herculean make.

The earl only lived to see his son emerging from infancy. Lady Raymond, after her husband's death, made the young Lord Raymond her sole care. He was her pride, and the darling object of her fondness. All other interests became indifferent to her, and selfishness and love of rule were (not for the first time) decked with the respectable name of maternal tenderness. *Her ladyship* was one of those persons who always *ask,* but never *take* advice. The whole family were therefore consulted in form, separately and collectively, on the mode of education most proper to be adopted for the young peer; and after listening to them with infinite politeness and attention, her own *predetermined* decision was followed without the smallest deviation, from which, as she was left sole guardian to her son, there was no appeal.

A public school was out of the question. Lord Raymond was *too delicate,* and his mother was convinced, that, whatever the mode adopted, if no expense were spared, his education *must be perfect.* A private tutor was in consequence sought for the young lord, and a set of attendants allotted to his particular service.

After much deliberation, the tutor chosen was a young man of family, a German, who from some disagreement with his relations, desirous to make him enter into ecclesiastic state, had left Vienna, and found it necessary to depend on his talents for bread, as his relations refused all assistance, hoping by these means to reduce him to obedience. He had accidentally been particularly known to an English family, then at Vienna, nearly connected with Lady Raymond's, by whom, on his arrival in England, he had been recommended to her, as a person well suited to the important charge of her son's education.

His manners were gentle, unassuming, and respectful, and being a good classic scholar, and having a considerable degree of knowledge in various branches of science, he was in many respects not ill fitted to the situation; but his character wanted energy, and by continually dwelling on the particular and unfortunate circumstances of his own life, he had weakened the powers of his mind, and rendered himself unequal to the task of forming with propriety that of another; yet the amiable qualities he possessed had so much endeared him to his pupil, that he became in everything fond of imitating him. He copied both his virtues and his faults, and often would fancy himself unhappy, while he sighed he knew not for what. Naturally of an indolent disposition, he preferred being taught *what* to think by another, to the trouble of learning *how* to think for himself.

When he arrived at the age of nineteen, it was judged proper to send Lord Raymond abroad, a measure much recommended by his tutor, who had gained no small degree of influence over Lady Raymond, not so much by flattery, as by his frequent and grateful acknowledgements of the benefits he had received from her; while she, on her side, considering him as her particular choice, placed by her in the situation he then occupied, was persuaded, that he could not err, and that his opinions were but the echo of her own dictates.

Lord Raymond, accompanied by his tutor, (then more in the character of a friend) whose family had at last consented to be reconciled to him, after stopping only a short time at Paris, went immediately to Vienna, where he passed some months; after which, having no inclinations to go on to Italy, particularly as he was obliged to relinquish his companion, then under the obligation of remaining with his relations, he returned to Paris, where he remained for above a year, and, having procured some letters of introduction from Vienna, was received there with particular attentions. Lord Raymond had an uncommonly pretty figure, and a certain negligence of manner, which happened to please. He was in consequence admitted to several societies, on a more intimate footing than is common to his countrymen, particularly at the *Marquise de Bellevue's. She* took him under her immediate protection, called him "*mon petit*," found fault with or praised his dress—told him what he was to do—laughed when he did wrong—"*c'est un enfant!*" she exclaimed—cried him up to the skies on even the slightest proof of merit—introduced him to the young women of her society with an air of familiarity, "*J'en fais les honneurs*"—as a person they *might* receive; and as he appeared to them a person, that they *might* extremely like to receive, he experienced none of that affected neglect, which would probably have effectually kept him at a distance; for, accustomed from his birth to be flattered, soothed, and caressed, the slightest check he received, or the least appearance of reserve or indifference, were considered by him almost as marks of aversion. However, if fame spoke truly, Lord Raymond was not in this case exposed to the possibility of such mistakes, and his conquests were as rapid, as they were uninteresting to himself. He had, on receiving some pressing letters from his mother, returned to England; but he stayed there only a short time, and with her consent, for in her opinion *he* was never wrong, *dawdled* back to Paris, and then again to Vienna, whence he was just returned for the second time, when he first met Emily at the *Marquise de Bellevue's.*

Such had been the life of Lord Raymond, and pleasures and indulgences had been so crowded upon him, that he neither knew their value, nor tasted their enjoyments. He was indeed without vice; but being also without emulation, and without energy, his virtues were at best but passive, and he was little sensible of, or grateful for the advantages of his own situation in life, further than as they enabled him to avoid *trouble.*—*Trouble* was his bane; and as a considerable estate is not managed *wholly* without, he was happy to find his mother still disposed to keep the reins of government in her hands for him; and knowing less now of his own country, than of those in which he had lately resided, he commenced *the lounging traveller;* for in his repeated visits to Paris and Vienna he had no other object, than to avoid that *ennui,* to which all decided enemies of *trouble* are invariably subject, and from which they find it still more difficult to escape.—Sensations far different to any he had yet experienced took place in his breast on the sight of Emily.—For the first time he felt a desire to please, before he was certain that desire was reciprocal.—He became her constant follower and attendant wherever she went; and Mrs. Stainville, by whom, as it may be supposed, his attentions were not unnoticed, never failed to invite him, and give him every encouragement in her power.—She was flattered with the idea of a marriage, which she doubted not would shortly be proposed, so brilliant and advantageous, so everything, it seemed to her, that could be wished for her friend.—Still Lord Raymond spoke not decisively, and a gloom often hung over his countenance, the cause of which Mrs. Stainville was at a loss to comprehend.—The time too drew near for her going into Italy.—She knew not what to think—one day had passed accidentally without their seeing Lord Raymond; and Emily, to Mrs. Stainville's surprise, had shown neither anxiety nor uneasiness; on the contrary, her spirits had on that day seemed better, than often was the case.—"You have been quite gay, my dear," said Mrs. Stainville, as they were returning home at night.—"Yet I fear this effort for you—I know what it is to feel as you do at this moment."—Emily was all astonishment.—"I was not aware," said she, "of being particularly gay; the day has indeed passed very agreeably; but what you mean further, for something you *do* mean, I really cannot guess!"—"Well," continued Mrs. Stainville, "if I am not to be your confidant, it shall be as you please."—"For Heaven's sake!" said Emily with earnestness, "dearest Madam, explain yourself; you seem offended!"—"Not I," said Mrs. Stainville; "but reserve is ever painful, and I suppose Lord Raymond's absence is not indifferent to you." "O!" said Emily, smiling, "is *that* what you mean!"—then, with a more serious air, taking Mrs. Stainville's hand, "I meant no reserve; can I be ungrateful enough to have any with you? on a subject too, on which your kind interest for me can alone make you curious!"—"I do not affect to deny," continued she, "that Lord Raymond's attentions have not been unnoticed by me, or pretend that they are disagreeable to me, but the contrary; yet to pass a day without seeing him, requires *no effort* on my side, nor do I know, that he has ever really entertained one serious thought about me!" "*Not know!*" said Mrs. Stainville, "strange *insensibility*! Is it not evident, that Lord Raymond loves you? Can anyone mistake his sentiments?—few, I believe, would see them with so much indifference!"—Saying this, Mrs. Stainville, folding her arms across her breast, sunk into the corner of her carriage, lost in a *tendre reverie,* and remained silent.

Emily had spoken from the honest openness of her heart, and knew no other language—seeing therefore, that her answers, instead of satisfying, had rather displeased her friend, she attempted not to renew the conversation.

Returned to the *hôtel,* and retired to her apartment, Emily for the first time began seriously to question her own heart on the subject of Lord Raymond; but on the strictest examination, she found nothing there, to contradict what she had said to Mrs. Stainville.

Lord Raymond did not make his appearance, till the next evening, at the *Marquise de Bellevue's.* Emily, who had arrived there early with Mrs. Stainville, received him with natural and unaffected ease—he was graver and more silent even than usual. Mrs. Stainville talked much of her journey to Italy, saying that on that day fortnight, at latest, she should set out.—"So soon?" said Lord Raymond, with a look of some surprise and disappointment.—"Why," replied Mrs. Stainville, "have I not told you this before, and that *the very best* thing you can do is to follow us?"—"I know not," said Lord Raymond, (looking at Emily with a sigh), "whether it be '*the very best*' thing I can do, but it is what I feel the greatest inclination to do."—"*Vous partez! est-il possible!—quitter Paris!—et dans cette saison!—vous milor!*" exclaimed the *Abbé,* who was at the moment walking about, and taking a view of his own person in each of the different looking-glasses, that ornamented the apartment. Then, recollecting himself, with a significant look cast towards Emily, he continued in a softer tone, "*Ah! qui n'en feroit pas autant!*"—He then began to *frêdonner* a French song, the words of which were of his own composition, beginning, "*C'est la beauté qui nous gouverne, &c.*"—Lord Raymond coloured—"*ce que vous dites la est affreux,*" cried the Marquise, "*ne parla pas de départ, vous me désoleriez; je n'ai pas encore osé seulement songer, que je vais la perdre!*" seizing one of Mrs. Stainville's hands, which she *tenderly* pressed, as she crossed the room in her way to meet a lady, at that moment just entering the door—"*Chere Comtesse, que je vous embrasse de tout mon coeur—quand se fera vôtre marriage—rien de si charmant que vôtre fille! Mon neveu,* (making a sign to the *Abbé* to approach) *que je vous le présente.*"—Here the conversation became general on the arrival of more company, and the *afflicting* subject of departure was wholly forgotten for the evening.

In little more than a fortnight, Mrs. Stainville, accompanied by Emily, actually set out for Italy; whither it was agreed that Lord Raymond, who had already ordered his travelling equipage and necessary preparations for the journey, should immediately follow them.—His attentions to Emily had now been so marked, that his sentiments were no longer to be mistaken; and Mrs. Stainville, who thought she saw that high tinge of romance so grateful to her imagination, in his still delaying any open declaration, while she satisfied her strict adherence to propriety, by not inviting him actually to accompany them on their journey, had, without reserve, shown herself every day more and more enchanted with him. "You are," said she to Emily, as they were continuing their route, "the happiest of women; and I rejoice at it from my heart.—Never was there such a being as Lord Raymond!—so different, so superiour to the young men one sees, so, in one word, *perfect.* But you do not, my dear, seem sensible to your own happiness. You, to *my* feelings, have often treated Lord Raymond with indifference, and *always* with reserve. It was but the other day, that you were warmly and openly expressing your satisfaction on the thoughts of shortly seeing Italy, though you knew our journey *must* cause a temporary separation, which I am sure *he* feels severely.—You are indeed strangely insensible!"—"Can you," replied Emily, with much gentleness, "wish my heart deeply engaged to a man, of whose serious intentions I am so uncertain?—and ought I not rather to curb than encourage any growing affection, of which I might be susceptible for Lord Raymond, who, I must think it not impossible, I may never see again?"—"And under such doubt you are composed!—quite composed!—well, such *prudence,*" continued Mrs. Stainville, shrugging up her shoulders, "*at eighteen I* did not possess!"—"Your situation," said Emily, her eyes filling with tears, "was far different from mine—alone and unprotected in the world, *misfortune* has thus early taught *me,* to think perhaps too seriously; for had not one kind friend stretched out his protecting hand to save me, what might not have been my fate!"—"Nay, now you quite affect me, dear Emily," said Mrs. Stainville, embracing her; "do not talk thus—have you not in *me* another friend, whose utmost *wish,* at least, is to serve you?"—"Forgive these tears!" said Emily, endeavouring to recover herself; "they are only an unavoidable tribute to the memory of an unhappy mother!—I know *your* goodness for me, and am not, believe me, ungrateful!"—Mrs. Stainville felt really sorry at having thus distressed her young friend, and endeavoured by repeated expressions of kindness and friendship, to dispel the melancholy she had excited in her breast.

A thoughtful silence then followed. Mrs. Stainville mused over the *wonder,* as it appeared to her, of a heart like Emily's, capable of the tenderest feelings, being insensible to the *uncommonly* interesting qualities of Lord Raymond—and Emily was much at a loss to comprehend the sentiments of her friend, and wherefore what appeared to her merely the effect of indecision in Lord Raymond's character, should excite so much admiration.—To her simple and unsophisticated mind there seemed no reason, why, if Lord Raymond took the interest in her, which Mrs. Stainville pretended, he should not have openly declared his sentiments for her, previously to her departure.—Their acquaintance had been of sufficient length, to authorise such a step; and if, on the contrary, her want of fortune and unprotected situation were objections to his more serious addresses, his attentions ought, surely, she thought, never to have been shown in so decided a manner, or with a view, in any degree, to captivate her affections. How unlike the anxious care of real friendship did the mistaken sentiments of Mrs. Stainville appear to Emily!—how superiour the rational solicitude of her old and dear Protector! and how, at this moment, did her heart overflow with gratitude and respect towards him!—The comparison before her seemed, if possible, to raise his value in her eyes; and to increase that tenderness, and truly filial affection, which she so deeply felt for him—from his idea, her imagination naturally transported itself to the scenes of her childhood, when her hours, rendered happy by his care, passed in playful gayety and content.—Here, thought she, could I have stopped! nor ever heard the sad story of my unfortunate parents, over whose memory I so soon learned to weep, without having known the charm of their endearments! Mrs. Stainville however regretted the pang she had inadvertently given to Emily, and became more cautious in her expressions of zeal for Lord Raymond.

The variety of country, through which they passed, even at that late season of the year, served to occupy and delight the mind of Emily; she had no wish as to the journey, but to follow Mrs. Stainville's inclinations; all was to her new, all was interesting. They stopped nowhere, for more than a few days, till they arrived at Rome, where Mrs. Stainville proposed for some months, and, having changed her original plan, then proceeding to Naples for the summer; in the vicinity of which, should the heat there prove troublesome, she doubted not but that she should find some sufficiently cool retreat.

They had crossed the Alps by the way of Lyons and Turin; reserving, as Mrs. Stainville said, for their return, a second and more detailed view of Florence, and some considerable stay at Venice, where several Roman Catholic relations of Mr. Stainville's were settled, some of whom she had formerly seen in England.

Mrs. Stainville was no sooner at Rome, than her love, her enthusiasm for the arts, her fondness for literature and science, returned to her with redoubled force; she avoided all English society, and was surrounded by *Abbati* and *literati;* among whom were to be found several men of deep learning and real information, such as, in that country, have both the desire and the leisure to communicate their knowledge to those, who really wish to profit by their instruction.

The mornings were employed in visiting the curious and magnificent remains of antiquity, still extant in that celebrated city, and its *environs:* and the evenings were passed at her own lodgings with her literary friends, and some artists and musicians of eminence; except when she occasionally attended the *accademias* and *assemblies,* with the *illustrissima,* destined, in consequence of letters of introduction, to present her to all the *good company* of Rome, or, in their phrase, *per servir la.*

Nothing could be more fortunate for Emily than this plan, or more consonant to her taste and disposition. Her intelligent mind, eager thirst after knowledge, genius for the fine arts, and the gentle unaffected simplicity of her manners, were soon observed by the society in which she lived. A respectable old ecclesiastic, in the kindest manner, undertook to perfect her knowledge of the Italian language, as well as to continue her classical studies. "I must," said he, "take charge *myself* of instructing this *bellissima donna,* to save my younger companions from the danger, to which they must be exposed in such an attempt—*Ecco,*" continued he, pointing to his white hair, "*la mia aegide.*" But Emily knew neither coquetry nor affectation, and was indeed only likely to become really dangerous to those few exalted spirits, capable of the pure flame of real love.

Lord Raymond, who had agreed with Mrs. Stainville to follow her steps, still came not. Several letters had passed between them, which were not always wholly communicated to Emily; but of this she took little notice, concluding (which, indeed, was partly the case,) that the letters might contain some foolish complaints of her indifference; which Mrs. Stainville, knowing her opinion on the subject, might naturally wish to avoid showing her.

Three months passed in this manner, to the infinite satisfaction of Emily, who felt unbounded gratitude towards her friend for the advantages she derived from her: while Mrs. Stainville really felt a pride in the uncommon degree of progress her young *protegée* made with the several masters she had procured for her; and her *prodigious friendship,* which had sometimes been a little on the wane at Paris, now returned with redoubled expressions of kindness and affection, which were at the moment all sincere. Emily, *at Rome,* instead of interfering with, served rather to establish the pretensions of her friend. The sonnets and verses of the obsequious *Abbati* were all addressed to Mrs. Stainville; and *her* charms, *her* merits, and *her* munificence, repeated by them in every species of rhyme.—If Emily sang or played, or, at Mrs. Stainville's express desire, produced any of the masterly sketches, which she made, of the remarkable buildings, or other picturesque scenes, the praises justly lavished on Emily seemed to redound also to the honour of her own superiour taste; and she reflected with much self-complacency, that *she* had drawn from obscurity a Being so much admired. In short, most of those about her knew so well how to qualify their expressions of delight at Emily's beauty and talents, as not to offend the vanity of the *padrona illustrissima,* at whose house they were entertained, and always received with the most flattering attentions and politeness; for nobody knew better than Mrs. Stainville, what, in the common way of the world, was due both to herself and others.

So much time had now elapsed since they left Paris, that Mrs. Stainville began to accustom herself to the idea of Lord Raymond's not following them at all; and this, from her *absorption in vertù,* with less difficulty than might have been supposed. Emily, who had always doubted his coming, considered this merely as proof of her having formed a just estimation of the *passion,* which her friend supposed him to entertain for her, and of course felt little disappointment and less surprise—when at last a letter, sent to Mrs. Stainville by an *avant-courier,* dispatched to secure lodgings for Lord Raymond, announced his being not only on the road, but actually arrived in Florence, where he meant to rest for a day or two, having travelled thither from Paris without stopping, night and day.—A method of seeing foreign countries, however strange it may seem, frequently adopted by persons wholly idle, and whose time is *too much* at their own disposal.

"There!" said Mrs. Stainville, on opening the letter, with an air of triumph—"Lord Raymond *is* coming, after all—*I* never doubted him!"—A slight blush overspread the cheek of Emily at these words; but more from the idea of what she thought might be supposed to be excited in her breast on this intelligence, than from any real agitation which she felt.

The *day or two,* which Lord Raymond was to pass at Florence, had already exceeded a fortnight, when, at last, towards evening, his chaise drove up to Mrs. Stainville's door, lodgings having been taken up for him at the same house. He had no sooner alighted, than he inquired for the *English ladies,* and was instantly shown into Mrs. Stainville's apartment. It happened that Emily had that morning been sitting for her portrait; and Mrs. Stainville had insisted on her continuing for the day in the same dress, which she said so particularly became her. Lord Raymond, on entering the room, was struck with the novelty of Emily's appearance, and, if possible, with the increased beauty of her figure. Her dress, that of a Tuscan peasant, with the large hat, and her hair arranged exactly in their *costume,* gave somewhat a different character to her face, and she was that evening *prettier,* than she had ever before appeared; for *prettiness* certainly was not the characteristic excellence of her countenance. Lord Raymond had no sooner paid his compliments to Mrs. Stainville, than he came up to Emily, with a look of so much admiration, as nearly to embarrass her. He wondered within himself how he could have remained so long behind, for the very causes of his delay were then almost forgotten by him.—These were no other than that to Paris he was accustomed, and *therefore* he liked it; and that with a mistress it was troublesome to part, and *therefore* he kept her. *Mademoiselle Albinie,* however, suspecting that the *Milor Anglais* might shortly desert her, although one of the most fashionable ladies *de son état* at Paris; and having an offer of a permanent settlement from a *fermier général,* thought proper to *resign,* rather than wait the chance of being dismissed; at which Lord Raymond fancying himself offended, determined to leave Paris; and *recollected,* that some months before, he had promised, to take a journey to Rome. Absence and distance had pretty nearly erased the impressions made by Emily on his heart, when the sight of her again revived them with additional force. Yet, though seeing her every day in those habits of intimacy, in which persons before acquainted naturally live when meeting in a foreign country, still in the course of above six weeks passed at Rome, he had not entirely brought himself to the final decision of making a serious engagement. It was not Emily's want of fortune, or the situation in which she was placed, to which he objected. Without being really generous, he cared not for money; he had always had more than he knew what to do with, which he continued to squander away without discrimination, or considering that others ever felt the want of it; and even had the name of Melville not been such as could with propriety be joined to that of any other family, however noble, he would have thought the rank he gave his wife always nobility sufficient. But his character was by nature undecided, and from never having been obliged to do anything he did not like, he seldom clearly knew what he *did* like, and still less what he *should* like.—Besides, Emily was not dying for him, she neither flattered him, nor encouraged him in the thousand little whims and fancies, in which he had been accustomed to be indulged: of this, under the borrowed names of *want of feeling* and *indifference,* he would sometimes complain to Mrs. Stainville, as to a common friend; and she, from thinking it *sentimental* to pity him, confirmed him in errour; for Emily's heart was free, and had Lord Raymond's affections been sincere and ready, it would have excited and confirmed hers; and he might have permanently attached and united to his destiny a woman, whose infinite worth his mind, indeed, was incapable of ever justly appreciating.

Mrs. Stainville, from the time of Lord Raymond's arrival, became gradually more indifferent to the objects which had of late so much engrossed her mind, while Emily continued the same sedulous attention to all the pursuits in which she was engaged.

Lord Raymond saw nothing in the remains of antiquity, that attracted his notice: pictures and statues little interested him, and he thought the Italians "the most horribly stupid set of people in the world"—which was indeed, the less extraordinary, as he understood scarcely a single word of their language—*a Cicerone's* lectures he *protested* against, but accompanied Mrs. Stainville and Emily constantly, in their morning excursions. Emily, as occasion offered, sometimes rallied him, sometimes endeavoured to reason with him on his fancies and follies, but with little success; on the contrary, this was considered by him as something little short of offence, and fresh complaints were in consequence always made to Mrs. Stainville. *She understood him, felt for him,* and seldom failed to lament that "*such sentiments* as his should ever be treated with *indifference,* or not as they deserved," for she "confessed they were *her own*!"—"We see no faults," said she, with a sigh, "in what we love!—therefore *love not* where we see faults!"

Thus, without at first intending it, did Mrs. Stainville gradually undermine the passion of a lover for her friend, whose rank and fortune would have placed her in a brilliant situation, and whose naturally harmless character, guided by Emily's good sense, affection, and judgment, might have materially improved, to the increase not only of the consequence to which his rank and fortune entitled him, but of his own real happiness. Mrs. Stainville had originally been perfectly sincere in her wish to see Emily united to Lord Raymond: she felt a pride in the idea of bringing her back to Dr. Stanmore, *Countess of Raymond,* and in thus showing at once the value of *her* protection, and, as she thought, the triumph of friendship.—But the dangerous indulgence of listening to the passionate complaints of a young man, whose elegance of figure, and gentleness of manner, rendered him in some respects very captivating, she found too difficult to resist. She heard and applauded the expression of sentiments for another, till she began to feel how much she wished such sentiments addressed to herself; her manner to Lord Raymond became more tender, and her interest in all he said increased. Emily's *insensibility* was more *wondered at;* more severely condemned. Lord Raymond began to discover, that Mrs. Stainville was still extremely handsome, and knew not how it happened, that he had till then so little noticed her beauty. Their conversations became more and more frequent, and they often passed whole hours together, while Emily was engaged in study, in music, or in drawing with her masters.—In the scientific meetings, of which Mrs. Stainville had been so fond, Lord Raymond took no delight; yet without the *abbati* and *literati,* such even as they now appeared to Mrs. Stainville, the evenings would have passed but awkwardly with the *trio* only, circumstanced as they then were. After the company had taken their leave, a moonlight walk was often proposed and accepted, even when Emily thought it too late, and herself retired to bed.

In this predicament, no other society offering itself but that of a few awkward English lads and their tutors, and the time not being far distant, at which Mrs. Stainville had originally proposed going to Naples, after sounding Lord Raymond on the subject, who entirely approved it, she signified her intention of proceeding thither immediately to Emily; and everything being shortly arranged for the journey, they set out for that place.

Chapter 29

FOR SOME TIME AFTER THEIR ARRIVAL at Naples, the beauty of the scene, the variety of new objects, and the bustle of that immense and populous city, completely occupied Emily's attention; and the constant crowds in which the evenings were passed, it being then the time of Carnival, facilitated the *manege* carried on between Mrs. Stainville and Lord Raymond. But Emily's quickness could not suffer her long to be wholly blinded, though the innocence of her own unsuspecting and upright mind made her doubt for some time the cause of Mrs. Stainville's altered manner to her, and Lord Raymond's coldness, and often forced civility.

The first lesson is always severe, which teaches a youthful mind, that *friendship can be false;* and Emily felt more deeply the insincerity and want of confidence in Mrs. Stainville, than the loss of her lover. There her heart fortunately had not been too far engaged, and she rejoiced at having been able exactly to follow Dr. Stanmore's advice, who, all intelligence, and alive to everything even the most minute, that might interest or affect his child, had before suspected what was passing at Paris, both from Emily's letters, and indistinct hints dropped without intention in Mrs. Stainville's, (who from time to time had written to him) for her plan was to surprise him, when Lord Raymond had made his proposals in form, by announcing to him the future countess.

But Dr. Stanmore, fearing the possible consequences of perhaps too sanguine hopes of an establishment every way so advantageous (for he was acquainted, though not personally, with Lord Raymond's family), had, with earnestness in his letters to Emily, exhorted her so far to guard her heart, if possible, against captivation, as not to endanger her own piece of mind, should Lord Raymond's intentions not be serious.—Young men, he said, often neither knew their own minds, nor the mischief they did by attentions shown through mere idleness, or caused by temporary admiration. He advised her to profit by the present circumstances, so advantageous to her education, and to lose no opportunity of acquiring knowledge and information; which would, he said, in whatever situation she might hereafter be placed, serve to strengthen and support her mind.—Emily, whose character was naturally turned to reflection, profited by his injunctions, and reserved, till their meeting, fully to explain what then really caused her uneasiness, for her situation became awkward and unpleasant.

Mrs. Stainville could not doubt, although Emily's honest pride prevented her complaining, but that she saw through the duplicity of her conduct, and had justly too high an opinion of her understanding, to attempt at an *excuse.* She had, indeed, at first tried to reconcile what she would have blamed in others, with what she was doing herself, by affecting an appearance of *interesting melancholy,* hinting at the *resistless powers* of *sympathy,* talking of *unfortunate, unconquerable sensations,* and all the *farrago* of false sentiment, so frequently offered, and so often received, as current coin in these cases. Measures, however, Mrs. Stainville, for her own sake, was determined to keep; and continued, to appearance, the same attentions to Emily; who with gratitude remembered the obligations she owed her, and felt without rancour, however painfully, that change towards her in Mrs. Stainville's heart, which from the state of her own she had so little expected or deserved.

Something Mrs. Stainville clearly saw must be done: for though Emily, from the consciousness of her own innocence, and the integrity of her mind, would have become gradually easier under the present circumstances, unpleasant as they were, it was by no means the same with Mrs. Stainville, who found the awkwardness of the situation in which she had placed herself daily increase; for though weak, and, from the want of steady principles, an easy prey to passion, her heart was not depraved, and she could not see Emily without a silent reproach to herself; besides, the attachment she now felt for Lord Raymond was not void of jealousy, and she dreaded the return of a passion he certainly *had* felt, were he allowed constantly to have the object of his former admiration before his eyes, the powers of whose dangerous charms, she could not sufficiently deceive herself, not seriously to fear.—In consequence of these reflections, a plan was formed in her head, the execution of which she entered upon immediately.—The first step towards this was quitting Naples, where she had originally declared her intention of passing a much more considerable time, without incurring a suspicion of the real cause of this change. For this purpose, she affected to be *more languid, more unwell,* and more in a *suffering state,* even than usual to her *extreme delicacy* of health, and *wretched nerves.* The sulphureous air of Naples *killed* her; the *oppression* of a *scirocco* was intolerable; and in a *tramontana, with her lungs, how could she breathe?*

All this was so well acted, that Emily believed her really ill, and, forgetting all idea of injuries, remembered only her former extreme kindness, and was under serious anxiety about her.—"Since the air of this place disagrees with you," said Emily affectionately, "why should you not, dearest Madam, change it immediately?"—"I believe you are right, dear Emily, I will take your advice," replied Mrs. Stainville, "it is certain, that here I cannot *exist.*" Preparations for the journey were immediately commenced, and, *if she revived,* as she said was often the case from change of place, Venice was to be the object, but they were to be a longer or shorter time in their way thither, according as Mrs. Stainville's health required. About this time, too, a circumstance happened, which made her doubly anxious to be gone, as she thought it indicated the necessity of separating Lord Raymond from Emily. She had one day been giving some directions to her servants in another room, when, returning to her own apartment, she found Lord Raymond, whom she had left there, leaning carelessly out of the window, sitting in another part of the room, and holding something in his hand, which she perceived was a picture, and which he was examining with so much attention and seeming admiration, that he neither heard her come in, nor knew she was near him, till she tapped him on the shoulder.—He started, coloured, and immediately getting up, replaced the picture on the table, from which he had taken it, without speaking.—It was the very portrait of Emily, for which she had sitten in the dress of a Florentine peasant, before mentioned; a miniature which Mrs. Stainville usually carried in her pocket, but had accidentally left on her table.—Mrs. Stainville, on perceiving what the picture was, which had so much absorbed Lord Raymond's attention, and the embarrassment of his manner on being discovered, was too much agitated herself to address him, and they both felt relieved *for once,* by Emily's entering and interrupting their *tête-a-tête.*

The leaving Naples was now with still more earnestness accelerated, and though a temporary separation with Lord Raymond was to be the consequence (as Mrs. Stainville's attention to the rules of propriety allowed her not to admit of his then accompanying them on the road), she felt much relieved when the day of their departure was come. The first place of rendezvous was fixed for Bologna, which place Mrs. Stainville and Emily reached without any occurrence worth mentioning, having taken their road by the Adriatic coast, and stopped at the different places most worthy of notice, for what Mrs. Stainville reckoned a *decent time.*

Lord Raymond, by another road, arrived on the very same day, and was ready at the door of the inn where they alighted, to hand them out of the carriage; but so tormented was Mrs. Stainville now by her jealousy of Emily, that, not knowing how exactly to interpret a punctuality she had not expected, she enjoyed not, as she otherwise would have done, their reunion. Lord Raymond's attentions to her, however, were continued; and Emily, she plainly saw, was above making the slightest advances on her side towards an attempt to regain the power she once had over him;—her manner to him now was that of perfect civility, and perfect indifference.

About a week had passed, since their arrival at Bologna, when one evening that they happened to be at the opera, about the middle of the performance, the door of one of the boxes near her was opened, and several men entered, who, by their dress and manner, seemed to be English.—One in particular, from the remarkable elegance of his appearance, and beauty of his figure, attracted Emily's notice.—He sat silently, and, as it seemed, wholly occupied by the performance.—Emily, after considering him for some time, asked Mrs. Stainville, if she knew who that young man was; pointing to the stranger—Mrs. Stainville answered in the negative, but almost without even turning her head to look towards the person.—On this Emily, addressing herself to Lord Raymond, repeated her question—Lord Raymond answered her also in the negative, but with a smile, or half sneer, which made her colour.—"The *Gentleman,*" said he to Emily, lowering his voice, "whoever he may be, has reason to be flattered with the attention he has excited in Miss Melville—everyone is not so fortunate!"

Emily, however, frequently again looked towards the stranger, who continued the same seeming attention to the performance; then, a little before the opera ended, got up, and taking leave of his companions, retired.

On the morning following, Mrs. Stainville announced her intention of leaving Bologna on the next day but one.—"So soon, Madam!" exclaimed Emily, with an involuntary expression of surprise.—"Have you any objection, my dear?" replied Mrs. Stainville, surprised in her turn at something, she could not define *what,* that struck her as unusual in Emily's manner.—"O! far from it," said Emily, colouring deeply, as she recollected herself—"how can I possibly have any objection either to going or staying, as it may be most agreeable to you? Every place I have yet seen in Italy has afforded fresh objects of admiration, and those which, owing to your kindness, I am still to see, will not, I am convinced, prove less interesting—I only—I"—"Well, my dear, Emily," said Mrs. Stainville, wishing to end the conversation, as she saw Lord Raymond coming—"since you like it, we will set out the day after tomorrow." She then walked to the other end of the room, and began talking to Lord Raymond.

The next day a box at the opera was proposed to Mrs. Stainville for that evening, who, turning to Emily, said—"Do you wish to go, Emily?" and then without waiting for her answer, continued, "I confess I feel very unwell."—"By no means," said Emily with quickness, wishing to repair her fault of the preceding day.—"I really prefer staying at home." This was not *quite* the case, for Emily had *depended* on going to the opera, as Mrs. Stainville had appeared for some time to avoid staying at home in the evenings, unless with more company than Lord Raymond and herself; and in going to the opera Emily thought it probable, that she might again see the stranger, and perhaps learn who he was; yet thought she to herself, how can I be so childish!—he is some Englishman of rank, travelling, it is evident; and what can his name or title ever signify to me?

Mrs. Stainville was uncommonly thoughtful, and out of spirits that whole day; when in the evening, after a long conversation between her and Lord Raymond, which was continued in a low voice, Emily was surprised to find, that it was then determined, that Lord Raymond should not merely meet them at the different towns where they made any stay, as she had understood to have been settled between them, when they all left Naples, but actually accompany them on the road. Emily felt this as an impropriety, and as what was extremely unpleasant to herself; but setting apart the fear of appearing to be governed by pique, she could not presume to make any objection to this plan; as her pretending to know better than Mrs. Stainville on such a subject, must, she thought, appear like the greatest impertinence. Mrs. Stainville had, however, looked extremely disconcerted when she spoke, which Emily, wishing not further to distress her, affected not to observe.—*Her* mind was of that generous nature, which in no case does not, in some degree, participate in the unhappiness of others.—She feels, thought Emily to herself, a passion for this young man, by whom, perhaps, that passion is but half returned, too powerful for her to reason to resist!—is she not then deserving also of pity, however much she may be deserving of censure?

Emily retired to her own room, saying, she was going to write.—Her situation was become seriously distressing, and she felt she wanted the advice of her absent and her only friend.—She sighed deeply; and the reflection of the impossibility of now recurring to the immediate support and comfort of Dr. Stanmore's friendship and affection, quite overcame her spirits. She several times took up her pen to address him, and then again laid it down, unable to begin her letter from the tears, which incessantly filled her eyes. In this situation she was interrupted by *Mademoiselle Jaqueline,* who tripped into the room, humming a French *vaudeville.*—She was, she said, come to inquire, "*Si mademoiselle n'avoit rien à emballer,*" as she found that *madame* intended to set out the next day, at which she was rather *étonnée;* but she had no sooner cast her eyes on Emily, than coming up to her, and resting both her hands on the table at which Emily was sitting, she exclaimed "*Ah! mon Dieu! ma chère demoiselle, vous pleurez, qu'avez vous?—mais ne pleurez pas—ma mère me disoit toujours, 'Jaqueline, ne pleure pas, cela gâte les yeux'—et vous les avez si beaux, mademoiselle!*" Emily smiled, then thanking *Mademoiselle Jaqueline* for her attention, told her, that she had nothing to trouble her with, and that what few things she had to pack up, she would bring to her presently, hoping by these means to get rid of her. But *Mademoiselle Jaqueline* was not disposed to go; she kept turning and turning about the room, first taking up one thing, and then another, and laying them down again, where she found them.—Poor Emily, who wanted to write in quiet, every now and then cast a melancholy look towards her, not choosing directly to say, that she wished to be left alone.—"*Vous voilà bien triste!*" said *Mademoiselle Jaqueline,* half muttering to herself—"*c'est bien dur, aussi! mais tout s'arrangera.*"—Emily cast a look of some surprise at her, but said nothing, thinking that the best chance of silencing her. "*O!*" continued she, still half to herself, "*vous faitez l'étonnée, mademoiselle, mais je sais bien ce que je sais;*" saying this, as she was near the door, and could find no tolerable pretence for stopping any longer, she left the room. Emily easily guessed at what *Mademoiselle Jaqueline* meant, as she had once or twice before given hints of her own surmises; but never having received the slightest encouragement to talk on the subject, from Emily, she had hitherto been kept within bounds.—"Good Heavens!" said Emily to herself, "to what will not Mrs. Stainville's imprudence expose me!" Emily then began her letter to Dr. Stanmore.—It was long and explicit, written in the warmth and fullness of her heart; yet no one harsh expression escaped her against Mrs. Stainville: she lamented indeed the change, that had, she feared, taken place in her mind towards herself, and entreated Dr. Stanmore's advice, in what manner she ought to act in so delicate a situation, as that in which she was now unfortunately placed. She had just finished her letter, when she was called to supper.—"What have you been doing," said Mrs. Stainville, "all this time? you must have written *volumes,*—for my part I am half asleep, and Lord Raymond, there, has actually been snoring upon the sofa."—"You are determined," said Lord Raymond, "not to leave Miss Melville any *regret* for the company she has lost."—"*O!*" replied Mrs. Stainville, a little dryly, "*the company might* have proved *rather* more lively, had *she* been here." The conversation for the rest of the evening turned wholly on the arrangements for their journey, which took place, as it had been settled, on the day following.

Chapter 30

VENICE WAS THE PLACE, where Mrs. Stainville had always said, that she meant to make her longest residence, before she returned to England; and there they arrived, after a journey which would have been in every respect delightful to Emily, if she had not been placed in so singular a situation. Mrs. Stainville affected to treat her with the greatest kindness; but Emily felt, that her professions were no longer sincere, and that fine thread, by which they had been united, which forms the bond of real friendship, and which, in a mind like Emily's, no false substitute could supply, was now snapped asunder.

Mrs. Stainville's flattery to Lord Raymond, too, became almost disgusting.—She seemed to study his every look, and caught at every word he uttered, with an attention and delight, that were often almost ridiculous: yet it seemed to please him; he talked to her with apparent confidence, and consulted her on every subject, that respected himself, even to the minutest trifle.—To *amuse* him was not so easy; for he took little delight in anything he saw during the journey, and slept half the way in the carriage; where, according to Mrs. Stainville's arrangements, he was placed with Emily and herself in her *berline;* and *Mademoiselle Jaqueline,* accompanied by Lord Raymond's *valet-de-chambre,* in his chaise.

During the journey, the image of the stranger, whom she had by chance seen at Bologna, sometimes recurred to Emily's imagination; and she could not help comparing his figure with that of Lord Raymond, who was certainly a very handsome man; but still he always lost by the comparison.—In the stranger there was so much dignity and grace, a look so commanding, and yet so sweet, and, she thought, as he occasionally half turned his face towards the side where she sat, that there was a melancholy spread over his countenance, which rendered his appearance still more interesting.—His attention to the performance, too, seemed to indicate a mind less volatile than that of the other Englishmen, who were in the box with him; and who kept talking together, and staring about the whole time they were in the theatre.—Emily could have been seen by none of them; having, on the account of a headache, from which she had suffered in the morning, placed herself behind Mrs. Stainville; and there were no lights in the box, an Italian custom at the theatres, to which Mrs. Stainville had a particular dislike, and always complained of her *lungs*, whenever they were proposed.—Emily was thus wholly concealed from the persons who sat on the same side of the house with herself.—But although the recollection of the stranger's figure did recur, her mind was too rational, not to discourage in herself an impression, the folly of which she felt she should so much condemn in another.

They were no sooner at Venice, than Mrs. Stainville began to prosecute a plan, which she thought would afford her much liberty, and certainly relieve her in a great degree from her dread of the renewal of Lord Raymond's sentiments for Emily, by removing her from his presence.—She immediately sought the relations of her late husband, and, exerting all the powers of her captivating manner, became shortly on an intimate footing even with those, whom she had not before seen; and prepared them for thinking, that whatever she might do, her conduct *could not be wrong.*—She redoubled her expressions of kindness for Emily, affected to be wholly occupied with her education, and earnest to bring about a marriage, of which she pretended to have little doubt, between her and Lord Raymond; all which was easily believed by persons uninformed of the real circumstances relative to their different situations. She then introduced Emily to the particular notice of a lady, who had formerly travelled into England, and being a near relation of Mr. Stainville's, resided for a considerable time with them at their house in the country.—Nothing, in general, giving Mr. Stainville greater satisfaction, than the idea of having many foreign relations, which, he thought, set forth the antiquity and former consequence of his family—he was constantly talking of them, writing to them on every event, which in any way affected *the family;* and was never so happy, as when he had an opportunity of exhibiting some of them to the *vulgar* neighbours, by whom he was surrounded in England.

This lady was by birth a Venetian, and had been contracted in her cradle, and afterward married to a Frenchman of distinction, who, notwithstanding the beauty, which, when young, she possessed, and the perfections of her mind, had always neglected her, and even obliged her after a time to live wholly separated from him. Disgusted with a treatment she so little deserved, and as, from being an Italian, and consequently not having, in every little particular the precise manners of a *French woman,* she had no opportunity of displaying the real merits of her character; she was not taken much notice of by the family of her husband, or by any of the other societies of Paris.—Thus uncomfortably situated, she requested to return to her own country, which was readily granted; and at Venice (her journey to England excepted) she had ever since resided—Being of a retired turn, and little fond of company in general, she passed much of her time with her only sister, who was then superiour of the seminary called *de'Mendicanti,* celebrated for the admirable school of music, which it contains.

Madame de Saint Valory (for that was the lady's name), being a woman of superiour understanding, failed not shortly to distinguish Emily.—She was charmed with the native simplicity of her mind, which formed, she thought, a striking contrast with Mrs. Stainville's, *not wholly* advantageous to the latter.—Mrs. Stainville's manner was not the more engaging to *Madame de Saint Valory,* from forcibly recalling the manners of Paris to her recollection, where the indignities she had suffered from the neglect of a husband, unfortunately *not* indifferent to her, and the impertinence of his family, had been too deeply impressed on her mind, to be forgotten.

Emily would have been more open to the impressions of friendship, from a character so amiable as that of *Madame de Saint Valory,* had not her heart lately been wounded by the conduct of Mrs. Stainville; a conduct which the generosity of her own disposition condemned, more than she chose to avow to herself.

Similarity of taste, however, united Emily and *Madame de Saint Valory* in a thousand instances, and particularly in their love of music, in which science Emily began now eminently to excel.—*Madame de Saint Valory,* enchanted with the melody of her voice, introduced her to her sister, by whom she was often placed in the grated gallery of the church of the *Mendicanti,* where, concealed with the proficients of the seminary, she often delighted the listening crowd below.

Mrs. Stainville had been from the first much pleased with the attentions, which *Madame de Saint Valory* showed to Emily; and affecting to give way to her wishes, she would often leave Emily for days under her care, who, on such occasions, resided in her house with her. By degrees, from days to weeks, nearly three months passed, during which time Mrs. Stainville, what with parties by water to *terra-firma* (as it is termed), the fair of Padua, and other excursions, all of which she said Emily, she was sure, would not like, had scarcely seen her.—Emily, on her side, was determined to make every advantage she could of her present situation, being strongly supported by the letters of Dr. Stanmore, in which he often repeated to Emily, that Mrs. Stainville, for her own sake, would behave to her at least with propriety; and that to the conscious rectitude of her own conduct, she must in every other respect look for consolation.

While Mrs. Stainville was thus devoting her time to *amusing* Lord Raymond, who knew not how to amuse himself, Emily was passing whole days in the exercise of a talent, which she thought might one day serve to beguile the melancholy of future hours; and as she never could have so favourable an opportunity of perfecting this talent, she gave up most of her time to the study of music.

Emily had been for some weeks with *Madame de Saint Valory*, and in the constant habit of attending with the other scholars and proficients in the gallery of the *Mendicanti*, already mentioned, when one day of performance it happened, that there were at first only a few persons scattered here and there below in the body of the church. A *motet* was to be sung, in which she had a considerable part, when, just as they commenced, from the lattice placed before the musicians, which wholly prevents them from being distinguished from below, Emily saw enter the church, the very stranger, whose figure had attracted her notice at Bologna.—He had on the Venetian white cloak, gracefully thrown over his shoulder.—His countenance Emily had now an opportunity fully to examine, as he seated himself so as to be more than half turned towards the music gallery, to which his eyes were often directed; and, she thought, though at the idea she accused herself of vanity, that on the sound of her voice, when, in the particular parts of the *motet*, she sang alone, he listened with redoubled attention.—The look of melancholy spread over his countenance, which Emily thought she had perceived when at Bologna, and which was now not to be mistaken, and the negligent ease and grace of his figure, rendered his appearance more than commonly interesting.—The music over, Emily still lingered in the gallery—she saw the stranger rise, and walk leisurely round the church, examining every part with attention, and as if the objects were not familiar to him.—He is newly come to Venice, thought Emily to herself; and she hoped, that her curiosity to know his name would probably now be satisfied.—Though Emily, when Mrs. Stainville was away on any of her excursions, scarcely went out, and never but with *Madame de Saint Valory,* in her *gondola,* who sometimes, indeed, to amuse Emily, walked with her in the *Place San Marc,* or revisited the churches and other objects of curiosity dispersed about the town.

When again a day for music at the *Mendicanti* was announced, Emily felt her heart beat.—She was, on this occasion, more than ever sedulous in her attendance at the rehearsals, and practiced over and over the part allotted to her for performance.—The day came, and brought again the stranger to the church, which was this time uncommonly crowded; but he found means to seat himself precisely in the same place.—His attention to the music was the same, and the evident expression of pleasure on his countenance, whenever the melodious voice of Emily was heard above the rest, was plainly distinguishable.

For several times subsequent, whenever music was repeated in the church, the stranger failed not in his attendance, took the same place, and expressed the same attention and delight; but when, after a vacation, music was again given there, Emily's eyes in vain sought the stranger—he returned no more. She doubted not but that he had left Venice; and concluded, as it indeed seemed determined, that she never was to discover even his name.

Although *Madame de Saint Valory* was commonly in the music gallery with her, where, as a privilege from her near relationship to the superiour, she was allowed to sit, Emily had not ventured to make her remark the stranger, or express her curiosity about him; she feared the keen and piercing eye of her friend, who was all quickness, and would, she thought, discover even the slightest expression of emotion as she spoke, should any appear in her countenance.—Emily one day, however, *ventured* to observe to one of her young companions, that there was a *forestiere* seated below; and asked her (as she happened to have some connection with an English family then at Venice), if she knew who he was.—"No," said the girl, looking at him, "*ma è bellissimo*"—she then again, without further remark, continued the occupation of tuning the instrument, on which she was going to perform, which Emily, by her question, had interrupted.

Although Emily now wholly abandoned the idea of discovering the stranger's name, and even the probability of ever seeing him again, still she retained his image in her mind, with a mixture of pleasure and melancholy; in which, in spite of reason, she felt a sort of satisfaction.

She amused herself with retracing everything that recalled him to her imagination—the church of the *Mendicanti* afforded subjects for her pencil; and numberless views of it were taken by her, particularly of the inside, where the figure of the stranger, as he sat wrapped up in his cloak, was not omitted.—The masterly manner, in which Emily could exert the various talents she possessed, rendered them a serious advantage to her, and increased that independence of mind, which belongs to superiour characters.—Of these talents Emily now availed herself, and in the society of *Madame de Saint Valory,* who rose daily in her opinion, time glided gently on: yet Emily's mind was not free from anxiety; the time was elapsed, which Mrs. Stainville had fixed for her return to England; and although

Dr. Stanmore gave not the slightest hint of impatience at this delay, Emily, both for his sake and her own, severely felt the length of such a separation. She felt too all she was to him, and her affectionate heart made her regret for him that comfort and consolation, of which, by her absence, he was so long deprived.—His age too, and frequent illnesses, would often, with a still sharper pang, recur to her imagination; and at these moments Mrs. Stainville's conduct, her uncertainty, and evident dependence on the caprice of another, presented her character under worse colours, even than it might otherwise have been viewed under by Emily; for although, as has already been observed, it bore not the nice inspection of truth and penetration, Mrs. Stainville's character was admirably calculated for the world, and its common intercourse—and, even now, while indulging in the plan she had formed for separating Lord Raymond from Emily, and attaching him to herself; she omitted not to give all the necessary air of propriety to their intimacy, and always repeated to the persons, whom she had joined to her society, that her young companion, both by her own choice and the express desire of her relations, followed the plan of education she had adopted for her.

How long this might have continued, it is difficult to say; for Mrs. Stainville became every day more and more captivated with her young admirer, and ceased even to talk of her return to England.

When, fortunately for Emily, as her situation began to be really distressing, letters were brought to Lord Raymond from his mother, informing him, that his presence was absolutely necessary in England, on business essential to his fortune, which could not be deferred.—As Lord Raymond's state of *captivation* was not *quite* so strong as that of Mrs. Stainville, he bore this *unexpected stroke* with great fortitude—all the regular forms, however, of *adieux,* on parting on these occasions, were strictly observed between them. Three days after the arrival of the letters, Lord Raymond was actually on his road to England. Mrs. Stainville, now reduced to the slender *aliment* of old *billets doux, rings, bracelets, and pictures,* found all the extreme delicacy of her health return;—she found, in spite of her *desire* to remain at Venice, that the air was so absolutely *contrary to her,* that she *must* change it, and try the well-known recipe of actual travelling; and thus, without communicating her intention of immediately returning to England, except to Emily, she ordered every preparation for her journey.

When the time came fixed on by Mrs. Stainville for their departure, Emily shed many tears upon embracing, for the last time, *Madame de Saint Valory,* who had so much distinguished her, and to whose society she owed the only agreeable hours she had passed at Venice.

Madame de Saint Valory, as they parted, taking her hand, said—"We will not, my young friend, *correspond:*—I know enough of the world, to be sensible, that, circumstanced as we both are, writing must become a task to you; and therefore could not contribute to any satisfaction of mind;—but *on* any event, that really interests you, I *do* request to hear from you, and to be remembered; as my admiration for you, and my sincere friendship deserves."—Saying this, she again pressed Emily to her bosom, and hastily retired.

Chapter 31

DURING THE JOURNEY, Mrs. Stainville, wishing to obliterate, as much as possible, the remembrance of her own misconduct, which she was sensible Emily must have perceived, and dreading the report she might make of her after their return to England, omitted no attention or appearance of kindness; though she no longer affected that *engouement* which she no longer felt, and which she was certain could no longer impose on Emily, before whose superiour understanding and penetration the weakness of her mind had long shrunk.—But she knew not the true greatness of Emily's character—knew not that she was incapable of the mean revenge, which Mrs. Stainville's imprudence had, indeed, put into her power; and that, far from wishing to expose the foibles of her character, she remembered only to lament its loss the dream of that former kindness towards her, which her youth and inexperience had once made her hope was friendship.

They travelled by the way of the Tyrol, and a part of Switzerland, into which enchanting and *then* happy country Mrs. Stainville made an excursion, purposely, as she said, for Emily's amusement; but in fact, Mrs. Stainville, though now impatient to return to England, wished still, by immediately following Lord Raymond's steps, to make that impatience at least as little visible as she could.

This excursion in Switzerland however excepted, they stopped nowhere for above a day or two, till they came to Paris, and there only for a fortnight.—*The Marquise de Bellevue* and her society were now no longer objects even of the slightest interest—Mrs. Stainville met them without pleasure, and quitted them without regret—even the *charming Abbé* sighed forth *sou désespoir* at the cruelty of her departure, and her making only "*une apparition a Paris,*" without producing the slightest effect.—To England Mrs. Stainville now directed all her wishes, and thither she was determined to return; although, during her journey, she had had time sufficient; to reason on the little chance she there had of meeting Lord Raymond still equally occupied with her, and of ever passing days to her so enchanting as those of Venice; at the worst, however, there always remained the *derniere ressource* of a *belle passion* and a *sentimental* distress.

In short, Mrs. Stainville's chief reason, for stopping above the time necessary to procure a passport at Paris, was to equip herself properly in every article of dress, and the study in that first of schools the newest fashions of the day.—She in vain wished to force presents on Emily—brought milliners and mantua-makers into her room, and wanted to insist on their being employed at her expense—"What can it signify, dearest Emily?" said she: "you know, that what I venture to offer are the merest trifles—a gown of this or that, a *chiffon;*"—but Emily, except here and there something in reality of the most trifling value, and merely not to appear impolite, steadily refused.—"My dress," said she, with a smile full of sweetness "will henceforward be simple *indeed,* and you therefore must excuse me." A sigh would have risen in Emily's bosom, which she repressed.—She could not but reflect, with a sensation of melancholy, on her own situation, when from any occurrence it was recalled to her mind, though her thoughts were at this time chiefly directed to the consoling hope of again seeing her kind benefactor. "You are an obstinate girl," said Mrs. Stainville (who, however, too well guessed, that the motive of Emily's extreme delicacy on the subject of her presents was her wishing to avoid obligations to her), "but if I can help it, you shall not have quite your own way in this." She then ordered a dress or two of the most simple, but elegant, make for Emily; which she enjoined *Mademoiselle Jaqueline* secretly to put up with Emily's clothes, and to take particular care, that the discovery should not be made, till she had safely deposited Emily at Dr. Stanmore's. Mrs. Stainville, in short, omitted no little art or attention, by which she fancied she might in some measure again ingratiate herself with Emily, hoping, at least, by these means, that she might be induced to give a more favourable turn to all that had passed, than she felt she had in reality any right to expect.

Chapter 32

EVERYTHING BEING READY, they left Paris; and a few days, with a favourable passage, brought them to England.—Ms. Stainville insisted on reconducting Emily herself to Dr. Stanmore, into whose arms Emily, on her arrival at her ancient habitation, fell almost breathless with agitation.—Dr. Stanmore pressed her long and affectionately to his bosom, while the tears rolled fast down his aged cheeks.—For what do not moments like these repay the feeling heart!—Emily then earnestly looking at Dr. Stanmore, examined his features;—she feared the increased decay, which after two years' absence, she might discover on them;—but from the pure and unruffled spirit within, his features seemed almost to defy the ravages of time, and to acquire only additional dignity from age. Yet Emily's heart at the moment suggested to her, how often, in so long an absence, he must have wanted her affectionate care, and what he must have suffered from anxiety for her.

The next morning Mrs. Stainville took her leave. Had she, indeed, been disposed to stay longer with them, she could not have done so without evident inconvenience, as the parsonage-house was too small, to admit of even one permanent guest.

Emily now returned with composure and activity to her former employments; she had fortunately lost none of the simple tastes, which, in a youth of innocence, she had acquired; and little regretted the gayer scenes, in which she had lately been engaged.—Mrs. Stainville's falsehood and insincerity, indeed for a time continued to affect her; but the diversity of objects she had seen during the course of her journey, the knowledge of the world which she had acquired, and her own increased information and improved talents, were to a mind like hers, considerations of serious importance and advantage, of which she had learned well to know the value. Dwelling thus on the scenes through which she had passed, the image of the stranger still often recurred to her memory; such as to her imagination he had appeared.—The drawings she had made of the *Mendicanti* were carefully framed, and hung up round her room and she insensibly took a sort of pleasure in retracing to her thoughts the circumstances, which had attended her seeing him, and everything that recalled him to her mind. She would, however, perhaps, have been less aware of this impression on her imagination, had not an accidental circumstance served to show her, that it was not so slight as she supposed.—Dr. Stanmore, whom nothing escaped in which Emily was concerned, had, in their various conversations on the occurrences during her journey, and her residence in Italy, often closely questioned her on the subject of Lord Raymond; fearing that an impression might have been made on her heart deeper than she was willing to avow, even to herself:—but her answers, her unembarrassed look, and her every expression, had always strictly confirmed what she had said on this subject in her letters. When, one day, after having with more than usual anxiety again engaged Emily in the recital of all that had passed relative to Lord Raymond, he added—"and is your heart then, my Emily, indeed so wholly unoccupied?—but you would not, I know, deceive me!"—Emily coloured.—"My child," said Dr. Stanmore, drawing nearer to her—and affectionately taking her hand, "what does this mean, has any other?"—"No, dearest sir," said she, "my colouring, which I feel that I do at this moment, means nothing—I do assure you,—it is too foolish—but"—"But what?" said Dr. Stanmore, "for *something* I am *sure* there is."—"No, indeed," repeated Emily, "it is too foolish!"—Dr. Stanmore, as it will be supposed, felt his curiosity increased by Emily's evident embarrassment, and insisted on knowing the real cause.—Emily then related her story, as briefly as she could, and ended by entreating of him not for a moment to consider what she had told him as serious—"I am not, indeed, so romantic," said she, "so childish."—"Come, come," said Dr. Stanmore, shaking his head, at the same time that his looks were expressive both of kindness and pity—"say more on this subject; I perfectly understand the whole, and allow for that singularity of circumstance, which, I observe," continued he smiling, "you have not very clearly detailed, and which, perhaps, has not merely increased, but actually *caused* this impression on your mind:—nay, do not interrupt me," continued he, seeing that Emily was attempting to speak,—"it is *not* that I consider what you have now told me as deserving of any serious attention, nor do I fear for you this stranger, whom, probably, you may never again see; or if you should, under appearances so different, that you would scarcely recognize him for the same person;—but, I *do* fear for thee, and must exhort thee, my child, carefully to guard against any strong impressions of this sort; unless it were, indeed, under circumstances, of which, alas! I cannot now foresee a chance for thee.—Well do I know thee! thou hast not one single grain of coquetry in thy whole composition; but thou hast a tender, feeling, susceptible heart; a strong, thoughtful, and reflecting mind; and it is on such characters that impressions are to be feared, as they are ever deep and lasting.—I shall not foolishly request of you, to *forget* this stranger, nor do I mean further to distress you on the subject—*remember* him you will, in the present state of your mind; but let not that remembrance be nursed into romance—it is all I now ask." Saying this, Dr. Stanmore walked slowly and thoughtfully out of the room.

Emily felt provoked with herself.—"Had I not," thought she, "betrayed so foolish an emotion, I might have convinced Dr. Stanmore how little necessary were his cautions." This subject was not, however, again renewed by Dr. Stanmore, except occasionally, and then only in general terms—he thought, as he had said, that it was improbable Emily, circumstanced as she was, should ever again meet with the stranger; and that dwelling unnecessarily on such a subject was not a likely way, to lessen the impression already made on her mind.

Chapter 33

A YEAR HAD NOW ELAPSED since Emily's return to England, and the hours had passed on her side in quiet occupation and content. But Dr. Stanmore, although too wise to lose the enjoyment of present moments in idle fears for the future, could not, without the most serious anxiety, reflect on Emily's situation, dependant on his frail existence, which age rendered every day more precarious, for support; for his living was little more than sufficient for his establishment, and for that ready assistance to such of his parishioners as required and deserved his care.

This he had frequently hinted to Emily, and thought it now an indispensable duty, not only strongly to set before her eyes, but to recommend to her sound understanding the only means of preserving to herself that independence of spirit, necessary to noble minds.—"I have been disappointed, I will confess," said he to Emily, "in the hope, which circumstances seemed, while you were abroad, to favour, a suitable establishment for you; but, my child, happiness depends not on situation, and *your* mind prone, I well know, to thought and reflection, will prevent you from now starting at the idea of acquiring support and independence by your own talents.—They are such, and it has been the study of my life to render them so, as may adapt themselves to any situation.—In short, my child, such is the pain and anxiety which I feel at the thoughts of leaving you exposed to this unfeeling world, unprotected as you will be, that I must, with your concurrence, consider seriously in what way at some future period of time those talents can best be employed for your support.—This is not a brilliant prospect," continued he with a sigh, "but you will ever, I feel *certain,* in any situation possess that first of blessings, which virtue and innocence alone can give, a clear and unsullied conscience; and for the rest we must trust to that merciful and all-seeing Providence, on whom all things depend."

Emily answered Dr. Stanmore with calmness and resignation, assuring him, that on all occasions she was ready, to be guided by his judgment.—"I should ill have profited," added she affectionately, "by your precepts, had I not so governed my mind, as to be prepared for the mere frowns of fortune!—Let me but now enjoy with you the flattering satisfaction of contributing to your comfort, and endeavouring in some degree to repay your infinite care and tenderness.—I ask no more,—you shall hereafter, as you please, dispose of me; and by *your* wisdom and advice, long, long may my future days be governed."

Though Emily had with fortitude supported this conversation, yet, after she had quitted Dr. Stanmore, she felt many melancholy reflections crowd on her mind: it was not the want of fortune, or even the necessity of employing her talents for subsistence, that deeply affected her; but the idea, that when she lost her kind protector, she lost her all on earth, and should remain a lonely, insulated, wandering being in this wide world!—she whose heart was formed for every tender, every social affection. The time, too, now drew near, when she knew that a temporary separation at least must take place between her and Dr. Stanmore, which did not serve to *raise* her spirits.

The parsonage required some necessary and considerable repairs, which would for a time render the house not habitable.—Dr. Stanmore too had some affairs to settle in Cornwall (his native country) concerning the property of a small house which he had sold; but for which, from some difficulty in proving the title, he had never received payment. This difficulty being likely to be removed were he on the spot, he thought this a good opportunity for taking the journey, particularly as he knew, that he could himself be lodged at the house of a distant relation for the time during which his affairs should require his presence. But where to place Emily till his return, was to him a consideration of no small embarrassment; at last, after thinking it over and over, he recollected his old acquaintance Mr. Rycot, who had repeatedly entreated a visit from him, telling him, that he had a spare room at his service, and assuring him of a hearty welcome as long as he chose to stay. Mr. Rycot, having serious obligations to him, he thought would surely, on such an occasion as the present, have a pleasure in obliging him; and it occurred to him, that by making the proper arrangements, he might, without scruple, propose to Mr. Rycot, to admit of Emily's occupying the room he had so often offered him for himself; he, therefore, with Emily's consent, wrote in consequence to Mr. Rycot, from whom he received a favourable answer.

The rector and his wife, though vulgar, and in no respect companions suited to Emily, were decent persons, with whom Dr. Stanmore considered, that she might remain without impropriety, during the time of his absence from the parsonage.—He thought also, that, as it was but too probable she might hereafter be obliged to pass much of her life in a situation very inferiour to that, to which her birth had entitled her, there was no harm in thus, by degrees, accustoming her to the nearer view of manners less polished than her own, that she might be less likely in future to start at the difference, or give that difference still more consequence than it deserved.

When Dr. Stanmore arrived at the rectory, on observing its vicinity to the castle, of which he had not been aware, he was glad to find, that the earl and his family were not expected there till the latter end of the summer; before which time, he hoped to be able to fetch Emily away; for he wished her, circumstanced as she then was, rather to shun any particular notice from persons of that description, and cautioned her against making any acquaintance, which might expose her to the necessity of entering into details concerning her own situation.

Emily perfectly entered into these ideas. She wished not to relate *her* melancholy story, where its truth might be doubted, or where it might serve only for the gratification of idle curiosity.—Hence, the rector's *doubts* of *who* Emily really was, which, as it is often the case with those, who like him are curious from mere idleness and want of better occupation, he improved into a story, which to him appeared probable, aided by a little degree of pique at not being, as he thought, himself let into the whole of the secret.

What afterward passed at Belmour Castle has already been related, and it will easily have been guessed, that the stranger was no other than Lord Belmour, whom Emily first unexpectedly met there, as she was viewing the portraits in the library of the castle. Various were her sensations at the moment, and so familiar to her mind was the image of the person, whom she then saw before her, that her first impulse was rather to recognize Belmour with a smile as an acquaintance, than to receive him as a perfect stranger; and this impression, marked as it was on Emily's countenance, though instantly checked by reflection, was not (as was before observed) wholly unperceived by Belmour.

Emily failed not to acquaint Dr. Stanmore with this unexpected discovery, dwelling, as it seemed to him, on the singularity of the circumstance, with a degree of interest, which awakened in him all his fears for her on the subject; and he, in return to her letter, wrote with much expression of anxiety, and entreated her to avoid going to the castle, to refuse, if possible, any invitation thither, that might be given to her. He then set before her, in the most serious light, the danger, in which he felt she was exposed, should she allow herself to encourage an interest, which it was so very improbable ever could tend to anything but her future misery.—"The Earl of Delavere," continued he in his letter, "I have always heard spoken of as being a proud, ostentatious man, and it is not therefore to be doubted what must be his views in the establishment of his only son; but I, perhaps, go too far," added he, "forgive me, my Emily, I can view nothing, lightly, where you are concerned."

Emily, when she received this letter from Dr. Stanmore, already felt the justness of the caution it contained, which subsequent events seemed to her still more to confirm.

She was at first, it is true, pleased to discover in the manners and distinguished character of Belmour, what she thought justified the idea she had formed to herself of him, when wholly unknown to her; nor could she be insensible to the admiration, which, however restrained, Belmour had, from the first moment he saw her, conveyed by every expression, that could most flatter the delicacy of a mind like hers. But what were her reflections, it will easily be imagined, when, after this conviction, she saw herself, as she thought, brought by the most unlooked-for accident, to witness, as it were, the marriage with another, of the very person, whose image had so long occupied her thoughts; for Mr. Rycot's intelligence, and other concurrent circumstances, left her without a doubt, that Belmour's marriage with Lady Clementina was determined on, and shortly to take place.—Still something in Belmour's manner, and a marked attention to herself at times, contradicted, she felt, the opinion of his preoccupation for another; but this idea only added to the painful sensations of her heart, whether she allowed herself to nourish or discard it from her breast; the melancholy, grown habitual to her, increased, and her spirits at last grew almost unequal to the talk of supporting, in any degree, the necessary appearance of unconcern on this occasion, which her situation, she was aware, demanded: she was therefore glad to have the sanction of Dr. Stanmore's advice for quitting the rectory, as she did, without further previous notice to her hosts, and without personally taking leave at the castle.

Dr. Stanmore had been again much embarrassed where to place Emily, when she should leave the rectory; a measure, however, on which everything more and more determined him.—The rector, in writing to him, had actually, with the utmost exultation, announced the *future joyful* event of the supposed marriage; and everything, that Emily had told him of the persons, whom she had seen on her visits to the castle, confirmed the intelligence; all which increased Dr. Stanmore's anxiety. In this dilemma, he recollected a Mr. Enstine, a lawyer, who resided near St. Alban's, and who, with a sister then living with him, took in sometimes an occasional boarder. This man, though not very particularly known to Dr. Stanmore, was sufficiently so to allow him to make the proposal of admitting Emily for a time as his lodger; which on Mr. Enstine's side was accepted, his room then being vacant. This being settled, Dr. Stanmore had only to arrange the method of conveying Emily thither;—in all which, he wished her to avoid the impertinent curiosity of indifferent persons; and thought it unnecessary, and indeed much better, that Mr. Rycot should not be informed of the place, to which she was going, rather choosing, that he should suppose her to have accepted of an invitation from some acquaintance; as her quitting the rectory thus suddenly, merely to go and board at Mr. Enstine's might excite Rycot's curiosity, and occasion him to make some unpleasant surmise.

It happened just at this time, that a cousin of Emily's, a Monsieur la Tour, son of a brother of her grandmother's in France, who had been supposed to have been lost in a voyage to the East Indies, came over to England, on some mercantile business, and likewise to endeavour to persuade Emily to sign a release to the claim of some trifling property, which he could not dispose of without her consent; and being now in very indifferent circumstances, from having failed in his voyage, this property, trifling as it was, became an object to him. Although Dr. Stanmore, to whom he applied on the business, was aware, that this man was not likely ever to afford the smallest protection to Emily; as he thought the request a just one, to say nothing, from the circumstances of the case, of the extreme improbability, that she should ever be benefited in the pecuniary way by a refusal, he advised her by all means to comply, and to sign the release. The young man having purposely sought him, where he was, in order to better explain the business, and being about the return to London when it should be settled, it occurred to him, that he might be of some use to Emily, by meeting her on the road, when she had quitted the rectory, and conducting her to Mr. Enstine's, where the whole business of the signing, &c. might be transacted immediately. To this la Tour willingly agreed, and Dr. Stanmore communicated the plan to Emily, desiring her, simply, to take a place for herself in the stagecoach for the first part of her journey, and come immediately to Staines, where she would find her cousin waiting for her to conduct her to Mr. Enstine's—and it was walking with this cousin, that Belmour saw Emily, when he went in search of her, directed by the master of the inn to the house where she then was; and where, as the innkeeper had informed him, she had been detained by being ill, and unable to proceed on her journey. Her conduct to Belmour on this occasion is easily accounted for.—Emily, circumstanced as she supposed him to be on the eve of his marriage with Lady Clementine, could only attribute this, as it appeared, clandestine pursuit of her, to motives the most offensive—an attempt to take advantage of her low, as he perhaps thought it, and unprotected situation; and she felt the keenest sense of mortification, at the idea of having inspired Lord Belmour with such sentiments, as she then supposed him to feel for her. Hence her desire to avoid him, which, without explaining the cause, she, in the general terms of choosing to see nobody, expressed with some warmth to her companion; who, by her manner, and her retiring into the house, imagined, that he was to defend her from some impertinent intrusion; which, as his natural disposition was rough and unpleasant, occasioned his speaking with so little restraint of civility to Belmour. Emily felt relieved at the thought, that, if she could get away unnoticed from the place where she was, as Mr. Enstine's chaise was to meet her on the road by appointment on the day following, Belmour must lose all trace of her, at least for the present; as she had not, by Dr. Stanmore's directions, told the rector and his wife whither she was going, the only persons who were the least likely, to give any information of her to Lord Belmour.

Having, as it was before mentioned, left the house near Staines unperceived; she rejoiced that she had, as it seemed to her, thus escaped further insult.—But a thousand painful recollections weighed heavily at her heart: ill could she reconcile the apparent lightness of Belmour's present conduct with all she had hitherto seen of him—his acknowledged character, his appearance, the respect of his attentions to her, could all this be put on!—could it be false!—Lost in reflections of this sort, she arrived at Mr. Enstine's who received her at the door.—Mr. Enstine had a smart little figure, with a sharp and rather intelligent eye; but the familiarity, with which he introduced himself to Emily, was by no means calculated to prejudice her in his favour. He conducted her immediately to his sister, who was in the parlour, sitting leaning in a chair with a dawdling air of indifference.—She rose, however, on Emily's appearing, as it seemed with a quicker motion than she had intended, and with an involuntary expression of surprise at her figure, and taking her by the hand, desired her to be seated. After some conversation on the *weather, roads,* &c.—"You must be *amazingly* fatigued with your journey," said Miss Enstine, "and my brother's chariot is a perfect *tumbril,* enough to dislocate one's bones, as I always tell him."—"Not in the least fatigued," said Emily, "I have, indeed, not been quite well of late."—"Indeed, you do not look so," resumed Miss Enstine, observing Emily's pale cheek, "you perhaps would like to repose yourself till dinner time—I am *sure* you would—here, Betty," cried she, opening the door, "show the lady into her apartment."—She then, without offering to accompany her, waved her hand, saying carelessly—"We shall soon meet again," and resumed her seat—Emily, sick at heart, and requiring time to recover her spirits, was not sorry to accept of the liberty offered her of withdrawing from the company. Mr. Enstine, who had always a considerable deal of business on his hands, and never chose unnecessarily to lose time, instantly took la Tour into his closet, to talk over the business, about which he was come, and of which he had had notice from Dr. Stanmore; and Miss Enstine, thus remaining alone, could not *communicate* either what she thought, or *chose* to *think,* of Emily's appearance and beauty, which had, in spite of herself, not a little surprised her. Miss Enstine's ambition was to be thought a *fine lady,* the means of effecting which she conceived chiefly to consist in appearing extremely idle, and extremely indifferent; and these specifics she produced on all possible occasions, which, together with a drawling and monotonous voice, and a half-languishing air, she thought rendered the character complete. Her idea of it she had much perfected by studying to make herself in every respect the reverse of her brother, whom she reckoned extremely vulgar; and he, on his side, holding in utter contempt manners so different from his own, seldom failed any opportunity of throwing a ridicule *indirectly* on his sister, sometimes not without a degree of dry humour, which she retorted as she could, and often, when exasperated, by downright abuse.

The contrast of such a society with that of Belmour Castle was ill calculated, to assist in obliterating recollections already too forcibly impressed on Emily's mind; and she looked forward only with the hope of again joining Dr. Stanmore, and regaining, in the exercise of constant and rational occupations, that quiet, and peace of mind, of which she felt herself almost wholly robbed.

Chapter 34

IT WAS AMONG THE PERSONS who occasionally came to Mr. Enstine's, that Emily first saw Mr. Courtenay, who came thither one day on business, and had accidentally agreed to stay to dinner, wholly ignorant of whom he was to meet at Mr. Enstine's table. It is needless to remark what must have been his astonishment on Emily's appearance, without previous notice, just at the instant of their sitting down to dinner;—but accustomed to curb the expression of the strongest feelings, nay, even almost wholly to suppress them, when not likely to prove conducive to his own gratification, he contented himself during dinner with endeavouring to guess who Emily could be; having no opportunity, then seated as they were at a small table, of asking such a question, without being overheard by her; the impoliteness of which rendered it, as he thought, impossible.

Mr. Courtenay's conversation was lively, uncommonly agreeable when he chose it, and always full of sense and information:—he possessed a perfect knowledge of human nature, and a nice discrimination of character even on the shortest observation.—He easily discovered, therefore, that Emily was not only distinguished by her beauty, but by a more than common share of understanding; and finding in himself a strong desire to please, he took not the common and trite method of avowed and open admiration, but endeavoured by frequently, though in a most respectful manner, addressing Emily, to draw her into conversation with him, in which, he without much difficulty succeeded; as she, on her side, was struck with the superiour polish of his manner, and the clearness and justness of his observations on the various subjects, on which their discourse turned; for Mr. Enstine was in his way clever, and at least afforded matter, on which Mr. Courtenay might work for the display of his own talents in conversation. On Dr. Stanmore's name being mentioned, Mr. Courtenay, with a visible expression of pleasure, took occasion to say, that he was one of his earliest acquaintances in life, and a person of all others whom he the most respected.—This, as it may be imagined, increased Emily's confidence, and she talked with still greater ease and liberty, than she might otherwise have done, to a person wholly till then unknown to her.

After dinner, when the gentlemen joined Emily in the parlour, where they found her with Miss Enstine, gaping with *ennui* from having been wholly *thrown out* that day, and completely unnoticed by Mr. Courtenay, on whom, as a man of distinction, she had cast her softest glances, without the slightest effect. Mr. Courtenay, who had procured what intelligence he could of Mr. Enstine concerning Emily, which, though only general, was all he wished to know, came immediately up to her with the ease of a man of the world, saying, "that he hoped, in consideration of his former acquaintance, he *dared* not venture to say *friendship,* with Dr. Stanmore, he might be received by her not wholly as a stranger, when he had the pleasure of coming to Mr. Enstine's;—and," continued he, turning to him, "you are going, I believe, Enstine, to find me a very troublesome fellow, for I am now with Williams only, you know, a few miles off, where I shall be for some time; and I mean to avail myself, with your leave, of this opportunity of terminating all our business together, which I think I can do more conveniently both for you and myself, than by carrying you, as I had intended, to Dean Abbey."—In answer to this speech Mr. Enstine, bowing as if much flattered, assured Mr. Courtenay, that he was at all times welcome, and that he hoped he would study only his own convenience.—"And if you can take up with our dinner, sir," said Enstine, "Kate and I" (turning towards his sister, who cast a disdainful look of disapprobation at this too familiar appellation) "shall be most happy whenever you will honour us, and then you will be in a manner sure at that time of finding *me,* without troubling yourself to send previous notice."—This seemed to be precisely what Mr. Courtenay wished, and under the pretence of *business,* which indeed was not without foundation, his visits to Mr. Enstine became extremely frequent. Emily always saw him with pleasure, as his coming gave a degree of life to the society at Mr. Enstine's, of which it would otherwise have been to her totally void.—She recollected too having heard Dr. Stanmore speak of Mr. Courtenay, as a man of uncommonly promising genius and understanding, which he now in his letters, on her mentioning having seen him at Mr. Enstine's confirmed, adding, that he should at any time be happy to renew his acquaintance with him.—And as Mr. Courtenay, in his attention to her, seemed actuated by no other motive than the pleasure he took in her conversation and society; she by degrees, grew to listen to him with the ease and familiarity inspired by an agreeable acquaintance.

In this manner above six weeks passed, when Emily, to her no small satisfaction, received a letter from Dr. Stanmore, announcing his return to the parsonage, and appointing a day for meeting her there.—She immediately communicated the contents of her letter to Mr. Enstine, who, she thought, seemed not much pleased with the intelligence: this, however, she attributed only to his not perhaps being provided with another lodger, to occupy the room she left, or some other reason of that sort.—A gloom too, as she spoke, was spread over Mr. Courtenay's countenance, who happened to be at the time with Mr. Enstine, which he appeared anxious to conceal, and affected to talk with an indifference of her ensuing departure, which she began to suspect he did not feel. This was the first time that any idea of the kind had struck her with regard to Mr. Courtenay; and many vague recollections now rushed on her mind, of different things which he had said to her in conversation, which seemed to corroborate this opinion. Such a supposition left her by no means without anxiety—she felt averse to engaging herself; yet was sensible, that to such a man as Mr. Courtenay appeared, should his intentions become serious, it was probable no reasonable objection could be opposed. All this she hoped might be fancy, and the effect of her too quick imagination; prone often to foresee even imaginary evils—and she determined, if possible, to mix no alloy in the sincere and heartfelt joy of again seeing her old and beloved friend;—and in the only hope to which she looked forward with a shadow even of satisfaction for herself, the contributing, by her care and tenderness, to his future comfort and happiness.

Chapter 35

OF SHORT DURATION were Emily's doubts respecting Mr. Courtenay's sentiments, as scarcely a fortnight had elapsed after her return to the parsonage, when he presented himself there evidently to seek her, as he offered no other pretext for coming, than his desire of renewing his former acquaintance with Dr. Stanmore.—This could not be mistaken.—Mr. Courtenay, however, for some time ventured not to avow the real motive of his visits, till sufficiently, as he thought, authorised by Dr. Stanmore, who, from the first, had received him with every expression of cordiality and regard. To him, therefore, he preferred his suit, entreating to be his advocate with Emily, on whom, he said, depended the future happiness of his life.

Mr. Courtenay spoke with manly sense and feeling—he was, he said, aware of the difference of age, and the little pretensions *he* could have to excite in the breast of Emily an interest more lively than that of friendship and esteem; still, he said, he was not without hope, that by making it the first study of his life, by every care and attention, to merit some share in her affection, he might, from a character like hers, meet with that return, which would satisfy the utmost of *his* ambition—and that, should he succeed in promoting the happiness he so sincerely wished her, he should consider himself as the most fortunate of men. Dr. Stanmore, having assured him of *his* good wishes, and of the satisfaction that for every reason such a union would give him, left Mr. Courtenay; impatient to communicate to Emily all that he had said, and obtain her consent to what he himself had so much at heart for her, a union with Mr. Courtenay; whom he considered as a man both of sense and honour, certainly of one of the most ancient families in this kingdom, and possessed still of no inconsiderable estate, though, as he understood, somewhat lessened by imprudences in his youth. A very affecting scene followed between him and the child of his adoption.—Poor Emily, though not surprised, was much agitated at what she heard, and affected at the disinterested anxiety of Dr. Stanmore, which, on every occasion, so manifestly showed itself for her.

Though in Mr. Courtenay she saw a protector, a man of sense, and an agreeable companion, she felt, indeed, that her wishes led her rather to prefer the pleasing task of contributing, by her care and attention, to the comfort of Dr. Stanmore, and devoting her life solely to quiet and retirement.—But Emily deceived not herself: she mistook not the secret cause, which, in a great measure, she was sensible, influenced her mind on this occasion; and determined, that what appeared to her only as a weakness, which time insensibly must conquer, should not govern her decisions, or destroy the prospects she might have of future and rational happiness.—For one only being, she was persuaded, could sensations more lively than those of friendship and affection ever have been excited in her bosom; and the vision of youthful fancy seemed there to have wholly faded before her eyes—Belmour she then believed actually married to Lady Clementina; for when the Earl of Delavere (then Marquis of Belmour) died, the newspapers were filled with accounts of his will, his funeral, its magnificence, and an enumeration of his titles, honours, and immense estates, all which devolved to his only son; to which was added a no less circumstantial detail of Belmour's marriage with Lady Clementina, which had (as it was supposed) taken place at the request of his father, while on his deathbed—the speech which Belmour had made on the occasion—Lady Clementina's wedding dress, all was exactly and accurately described; and their being together to accompany Lady Caroline, his sister, to Lisbon, whither she was ordered for the re-establishment of her health. This jumble of facts and falsehood, as it but too often happens, was, for a considerable time, generally talked of, and generally believed; as those whom the account most nearly concerned, either heard not of it themselves, or, as immaterial, thought the report not worth formally contradicting. In short, Emily, confirmed by the dictates of her own reason, and having nothing to oppose to the arguments, which Dr. Stanmore's anxious zeal and disinterested friendship adduced for her compliance to the proposal, consented to receive Mr. Courtenay as her future husband. No sooner had Emily taken her resolution, than she determined to fulfill, according to the utmost strictness of her own conscience, every serious duty of the engagement she was shortly to make for life; *certain,* that in so doing alone, she could ever hope to attain that sacred peace of mind, to which she looked forward as her consolation and reward.

Mr. Courtenay, by the restrained expressions of the more lively sense he felt of his own happiness, and the most respectful attentions to Emily every day, gained ground in her good opinion, and gave her cause not to regret the consent she had given to his addresses; yet the first and best reason Emily still felt for the step she had taken was her reliance on Dr. Stanmore's better judgment, who knew the inmost recesses of her soul—*he* advised, *he* even entreated;—and that her welfare and happiness were dearer to him than to herself, she never for a single instant doubted.

Dr. Stanmore, on his part, relieved from the painful anxiety, under which he had so long laboured on Emily's account, and from grudging, as it were, every passing day, which, by robbing him of a portion of his frail existence, must also rob his darling child of her only support, seemed to revive—it was rejuvenescence, and he talked of nothing but future plans.

Mr. Courtenay's intention, which he had before declared, of residing wholly in the country, was by no means displeasing to Emily.—Of London she knew nothing; her curiosity was not much excited by anything she had heard of its society or amusements, and she despised that vanity arising from indiscriminate admiration, which, from her extreme beauty, she could not but know, that she might everywhere command;—on such admiration she knew happiness depended not—*that* happiness, or rather *content,* she was determined to seek within herself, and, if denied her to enjoy, at least to deserve.

Chapter 36

SETTLEMENTS WERE, by Mr. Courtenay's direction, immediately drawn up by Mr. Enstine, and shown to Dr. Stanmore for his approbation. The provision for Emily appeared uncommonly handsome; and it is not to be supposed, that Dr. Stanmore, in such a case, inquired narrowly into the powers of the estate with an eye of suspicion: he could have no doubt of their validity, and Emily had nothing.

Soon after their marriage, which immediately took place, Emily set out with her husband for Dean Abbey, his family seat.

She had to the utmost endeavoured to support her spirits; yet her parting with Dr. Stanmore was a heavy trial—the mutual promises, which had passed between Dr. Stanmore and Mr. Courtenay, of meeting from time to time at their respective habitations, were little calculated, by imposing on her mind, to afford so consoling a hope. Dr. Stanmore's duty she knew seldom, indeed, allowed him to leave the parsonage, and of Mr. Courtenay's predilection and design uninterruptedly to reside at Dean Abbey, she was aware.

During the journey, Mr. Courtenay attempted, not foolishly to comfort or *console* Emily, but rather appeared to pity and respect her distress; and by every expression in his power, endeavoured to convince her, that such marks of the tenderness and affection of her heart were by no means displeasing to him.

When they arrived at Dean Abbey, it was already late, the distance from the parsonage being nearly a hundred miles.—On alighting, Emily perceived evident signs of confusion among the servants; some ran one way, some another, and no preparations seemed made for their reception. Mr. Courtenay led Emily on through an immense Gothic hall, from the opposite end of which they saw the fat housekeeper come waddling towards them with a candle in her hand, the only light, two half-extinguished lamps excepted, in the place.

"Warner," said Mr. Courtenay, as she came up to them, "I believe all the servants have lost their senses—none of them appear to attend us—here is your lady."—"And a sweet one, I am sure," said Mrs. Warner, holding up the candle, which she had in her hand, to Emily's face as she spoke,—"God bless her! say I, and your honour."—Saying this, she curtsied low, Emily smiled, then turning to Mr. Courtenay,—"Do not be distressed," said she, "the servants probably did not expect us after it was so late; Mrs. Warner will, I am sure, take sufficient care of us."—As she spoke, Emily accidentally laid her hand on Mr. Courtenay's arm; she felt that he trembled, as it seemed with vexation. He then drew Mrs. Warner on one side, and said something to her in a low voice, which she answered in the same tone. Afterward collecting himself, and turning towards Emily—"The servants," said he, "as Warner informs me, have all been quarrelling together today, a damned set of rascals!—but she has, however, prepared our room, and some supper for us." Saying this, he made the housekeeper a sign to advance, and they followed her through the hall to the bottom of a stair-case—all was dark.—"Your honour," said the housekeeper, stopping, "would it not be better, if you and my lady would come into your honour's study? there is a good fire there, and I can bring your honour and my lady the things for supper, while the maids are getting all ready above?"—To this Emily begged they might assent.—"We shall," said she mildly, and with perfect composure of countenance, "I have no doubt, I will find the room extremely comfortable, and all will be perfectly set right tomorrow.—I have not, you know," continued she, addressing herself to Mr. Courtenay, "been accustomed to *many* servants, and be assured, that *your* feeling for a moment disturbed at this little accident can alone even in the slightest degree distress me."—Mr. Courtenay gently pressed her hand, casting towards her a look of infinite admiration.

Emily's spirits seemed to rise on this little occurrence, as she found a necessity for exerting them, lest Mr. Courtenay, who she plainly saw was himself much vexed, should imagine her affected by difficulties of so trifling a nature in themselves, as these appeared to her.

The next day, Mr. Courtenay told Emily, that he had turned some of the rascals away, and that the whole was settled; but entered not into the least detail, and seemed rather desirous afterward to avoid the subject. Emily thought little more of what had passed at the moment, nor till further circumstances led her to think, that there was something mysterious in Mr. Courtenay's conduct, which subsequent events fully explained; convincing her, that former imprudences, want of arrangement in his affairs, and above all a want of confidence inherent in his character, caused that inward uneasiness of mind, which he vainly strove to conceal.

Emily had heard much of the ancient magnificence of Dean Abbey, and of its picturesque beauties, both from others and from Mr. Courtenay, who seemed to take peculiar pleasure in detailing them. With the latter, indeed, Emily was much struck, as the views of the building on the outside were admirable; and she could easily trace the remains of the former: but internally the long train of uninhabited apartments, the numberless passages and stair-cases leading to useless turrets and towers, were little calculated to inspire any ideas but those of melancholy and discomfort.

The same appearance of decay and neglect was visible throughout the park and the gardens, some nicely trimmed yew-hedges near the house excepted.—Yet Mr. Courtenay kept a considerable number of servants, distinguished in strict form according to their different capacities, as steward, game-keeper, &c.; but they seemed all to be equally unacquainted with their business, and with the respect and attentions due from them to their master. Mrs. Warner, the housekeeper, was the only servant, who had resided for any time with him.—She had been born in the house, and her mother had been housekeeper to his father.—In her Mr. Courtenay seemed to place no small degree of confidence; but with the rest of his servants he was impatient, and often violent; and they appeared to obey him rather through fear than attachment.

Emily, who had a spirit of order, without which no abilities can be really useful, seeing his impatience at being so ill served, several times offered to take upon herself the care of his house; but this Mr. Courtenay declined, saying, that *to Warner* he had consigned the whole of that business, and as to servants in general they were "*all alike.*" Emily, after a time, seeing that Mr. Courtenay always avoided the subject, desisted from any further offers. The evils in themselves she considered not as great, but regretted that reserve of disposition in Mr. Courtenay, which would, she foresaw, on any future occasion, prevent her from affording to his mind that support and relief, which might otherwise have been in her power, and which, both from duty and inclination, she felt so much disposed to give.

Emily, from the time of her marriage, and her arrival at Dean Abbey, continued to live in what might be called almost total solitude, till the period of her going to Cheltenham.—There were few neighbours near enough to make any intercourse with them of much resource; particularly as Mr. Courtenay appeared not to wish to cultivate their acquaintance—a visit of form received and returned ended the business; and now and then a dinner given at the Abbey, when Mr. Courtenay always seemed anxious to maintain an appearance, not only of opulence, but even of state; which Warner, aware of the humour and disposition of her master, endeavoured, as much as it was in her power, to promote. On these occasions, under her direction, the servants were *drilled* for a week previous to the day of invitation; and the old family plate, of which there was a considerable quantity, was cleaned up, and placed on the sideboard in the most exact order.—Warner prepared everything, and, in fact, had the care of everything; which was extremely necessary, as the different servants, though *dignified* by the most honourable appellations, as steward, groom of the chambers, &c., were a set of awkward clowns, who were totally strangers to the duties attached to the situations, in which they were misplaced.

Mr. Courtenay always affected the greatest indifference at the moment when anything went wrong, but evidently felt it much more severely than the subject deserved, and would afterward chastise his servants in a manner that added to their stupidity, by inspiring them with terrour, and deprived them of what little powers they might have had, under gentler treatment, of serving him more to his own satisfaction.

To Emily, Mr. Courtenay always appeared kind and attentive, and seemed, earnest to curb the violence of his disposition in her presence, though unwilling to disclose the cause of that gloom, and inward uneasiness, which so often hung over his countenance—He sought indeed at times, as it appeared, entire solitude, and would take long rambles alone, sometimes on foot, and sometimes on horseback, unaccompanied by any servant, and often did not return till it was dark. On these occasions, Emily perceived that it was displeasing to him to have any remarks made on the lateness of the hour, or length of his absence, at his return; and therefore endeavoured not to meet him with a countenance expressive of the uneasiness she often really felt, at the disordered state of mind under which at times he appeared to labour. Mr. Courtenay also made occasional journeys to town, and to Mr. Enstine's, with whom he seemed to have frequent business. Emily, by these means, passed many solitary hours, which she, however, had the advantage of being able to employ in the further cultivation of her mind, and in the pursuit and exercise of her various talents. Her music was no small resource, though as she made the soft notes of the organ resound to her voice, the image of Belmour would sometimes involuntarily present itself to her mind, and, by recollections at the same time dear and painful to her, increase that melancholy, which no surrounding object was then calculated to diminish.—To no one could she complain; for the susceptible heart of her only friend she feared to wound, by dwelling in any degree on the gloom of her present situation; since he, anxious for her welfare, had so earnestly pressed an union, which he thought every way likely to conduce to her future advantage and happiness, and to which he had sacrificed every selfish view, in thus promoting a plan, which separated him from all he held most dear on earth.

Emily had learnt with surprise, and a mixture of confused sensations, which she could not exactly define to herself, the marriage of Lady Clementina with Melford. This, of course, contradicted the persuasion of Belmour's engagement, of which she had hitherto entertained no doubt—but as of these events she knew nothing except from common report, she was at a loss what to credit, or what to disbelieve.

About this time her health, which was always delicate, had visibly declined, and Mr. Courtenay, anxious for her in the extreme, had insisted on having medical advice. The consequence of this was her being ordered to Cheltenham, where she so unexpectedly again saw Belmour—destined, as it were, to renew with so much additional interest, from a further knowledge of his character, from his passionate admiration of her, which she could no longer doubt, and from the thousand amiable qualities he possessed, those sentiments, which she had so often vainly endeavoured to banish from her heart.

Chapter 37

IT WAS NOW NEARLY THREE YEARS since Belmour had quitted England; during which time, he had not only visited great parts of Europe, but extended his travels into Asia and Egypt. From Constantinople he had sailed to Smyrna, where he had by chance met with a Greek, a man of profound erudition, who had made it his particular study, to trace the remains of Grecian art, science, and grandeur, on the very spots where they had existed. He had already made several voyages and journeys for this purpose, was particularly acquainted with the different islands in the Archipelago, and had, with the enthusiasm of national pride, more than once visited that part of the Asiatic coast, where still are to be traced the ever memorable plains of Troy. He had even gone farther than any other traveller into the interior of the country, which afforded him the most curious speculations from the still remaining language and customs of ancient Greece.—On conversing with this man, Belmour found, that his circumstances, which were contracted, alone hindered his further prosecuting his travels and observation; and that if proper opportunity offered, he would not even object again to go over such parts of Greece and Asia, as he had already visited.—Such a companion, it appeared to

Belmour, would be of infinite use to him; and circumstances thus uniting to make it the advantage of both, their plan was easily settled, and they agreed to travel together.—The Greek was a man of a thoughtful and serious turn, who, in addition, having had misfortunes in his youth, was uncommonly silent, though without any unpleasant reserve, when once engaged to enter into conversation.—Yet as there existed not that sympathy between them, which renders confidence the necessary consequence of intimacy, without further investigation of Belmour's character, he considered him in the light only of a young Englishman of fortune, who travelled for amusement, and to dissipate some secret chagrin, the cause of which he had no wish to penetrate.

Belmour, often in the course of their travels, when for any time they remained at particular places, made solitary rambles for several days, and even weeks together;—when he returned, he found the Greek void of surprise or curiosity at the length of his absence; and to appearance indifferent as to his return.—Love, when occasionally the subject occurred, he treated as a mere delirium of the imagination; and admitted of no circumstances, which could make it otherwise.—This did not encourage confidence on the part of Belmour—his sorrows remained wholly locked up in his own bosom—those sorrows time had only more deeply impressed on his heart, where Emily still reigned without control.—To muse over his own hard fate, and to recall to his mind her perfections, was the great charm of his life, and could, he thought, best be indulged, while thus far distant from that vain and insignificant society of the world, for which he then felt only disgust.—While his eyes wandered over the various new and interesting scenes everywhere presented to his view, a calm and composed sensation often took place in his breast, which, by leading to the consolations of philosophy and virtue, so softened his melancholy, as to allow it almost to merit the name of pleasure.

From that spice too of romance inherent in his character, the gratification of every act of benevolence, which, when the occasion occurred, he never neglected, was redoubled to him by his name and fortune not being known, and consequently less expectations formed of his powers to relieve by munificence. On one occasion, in particular, he had the satisfaction, so touching to his own heart, of completing the happiness of another.

A young man of the name of Wilmot, with whom he happened to form some degree of acquaintance on his first coming to Smyrna, (where Belmour now was for the second time) had, during his absence, become passionately in love with a Turkish girl, whom a merchant there, of that nation, had bred up from a child, and intended for the seraglio of the Grand Seignior.—Wilmot had seen her by chance; but afterward found means to converse with her in secret from her window, which looked into a garden, over the wall of which, to his no small risk, Wilmot used to climb when the nights were dark, on a given signal agreed upon between them.—This intercourse had continued for a considerable time; when Wilmot, certain of his passion being returned, and without the smallest hope of openly obtaining the object of his wishes, determined, with the young girl's consent, to carry her off secretly.—The plan was laid, and everything, as they thought, secure, when, after she had actually left the house with her lover, they found themselves pursued, a fray ensued in the street, and with difficulty, by the interference of the English factory, Wilmot was allowed to escape without being thrown into prison.—Belmour, who had only been entrusted on the very night on which the affair took place, had accompanied Wilmot, and been the means actually of saving him from the fury of the pursuers, in effecting which he had been himself wounded.

On the next day, his wound not being of consequence sufficient to confine him, Belmour visited Wilmot with an intention of inquiring into his further hopes. He found him the picture of despair, and in a state almost of insensibility.—"Would not money do much, secretly and judiciously employed?" asked Belmour in a comforting voice of encouragement.—"Money!" exclaimed Wilmot, frantically starting, "Yes, *money would do*—but I am sufficiently cursed! not double the sum of all I possess on earth, or possibly could raise, would satisfy the rapacious demands of this infernal tribe!"

Belmour made no reply, but instantly hurried out of the room—"Ay, ay!" cried Wilmot with a forced smile, following him with his eyes as he quitted the room—"even the noble spirit of an Englishman shrinks from the sight of such a wretch as I am! unable as he now is to assist me."

Wilmot had remained in such a situation of mind, as made it necessary he should be watched, lest from the despair he should be tempted to some rash act against himself—a care which, as he was much beloved, some gentlemen of the English factory had undertaken; when, after some hours, the door flew open, and Belmour, like a protecting angel, appeared, leading the beautiful slave by the hand.—Wilmot, at first, thought himself in a dream; and still, though encircled by the tender arms of his mistress, he continued to stare wildly, unable to collect his scattered senses, and turn at once from misery to happiness.

When he had, in some degree, recovered, turning to Belmour—"Far, far beyond all power of thanks, are such benefits!" said he, pressing his hands closely to his eyes—then to his bosom—"here, here, I feel my obligation."—He could say no more; and Belmour, much affected himself, hastily left him.

The next day, Wilmot having procured the proper draught for a sum to the full extent of all he possessed, carried it to Belmour. "So much," said he, "of your generous benefaction I can repay—for the rest I shall willingly remain *your* debtor—have no scruple in the acceptance—I am young, and can easily find employment."—Belmour, smiling, returned him his draught, and gently pressing his hand—"Rest secure," said he, "my young friend, I am already more than repaid—as to the money, it was to me of no importance—of this I assure you, on my honour.—One day, perhaps, I shall explain my situation to you."—Seeing that Wilmot was going to reply, Belmour begged to be no farther pressed on the subject at which he had hinted; and shortly afterward took his leave.

Wilmot attempted not to penetrate a secret, whatever it might be, which Belmour wished to conceal.—His surprise was, indeed, extreme at the facility, with which Belmour, who, under the name of Hubert, passed for an English gentleman of no considerable fortune, had procured so large a sum; and the ease with which he had thus bestowed it on one, who was in reality so little known to him, merely to satisfy the generosity and benevolence of his own disposition.

Wilmot's thoughts were, however, soon turned to the necessary preparations for leaving Smyrna, and going to England, whither he was to carry his newly married wife, trusting he had recommendations, to enable him to find employment in the line of business which he meant to follow. A vessel was shortly to sail for England, and in it he took his passage.

These preparations—the name of England, which contained all that was most dear to him, so often repeated, strangely affected Belmour, and brought past remembrances, as it seemed, with new force to his mind.—A thousand vague plans, in consequence, successively presented themselves to his imagination, and were as soon rejected by him.—In this unsettled state of mind, he was one day walking alone near the outskirts of the town, when he saw a figure moving slowly on in pensive meditation, which appeared not unknown to him,—again he looked.—"Good Heavens!" he exclaimed, "is this possible, or do my eyes deceive me!"—at the sound of his voice, the friar of Cintra (for it was he), suddenly started, and easily recognizing

Belmour, advanced towards him with open arms, then held him closely pressed to his bosom—"These are the rewards," said he, devoutly raising his eyes, "which bounteous Heaven, when least expected, sends to soften and mitigate our sorrows!—that we should meet in these distant regions; or that we should again meet at all, my son," continued he, as a tear stole gently down his cheek; "is wonderful!"—After the first expressions of surprise were over, they mutually, as may be supposed, inquired into each other's history.

The friar informed Belmour, that about a year after he had seen him, their convent having fallen much into decay, and the funds belonging to it being by no means adequate to the necessary repairs, added to which, a contagious malady had carried off several of the brothers; it was determined by those who had the supreme power, that the remainder of the brotherhood should be transferred to another monastery of the same order, then labouring under nearly similar difficulties; as by this incorporation of the two monasteries, their united income would prove sufficient for their support. On this occasion, a strict inquiry was made into everything relative to each of the friars, their names, ages, and other particulars; and the family of Don Juan de Colavrado (for that was the friar's name), became fully acquainted with the place of his concealment, which had been till then but suspected. The head of the family, who, by the death of his elder brother, had very lately become possessed of a large property, being a man of a humane and generous disposition; and at the same time feeling his pride hurt by the seeming neglect, into which his near relation, and the real heir of all his riches, had fallen; immediately sought him out, and endeavoured, by every means, to persuade him to partake at least of his fortune: hoping by his interest, which was considerable at court, being one of the first and most powerful of the grandees of Spain, if not to obtain a dispensation from his vows, for Don Juan at least was to be denied a mitigation of what he considered as his sufferings, by his removal to some richer and more considerable monastery of an order less severe; where, although deprived of liberty, he might still enjoy many of the comforts of life, of which he now was wholly deprived.—"My melancholy story," continued the friar, "which was now revived and publicly talked of, rendered me an object of curiosity; and besides many relations who sought me, I found myself continually molested by persons, who, under pretence of visiting the convent, came in fact merely to look at me. This, and the distance of the new monastery, to which I was to be transferred from the sad urn, and the remains of all that attached me to earth,—the silence and solitude, to which my soul was accustomed, wholly broken into—these considerations made me at last listen to a proposal of my really kind relation, Don Lewis; who offered to procure me the nominal charge of a mission to the Levant, under cover of which I might avoid again entering the dark walls of a monastery.—His affection touched me, and I gave way—nor have I repented.—Heaven, my son, is merciful!—thirty years of suffering have, I trust, expiated the crimes and errours of my youth; and I find my sad heart composed—this canopy," said he, pointing to the sky, "is glorious! and the repose in which I am allowed to pass the remnant of my life, soothes and mitigates my sorrows!—But on *your* countenance," looking with some earnestness at Belmour—"if I mistake not, I see traces of sorrow, which my heart tells me you have not deserved!—I would know more," continued he, "and surely may be trusted!" "You are kind," replied Belmour, "let us retire to my house, we shall there be freer from interruption."—"Today, I cannot," said the friar, "but for tomorrow, name your time; consider me as a friend, as one in whom you may confide; on that condition I will attend you."

The next day, at the appointed time, the friar came to him; and Belmour, having no fear of any indiscretion from such a confidant, made no scruple to relate to him, without reserve, the whole of his story—and as he found a sympathizing heart, the recital was not made without some relief to his own bosom.—When Belmour had finished his relation—"Much, much I pity you," said the friar; "but oh! how different is our fate!—*you* may still again behold the object of your love!"—the tears, which already stood in his eyes, now flowed so fast, that he was unable to continue, but turning his head on one side, he remained for a considerable time without speaking; then, after exchanging a promise with Belmour of shortly meeting, he took his leave.

"I *may* again see the object of my love," repeated Belmour to himself, as the friar left the room—and this reflection of the unfortunate Don Juan, so exactly coincided with the ideas, which had of late occupied his own mind, that giving way to an almost irresistible impulse, he determined to take advantage of the opportunity of the vessel in which Wilmot was to sail; and, under the pretence of business, which required his presence for a short time in England, contrive once again to see Emily—"But that peace of mind," said he, sighing heavily, "which she, fortunately, may have regained, must never be disturbed by me—such were her last injunctions—and they shall be religiously observed;—yet I may behold her!—*I* cannot *renew* sensations, which have long since become a part of my existence, and which melancholy seems but to have endeared to me!"—The resolution once taken, everything necessary for the voyage was easily settled, to the no small satisfaction of Wilmot, who rejoiced at the idea of being accompanied by his generous benefactor.

Belmour thought only of the means of putting his plan in execution, after he should arrive in England—he had left Emily at Dean Abbey, and doubted not but that, from every circumstance he had observed relative to Mr. Courtenay's character and disposition, to that spot her residence was fixed.—On this supposition his plan was formed; the execution of which appeared to him attended with little difficulty, acquainted as he was with the place, and the different roads leading to it.

Much of the remainder of his time, during his stay at Smyrna, was passed with Don Juan, in whom he every day discovered fresh proofs of those amiable and generous qualities, which were inherent in his nature.—The noble enthusiasm of the Spaniard was not diminished either by the superstitious observances of a monastic life, or by his own misfortunes; he listened with interest to the sufferings of real passion, and though time had in part conquered the acuteness of his own griefs, he knew not how to condemn in another a sentiment, which had imperiously governed the fate of his own life.

They parted with regret on both sides, yet Belmour was much relieved on his friend's account, from the infinite difference between his present situation and that in which he saw him when first they met at Cintra; where, condemned almost to total solitude, the unfortunate Don Juan was surrounded only by objects tending to increase his melancholy, and depress the natural powers of his mind.

Chapter 38

IN THREE WEEKS from the time of Wilmot's adventure, the vessel already mentioned set sail, and, after an uncommonly prosperous voyage, arrived at Portsmouth, where it had been agreed, that, circumstances permitting, the passengers were to be landed.

Wilmot went immediately to London; and Belmour, leaving Bertram at Portsmouth, under strict charge of secrecy, crossed the country alone. By the help of a slouched hat, and great coat, which he procured for the occasion, he was, he thought, sufficiently disguised, not to fear a discovery from those, whom he might accidentally meet in his way.—When he got to an inn, or rather halfway-house, within about fifteen miles of the Abbey, he took a horse for the remainder of the day, and for as much of the next as he should want it; leaving his portmanteau and watch for a security: having, as he thought, calculated his time so, as by leaving the horse at a cottage he recollected to have seen, and continuing the rest of the way about three miles on foot, he should just arrive at the close of day near the Abbey.—"On the terrace, she will take her accustomed walk—I shall there behold her!" said he to himself. It must be observed, that an unfrequented hollow road led immediately below the terrace, from which those who walked on the terrace were easily seen, while the persons in the road, from a high neglected hedge-row, that overshadowed it on each side, were completely concealed.

Belmour left the inn with almost breathless impatience, and hurrying on his horse, scarcely sensible of what he did, the poor animal struck its foot with so much violence against the stump of a tree, which accidentally stood up in the road, that it became suddenly lame. To this accident Belmour's attention was of necessity called—he alighted, examined the foot, and plainly saw, that on horseback it was impossible for him to proceed. He was then on an open common, and how many miles precisely from Dean Abbey he knew not.

"I shall still perhaps be able to arrive, even on foot, before it is quite dark," thought he to himself;—and leaving his horse at a farm-house, which he perceived at a small distance, he hastened away on foot.—After crossing several fields, by which, he imagined, he should shorten his road, he found, that he had missed his way, and was actually obliged to return to the very spot, where he had left his horse, in order with certainty to regain his track. The evening (it being now towards the end of July) was warm and serene, but the sky somewhat lowering and overcast; whence, added to the extreme agitation of his mind, Belmour guessed not at the hour, and found himself, long after sunset, contrary to his expectation, some miles from the Abbey. He still continued to hurry forward, for his imagination was by this time worked up to the utmost, and he thought that if he could but even distinguish the walls which enclosed Emily, see but a light in some one of the chambers, it would be happiness compared to what he then felt.

The moon, which was not risen, shone in her brightest orb, and seemed for a while to dispel the gathering clouds, but the evident signs of an approaching storm were shortly afterward not to be mistaken.—An awful sound of distant thunder first struck the ear, then gradually rolling onwards, became louder and louder, accompanied by streams of forked lightning falling from every side, till collecting, as it were, all its force, the storm seemed to threaten destruction over Belmour's head.—Torrents of rain now fell, and a total darkness prevailed, interrupted only by the lightning, which served, however, still to enable him, though slowly and by intervals, to pursue his way.—Belmour had already reached the great avenue, which led immediately to the Abbey, when the lightning became so much less frequent, though the darkness still continued, that it was only by very slow degrees he could advance.—At last being arrived at the iron gates in front of the entrance, a still louder peal of thunder than the preceding was heard, accompanied by a short vivid flash of lightning, which, darting across the walls of the Abbey, discovered to his almost frantic sight a large hatchment, suspended over the principal door. A deadly chill instantly seized his limbs, they shook, and he could scarcely support himself. With his eyes still strained towards the fatal object, which he could no longer discern, he for some time waited for a second flash.—All was darkness.

"Oh God!" he exclaimed, "Emily is no more!—all, all is over!"—but a shadow of suspense was now become intolerable, and rushing forward with violence through the iron gates, which were open, he flew with impetuosity to the door immediately under the dreadful hatchment.—Vainly he attempted to force it, and knocker there was none—then recollecting, that, nearly on the opposite side, was a small door commonly open, by which the servants passed, he endeavoured to hurry round half the immense circumference of the building; but in the attempt, having, from agitation of mind, wandered he knew not where, he found himself, after scrambling through thorns and brambles, and over fragments of broken stone, wholly at a loss which way to turn.—At this instant, supporting himself by chance against the door of a small porch, which had formerly led to a chapel, then in ruins, and where hay and straw were sometimes kept for the use of the stables, he felt the door give way, and through excess of fatigue, confusion, and disorder of mind, fell senseless on the ground, where he remained in a state between stupor and sleep, which wholly deprived him for a time of recollection.—After some hours, when he first began to recover, he knew not where he was; the trees were so thick, which closely overshadowed the little porch, that scarcely a ray of light could penetrate its recess; and when he arose and quitted his unsought for shelter, he was astonished to see the morning sun already shining brightly.—With his recollection, had returned his misery and agitation—unmindful of the consequences, and forgetful of his disguise, he wildly rushed in, determined to know the worst.—After entering the back door already mentioned, he ran swiftly through the house, without meeting a single creature, till at the end of a long passage, which terminated in the hall, he saw an old man, whom he remembered to have been a gardener.—The man had a bundle of faggots and a candle in his hand; and alarmed, as it seemed, at Belmour's sudden appearance, endeavoured to stop him. But

Belmour, pushing him aside without uttering a word, darted onwards, past the hall, flew up the great stair-case, and already had gotten some way along the gallery, when, stopping to take breath, and resting his arm against the wall, a soft and gentle sound proceeding from the apartment at the further end of the gallery, struck his ear.—He paused—again he listened—it was not a delusion—distinctly he heard the well-known voice of Emily. Plaintively she sang, and it was the very ballad he had with so much surprise listened to, when accidentally walking out alone on the evening he arrived at Belmour Castle—sounds never to be forgotten!—He was now for some moments unable to proceed—his sensations were too strong for him, and the quick transition from wretchedness and horrour, to the most enchanting hope, suspended all his faculties.—Twice she had gone over the same air, when Belmour, somewhat recovering, softly advanced towards the door whence the sound proceeded.—The door was not entirely closed, and a gentle breeze at the moment blowing it open, discovered Emily seated at the organ, her head half turned the other way.—Never did she appear to Belmour's sight so lovely! She was in the slight and simple dress, which she had first thrown on as she rose in the morning—her fine flowing hair hung negligently over her shoulders, and her whole figure had that character of natural elegance, which baffles all description. An old-fashioned bow-window, which occupied nearly the whole side of the room opposite the door, was filled with plants and flowers, and a small table was set ready with breakfast for her.—The soft refreshing feel of air was that of the early morning, which precedes a sultry day—the whole, indeed, of this scene was to Belmour one of enchantment and delight—he stopped—he stood gazing in silent rapture.—Having finished singing, Emily rose, and as she turned, Belmour's figure appeared before her.—"Oh Heavens!" she exclaimed—"is this a dream, or is it!"—Belmour was at her feet.

The unalloyed satisfaction which they now experienced, in again seeing each other after so long a separation, for a time suspended their mutual inquiries into the circumstances, which had finally united them.—Belmour could not mistake, that Emily was free—nor could she doubt the tender affecting submission, and tried constancy of Belmour; and no longer at variance with herself, she wished not to disguise either the feelings or intentions of her heart.—Emily then with earnestness inquired of Belmour into all that had passed relative to himself since their last melancholy parting. His simple narrative, in which he dwelt not either on his illness, when first he left her, or on his sufferings since, drew many tears from Emily's eyes.—"Nothing," said she, holding out her hand to Belmour, which he kissed with rapture, "is lost upon me; and all that you have omitted saying is only the more deeply felt by me—words are unnecessary, when sympathy like ours supplies their place! *My* history," continued she, seeing that his eyes were fixed on her with a look of inexpressible anxiety, to know what more she had to say—"*My* history is short. I have not once quitted this place, since we parted; and for this last year, two visits from Dr. Stanmore, and some persons of business excepted, I have remained wholly alone. On this very day I again expect him; and with him in a few days more I am to take leave of Dean Abbey, which now is the property of a distant relation of Mr. Courtenay's."—On the mention of Dr. Stanmore's coming, Belmour showed evident signs of satisfaction; something whispered to his mind, that in him he should find a friend to his earnest wishes of being shortly united to Emily.

A day of enchantment thus passed, when towards evening, as Emily and Belmour were seated on the terrace, the noise of a carriage was heard—Emily's colour went and came—Belmour was for hastily advancing to meet him—"Stay," said she, gently stopping Belmour, "the surprise of seeing you thus suddenly might be too much for him—I know the acuteness of his feelings for all that interests his child!"—Saying this, she went forward and came up to Dr. Stanmore just as he alighted from the chaise. As he pressed her to his bosom, he perceived her agitation—then looking earnestly at her, it was not grief he plainly saw. Scarcely had she time to prepare him for seeing Belmour, when, unable longer to restrain his impatience, he flew forward. Dr. Stanmore advanced towards him, as quickly as his steps would allow, with extended arms—tears streamed down his aged cheeks. "My children, my children!" he exclaimed, unable to utter more, as he pressed them together to his bosom; then turning to Emily, "I have not then," said he, "caused thy unhappiness!—thy virtues now will be rewarded!"—He then seated himself between them. "I must recover myself a little," said he, "this is almost too much for me!"—After a short pause, he continued, "not that I am *surprised* (you will forgive the liberty an old man takes), but the first and only time I saw you, a prepossession for you took place in my mind, which the subsequent knowledge of your character had indeed fully justified. Do not wonder that I am so well informed," said he, smiling, as he looked at Belmour—"You may be easy—consider me only as your *confessor*." "I consider you as my *father*," said Belmour, with warmth, pressing his hand to his lips with an expression of the tenderest respect, "as the father of my Emily!" "Amiable being!" said Dr. Stanmore, wiping away the tears from his eyes—"long mayest thou live to enjoy that happiness, thou hast so well deserved!"—Emily presently afterward interrupted them, by saying, that as the evening was so far advanced, she feared the dampness of the air and overfatigue for Dr. Stanmore. "I feel as if I could sit here forever," said he, "but must obey my monitress."—They then all three retired into the house; and such were the feelings of their gratified hearts, that the mouldering and dismal walls of Dean Abbey assumed to their imagination an aspect of cheerfulness and content.

Chapter 39

IN THE COURSE OF THE FOLLOWING DAY, Dr. Stanmore informed Belmour of the particulars, which had passed since his absence, relative to Emily, and to Mr. Courtenay's death. Not long after Belmour had left Dean Abbey, Dr. Stanmore had passed a few weeks there, and to him Emily had not disguised the oppression of her heart.—She knew, that her conduct would be approved by him; and that the rectitude of her intentions would be strengthened and supported by his counsel and advice.—She knew too, that he would shed a tear of pity and affection over her; and not harshly condemn a weakness, which, if she could not conquer, she had determined to suffer without reproach to herself: for such was the basis of that sound yet gentle philosophy, which he had taken for the guide of his own life; and was the approved maxim, which he had always forcibly inculcated into his pupil.—"From circumstances and events, my child," he would say, "it is more than probable, thou hast much to labour through in life; nor would I, even were it in my power, steel thy tender susceptible heart against the sufferings of humanity—for can we lessen the woes of others, without partaking theirs? or can we hope otherwise to receive that alleviation of our own miseries, which sympathy alone can give! But," he would continue, assuming a graver aspect, "although we cannot govern events, we *can* govern our own conduct—let us only remember, that the force of our passions is commonly proportioned to the force of our minds, and consequently, that those passions may be controlled.—Youth and inexperience, indeed, are often to be pitied for the errours, into which they may have been led, and from which the timely hand of friendly admonition might have saved them, by setting before their eyes that one great truth, that with a guiltless conscience all mental sufferings become supportable. But it is the argument of lurking vice, when *weakness* is pleaded as an excuse for the little resistance, made to *supposed* uncontrollable passions."

To Mr. Courtenay, Emily's manner was uniformly gentle and attentive; and she was studious, by every means in her power, to render the solitary life he had chosen, such as might best contribute to his comfort and satisfaction; but as he had made his opinion more from disgust for the world, than taste for retirement, and felt not that internal glow of content, which alone can give real charms to quiet, and seclusion from the busier scenes of life, even her judicious endeavours could not always ensure success.

Sometimes, from slight causes, the violence of his temper would break out; and whenever that had been the case, discontented with himself, he became silent and sullen, and avoided even the sight of Emily. He would then often take long solitary rambles over his park, which, in its then neglected state, could only convey to his mind ideas of melancholy and regret; since to the follies and extravagance of his youth it owed its present desolate appearance. At other times, however, he found in the society of Emily, whose well-cultivated mind and improved talents rendered her a companion to her husband, that relief and advantage, of which his own sense and taste made him fully sensible.—Emily had, in addition, the satisfaction of knowing, that Mr. Courtenay did her justice, and that he felt that confidence in her character, which she so well deserved.

When Belmour left England after his long illness in town, a paragraph appeared in the papers, mentioning his going, which ended in these words: "We know not positively the cause of this young nobleman's going abroad, he having already twice made the *grand tour;* but we have reason to suppose, that a secret mission from our cabinet to Russia is the real object of his journey, in which case, his being *personally* well received at that court cannot be doubted."

"Stuff!" cried Mr. Courtenay, who had just glanced over the newspaper, when his eye met this paragraph. "Yet," said he, giving the paper to Emily, who was sitting near him on a bench on the terrace, "I doubt not, but that Lord Belmour may be gone abroad—it is a subject on which I will not trust myself—but you understand me—and let me, my Emily, take this opportunity, once for all to assure you, that my mind is now at ease, perfectly at ease—you have acted like yourself—can I say more?"—He then, holding out his hand to signify that he would not be answered, walked away, and she shortly afterward saw him with his gun, and heard him speaking in his usual voice and manner to his game-keeper.

Emily doubted not but that Belmour was indeed gone abroad—doubted not the cause—and the delicacy of his forbearance, in not writing to her, more affected her than could have done the most expressive words of a letter.—The strictness of her principles, and the purity of her mind, had left her no doubt as to her own conduct; but over the sufferings of one, for whom she felt both tenderness and admiration, she shed many a silent tear. Yet still she knew not how wholly to regret an attachment, which touched and gratified, not that idle vanity to which indeed she was a stranger, but her heart.

A few months had passed in the manner already mentioned at Dean Abbey, when Emily had an opportunity of exercising that strength of mind, for which her character was so conspicuous, as well as of gratifying an exalted idea of delicacy, which converted a subject of serious uneasiness into one little short of satisfaction.

Mr. Courtenay had appeared more than usually thoughtful for some days past. This Emily plainly perceived, yet, as it seemed to be from some cause, which he chose should be secret, she ventured but slightly to hint at her observation: for in spite of his high opinion of Emily's understanding, his temper never would allow him, to be what he called *admonished* even by her; and advice was never to be given, unless, which indeed not unfrequently happened, he asked it of her himself.

A patient silence, in cases like the present, was her only resource.—It happened one morning, that Mr. Courtenay having gone out the moment after breakfast, Emily had omitted to ask him some intended question—when going to the terrace, the way by which she thought he would probably return, in order to meet him, as she walked slowly on, an open letter, fallen accidentally on the ground, met her eye, and she had glanced over nearly a page, unconscious of what she was doing, when the letter, suddenly, from its contents, called forth all her attention. It began with excuses for being under the necessity of pressing an unpleasant subject—then reminded the person, to whom it was addressed (and whom she afterward found to be her husband) of the promise of a *premium,* "for business done, if not *honestly,* at least *cleverly;* and without which, my good sir, you well know, that the finest woman in the world would never have been yours, nor you have shown your face with credit; for, notwithstanding your own confidence then in the expectations you had from your uncle, who since was so *obliging* to you as to marry, and his wife so *obliging* to him as to find him an heir, the parson would never, in common prudence, have consented to a marriage for his ward, on such really uncertain grounds.—But I held out your rent-roll, above three good thousand pounds per annum! which your father bequeathed to you at his death! and then *nicked* the young practitioner, whom Dr. Stanmore employed to examine into it, by keeping all the debts, post obits, bonds, and mortgages, carefully out of his sight—and now you may go on tolerably for your own life—therefore, according to your own maxim, *take care of today,* and *tomorrow may shift for itself. Your* conscience may be tolerably easy—but, sir, I must have *my premium;* I can now buy in with advantage, and it is but ordering down some more of your old timber.—This, I know, goes rather against you, and am sorry therefore to insist, but it is the only way I can think of: and thus you will, at least, be no more plagued by, sir, your most sincere and respectful, '*R. Enstine.*' "

Emily had no sooner recovered from the surprise, which this letter occasioned her, than, actuated by the noble and disinterested generosity of her spirit, she began to frame excuses for the conduct of her husband.—She wished, indeed, that on such an occasion he had entrusted her, and treated her with that confidence, which a subsequent knowledge of her character, she thought, might have deserved. But still, said she to herself, *interested* motives were certainly not Mr. Courtenay's object in this fraud, the idea of which could only have been suggested to him by sentiments flattering in themselves to me.—*I* brought him only additional expenses, and had his uncle, as he expected, left him his heir, that provision for me, which was merely nominal, he, doubtless, intended to make real. In short, Emily determined to act with that candour and disinterested generosity, which her heart at the moment suggested; and even felt a secret satisfaction in having thus something to *forgive* Mr. Courtenay, which seemed in a degree to relieve her mind from the sort of reproach, that she often felt heavily at her heart, from the sentiments she had hitherto found unconquerable for another. Willingly would she have indulged the open frankness of her disposition on this occasion, and have instantly assured her husband of the perfect indifference, with which she viewed this possible future diminution of fortune for herself: but wishing rather to consult *his* disposition than her own, she resolved on silence at least for the present; fearing, that, however palliated by her own real disinterested sentiments and sincerity, this discovery might appear to him as a detection of his conduct, and serve only to irritate his mind, already too susceptible on the slightest contradiction.

Emily was at first embarrassed how to dispose of the letter—should she secrete it, the loss, and uncertainty of what might have become of it, would undoubtedly distress Mr. Courtenay—she preferred, therefore, leaving the letter exactly where she found it; as she knew it was unlikely, that anyone, Mr. Courtenay himself excepted, should then come that way. She seated herself in a window, whence she could observe what passed below, and shortly afterward actually saw Mr. Courtenay at the further end of the terrace. With quick steps he advanced, looking round him, as it seemed, with much anxiety; then, seeing the letter, he snatched it up, and having put it hastily into his pocket, advanced towards the house. Emily retired to her room, whither he soon followed; her cheerful and open countenance, which a conscious sensation of the rectitude of her own intentions inspired, instantly removed the most distant idea of her having seen the letter, and relieved his mind; for although Mr. Courtenay loved, respected, and admired Emily, his own character was not calculated fully to understand and do justice to the superiourity of hers.

Emily determined not to mention the circumstance of the letter even to Dr. Stanmore—she knew the pain such a discovery would give him, and for herself feared not poverty, were it coming with a nearer and more certain approach, than at that time there was reason to expect.

Nearly two years passed without any material incident, when Mr. Courtenay's temper growing daily more fretful and uneasy to himself, and some symptoms of his impaired health occasioning Emily considerable alarm, she entreated of Dr. Stanmore, to come to her assistance, and endeavour (an attempt in which she herself had not been able to succeed), to persuade him to see some physician.—"All stuff," he would say, "I am perfectly well, and were I otherwise, the farrago of nonsense I must hear from a physician, by irritating my unfortunate nerves, would do me more harm, than all his medicines could do me good."

Still this satisfied not Emily, and she perceived, that Mr. Courtenay by no means thought so lightly of his own indisposition, as he pretended. The frequent giddiness in his head, with which he was seized, sometimes occasioned a loss of sense and recollection for some hours, and his recovery from these fits was by no means immediate.—Dr. Stanmore flew to Emily the very moment it was in his power—he found her anxious and uneasy, and waiting his friendly presence with impatience.—With regard to Mr. Courtenay, he felt he could give him no real comfort, as the whole appearance of his complaint seemed threatening in the extreme, while he continued nearly in the same state of obstinacy with respect to any medical advice. Once or twice, however, at Emily's earnest request, he did see a physician; who, being a man of knowledge and integrity, averse from trifling in any way with the feelings of others, plainly told Dr. Stanmore and Emily, that there was little hope of final recovery for the patient; but that with care on his own part, and occasional bleeding, he might prevent the rapid progress of the disorder.—Mr. Courtenay, however, was not to be persuaded to any alteration of this sort, and would, whenever his fancy led him, go out in his usual manner, and wander whole hours alone. Having on one of these solitary rambles, and after appearing extremely unwell in the morning, outstayed by far even the probable time of his return, Emily, who from one moment to another grew more and more uneasy at the length of his absence, at last went out into the park, accompanied by his servant, in search of him.—Dr. Stanmore, who had little doubt but that in truth some accident had happened, also followed,—Emily and the servant advanced rapidly, and they had not gone very far, when they actually saw Mr. Courtenay lying extended on the ground—They found, on raising him, that he still breathed, carried him home, put him to bed, and got the physician's assistance, but all was vain—he expired a few hours afterward, having scarcely again spoken—The words, which he with difficulty uttered, were to thank Emily for the only really happy days he had ever passed—"Thy own virtues will, I trust, reward thee!—may'st thou be happy!"—and then lowering his voice, he whispered, "I want forgiveness of you—you know not."—"I *know* all," earnestly pressing his hand, said Emily.—"I more—more than forgive!"—Tears then choked her voice, and she sunk almost senseless by the side of her husband.—When all was over, Dr. Stanmore removed her from the melancholy apartment, and recalled her mind to the calmer dictates of reason and resignation.

He sent shortly after for a lawyer, and before his arrival, as it then became necessary, Emily informed him of what she concluded must be the real state of Mr. Courtenay's fortune, and of the accidental circumstance, by which she had come to this knowledge.—Dr. Stanmore, on finding that he had been thus trifled with, and cruelly imposed upon, and that Emily, through his means, was in all probability, after consenting to a marriage not particularly agreeable to herself, chiefly in compliance to his entreaties and decided opinion, now almost unprovided for, nearly lost his wonted fortitude.—With difficulty it was that Emily, even by the tenderest expressions of affection for him, which her heart could suggest, and the most perfect sense of disinterestedness for her own situation, could comfort him, or even recall him to himself.

The lawyer, who had now been sent for by Dr. Stanmore, proved a man of honour and integrity, and perfectly versed in every branch of his profession. He already knew something of Mr. Courtenay's affairs, had seen Emily several times on different occasions, and charmed with her character, her intelligence, and her manners, undertook the business entrusted to him with the alacrity of a friend. After wading through a troublesome and almost endless investigation of papers and parchments, he, at the end of the year, in spite of the utmost care and diligence, when the debts were settled, could with difficulty collect, out of the remains of the whole supposed considerable property, more than a bare sufficiency for her future support.—The estate of Dean Abbey, indeed, might have been sold for a greater sum than it was, which would have made a considerable difference to her; but of two bidders she preferred the one, who offered the least for the purchase, because he was a near relation, of the name of Courtenay, and her husband had often expressed much uneasiness at the idea of that place, which, he said, had descended to him from a long succession of ancestors, ever passing into another family.

After Dr. Stanmore had, as far as they were known to him, related these particulars, he added, with emotion—"Thus has my child, in every stage of life through which she has hitherto passed, acquitted herself of her duty with that nice sense of delicacy and integrity, which would do honour to the strictest moralist; and while dispensing blessings to all around her, by the warmth of her generous and benevolent heart, the powers of her understanding, and the charm of her society, her last thought, and care least attended to, have ever been for herself!—Yet Fortune, alas! has not smiled upon her—her life, from early youth, has been one of exertion—but I now trust," said he, looking with affection at Belmour, "that it will become a life only of happiness and content!"—"O! could I render it so!" exclaimed Belmour with extreme eagerness, "how should I not myself be blessed!—long, long has *my* life been devoted to her—my every thought, my every care!—in absence *she* was ever present before me, and even my sufferings for *her* became dearer to my heart, than could have done all other joys!—But," continued he, "may I not hope to shorten unnecessary delays! enough of time, if I mistake not, has already been granted to propriety—and to vain forms Emily cannot be attached—in a few days you were together to leave this place."—Here Belmour looked at Dr. Stanmore with an almost trembling anxiety—"May I not then—may I not, seconded by you, venture to propose, that together we proceed immediately to Belmour Castle?—You alone must give Emily to my wishes—sanction and confirm, by every sacred tie, those vows my heart has long made to her!"—Dr. Stanmore, almost wholly overcome by the sensations of satisfaction and joy, with which the tenderness, the open, and generous spirit of Belmour inspired him—without speaking, took his hand, and led him to Emily's apartment.—Belmour fell at her feet, and then, in the presence of Dr. Stanmore, renewed his suit.—Emily, although herself much affected, half smiling at his extreme earnestness, gave him her hand.—"Affectation," said she, "I despise!—and since my first and dear monitor," looking towards Dr. Stanmore, "approves, think not that I shall longer oppose my own happiness—to *you,* Belmour, I henceforward look for a protector—*you* will not, I am sure, while you regulate the future tenour of *my* life, forget how much in that your own honour and happiness are now involved!"

Belmour, enchanted with what he heard, flew instantly to give the necessary orders for their departure.—Messengers were sent for from the nearest post-town, and dispatched with their separate directions; one to Portsmouth, where his servant Bertram had remained; one to Belmour Castle, with orders to his steward, to prepare everything for Emily's reception; and another to London for his equipage. In short, it was not many days before all was ready for their journey, and on the day week from that on which Belmour had again seen Emily after his long absence, they actually set out together, accompanied by Dr. Stanmore, no more to part; blessed not only in the certainty of each other's tenderness and affection, but in the certainty of each other's worth, and in that mutual confidence, without which no happiness can be complete.

As from the carriage, by a turn in the road, they caught the last glimpse of the walls and turrets of Dean Abbey, Emily's eyes filled with tears.—"*You* will not," said she, recovering herself and turning to Belmour, "condemn this last tribute to the memory of a place I have so long inhabited, and may never more now behold!"—Belmour tenderly pressed her hand to his lips, but was not sorry shortly afterward to see her regain the natural composure of her spirits.

Dr. Stanmore bore the journey almost without fatigue, and when they entered the park-gates of Belmour Castle—"This air," said he, "revives me."—Emily and Belmour, with whom he was in the coach, looked at each other, then at him, with an expression of infinite affection—"Long may this air agree with you," said Belmour, "try but its salubrity sufficiently."—Their attention was now called off by the numbers of the tenants and cottagers, who flocked to receive their lord, meeting the carriage, and following it, many of them with uplifted hands and streaming eyes!—These evident marks of joy, which his arrival occasioned, much affected Belmour, and still more Emily.—"How deeply am I not already in debt to these good people," said she, "since I have been the cause of so long detaining their protector from them!"—Yet Belmour, even amid these grateful expressions of universal joy and satisfaction, still felt one latent cause of anxiety, which the very scene before him seemed doubly to recall to his mind.—It was several months since he had heard from his sister, and her last letters by no means gave him satisfactory accounts of her health.—She wrote them from Pisa, and with uncertainty as to her future plans, whether she should continue in Italy, again return to Lisbon, or come, which seemed by what she said most unlikely, to England.—He had been much disappointed at receiving no letters from London, which he had expected he should; and now dreaded the intelligence, which at that moment he might find of her at Belmour Castle.—Let the reader then judge what must have been the feelings of a heart like his, when, on alighting from the carriage, he found himself in his sister's arms.—She had arrived from Lisbon, where several packets having been detained by contrary winds, none of her last letters had preceded her; and had stopped with an intention of remaining at Belmour Castle, while she made some inquiries about her brother; when, a few days after her arrival there, she was met by the first messenger dispatched by Belmour, who shortly afterward was followed by Bertram, from whom she heard all that his breathless impatience, and extravagant expressions of joy, allowed him to detail of what he had learned at Dean Abbey. This intelligence had given her, for every reason, the most unfeigned satisfaction. She was herself tired of the desultory life she had so long led abroad, and sighed for what then appeared to her the more rational enjoyments of life, quiet and retirement—and all the mystery of her brother's conduct, and the secret cause of that melancholy, which she never failed to trace in his letters, being now explained, and the immediate prospect of his happiness taking place, she looked forward for herself, in the society and protection of her brother, to scenes of calm content and comfort, which had been long strangers to her imagination.

Lady Caroline had expressly forbidden, on this occasion, that the least hint should be given to her brother of her return, reserving to herself the full pleasure of surprising him.—Belmour held his sister long pressed to his bosom—then, scarcely recovering from the delightful emotion the surprise of seeing her thus unexpectedly had occasioned, he took Emily's hand, and leading her to Lady Caroline, who at the same instant advanced towards her—"Receive," said he, "a *sister.*"—"I *do* receive her," returned Lady Caroline extremely affected at this scene, "and take her to my heart!—I shall now no longer have to *fear* her charms, their power will be employed, by all I have heard, by all I hope, only to bless *my* happy brother!"

Heartley and Mortimer, who having heard of Belmour's return, had hastened to meet him, now advanced, wishing to express their congratulations; and, according to their different characters and dispositions, their sense of the present joy and satisfaction. Heartley, simple in his ideas, open and generous in every thought, felt the most cordial satisfaction at seeing the son of his late friend and patron restored to his country and to his family, with the prospect of so much happiness to himself, in his union with a woman, whose superiour merit had by no means escaped his penetration, even in the few opportunities he had of seeing her formerly at Belmour Castle.—Nor had he then been without suspicions of Belmour's sentiments for her; but, had secretly regretted, that shackles imposed by pride and prejudice perhaps then alone prevented an explanation, which might tend to the future happiness of both. And Mortimer, who wished others those blessings, which he had never hoped himself to obtain, felt infinite satisfaction in the prospect of renewing the only gratification he had ever known; the liberty of contemplating the object of his wishes in silent admiration.

It had been settled by Belmour, with the concurrence of Dr. Stanmore and the consent of Emily, that on the day subsequent to their arrival at Belmour Castle, which was in the morning, their marriage should take place, and that the ceremony should be performed in the chapel of the castle as privately as possible.

On the evening of that day, the company already mentioned being assembled in the drawing-room, Dr. Stanmore, looking round him, desired to know who was to take *his* place on the ensuing day—"for," continued he, "tomorrow my Emily will want a *father,* a place that my affection at least has ever, I trust, supplied."—Belmour immediately started up, and flying across the room to Heartley—"On *you,*" said he, seizing his hand, "my best and oldest friend, can I with most satisfaction to myself impose this grateful office!—you, Heartley, must give Emily to your friend."—Heartley, surprised and affected at a compliment he so little expected, having concluded that some at *least right honourable relation* would have been sent for on such an occasion, silently pressed Belmour's hand to his heart, as his eyes filled with tears.

Here they were interrupted by the entrance of Mr. Rycot, who, after skipping about with the most ludicrous expression of intended respect, from one side of the room to the other, advanced, bowing as lowly as the increased corpulence of his person would possibly admit; paying his obedience first to Belmour, and then to Emily; to the latter, not without a considerable feeling of awkwardness at the thoughts of not having treated her, while with him, *quite* as he would have treated a future *Lady Belmour;* which he feared would be remembered by her to his disadvantage, and inwardly cursed his own folly, for having, as he thought, missed an opportunity of securing to himself the protection and favour of so powerful a patroness.—This was, moreover, the only occasion, on which his wife had ever ventured openly to controvert his *supposed* better judgment.—"There!" said she, when the news of Belmour's arrival and intended marriage reached the parsonage—"there you have made a fine *spot o' work,* with all your cleverness! didn't I always tell you *Miss* was summone more than she chose to say?—I am sure you never were half civil enough to her, a sweet lady! and so I told you every day—but you was only for scolding me, never to be ruled but by your own pate."—"Poh, poh!" cried he, giving his wig a sharp twist at the ear, and endeavouring to conceal his not thinking her *for once* quite in the wrong—"you are a fool—always told ye so—know not what ye're talking about—never did, so best hold your tongue once for all!"—But Mrs. Rycot, proud of conquest, had already often renewed this conversation, as in spite of her husband's affected unconcern, she plainly saw, and exulted in her triumph over him.

The rector was, therefore, not a little relieved by the reception, which he met with from Emily, who remembered only the obligations she owed him; and by Dr. Stanmore's acknowledging him as an old friend, and thanking him for the protection he said he had given to his child, in the most cordial terms of gratitude.

Things taking this turn, so much beyond his expectation, gave him a flow of spirits, which it required nothing less than the *awe* and respect, with which he was inspired for the company, in any degree to repress.—After having paid his compliments of congratulation, separately and collectively, to everybody, he came again to Dr. Stanmore.—" 'Pon my word, doctor," said he, taking hold of his coat with each hand, as he held him at arm's length, and looking up at him in the face, "Why, you are not grown much older, nor much fatter, nor much thinner, all these years!—egad! look at me here," clapping his hands to his sides, "my wife says she can't let my waistcoats out fast enough!—Well, Heaven be praised for all things, as they say, and I am sure, I never should have thought of seeing *you* here!"—he then said something in a whisper to Dr. Stanmore, who himself wishing to speak to him on the subject of the ceremony, which was to take place on the ensuing day, walked with him into another room.

They presently returned together, but the rector had, instead of the usual smirk which distinguished his countenance, now assumed a more consequential air of gravity, and walking up with solemnity, he bowed, first to Emily, then to Belmour.—"Wait your lordship's commands, my lord, for tomorrow"—Emily coloured.—"O!" said Belmour, who could not help smiling at his solemnity—"my requests for tomorrow Dr. Stanmore will tell you, and you will have the goodness to take your directions from him."

"I will follow you immediately to the parsonage," said Dr. Stanmore, making him a sign to go; "the walk will do me good this fine evening, I understand it is but a short distance; and I shall be glad to pay my compliments to Mrs. Rycot.—I will follow you immediately," Dr. Stanmore repeated (wishing to relieve Emily from his presence) "and we will settle everything together."—On this, the rector bowing round to all the company, with the most affected air of gravity, left the room.

On the morning following, Dr. Stanmore, with that unaffected dignity peculiar to his manner, joined in sacred and indissoluble bands two beings formed for the support and comfort of each other, whose hearts had long been united—and who thus presented to the world a bright example of that reward, which bounteous Heaven can alone bestow on virtue, constancy, and truth.

Chapter 40

ALMOST ON THEIR ARRIVAL at Belmour Castle, both Emily and Belmour had been anxious to dispatch letters to Lady Clementina, to announce their marriage to her, and with every expression of affection and kindness towards her, to entreat her presence, as the completion of their own happiness.—For setting apart the charm of her society, to her they both felt much was owing, and were both impatient to thank her—she had ever, with that natural frankness peculiar to her character, expressed her admiration of Emily, and had in no small degree contributed while at Cheltenham to promote that degree of intimacy between her and Belmour, which, by necessarily raising them in each other's opinion, proved finally the source of all the happiness they now enjoyed.

In little more than a fortnight, Lady Clementina's speedy arrival was announced, with that shortly afterward of some other near relations of Belmour's desirous of expressing personally their satisfaction on his marriage.

Amid the general content and satisfaction which prevailed, one thought, and one only, weighed on Emily's mind, for not like those over-susceptible dispositions, who seem to languish after subjects of distress, often when farthest removed from them, she was fully sensible of all the blessings she possessed: but to Dr. Stanmore she felt her obligations incalculable; and to her it had ever seemed, that the only return in her power, in any degree adequate to what she owed him, was to attend and watch over his latter days, to soothe and comfort him in the hour of sickness, or of death.—And her new tie, with all its charms, seemed to remove her still further from all chance of fulfilling these grateful duties to her friend, her benefactor, her more than father. Impressed with these ideas, Emily had been sitting for a time alone in her room, when Belmour entered with a letter in his hand from Lady Clementina, saying, that all impatience to see them she should be on the very next day at Belmour Castle.—The expression of satisfaction evident on his countenance, when he came to announce this news to Emily, was instantly damped by the sight of a recent tear, which had stolen down her cheek.—"My Emily," said he, advancing and taking her hand, "what has happened? you have something to distress you!"—"Nothing, thank Heaven!" she replied, with an expression of infinite affection, "which I may not partake with you!"—She then ingenuously told him what had affected her.—"Yet I feel," said she, "almost as ashamed to admit now even of this cause a grievance! it is a subject," continued she, "on which I never touched to Dr. Stanmore; nor would he, where my happiness was concerned, see a disappointment in any privation, which might be occasioned to himself—Yet."—"Yes, yes," said Belmour, "but this *is a grievance,* a *just* grievance, and what we must endeavour to remedy."—He had walked thoughtfully several times up and down the room without speaking.—When a gentle tap was heard at the door, and in came Dr. Stanmore.—"What," said he, on looking at them, after he had entered the room, "are the cares of matrimony already come upon you!—why, you both look as serious as if you had been married this twelvemonth!—but, come, come," continued he, smiling, "I must have you both in good humour, I am come to ask a favour of you;" saying this, he seated himself, making them sit on each side of him.—"It is not your interest for a bishoprick," continued he, turning to Belmour—"no, the favour I am going to ask is wholly in your own power—and it is by your countenance already granted!—but not longer shall I keep you in suspense, I will tell you my request—it is to make me your *almoner*—the place, I am aware, will not be a *sinecure*—but Emily, I have long known, can be a good assistant on these occasions."—He might have continued speaking much longer, for both Emily and Belmour were too much affected to reply.—"My most kind friends!" said he, "to be serious, I see, I *feel* that I have anticipated your wishes!—pity for a poor old man, alone and forlorn, distant from all he holds on earth most dear, would become a painful sensation to yourselves!—I know your hearts!—nor would I touch on this subject even to Emily, till I had fully weighed it; fully, to the best of my judgment, determined on the propriety of the step I am taking—but, like actors from the stage, we may, under certain circumstances, without disgrace retire from the busier scenes of life, when, from age or infirmity, no longer able to fulfill our part!—and nearly thus it is with me.—I cannot long expect, in any degree, to be able to discharge the duties of my station, with that inward satisfaction to myself, and hope of approbation from Heaven, which I have ever made the end and aim of all my actions.—Yet still I would go on to the last, persevere in my endeavours at least, were I not certain that my parishioners would, in their future pastor, find a father—in short, I know and reverence the virtuous young man who is to succeed me—admire his saint-like character! and feel that in *his* hands my flock will be secure!—I know that he has the promise of my living from my diocesan,—know, too, that on his preferment depends his marriage with an amiable, accomplished, and virtuous young woman, to whom his heart has long been engaged; and that prudence alone, from the state of their circumstances, too contracted even for their moderate wishes, has hitherto prevented their union—for them, therefore, by retiring, I prepare happiness, which long may Heaven continue to them!—and for myself, I secure that quiet scene of ease and comfort, which, at the close of life, is most grateful. To you and Emily I am willing to owe much more than would be sufficient for my support.—Have I made my cause good? and is my request granted?" continued he.—Emily, still unable to speak, hung on his neck, and bathed him with her tears—and Belmour, scarcely less affected, left him no doubt how he felt this last kind mark of real confidence and friendship, which, by adding to his society a man whom he loved, honoured, and admired, relieved him from the painful idea of having caused one single sensation of regret, anxiety, or uneasiness to Emily, in the completion of his own happiness.

Chapter 41

THE NEXT DAY Emily, Belmour, and the rest of the party, took their evening walk in the park, following the road by which Lady Clementina was expected, and accordingly ere long the carriage appeared.—Scarcely would Lady Clementina allow it to stop, and the door to be opened, before she flew out, and in an instant was in Emily's arms.—"I hardly know which way to turn," she then said, "but my *new* cousin claims my first attentions.—Caroline," she continued, tenderly embracing her cousin, "how I rejoice to see you! and looking, I protest, better than I ever recollect to have seen you—no more running away from us! you shall stay now with this *will o' the wisp,*" looking towards Emily, "whom at last we have caught!—Well, I hope you will none of you grow tired of me, for," turning to Belmour, "I am come to stay the whole summer with you.—Aunt Eliza is following me with my little boy, and will be here tomorrow or the next day, for I travelled too fast for him, poor dear little fellow! and she is as good a nurse as she was a chaperon.—You see what liberties I take with you, but Melford's regiment is quartered near, and I was so glad, so delighted to come, that I am sure you cannot be *sorry* to see me.—Melford," she continued, "would not come with me; he said, that we should all be so foolish, so ridiculous, and so fond of each other, that he would stay till the first nonsensical days were over.—You know he always laughs at one, but I never mind him, for 'tis only that he hates the trouble himself of being either very glad, or very sorry—but Aunt Eliza, I can tell you, will be quite disappointed, if you have not saved her a bit of wedding cake—she thinks it's lucky, and I know not what, and has talked of nothing but on which side of her pillow she should put it ever since we heard of your marriage, and of my bringing her here."—"I trust," said Belmour, casting a significant look towards Lady Caroline, that we *may* find her a bit of fresh cakes, should none of ours remain."—"No, you don't say so! well, I am so glad!" exclaimed Lady Clementina, flying again up to Lady Caroline, who, colouring violently, turned her head the other way.—"Is it really all settled? for *I* guess—poor dear Mr. Mortimer!—well he does deserve this, for never, surely, was there so constant an admirer!—you're nothing to him, Belmour, and then he used to be so melancholy, and so respectful and so hopeless!—now do tell me, Caroline, how long is it since he has been dying for you? for the years are beyond my counting!"—"How can you be so ridiculous," replied Lady Caroline, affecting to laugh—

then with a more serious look, turning to Belmour, "upon my word, brother," said she, "this is too much—and I don't guess what you mean!—not a word has passed, and"—"Come, come, sister," said Belmour, "do not let us trifle any longer, you know very well what I mean—we will talk this over as we walk along—but for the present, our conference on this subject must be short I believe, for, if I mistake not, I see Mortimer himself at a distance, coming out of the castle gate towards us—but let me, my dear sister," said Belmour, taking Lady Caroline affectionately by the hand, "just say, that you have ever known my sentiments with respect to Mortimer.—I admire his virtues, and the modest gentleness of his character, and saw with pleasure his growing attachment for you, from a hope, that time at least would render you sensible to his merit—and, by your altered manner, which has not escaped me, you at last feel, as indeed you ought, the constant, sincere, and respectful attachment of one, who has long deserved a better return from you; and should fortune by an objection to such of our relations as may think they have a right to interfere on this occasion, for to your own generous mind, I am sure *that* can be none, I intend to make that matter easy—the addition of the farm you have so often admired, which joins his estate, and which, from my friendship and esteem, he will not refuse, will certainly make the offer of his hand such as you may, even with prudence and propriety, accept—a selfish plan of my own, you see, to secure you to myself, by marrying you to my nearest neighbour!"—Lady Caroline, surprised and overcome by so much kindness and noble generosity, abandoning her reserve and seeming indifference, tenderly embraced her brother, then, wishing to conceal her emotion, she took his arm, and walked on with him, in silence.—"This is all very well," cried Lady Clementina, skipping on lightly before them, "but I am in such spirits myself, that I will have every other creature here happy too; and I give you notice, that if I see poor Mortimer with his usual melancholy face, I shall tell him all, this instant—but I shall," cried she, running on towards him, in spite of Lady Caroline's efforts to stop her.—"Emily and Belmour can scarcely help laughing, I see, and as for you, my dear grave cousin, I don't care—and so away I go."—Saying this, she sprang forward, and returned not long afterward to them, dragging Mortimer by the arm, who, fearing to trust what he heard, and still unable to believe in happiness almost beyond his hope, looked with earnest anxiety first at the one, and then at the other of the company.—Belmour then advancing, took his sister's hand, which Mortimer received from him, and pressed with ecstasy to his lips.—"Come," said Lady Clementina, at first not quite sure if she should cry or laugh, but determining for the latter—"No more fuss, nor talking this over now—you may thank me for making you know your own minds, and not letting you dawdle on till doomsday, which you both would have done, I believe, if you had been left to yourselves—so I will have my own way."—"Upon my word, my pretty cousin," said Belmour, smiling, " 'tis well our aunt Eliza is coming tomorrow, to keep you in better order."—"Oh! she's too busy now with the child to trouble her head much about me and that she thinks is still better sport, for as the poor little fellow can't speak yet, you know he can't contradict her; so she talks to him all day, and lets me alone, except now and then, to be sure, just making a face at me when I am *very bad indeed.*"—"Most amiable of beings!" said Emily, affectionately, taking her hand, "the correction of *your faults* can be but a lesson of philanthropy to others, since your gentleness in bearing reproof for errours, if they be such, serves but to endear you the more to all who admire, to all who love you—nor is it gratitude alone, believe me, which ranks me foremost in that number!"—"Nay, if you praise me," said Lady Clementina to Emily, embracing her, "I shall be too vain; and all Aunt Eliza's *nods* and *winks,* or even her scoldings, will go for nothing, I can assure you; so take care what you do, and don't quite spoil me for your own sakes, as you see that I have settled myself among you."

Belmour's sensations, on thus finding all combine to justify his choice, to grace and honour the long wished for object of his tenderest affection, those only can imagine, whose feeling hearts and exalted minds render them incapable of enjoying blessings, where they endanger the peace of others, and who despise the mere advantages of fortune, when unaccompanied by what alone can give them real value—the power of contributing to the happiness of those whom they love.

The remainder of Belmour's family, as it may be supposed, failed not in their congratulations and attentions of the occasion of his marriage, an event which gave universal satisfaction; and Emily's relations made advances towards her, which were on her side received, as they deserved, with cold and distant civility.—Mrs. Stainville, whom she afterward occasionally saw in London, she ever treated with expressions of kindness, and was pleased to receive as an agreeable companion, remembering past occurrences only with gratitude.—To her, indeed, and even to her weakness, Emily felt that she probably owed the happiness she now enjoyed in being united for life to the dear and only real partner of her heart.

Chapter 1

6 *Spa* The name of a watering-place in the province of Liège, Belgium, celebrated for the curative properties of its mineral springs (*OED*). It was frequented by women wishing to become pregnant, or for those who were pregnant, to facilitate delivery. Anne Damer's friend Georgiana, Duchess of Devonshire, visited the waters at Spa.

7 *ton* The fashion, the vogue, the mode; fashionable air or style (*OED*). Derville is a fop and his libertine attentions are themselves a form of fashion.

9 *figurante* Attractive mistress.

12 *parterres* Level spaces in a garden occupied by an ornamental arrangement of flowerbeds (*OED*).

12 *jets d'eau* Fountains.

14 *covers* The utensils laid for each person's use at table; the plate, napkin, knife, spoon, etc. (Not in *OED*.)

15 *dowdy* A woman or girl shabbily or unattractively dressed, without smartness or brightness (*OED*).

Chapter 2

19 *novices* A novice is a person who has entered a religious order and is under probation or trial before taking the required vows; a candidate for admission into a religious order; a probationer (*OED*).

20 *freaks* A sudden causeless change or turn of the mind; a capricious humor, notion, whim, or vagary (*OED*).

21 *chaperon* A person, especially a married or elderly woman, who, for the sake of propriety, accompanies a young unmarried lady in public, as guide and protector (*OED*).

Chapter 3

24 *whip Miss* Not in *OED;* perhaps a woman who moves quickly, like a whip.

25 *curricle* A light two-wheeled carriage, usually drawn by two horses abreast (*OED*).

25 *Cumberland* The name of the English county, now part of Cumbria (*OED*).

25 *Major Heartley . . . loss of an arm* Admiral Nelson certainly sat for Anne Damer in London in 1801, possibly as early as 1798 in Naples after defeating Napoleon, and this portrait of Major Heartley may owe something to their acquaintance.

27 *surtout* A man's greatcoat or overcoat (*OED*).

27 *made love* Expressed admiration for; flirted with.

28 *hanger-on* A follower or dependent (*OED*).

28 *led-captain* A hanger-on, dependent, parasite (*OED*).

28 *fatigues* The extra-professional duties of a soldier, sometimes allotted to him as punishment for misdemeanor; an instance of this (*OED*).

28 *frigates* In the Royal Navy, formerly vessels of the class next in size and equipment to ships of the line, carrying from 28 to 60 guns on the main deck and a raised quarter-deck and forecastle. As subsequently used, the term no longer denoted a distinct class of vessels, being often applied to ships of much larger size than those that were so designated early in the nineteenth century. Since 1943, a naval escort vessel, a large corvette (*OED*).

Chapter 4

32 *jessamine* A climbing or ascending shrub with fragrant white flowers, long naturalized in Southern Europe, and grown in England since the sixteenth century (*OED*).

32 *pyracanthus* Scarlet firethorn, *Pyracantha coccinea* (family Rosaceae), a southern European thorny evergreen shrub bearing clusters of white flowers and persistent orange-red berries, often grown as an ornamental wall shrub (*OED*).

32 *Flora* In Latin mythology, the goddess of flowers; hence, in modern poetical language, the personification of nature's power in producing flowers (*OED*). Here, also, an attractive woman.

33 *finical* Over-nice or particular, affectedly fastidious, excessively punctilious or precise, in speech, dress, manners, methods of work (*OED*).

33 *possets, caudles, and conserves* Medical remedies (not in *OED*).

36 *slurry* To dirty, soil, smear, daub (*OED*).

43 *tar* A familiar appellation for a sailor: perhaps an abbreviation of "tarpaulin" (for example, Jack-Tar) (*OED*).

45 *check-string* A string by which the occupant of a carriage may signal to the driver to stop (*OED*).

54 *black-friar* A member of the order of Dominican friars, founded at the beginning of the thirteenth century by St. Dominic, so called from the color of their dress (*OED*).

54 *domino* A kind of loose cloak, apparently of Venetian origin, chiefly worn at masquerades, with a small mask covering the upper part of the face, by persons not personating a character (*OED*). Sometimes "domino" means the half-mask itself, and that seems to be the intention here, since the disguise is not complete ("merely in a domino").

55 *hackney-chair* Formerly, a sedan chair, subsequently a bath chair or the like, plying publicly for hire (*OED*).

56–57 *"Oh! mon Dieu! mon cher maître, qu'est-il donc arrivé?—un duel?—Mais non, vous serier plus tranquille—je me rappelle quand."—"Ne parle pas si haut,"... "ce n'est rien—va te coucher, Bertram, et laisse moi."* "Oh, my God! My dear master, what has happened? A duel? No you would be more tranquil; I remember when."—"Do not speak so loud," . . . "it's nothing—go to sleep, Bertram, and leave me."

Chapter 5

61 *hollowed* laughed

62 *Rycot* Variants in spellings in the original, such as "Roycot" and "Rycott," have been changed to read "Rycot."

63 *guinea* Sum of money equal to the value of this coin. In present use, a name for the sum of £1.05 (21*s*) (*OED*).

Chapter 6

71 *commerce* A card game; a game in which exchange or barter is the chief feature (*OED*), as in these examples: "**1732** MRS. DELANY *Autobiog. & Corr.* (1861) I. 346, I played two pools at commerce. **1776** MRS. HARRIS in *Priv. Lett. 1st. Lord Malmesbury* I. 341 The *ton* here is the game of 'Commerce' which the fine people play immoderately high. **1779** *The Sylph* I. 238 My former

winnings are in the sweepstake-pool at the commerce-table. **1780** F. BURNEY *Diary* (1854) I. 270 Whist players in one, and a commerce party in the others."

72 *"Perche amor mio ben nascondi"* I have been unable to trace this song in the Italian repertoire.

74 *curvettes* Not in *OED*.

74 *"Sweet be the slumbers of the virtuous mind"* Joseph Addison, *Cato* 5:4.

Chapter 7

75 *marquisate* In Britain and Ireland: the rank or dignity of a marquess. Formerly also: the place from which a marquess takes his title (obsolete) (*OED*). A nobleman ranking below a duke and above an earl or count; the title for such a nobleman, the rank of a marquise.

Chapter 8

83 *allemande* A name given to various German dances; a figure in which the gentleman turns his partner, in square or country dancing (*OED*).

Chapter 9

86 *Staines* Residential city on the Thames in southeast England, Surrey (*Columbia Encyclopedia*).

87 *stock* An article of clerical attire, consisting of a piece of black silk or stuff (worn on the chest and secured by a band round the neck) over which the linen collar is fastened (*OED*); perhaps an obsolete usage is intended, because the man described in this passage is a "sea-faring person."

87 *hanger* A kind of short sword, originally hung from the belt (*OED,* third definition).

89 *Weymouth* Famous for its beaches, in southwest England, Dorset (*Columbia Encyclopedia*).

89 *chay* Perhaps slang for "chaise."

91 *"Mauvaises nouvelles milor"* "Bad news, milor."

94 *Falmouth* A warm port city in southwest England, Cornwall (*Columbia Encyclopedia*).

Chapter 10

99 *packets* Boats on a regular route that carry passengers, freight, and mail.

103 *fidalgo* "A Portugueze nobleman" (Damer's notation).

104 *lauristinus* An evergreen winter-flowering shrub (*OED*).

104 *Capuchins* Friars of the order of St. Francis, of the new rule of 1528. So called from the sharp-pointed capuche, adopted first in 1525, and confirmed to them by Pope Clement VII in 1528 (*OED*).

105 *Velasquez* Velaques in the original (2:18). Damer prided herself on discovering a Raphael while in Portugal (Notebooks, 2:34).

105 *padre* In Italy, Spain, Portugal, Latin America, and other areas of Spanish and Portuguese influence: a title of a Christian clergyman, especially a Roman Catholic priest (*OED*).

106 *"Rosaurae Sacer . . . posuit"* "Sacred Rosaura . . . passed."

109 *Adeya-Galega* "A small village, where passengers land, after crossing the harbour in their way to Spain." (Damer's notation).

109 *"Salve Domine"* "Hail, Lord" (*Oxford Dictionary of Latin Words and Phrases,* 1998).

110 *St. Benedict* Sixth-century monk regarded as the father of Western monasticism (*Encyclopaedia Britannica*).

114 *cenotaph* An empty tomb; a sepulchral monument erected in honor of a deceased person whose body is elsewhere (*OED*).

Chapter 11

121 *demur* Delay, lingering, waiting (*OED*).

121 *goth* One who behaves like a barbarian, especially in the destruction or neglect of works of art; a rude, uncivilized, or ignorant person; one devoid of culture and taste. Often associated with *Vandal* (*OED*).

124 *Mr. Courtenay* The spelling of Mr. Courtenay's name fluctuates in the original text. I use the "a" ending throughout; interested scholars can compare volume 2, pages 183, 184, 185, 186, 187, 189, 193, 197, 216, 217, 219, 220.

126 *battle of Culloden* April 16, 1746; culminating battle of the "Forty-five Rebellion" and last serious attempt by the Jacobites to restore the Stuart dynasty to the British throne in which the Jacobites under Charles Edward were defeated by British forces

under William Augustus, Duke of Cumberland (*Columbia Encyclopedia*). Damer's father participated in this battle.

138 *Gloucestershire* A county in central England (*OED*).

Chapter 12

139 *postillions* Those who stand behind the horses of a carriage-horses (not in *OED*).

141 *chay-seat* A light open carriage for one or two persons, often having a top or calash; those with four wheels resembling the phaeton, those with two the curricle; also loosely used for pleasure carts and light carriages generally (*OED*).

141 *Cheltenham* Town in Gloucestershire; the term Cheltenham is "used to designate the chalybeate [iron-rich] waters of the springs there or the salts left by the evaporation of these waters" (*OED*).

Chapter 13

142 *"Milor n'aura pas diné"* "You haven't eaten?" "Milor": An English nobleman in Europe; an Englishman traveling in Europe in aristocratic style; more generally: a wealthy Englishman; also as a title of respect (*OED*).

142 *"n'est pas tard, Bertram mais ordonne moi à diner, et dis que je compte passer la nuit ici"* "It is not late, Bertram, but order me something for dinner and say that I plan to spend the night here."

Chapter 14

146 *pattens* Wooden-soled footwear worn to make the wearer taller or keep them out of the mud (not in *OED*).

146 *casement* A frame or sash forming a window or part of a window, opening on hinges attached to the upright side of the frame in which it is fixed (not in *OED*).

146 *cravat* An article of dress worn round the neck, chiefly by men (*OED*).

147 *sociable* Designating an open, four-wheeled carriage that has two double seats facing each other and a box seat for the driver (*OED*).

Chapter 15

148 *saddle-horses* Horses which are used for riding (*OED*).
150 *quiz* An odd or eccentric person; a person whose appearance is peculiar or ridiculous (*OED*), as in "**?1781** C. A. BURNEY *Diary* ?24 June in F. Burney *Early Diary* (1889) II. 297 He's a droll quiz, and I rather like him."
150 *nabob* In extended use: a wealthy, influential, or powerful landowner or other person, especially one with an extravagantly luxurious lifestyle; specifically (now historical) a British person who acquired a large fortune in India during the period of British rule (*OED*).
150 *se'nnight* A period of seven (days and) nights; a week (*OED*).
150 *bosquets* Copses, groves (not in *OED*).

Chapter 16

152 *coiffeur* Hairdresser; the French word for hairdresser: affected by fashionable or artistic hairdressers, and their patrons (*OED*).
152 *chignon* A large coil or hump of hair, usually folded round a pad, which has, at various times (e.g., c. 1780, c. 1870), been worn by women on the nape of the neck or back of the head (*OED*).

Chapter 17

155 *bandeau* A narrow band or fillet worn by women to bind the hair, or as part of a headdress (*OED*).
156 *menuet de la cour* A court minuet.
159 *mutton pie, when you peached* The speaker uses the term "peached" to mean "blamed, out of spite, on."

Chapter 19

166 *Argo* The ship in which Jason sailed in search of the Golden Fleece in Greek mythology.
166 *arras* A rich tapestry fabric, in which figures and scenes are woven in colors (*OED*).
166 *airs* Melodies or tunes, especially in the soprano or tenor range; a solo (*OED*).

168 *massy* Massive (*OED*).
168 *tester* A canopy (*OED*).

Chapter 20

173 *sartain* Certain.

Chapter 21

178 *commands* Directions (not in *OED*).

Chapter 23

190 *cotillon* An elaborate ballroom dance with frequent changing of partners.
191 *minuets* A stately dance for two in triple time (*OED*).
192 *nabby* Not in *OED;* perhaps a version of nabob or of nobby, a person of wealth or social refinement (*OED*).
193 *sitten up* Been sitting up. Damer uses this form and the reviewer commented upon it as a peculiarity of her style; for this historic reason (as a feature that marked the manuscript when it was first reviewed), "sitten" has been retained.

Chapter 25

204 *Harberry* The seat of the Stainvilles (Damer's note).

Chapter 26

210 *"Ah! mon Dieu! nous allons perir"* "Oh my God! We will perish!"
211 *"Comment!" . . . "Madame n'a pas peur en voiture!"* "What!" . . . "Madame is not afraid to drive!"
211 *"Madame la marquise, que je viens de quitter, crioit toujours encore plus fort que moi, toutes les fois que la voiture panchoit seulment de côté. J'y suis si habituée que."* "Madame the marquise, whom I just left, always cries out louder than me when the coach lists even a little. I am used to it."

211 *"Il faut vous deshabituer, Jaqueline,"* . . . *"ou vous courez risque de crier toute seule, avec nous"* "It is necessary to get un-used to it, Jaqueline," . . . "or you will risk crying out all alone, among us."

Chapter 27

213 *passer au moins l'hiver* To spend at least the winter.
213 *embrassée* and *recherché* Embraced and sought after.
213 *"Mais qui est cette jeune personne?—une parente apparemment?—elle est charmante!—mais charmante! belle comme un Ange!"* "But who is this young person. A relative apparently? She is charming, just charming! As beautiful as an angel!"
213 *l'air d'une belle statue* The look of a beautiful statue.
213 *la belle Anglaise* The beautiful English girl.
214 *"ce sont des étrangères: apparement que c'est sa fille!"* "Those are foreign ladies: apparently that's her daughter."
214 *"Mais je vous trouve rajeunie et embellie, jamais je ne vous ai vue si bien!"* "But you seem younger and even more beautiful, never have I seen you looking so well!" (the original reads: *"jamais je en vous ai vu si bien"*).
215 *everyone had chacun sa chacune* Each had his lady.
215 *de bonne compagnie* Of good breeding.
215 *"Ah! vous voilà donc de retour."* "Oh, you've returned."
215 *"Mais vous êtes bien aimable de revenir,"* . . . *"nous ne vous attendions pas de si tôt—convenez en, vous vous êtes ennuyé à Vienne?"* . . . *"vous connaissez surement le petit Raymond, votre compatriote."* "But you are so good to have come back," . . . "though we admit we weren't expecting you so early. Were you bored in Vienna?" . . . "you surely know young Raymond, your compatriot."
215 *connaissez* The original reads *"connoisser."*
215 *"il faut donc que je vous le présente—c'est le meilleur enfant du monde!—venez, Milor, que je vous présente."* "I must introduce you—he's the most wonderful child in the world—come here, my lord, I want to introduce you."
216 *"le voilà amoureux de vôtre belle Demoiselle,"* . . . *"mais savez vous que ce seroit le plus joli parti du monde pour elle—il faut que nous arrangions cela ensemble—il est riche, et n'a personne à consulter que lui même!"* "There he goes falling in love with your beautiful friend," ... "but do you know that it would be the most attractive

match in the world for her—we must arrange this—he is rich, and has no one to consult but himself."

216 *"Mais vous y allez bienvite, ma chère amie"* "But you are hasty, my dear friend."

Chapter 28

217 *"Mille et mille pardons, Madame, je suis honteux!—je le vois, je me suis fait attendre!"* "A thousand pardons Madame. I'm ashamed—I see I made you wait!"

218 *"Ah, Milor!" . . . "charmé de vous revoir!—rien de si triste, que Vienne, à ce que l'on dit—la société du monde la plus choisie, à la vérité—mais d'une tristesse! d'une monotonie—c'est vôtre païs, par example, qui est beau!—je regrette encore le tem[p]s, que j'y ai passé!—j'étois bien jeune alors!"* "Ah Milor," . . . "wonderful to meet you; nothing so dull as Vienna, they say; the most pleasing society, truth be told. But dull, monotonous! It's your country that is beautiful; I wish I had spent more time there, but I was very young when I visited."

218 *"Rien de si charmant!"* "Nothing so charming."

218 *"On trouve moyen d'y remedier"* "One finds means to remedy that."

218 *"une affaire arrangée"* "A personal matter."

220 *"le philosophe des ames integres"* "The philosopher for honest souls"; a pretentious phrase with little meaning, characteristic of some superficial members of salon society.

220 *bonne* a (French) nursemaid (*OED*).

221 *"Vous etés étonnée, n'est-ce pas, mon coeur, de voir Madame de Vermont ici?"* "You are amazed, my dear, to see Madame de Vermont here?"

221 *"mais c'est mon neveu qui l'a voulû," . . . "Il me gouverne, comme vous savez!"* "But it is my nephew who wanted him here" . . . "he runs my life, as you well know."

221 *"Oh! elle est coquette comme on ne l'est pas!"* "Oh she is as flirtatious as can be!"

222 *"ce que la Duchesse ne pardonne jamais—mais je suis d'une étourderie!"* "This is something the duchess won't forgive, but I am an idiot."

222 *"les gens de Madame de Vermont!"* "The servants of Madame de Vermont!"

222 *fade compliment* An insipid compliment.

222 *"Si on nourissoit les vaches en Angleterre comme en France?"* "Are cows fed in England as they are in France?"

229 *"Vous partez! est-il possible!—quitter Paris!—et dans cette saison!—vous milor!"* "You leave! is it possible!—to leave Paris!—and in this season!—you milor!"

229 *"Ah! qui n'en feroit pas autant!"* . . . *"C'est la beauté qui nous gouverne, &c."* "What you say is terrible!" . . . "It's beauty which guides us."

229 *"ce que vous dites la est affreux,"* . . . *"ne parla pas de départ, vous me désoleriez; je n'ai pas encore osé seulement songer, que je vais la perdre!"* "What you say is awful," . . . "Don't speak of leaving; you depress me; I did not dare think that I would lose her!"

229 *"Chere Comtesse, que je vous embrasse de tout mon coeur—quand se fera vôtre marriage—rien de si charmant que vôtre fille! Mon neveu, . . . que je vous le présente."* "My dear comtesse, I embrace you with all my heart—when is your wedding—nothing so charming as your daughter! Please meet my nephew."

237 *Cicerone's* A guide who shows and explains the antiquities or curiosities of a place to strangers (*OED*).

Chapter 29

241 *scirocco* An oppressively hot and blighting wind, blowing from the north coast of Africa over the Mediterranean and affecting parts of southern Europe (where it is also moist and depressing). Usually with *the* (*OED*).

241 *tramontana* Of the wind: Coming across or from beyond the mountains; *spec.* in reference to Italy, blowing from beyond the Alps: cf. B. 2 (*OED*).

245 *"Si mademoiselle n'avoit rien à emballer."* "If mademoiselle has nothing else to pack up."

245 *"Ah! mon Dieu! ma chère demoiselle, vous pleurez, qu'avez vous?—mais ne pleurez pas—ma mère me disoit toujours, 'Jaqueline, ne pleure pas, cela gâte les yeux'—et vous les avez si beaux, mademoiselle!"* "Oh, my poor lady, you've been crying, have you? But don't cry, my mother always told me, 'Jaqueline, crying spoils your eyes.' And your eyes are beautiful, mademoiselle."

246 *"Vous voilà bien triste!"*. . . *"c'est bien dur, aussi! mais tout s'arrangera."* "You have become very sad" . . . "it's certainly been hard, but things will work out."

246 *"vous faitez l' étonnée, mademoiselle, mais je sais bien ce que je sais"* "You act surprised, but I know what I have seen."

Chapter 30

251 *motet* A short vocal composition, *esp.* a polyphonic piece for liturgical use or for setting a religious text. In early use also more generally: a melody, a song (*obs.*). Also in extended use (*OED*).

255 *aliment* Nourishment.

255 *billets doux* Love letters.

Chapter 33

269 *tumbril* Tumbrel, an instrument of punishment (*OED*); also, a device such as a wheelbarrow for dumping dirt (*OED*).

Chapter 37

283 *Smyrna* An ancient city, now in Turkey, that rose to prominence before the classical era.

Chapter 39

311 *pate* Usually derogatory. Denoting a person with a mind of a specified quality or an intellect of a particular type (*OED*).

Chapter 40

315 *bishoprick* An obsolete spelling of "bishopric," which refers to the province of a bishop; a diocese (*OED*).

315 *almoner* An official distributor of the alms of another; the name of a functionary in a religious house, in the household of a bishop, prince, or other person of rank. Sometimes applied to the chaplain of a hospital, or other institution (*OED*).

316 *preferment* Advancement to an office or position; promotion. Formerly also: the advancement of a son or daughter by marriage or a financial settlement (*obs.*) (*OED*).

Manuscripts

Damer, Anne Seymour. Notebooks, 1791–97. 4 vols. Lewis Walpole Library. Farmington, Conn.

Editions of *Belmour*

[Damer, Anne Seymour]. *Belmour.* 3 vols. London: Joseph Johnson, 1801.

Damer, Anne. *Belmour.* 3 vols. Dublin: B. Smith, 1801.

———. *Belmont.* Translated by Marie-Anne-Cécile Langlois Houdon. 2 vols. Paris: Demonville, 1804.

———. *Belmour.* 2nd ed. 2 vols. London: Henry Colburn, 1827.

Primary Sources

"The Author Is Supposed to Speak," a handwritten poem by Lady Ailesbury to her daughter included in the Lewis Walpole Library copy of Anne Seymour Damer, *Belmour,* 3 vols. London: Joseph Johnson, 1801.

Anon. "The Damerian Apollo." London: William Holland, 1789.

Anon. "Review of *Belmour.*" *Monthly Review,* n.s., 38 (July 1801): 314.

Berry, Mary. *The Berry Papers: Being the Correspondence Hitherto Unpublished of Mary and Agnes Berry, 1763–1852.* Edited by Lewis Melville. London: John Lane, 1914.

———. *England and France: A Comparative View of the Social Condition of Both Countries: From the Restoration of Charles the Second, to the Present Time.* 2 vols. London: R. Bentley, 1844.

———. *Extracts of the Journals and Correspondence of Miss Berry.* Ed. Lady Theresa Lewis. 3 vols. London: Longmans, Green, 1865. Reprint, New York: AMS Press, 1971.

———. *Fashionable Friends.* 3rd ed. London: J. Ridgway, 1802.

———. *Letters and Journals.* Edited by Leslie A. Marchand. 12 vols. London: John Murray, 1973–95.

Bibliotheca Britannica; or, A General Index to British and Foreign Literature. Edited by Robert Watt. 4 vols. Edinburgh: Archibald, Constable, 1824.

Cavendish, Jack. *A Sapphick Epistle, from Jack Cavendish to the Honourable and Most Beautiful Mrs. D****.* London: M. Smith, [1778]. [Cited as 1770 in *Dictionary of National Biography;* 1778 in Elfenbein, *Romantic Genius,* p. 100; 1782 in Donoghue, *Passions;* I follow *Bibliotheca Britannica,* which lists 1778.]

Cawthorne, Henry. "Life Unhappy, Because We Use It Improperly: A Moral Essay, Spoken at the Tunbridge School Anniversary, 1760." In *The Poems of Hill, Cawthorne, and Hill,* vol. 65. of *The British Poets, Including Translations.* 100 vols. London: C. Whittingham, 1822.

Collins, William. "Ode, To a Lady on the Death of Colonel Ross in the Action of Fontenoy." In *Odes on Several Descriptive and Allegoric Subjects.* London: A. Millar, 1747. Reprinted in *The Poems of Thomas Gray, William Collins, and Oliver Goldsmith.* Edited by Roger Lonsdale. Oxford: Longman, 1969.

Combe, William. *The First of April: or, the Triumphs of Folly.* London: J. Bew, 1771.

Congreve, William. *The Old Batchelour.* In *The Comedies of William Congreve,* edited by Eric S. Rump. New York: Penguin, 1985.

Cunningham, Alan. *The Lives of the Most Eminent British Painters, Sculptors, and Architects.* Vol. 3. London: John Murray, 1830.

Devonshire, Duchess of. *Emma, or the Unfortunate Attachment.* Edited by Jonathan David Gross. New York: SUNY Press, 2004.

———. *The Sylph.* Edited by Jonathan David Gross. Evanston, Ill.: Northwestern University Press, 2007.

"Domestic Occurrences." *Gentleman's Magazine* 57 (1787): 359–60.

Farington, Joseph. *The Joseph Farington Diary.* Edited by Kenneth Garlick, Angus D. Macintyre, and Kathryn Cave. 16 vols. New Haven: Published for the Paul Mellon Centre for Studies in British Art by Yale University Press, 1978–84.

Ferrier, Susan. *Marriage: A Novel.* 1818. Edited by Herbert Foltinek. London: Oxford University Press, 1997.

Freud, Sigmund. "Mourning and Melancholia." 1917. In The Standard Edition of the Complete Psychological Works of Sigmund Freud [or S.E.]. Edited and translated by James Strachey et al. 24 vols. London: Hogarth Press, 1953–74. S.E. 14:243–60.

Gray, Thomas. *The Works of Thomas Gray: In Prose and Verse.* 2 vols. Edited by Edmund Gosse. New York: Worthington Company, 1890.

Hobhouse, John Cam, Lord Broughton. *Recollections of a Long Life, with Additional Extracts from His Private Diaries, Ed. by His Daughter Lady Dorchester.* 2 vols. New York, AMS Press, 1968.

Keats, John. "Ode to Melancholy." In *Complete Works of John Keats.* Edited by Jack Stillinger. Cambridge: Belknap Press of Harvard University, 1978.

———. *Selected Letters of John Keats.* Edited by Grant F. Scott. Cambridge: Harvard University Press, 2002.

The Lesbian History Sourcebook: Love and Sex Between Women in Britain from 1780 to 1970. Edited by Alison Oram and Annmarie Turnbull. London: Routledge, 2001.

Lennox, Sarah. *Life and Letters of Lady Sarah Lennox, 1745–1826 . . .* Edited by the Countess of Ilchester and Lord Stavordale. 2 vols. London: John Murray, 1802.

Milbanke, Elizabeth, Lady Melbourne. *Byron's "Corbeau Blanc": The Life of Lady Melbourne.* Edited by Jonathan David Gross. Houston: Rice University Press, 1997.

Moore, John. *Zeluco: Various Views of Human Nature, Taken from Life and Manners, Foreign and Domestic.* New York: Oxford University Press, 1995.

[Pigott, Charles]. *The Whig Club; or, A Sketch of the Manners of the Age.* London, 1794.

Piozzi, Hester. *Thraliana: The Diary of Mrs. Hester Lynch Thrale.* Edited by Katharine C. Balderston. 2nd ed. 2 vols. Oxford: Clarendon, 1951.

Radcliffe, Ann. *The Mysteries of Udolpho: A Romance, Interspersed with Some Pieces of Poetry.* Edited by Jacqueline Howard. New York: Penguin, 2001.

———. *The Romance of the Forest.* Edited by Chloe Chard. New York: Oxford University Press, 1986.

Rosenfeld, Sybil Marion. *Temples of Thespis: Some Private Theatres and Theatricals in England and Wales, 1700–1820.* London: Society for Theatre Research, 1978.

Shelley, Percy. "Shelleys' Reading List." In *The Journals of Mary Shelley: 1814–1844.* Edited by Paula R. Feldman and Diana Scott. 631–85. 2 vols. Oxford: Oxford University Press, 1987.

Spencer, Georigana, Duchess of Devonshire. *Emma, or the Unfortunate Attachment.* Edited by Jonathan David Gross. New York: SUNY Press, 2004.

Staël, Madame de. *A Treatise on the Influence of the Passions upon the Happiness of Individuals and of Nations.* London: Cawthorn, 1798.

Walpole, Horace. *Correspondence.* 48 vols. Edited by W. S. Lewis. New Haven, Conn.: Yale University Press, 1937–83.
Williamson, George C. *Daniel Gardner.* New York: John Lane, 1921.

Secondary Sources

Benforado, Susan. "Anne Seymour Damer (1748–1828). Sculptor." Ph.D. diss., University of New Mexico, 1986.
Brown, Susan, Patricia Clements, and Isobel Grundy, eds. "Anne Damer." In *Orlando: Women's Writing in the British Isles from the Beginnings to the Present.* Cambridge: Cambridge University Press Online, 2006. http://orlando.cambridge.org/ (October 28, 2009).
Castle, Terry. *The Apparitional Lesbian: Female Homosexuality and Modern Culture.* New York: Columbia University Press, 1993.
———. *The Female Thermometer: Eighteenth-Century Culture and the Invention of the Uncanny.* New York: Oxford University Press, 1995.
Clark, Robert. "Mourning and Melancholia." *The Literary Encyclopedia.* October 22, 2005. http://www.litencyc.com/php/stopics.php?rec=true&UID=1606 (accessed November 6, 2009).
Clery, E. J. *The Rise of Supernatural Fiction, 1762–1800.* Cambridge: Cambridge University Press, 1995.
Concise Dictionary of National Biography. Edited by Sir Sidney Lee. Oxford: Oxford University Press, 1920.
Donoghue, Emma. *Life Mask.* New York: Houghton Mifflin Harcourt, 2004.
———. *Passions Between Women: British Lesbian Culture, 1668–1801.* London: Scarlet Press, 1993.
Donkin, Ellen. *Getting into the Act: Women Playwrights in London, 1776–1829.* London: Routledge, 1995.
Elfenbein, Andrew. "Lesbian Aestheticism on the Eighteenth-Century Stage," *Eighteenth-Century Life* 25, no. 1 (2001): 1–16.
———. *Romantic Genius: The Prehistory of a Homosexual Role.* New York: Columbia University Press, 1999.
Faderman, Lillian. *Surpassing the Love of Men: Romantic Friendship and Love Between Women from the Renaissance to the Present.* New York: William Morrow, 1981.
Fleenor, Juliann, ed. *The Female Gothic.* Montreal: Eden Press, 1983.
Fothergill, Brian. *The Strawberry Hill Set: Horace Walpole and His Circle.* London: Faber & Faber, 1983.

Gamer, Michael. *Romanticism and the Gothic.* Cambridge: Cambridge University Press, 2000.

George, Mary Dorothy. *Catalogue of Prints and Drawings in the British Museum: Division I. Political and Personal Satires.* 12 vols. London, 1870–1954.

Hoeveler, Diane Long. *Gothic Feminism: The Professionalization of Gender from Charlotte Smith to the Brontës.* University Park: Pennsylvania State University Press, 1998.

Jacobs, John. *Anne Damer: American Sculptress.* London: Inner London Education Authority, 1983.

Lewis, W. S. *Walpole.* New York: Pantheon, 1961.

Lipking, Lawrence. *The Ordering of the Arts in Eighteenth-Century England.* Princeton: Princeton University Press, 1970.

Mellor, Anne. *Romanticism and Gender.* New York: Routledge, 1993.

Memoirs of the Princess Daschkow Lady of Honour to Catherine II, Empress of All the Russias . . . Edited by Mrs. W. Bradford. 2 vols. London, 1840.

Miles, Robert. *The Gothic Novel, 1750–1820: A Genealogy.* Manchester, U.K.: Manchester University Press; New York: Palgrave, 2002.

Moore, Lisa A. *Dangerous Intimacies.* Durham, N.C.: Duke University Press, 2001.

Noble, Percy. *Anne Seymour Damer: A Woman of Art and Fashion, 1748–1828.* London: Kegan Paul, Trench, Trübner, 1908.

Pfau, Thomas. *Romantic Moods: Paranoia, Trauma, and Melancholy, 1790–1840.* Baltimore: Johns Hopkins University Press, 2005.

Ross, Marlon. *The Contours of Masculine Desire.* New York: Oxford University Press, 1989.

Salmon, Eric. "Crewe, Frances Anne, Lady Crewe (bap. 1748, d. 1818)," *Oxford Dictionary of National Biography.* Oxford University Press, 2004–9.

Sheppard, F. H. W., ed. *Survey of London.* London: Athlone Press, 1964.

Stephen, Leslie, ed. *Dictionary of National Biography.* 22 vols. London: Oxford University Press, 1964–65.

Trumbach, Randolph. "London's Sapphists: From Three Sexes to Four Genders in the Making of Modern Culture." In *Body Guards: The Cultural Politics of Gender Ambiguity,* edited by Julia Epstein and Kristina Straub, 112–41. New York: Routledge, 1991.

Vicinus, Mary. *Intimate Friends: Women Who Loved Women, 1778–1928.* Chicago: University of Chicago Press, 2004.

Williams, Anne. *Art of Darkness: A Poetics of Gothic.* Chicago: University of Chicago Press, 1995.

Wilson, Eric G. *Against Happiness.* New York: Farrar, Straus, & Giroux, 2008.

Yarrington, Alison. "Damer, Anne Seymour (1749–1828)," *Oxford Dictionary of National Biography.* Oxford: Oxford University Press, 2004–9.

———. "The Female Pygmalion: Anne Seymour Damer, Allan Cunningham, and the Writing of a Woman Sculptor's Life," *The Sculpture Journal* 1 (1997): 32–44.

With his new edition of *The Sylph*, Jonathan Gross recovered the work of novelist and biopic subject Georgiana, Duchess of Devonshire. With *Belmour*, Gross introduces the only novel of the English sculptress Anne Damer, another powerful eighteenth century woman, to a modern audience.

Belmour chronicles the tangled romances of a group of eighteenth-century English aristocrats. The plot centers on charismatic Lord Belmour, a man of intense feeling and quick perception, who goes to great lengths to gain the affection of the lovely and mysterious Emily Melville, only to learn that she has recently married another man. His heartache propels him on an extensive journey across Europe, until fate ultimately leads their paths to cross once more. Set against vivid backdrops in Paris, Lisbon, Venice, and Rome, *Belmour* is a rich, multifaceted story of forbidden love and erotic intrigue that will appeal to those interested in the gothic romances of Ann Radcliffe and the psychological novels of Elizabeth Inchbald. Like her contemporary Jane Austen, Anne Damer casts a sharp and critical eye on the foibles of the aristocracy, yielding a memorable portrait of romantic love in the age of sensibility.

"How fortunate we are to have this new edition of Anne Damer's novel *Belmour*—a book as fascinating as the many-talented woman who wrote it. And how fortunate as well to have the book framed for us by Jonathan Gross's critical and biographical commentaries, where the cultural significance of Damer and her work is set forth so well. Damer is an artist, a writer, and a personality of real importance, now more lapsed from attention than she ever should have been."

—Jerome McGann, University of Virginia

Anne Seymour Damer (1748–1828) was born in Kent to an aristocratic family. Her father's secretary, the philosopher David Hume, allegedly encouraged her to pursue a career as a sculptor at a time when few women did so. Among her best-known subjects are Lord Admiral Nelson and King George III. Giuseppe Ceracchi cast her as the Muse of Sculpture in a full-length statue that graced the entrance of the British Museum for more than one hundred years. *Belmour* (1801) was her only novel.

Jonathan David Gross is a professor of English at DePaul University and the director of the DePaul Humanities Center. He edited *The Sylph* (Northwestern, 2007) and *Emma; or, The Unfortunate Attachment*, both by Georgiana, Duchess of Devonshire. He is the editor of *Byron's "Corbeau Blanc": The Life and Letters of Lady Melbourne* and the author of *Byron: The Erotic Liberal*.

NORTHWESTERN WORLD CLASSICS

FICTION U.S. $24.95

ISBN 978-0-8101-2670-1

52495

9 780810 126701

Cover image: Jean-Francois de Troy, *Declaration of Love*, oil on canvas, 1731. Photograph © Jörg P. Anders, by permission of Bildarchiv Preussische Kulturbesitz / Art Resource, NY

Cover design: Marianne Jankowski

WWW.NUPRESS.NORTHWESTERN.EDU